Margaret Hasluck

The Hasluck Collection of Albanian Folktales

Edited by Robert Elsie

Centre for Albanian Studies, London

Publisher's Cataloging-in-Publication data

Hasluck, Margaret Masson Hardie, 1885-1948.
 The Hasluck collection of Albanian folktales / Margaret Hasluck ;
edited by Robert Elsie.
 472 p. cm.
 ISBN 978-1512002287
 Series : Albanian studies.
 Includes bibliographical references.

1. Tales --Albania. 2. Legends --Albania. 3. Folklore --Albania. I.
Elsie, Robert, 1950-. II. Series. III. Title.

GR251 .A4 2015
398.2/094965 --dc23

                    Albanian Studies, Vol. 14
                    ISBN 978-1512002287

Cover photo: Young Woman from Shkodra (photo: Giuseppe Massani,
1940).

Table of Contents

3

Introduction

Albanian Folktales

The folktales of this collection were gathered and translated into English by the noted Scottish anthropologist Margaret Hasluck (1885-1948) in the late 1920s and 1930s. She collected them, for the most part, not from experienced storytellers, but directly from the children, young people and elementary school teachers she met during her long years of stay in Albania. The narratives are accordingly simple, taken, so to speak, from the mouths of babes. They are, however, enough to enthrall the modern reader, adult or child, and provide sufficient material to keep experts and analysts of oral literature happy, who delve into the deeper structures behind them.

Pashas, beys and dervishes abound in Albanian folktales, as do noticeably passive and submissive female characters. This Oriental touch should come as no surprise since Albania, situated in southeastern Europe, was part of the Ottoman Empire for about five centuries and had a primarily Muslim population by the end of that period.

Albanian folktales were first recorded in the middle of the nineteenth century by European scholars such as the Austrian consul in Janina (Ioannina), Johann Georg von Hahn (1854); the German ethnographer and physician, Karl H. Reinhold (1855); and the Sicilian folklorist, Giuseppe Pitrè (1875). The next generation of scholars to take an interest in the collection of Albanian folktales were primarily philologists, among whom were well-known Indo-European linguists concerned with recording and analysing a hitherto little known European language: Auguste Dozon (1879, 1881), Jan Jarnik (1883), Gustav Meyer (1884, 1888), Holger Pedersen (1895), Gustav Weigand (1913) and August Leskien (1915).

The nationalist movement in Albania in the second half of the nineteenth century, the so-called Rilindja period, gave rise to native collections of folklore material such as the 'Albanian Bee' *(Albanikê melissa / Bêlietta sskiypêtare)* by Thimi Mitko (1878), the 'Albanian Spelling Book' *(Albanikon alfavêtarion / Avabatar arbëror)* by the Greco-Albanian Anastas Kullurioti (1882), and the 'Waves of the Sea' (*Valët e Detit*) by Spiro Dine (1908). In the second half of the twentieth century, much field work was done by the Institute of Folk Culture in Tirana and by the Institute of Albanian Studies in Prishtina, which published numerous collections of folktales and legends. Unfortunately, very little of this substantial material has been translated into other languages.

The only substantial collections of Albanian folk tales to have appeared in English up to the present are: *Tricks of Women and Other Albanian Tales* by Paul Fenimore Cooper (New York 1928), which was translated from the collections of Dozon and Pedersen, and *Albanian Wonder Tales* by Post Wheeler (London 1936). These classic editions were followed by my collection, *Albanian Folktales and Legends* (Peja 2001, 3rd edition 2015), which is also largely available at http://www.albanianliterature.net/en/oral_lit1.html. The present Hasluck collection, comprising 115 tales, is by far the largest ever to appear.

Who was Margaret Hasluck?

The Scottish scholar and anthropologist, Margaret Masson Hasluck, née Hardie, also known as Peggy Hasluck, was born of a strict Christian family at Chapelton, Drumblade, near Elgin in northern Scotland on 18 June 1885, and grew up in the Moray countryside. The eldest of nine children, she studied at the Elgin Academy, Aberdeen University and then at Newnham College, Cambridge, where she completed a degree in classics.

In 1910, as the first women ever, she won a scholarship to study at the British School of Archaeology in Athens and took part in

8

archaeological excavations in Anatolia under Sir William Ramsay (1851-1939). It was at the British School that she met the archaeologist and orientalist Frederick William Hasluck (1878-1920), whom she married in Scotland in September 1912. In 1915, her husband quit the British School and joined the Intelligence Department of the British Legation in Athens. He died of tuberculosis in a Swiss sanatorium in 1920, and it was Margaret who edited and published his works, including his *magnum opus* entitled *Christianity and Islam under the Sultans*, Oxford 1929.

In 1921, Margaret Hasluck received a fellowship from Aberdeen University that enabled her to travel and work in the Balkans, initially to collect folktales in Macedonia. From 1923 onwards, she spent most of her years in Albania, travelling much of the time in the back country. In 1935, she settled in Elbasan, where she bought land and built a house. She was a close friend of the Albanian political figure and scholar Lef Nosi (1877-1946) of Elbasan, with whom she shared interests in archaeology and ethnography. The claim put out by the communist dictator Enver Hoxha (1908-1985) after Nosi's execution that Hasluck was Nosi's mistress cannot be substantiated one way or the other. At any rate, Margaret Hasluck spent many years in Elbasan, returning once or twice a year to Britain to give lectures at the Folklore Society and to visit her family.

The British historian Nicholas Hammond (1907-2001) met Hasluck in 1931 during a tour of Epirus and southern Albania and records the following:

"I first met her [Mrs. Hasluck] at the Monastery of St. John's near Elbasan in Central Albania, when I went there to copy some Latin inscriptions. The monks told me that "an Englishwoman" was there. The usual meaning of such a remark is that an Albanian has returned from America and knows only enough English to say "Hallo, Johnny; you English?" So I said I did not wish to meet her. Then I heard an English voice calling to me. When I saw her on a balcony, I realised that she was the real thing, and went to greet her. The widow of a scholar who

9

had died young after writing an important book on the monasteries of Athos, she devoted the rest of her life to the Albanians living in the villages and making friend with the women. She asked me to stay that night in the monastery, as she was expecting a troubadour."[1]

In April 1939, King Zog (189-1961), pressured by the Italian government, demanded that Margaret Hasluck leave Albania. During the Italian invasion which followed immediately thereafter, she was forced to flee, leaving her home and her 3,000-book library to the care of her friend Lef Nosi, whom she was never to see again. In Athens, she worked for the press office of the British Embassy and, in view of her unique knowledge of Albania, was asked, in late April 1940, to help in preliminary work to organise an Albanian resistance movement. For this project she was able to establish contacts with Albanian resistance leaders. At the end of April 1942, when German forces invaded Greece, Hasluck managed to flee to Istanbul, where she replaced Colonel Walter Francis Stirling (1889-1958). There she sought contacts in occupied Albania and endeavoured to find young Albanians for infiltration operations. Also in 1942, she was recruited in Cairo to help set up an Albanian section of the Special Operations Executive (SOE). From 1943 to February 1944, she was thus active in writing reports and assessments on Albania and in teaching and briefing SOE operatives, who affectionately called her Fanny Hasluck.

The British military officer and writer, Julian Amery (1919-1996), mentions Margaret Hasluck in his book on British involvement in Albania during the Second World War:

"An Albanian office, similar to our own, was therefore opened in Athens, with Mrs. Hazluck, Edith Durham's friend, as its adviser. Mrs. Hazluck was one of those remarkable

---

[1] N. G. L. Hammond, Travels in Epirus and South Albania before World War II. in: *Ancient World*, 8 (1983), p. 26-27.

Englishwomen who make their homes in strange lands and gain the affection and respect of their inhabitants. She had crossed the Albanian border in 1919 in the course of anthropological researches in Macedonia, and, attracted by the country and its people, had made her permanent home near Elbasan. Her chief interest was folk-lore, but the Italians suspected that she was a spy, and expelled her from Albania in 1939. By so doing they threw her, for the first time, into the arms of the Secret Service."[2]

"His [Stirling's] place in Constantinople was taken by Mrs. Hasluck, but otherwise the whole organisation which had grown up to promote an Albanian revolt was dissolved. For close on two years, therefore, the responsibilities of observing the Albanian situation, keeping touch with the exiles and seeking to re-establish communications with Albania devolved upon Mrs. Hasluck alone. The triple barrier of German, Bulgarian and Italian counter-espionage proved a formidable obstacle to her efforts; and indeed informed opinion in the "D" Organisation long despaired of Albanian resistance. Mrs. Hasluck, however, remained convinced that a revolt was preparing in Albania, and worked tirelessly to glean information from the Albanian exiles and the rare Albanians who visited Constantinople. Also – and this was perhaps her greatest service – she despatched to Cairo a continuous series of reports, memoranda, and telegrams, which saved the increasingly bureaucratic headquarters of the "D" Organisation from altogether forgetting that Albania existed."[3]

Another British officer and writer, David Smiley (1916-2009), met Hasluck during the Second World War, too:

---

[2] Julian Amery. *Sons of the Eagle: A Study in Guerilla War*, London 1948, p. 26-27.
[3] idem, p. 48.

"The Albanian section [of M04] then consisted of one person only – Mrs Margaret Hasluck. She was an elderly lady, the widow of a famous archaeologist, with greying hair swept back into a bun and a pink complexion with bright blue eyes; she reminded me of an old-fashioned English nanny. Full of energy and enthusiasm, she was totally dedicated to her beloved Albania. She had lived for about twenty years in her home near Elbasan, studying Albanian anthropology and folklore, on which she was one of the greatest authorities. Her closest Albanian friend was Lef Nosi, a distinguished and patriotic figure who had taken a prominent part in the creation of an independent Albania after the First World War. In 1939, the Italians expelled Mrs Hasluck from Albania as a spy, which at that time she was not, but when she moved to Turkey she was recruited by British Intelligence. For the next two years she worked there collecting every scrap of information on Albania, keeping in touch with Albanians both in and out of the country, until finally she was brought to Cairo to set up the Albanian section of the SOE HQ."[4]

In May 1944, Margaret Hasluck returned to London when she was diagnosed with leukaemia. After spells in Cyprus and Switzerland for health reasons after the war, she moved to Dublin where she died of the disease on 18 October 1948. She is buried in the churchyard of Dallas, Scotland.

Of Margaret Hasluck's scholarly publications, mention may be made of the now rather outdated *Këndime Englisht-Shqip or Albanian-English Reader: Sixteen Albanian Folk-stories, Collected and Translated, with Two Grammars and Vocabularies*. Cambridge 1931; and the rare *Albanian Phrase Book*, London 1944. She published numerous articles on Albanian folk culture in *Man: the Journal of the Royal Anthropological Society* and elsewhere. Hasluck is remembered

---

[4] David Smiley, *Albanian Assignment*, London 1985, p. 8-9.

primarily for her *The Unwritten Law in Albania: a Record of the Customary Law of the Albanian Tribes,* Cambridge 1954, the first English-language monograph devoted to Albanian customary law and the *Kanun.* Her archives are kept at the Taylor Institution of Oxford University and her photography collection is preserved at the Royal Geographical Society in London.

The Hasluck Collection of Albanian Folktales

Margaret Hasluck was in Albania for the first time in or around 1919 and, when she returned to Scotland, she knew that her place was in the Balkans. With a scholarship from Aberdeen University as a Wilson Travelling Fellow (1921-1923, 1926-1928), she began collecting folklore in western Macedonia and increasingly in Albania, where she moved definitively in 1923. Her interest in Albanian folktales continued throughout her years of residence in Albania and, no doubt with the help of Lef Nosi, she amassed a substantial collection. Hasluck acquired a good knowledge of Albanian over the years and was therefore able to translate the material into English. This was a notable achievement in itself since the folktales, collected from peasant children and adults, were recorded in various dialect forms. Her material was augmented by a collection of folktales assembled by the Albanian Ministry of Education, gathered from school teachers throughout Albania, probably some time in the late 1920s.

With the exception of sixteen minor folktales that appeared as an appendix to her book *Këndime Englisht-Shqip or Albanian-English Reader* (1931), Margaret Hasluck's vast folktale material remained alas unpublished but was preserved after her death at the Taylor Institution of Oxford University. It is by far the largest collection of Albanian folktales ever translated into English.

We are grateful to Bejtullah Destani of the Centre for Albanian Studies in London for his discovery of the typescript, to the Taylor Institution in Oxford where it is preserved, and to Margaret Woodward

13

of the Hasluck estate in Scotland for the privilege of presenting this historic collection to the public.

Robert Elsie
Berlin, Germany
May 2015

The Hasluck Collection
of Albanian Folktales

Margaret Hasluck

Pahdivan

Once there were a young man and an old woman who were poor. One day, the young man set out for the forest to cut wood. He took his axe with him and on reaching the forest, lost no time in chopping down a tree. As he did so, he accidentally chopped off the tail of a serpent, which darted at him and bit his finger.

That done, the serpent turned and said: "I bit your finger and you cut off my tail. Shall be become blood-brothers now?" "Yes, that is a good idea," answered the young man.

After they became blood-brothers, they set out for the young man's house. When they reached it, the old woman, taking fright, said to him: "What is this, son?" "Nothing, mother, only my brother," he replied. "All right, then. Come to the fire and warm yourselves," she said. And they went into the house.

One fine day the serpent saw the king's daughter at her window and fell in love with her. So he said to the old woman: "Old lady, go and ask for the king's daughter for me."

The old woman, in obedience to her serpent son, set off for the royal palace. On reaching it, she made her way towards the apartments of the king. But when the servants saw her, a poor old woman, they began to push her back. Fortunately, the king came out on the balcony, saw her being beaten by the servants, and shouted angrily at them: "What has that old woman done to you?" "Nothing, emperor, but she wants to go and see you." "Well, let her come in," replied the king.

When the old woman heard this, she climbed the stairs and went to the king's room, saying: "As Your Majesty knows, I have a serpent son. He has fallen in love with your daughter and I've come today to settle the business." "That's easy, only I must make a certain condition. By tomorrow, his house must be better than mine, the road

17

to it must be spread with velvet, and the sides of the road must be lined with vines, with the grapes on them, and the grapes must be ripe. These conditions must be fulfilled. I'll then give him my daughter."

The old woman left him and went home, where she said to the serpent: "Oh, the king has made hard conditions!" "How so?" "He wants the house to be more beautiful than his palace is by tomorrow, the road must be spread with velvet, and the sides of the road must be lined with ripe grapes." "A plague on you, old woman! I'll carry out these conditions now, as soon as my brother comes home," said the serpent.

While they talked, the young man arrived. As soon as the serpent saw him, he said: "I say, young man, go and bring a bag of earth from the place where you cut off my tail." "All right," said the young man, and set off.

After he had gone some way, he reached the place indicated. With his hatchet he dug up some earth, which he put into his satchel and brought to the serpent. The latter took the satchel and during the night scattered the earth in the courtyard, on the road, and on the sides of the road.

Next morning, as the king was washing his face, something bothered his eyes. When he lifted them to look out, he saw that the serpent's house had been built in magnificent style, and he said to himself: "He's got my daughter."

While he was saying this, the old woman arrived at the palace. As soon as the king saw her, he said: "Go away, now. Tomorrow we'll have the betrothal, and two weeks later you shall come to fetch the bride." "Right, king," said the old woman, and went away.

When the serpent, who was waiting at the door, saw her, he said hastily: "Well, how did you manage things?" "Couldn't be better. It's all arranged. Tomorrow we'll betroth you and at the end of two weeks, we'll fetch the bride."

Next day, the king betrothed them, and when the two weeks were up, the serpent, as they had arranged, sent people to fetch the bride. To them he said: "Tell the bride's mother to dress her in seven chemises." The wedding party arrived at the king's, the bride was dressed up, mounted on a horse, and was sent to the serpent, who was shut up in a room apart.

When the time came, they called him and he came out, crawling on his belly. They carried out the usual customs and put him into the bride's room.

When everybody had gone and they were left alone, he said to the bride: "Take off a chemise!" She did so, and he took off a skin. When the time came for her to take off her seventh chemise, she became covered with gold and pearls, and when the serpent took off his seventh skin, a very handsome young man appeared by a miracle. He said: "They call me Pahdivan the Beautiful, but if you reveal my name, I'll run away."

Next day, he became a serpent again, and the bride put on her seven chemises. Afterwards, when the time for the first party came, the king invited him along with his daughter. The bride left in the morning and the serpent arrived at sundown. During the party, the bride was teased by her sisters, who called her 'a serpent's bride'. She lost her temper and said: "I am the wife of Pahdivan the Beautiful!"

As soon as she had said this, the serpent was turned into a ram, and ran away.

Next day, the bride said to her father: "Father, I want a suit of armour, an iron cap, a pair of iron shoes, and an iron stick. I'm going to look for my husband." Her father prepared everything for her, she put them on and set off to find her husband.

After she had travelled a long way, she came to the Sun's house and knocked at the door. Out came the daughter of the Sun. When the bride saw her, she said: "Where is Pahdivan's house?" "Upon my word, I don't know. Go a little farther on. The Moon's house is over there and they may be able to tell you."

The bride continued her journey, and after a long time reached the Moon's house, and knocked at the door. Out came the daughter of the Moon. When the bride saw her, she said: "Where is Pahdivan's house?" The daughter of the Moon said: "I don't know, but go on a little farther. The Wind's house is over there, and it's older than ours."

Again the bride continued her journey, and after a much longer time, she reached the Wind's house and knocked at the door. Out came the Wind's daughter. When the bride saw her, she said: "Where is Pahdivan's house?" The Wind's daughter replied: "Sister, it's forty years, forty months, forty weeks, forty days, forty hours and forty minutes away." The bride said: "But, girl, I've done forty years and forty months." "All right, but you still have the rest to do," she answered.

The bride again continued her journey and, after travelling forty weeks, forty days, forty hours and forty minutes, reached a large meadow, where she sat down to rest and then lay down to take a short nap.

While she slept, her husband arrived. He at once recognised her, went up to her, laying his head on her knees, and stayed there.

Two tear-drops escaped from his eyes and fell on her forehead. She at once woke up. Seeing her husband there, she turned and said: "You know me, don't you?" The young man said: "I know you. I know you, but where am I to take you now? Well, I'll turn you into an apple for the time being." With a slap, he turned her into an apple and put her in his pocket.

When he went home, his mother, the *kulshedra*, smelled her and said to him: "There's the smell of a human being here, son." "Yes, mother, I have somebody with me, but swear that you won't eat her," replied the young man. She said: "By spoons and bowls, by mountains and peaks, mother will not eat her." "No, no, you must say: by Pahdivan's head." And she said: "By Pahdivan's head, mother will not eat her." After binding her by this oath, he took the apple out of his pocket, turned it into a human being, and said to his mother: "This is my wife."

The *kulshedra*, who wanted to eat her, said one day to her: "Young wife, when I come back, let me find you neither in nor out," and went away. The young wife began to cry. But as she did so, her husband came in. "What makes you cry?" he said. She told him what the *kulshedra* had said. "Don't cry," he said. He put up a swing in the doorway, lifted her into it and, after giving her two or three pushes, went away. When the *kulshedra* came home, she saw the young wife was neither in nor out, and said to herself: "My rascally son taught you this!" But the wife said nothing in reply.

Next day, she said to her: "I'm going to see my daughters. When I get back, let me find these three casks full of tears." The poor young wife began to cry, beating her head with her fists, trying to fill the casks. At the very time she was beating her head, the husband came in. "What are you doing, you silly girl?" he asked. She told him what the *kulshedra* had said. "Don't cry," said he. He took a load of salt, divided it between the three casks, filled them with water, and went away. The *kulshedra* arrived and saw the casks full of tears, which were really salt water, she said: "My rascally son taught you this!"

The following day, the *kulshedra* said to her: "I'm going to see my daughters to invite them to come here tomorrow. Make a loaf for us, one half of it baked and the other not." So saying, she went away. The poor young wife began to cry. But again, as before, her husband came in and said: "Whatever's making you cry?" She told him what his mother, the *kulshedra*, had said. "It's quite easy," he said. "Don't cry." He took a baking pan and put it on the fire. Then he made two thin loaves, baked one, and put the other on top of it unbaked. After he had finished, he went away. When the *kulshedra* came home, she saw that the loaf was made as she had said, and said to her daughters: "My rascally son has taught her this."

Next day, before it was light, the young man said to the girl: "We've no luck here. Let's go away." So they put on armour and set off in the dark.

When it grew light, the *kulshedra* went to her son's room to tell him to get up. When she saw there was nobody there, she said: "The boy's gone. I'm off after him to catch him." And she set off.

After travelling for a long time, the *kulshedra* began to catch up to them. As she came near, the young man gave his wife a slap and turned her into a cypress tree. He himself became a very long serpent and wound himself around the tree so as to leave no part of it exposed.

When the *kulshedra* approached, she saw her serpent son, who had covered up his wife, and she said:

21

"If mother pecks your head,
Mother'll spoil your pearly cap,
Mother's beautiful Pahdivan.
It mother pecks your waist,
Mother'll spoil your silken sash,
Mother's beautiful Pahdivan.
If mother pecks your feet,
Mother'll spoil your golden sandals,
Mother's beautiful Pahdivan."

When she saw that she could do no harm to her son's wife, she said: "All right, son! One of you shall be the Morning Star and the other the Evening Star."

[told by Ismail Haxhi Musaj of Elbasan]

Saint Nicholas and the Prophet Elias

Once upon a time a peasant went to church and lit a candle to Saint Nicholas. Now the picture of Saint Nicholas was near the picture of the Prophet Elias. When the peasant came in, the Prophet Elias said to Saint Nicholas, "The peasant is coming to light a candle to you. What good turn will you do to him?" "He has a field in which he has sown wheat. There is a perfect sea of wheat in the field," replied Saint Nicholas. Then the Prophet Elias said, "I will let loose a great storm of hail and a great storm of wind and I will destroy all his wheat." Saint Nicholas appeared to the peasant in a dream, saying, "The Prophet Elias is going to destroy all your wheat. Sell it before you reap it."

In the morning, the peasant got up from sleep, took a candle to the church, and, after lighting it in honour of Saint Nicholas, stayed for the service. When church was over, he said to the priest, "Would you like me to sell my wheat to you?" "Yes, of course," said the priest. "How much do you want for it?" "Five hundred piastres," said the peasant. The priest drew out his purse and gave him this money.

Next day, it rained heavily and then hailed so that all the wheat was spoiled. The peasant went to church with another candle for Saint Nicholas. The Prophet Elias said to Saint Nicholas, "Just ask the farmer about his wheat." "Oh, he has sold it to the priest," replied Saint Nicholas. The Prophet Elias said, "I will make the wheat better than it ever was." Again Saint Nicholas appeared to the peasant in a dream and said, "Go to the priest and buy back your wheat from him because it is going to be much better than it ever was."

The peasant went to the priest and said, "You have lost money, priest. The wheat you bought has been ruined. Sell it back to me." "All right," said the priest, "I will, but I want 200 piastres." In this way, the peasant bought back the wheat from the priest.

23

The wheat then grew as tall and thick as a forest. The day after reaping it, the peasant again went to church with a candle which he lit in honour of Saint Nicholas. The Prophet Elias said to Saint Nicholas, "Has he seen how splendidly the wheat which the priest bought from him has grown?" "He has bought it back from the priest and has reaped it," replied Saint Nicholas.

The Prophet Elias said, "I will make a blast of wind which will scatter the sheaves all over the field, one here and one there." Again Saint Nicholas appeared to the peasant in a dream and this time said, "Make a fat candle and take it to the Prophet Elias. He means to blow all your wheat away."

The peasant made the fat candle and took it to the Prophet Elias in the church and lit it. "Saint Nicholas," said the Prophet Elias, "Now the man can eat his wheat in peace. He has brought me, too, a present."

[told at Shëngjin in the district of Elbasan]

The Hen and the Cock

Once a cock was perched on a cornel-tree, eating its fruit. A hen which happened to be underneath said, "Cock, cock, drop me a cornel." He let fall one of his own droppings and dirtied her leg.

The cock said to the thorn, "Thorn, thorn, wipe the leg of the hen, the short-legged hen." "I will neither wipe nor touch it."

"Goat, goat, eat the thorn. The thorn wouldn't wipe the leg of the hen, the short-legged hen." "I will neither eat nor touch it."

"Shepherd, shepherd, kill the goat. The goat wouldn't eat the thorn, the thorn wouldn't wipe the leg of the hen, the short-legged hen." "I will neither kill nor touch her."

"Dog, dog, bite the shepherd. The shepherd wouldn't kill the goat, the goat wouldn't eat the thorn, the thorn wouldn't wipe the leg of the hen, the short-legged hen." "I will neither bite nor touch him."

"Water, water, drown the dog. The dog wouldn't bite the shepherd, the shepherd wouldn't kill the goat, the goat wouldn't eat the thorn, the thorn wouldn't wipe the leg of the hen, the short-legged hen." "I will neither drown nor touch him."

"Buffaloes, buffaloes, drink the water. The water wouldn't drown the dog, the dog wouldn't bite the shepherd, the shepherd wouldn't kill the goat, the goat wouldn't eat the thorn, the thorn wouldn't wipe the leg of the hen, the short-legged hen." "We will neither drink nor touch it."

"Rope, rope, tie up the buffaloes. The buffaloes wouldn't drink the water, the water wouldn't drown the dog, the dog wouldn't bite the shepherd, the shepherd wouldn't kill the goat, the goat wouldn't eat the thorn, the thorn wouldn't wipe the leg of the hen, the short-legged hen." "I will neither tie up nor touch them."

"Mouse, mouse, gnaw the rope. The rope wouldn't tie up the buffaloes, the buffaloes wouldn't drink the water, the water wouldn't drown the dog, the dog wouldn't bite the shepherd, the shepherd wouldn't kill the goat, the goat wouldn't eat the thorn, the thorn wouldn't wipe the leg of the hen, the short-legged hen." "I will neither gnaw nor touch it."

"Cat, cat, chase the mouse. The mouse wouldn't gnaw the rope, the rope wouldn't tie up the buffaloes, the buffaloes wouldn't drink the water, the water wouldn't drown the dog, the dog wouldn't bite the shepherd, the shepherd wouldn't kill the goat, the goat wouldn't eat the thorn, the thorn wouldn't wipe the leg of the hen, the short-legged hen."

The cat rushed to catch the mouse, the mouse rushed to gnaw the rope, the rope rushed to tie up the buffaloes, the buffaloes rushed to drink the water, the water rushed to drown the dog, the dog rushed to bite the shepherd, the shepherd rushed to kill the goat, the goat rushed to eat the thorn, the thorn wiped the leg of the hen, the short-legged hen.

So it was seen that the thorn had the worst of it.

[told by Mahmud Verrçani]

The Baldhead and the Giant

Once upon a time there was an old woman who had three sons. The two eldest who were well doing, worked as servants with the king. The youngest was a wretched baldhead, and his brothers did not like him at all because they were ashamed of his bald head.

One day, the two brothers said to the king, "You should have the Giant's broom which sweeps by itself." "Who will fetch it?" said the king. "Haran," they said. "Call him in. Who is he?" said the king. The brothers went and called him in.

They brought him to the king who said, "You must get me the Giant's broom." "How can one get to the Giant, Your Majesty?" he pleaded. "You must go. If you don't, I'll have your head cut off." "Well, give me ten Napoleons or so." He got this sum from the king and gave it to his mother who needed to be provided for, and then he went away.

He became a fly and settled on the broom. The broom said to the Giant, "He is taking me away!" "Who is taking you away?" asked the Giant. "I don't know. I can't see anyone," said the broom. The Giant came and looked around but saw no one. The baldhead again pulled at the broom to carry it off. Again the broom said, "He is carrying me off!" "But who is carrying you off?" said the Giant. "I don't know," replied the broom. The Giant picked up the broom and flung it away. He thought it was making fun of him.

The baldhead picked up the broom and went away. He took it to the king. His brothers were bursting with anger and wished to kill him.

They next said to the king, "You should have the Giant's jug and basin!" "But who can fetch them?" said the king. "Haran." They called in Haran again and took him to the king, who said, "You are to get me the Giant's jug and basin." "Give me ten Napoleons," said the

27

baldhead. The king gave him this sum and he handed it to his mother. Then, disguised as a fly, he went to the Giant for a second time.

As the jug and basin were outside, he tried to steal them. They said to the Giant, "He is carrying us off!" The Giant went to see, and said, "Who is?" "We can't see anyone," they complained. The Giant came there again to see. They shouted, "He is carrying us off!" The Giant picked up the jug and basin and flung them away. Haran picked them up and took them to the king.

Then the brothers said to the king, "You should have the Giant's ring!" "Who can get it?" "Haran." "Call him in," ordered the king. They called him in and brought him to the king. "I want you to get me the Giant's ring," said the king. "How can I, Your Majesty? The Giant keeps the ring on his finger." "I want the ring. If you don't get it, I'll kill you," said the king. A third time he gave him ten Napoleons, and the baldhead gave them to his mother. Disguised as a fly, he again set off and went to the Giant.

He landed on his finger and fumbled with his ring, but the Giant saw him and brushed him off. He did not give up, but again settled on his finger. Then the Giant understood and caught the fly. "Ah!" he exclaimed, "It's you who stole my broom and my jug and basin!" "Yes, it was," said the fly and turned into a man.

The Giant dug a large hole and put him into it. After placing a big stone on top of the hole to prevent Haran from escaping, he said to his wife, "Put a pot of water on the fire to boil, and sharpen the knife. I am going to call in two of our neighbours to kill the man and eat him." "All right," said the Giant's wife.

She put a pot of water on the fire and began to sharpen the knife. The baldhead called out to her from the pit, "Sharpen the knife properly so that it will kill me at once. I don't want to suffer." "I don't know how to sharpen it," she said. "Help me out of this hole," pleaded the baldhead. "Let me sharpen it with my own hands." The Giant's wife helped him out, he sharpened the knife, then seized the Giant's wife, and killed her. He cut her into pieces, and flung the pieces into the pot of water.

He then climbed onto the rafters and turned into a fly. The Giant arrived, together with his neighbours. "Oh," he said, "my wife has already killed the baldhead and put him on to boil. She has boiled him just as we would have wished. Let me fill a big tray with the meat!" He did so, and they ate a hearty meal.

He then looked around for his wife, but she was nowhere to be found. He called out, "Haran, Haran!" "Yes?" cried Haran from over his head. "Did you steal my broom?" "Yes, I did." "Did you steal my jug and basin?" "Yes, I did." "Did you kill my wife?" "Yes, I did." "Won't you come again to see me?" "Why not, if I chance to pass this way again?" And Haran went away home.

He went to the king and said, "I could not steal the ring from his finger, but I will go and bring the Giant himself here. Then I'll kill him and get his ring. I need, however, two good axes and about two hundred big nails. If I get these, I will fetch the Giant and bring him here." The king supplied him with the axes and the nails. He took them with him and went to the Giant's forest.

He began to cut down a few big trees. The Giant heard him felling them and shouted at him, but he pretended not to hear. The Giant came there himself and said, "What are you doing?" "I have been sent to your forest to cut some good, big boards. Our Haran is dead," the baldhead said. "Oh, is Haran dead?" exclaimed the Giant. "He is," said the baldhead. "What a lot of harm he did to me!" said the Giant, and began to help him cut the wood.

The baldhead made a big coffin with the boards and said to the Giant, "Sir, get into the coffin a moment to see how big it is. Haran was a huge fellow." The Giant got into the coffin and immediately the baldhead nailed down the lid thoroughly. "Now try to break out!" he said. The Giant tried, but could not break the coffin open.

The baldhead then said, "I'm Haran, and I'm carrying the Giant on my shoulder." He took the Giant in the coffin to the king and said, "Come and see the Giant. I have him here." the king and the baldhead's two brothers, who were the king's servants, all went to see the coffin. "Line up here," said the baldhead and, hiding himself behind the lid, he opened the coffin. The Giant came out, saw the king standing near, and ate him and his two servants. Haran escaped because he had hidden himself.

He ascended the throne of the king. "Fire cannons and make merry. I'm your new king," he cried. And so the baldhead became a king.

[told at Shëngjin in the district of Elbasan]

The Fox

Once there was a fox which grew hungry and went to a wild figtree to pick figs. She strung them on a thread like a rosary and hung them round her neck. Her aim was to find food.

As she walked along, she met a hen, which ran away very fast when she saw the fox. But the fox said, "Don't be afraid. I don't eat hens now. See, I'm going on a pilgrimage! I'm going to be a *hadji*. Look at the rosary I have hung round my neck. Please walk down the hill a little way with me and see me off."

She went on a little further and met a cock. As soon as he saw her, he ran away. Then the fox said to the hen, "Tell the cock not to be frightened because I'm going on a pilgrimage." The cock stopped, and the fox said to him, "Come along with the hen and see me off."

They went on a little and met a turkey cock. As soon as he saw the fox, he ran away. Then the fox said to the hen and the cock, "Tell the turkey not to be frightened because you know that I'm going on a pilgrimage." The turkey stopped, and the fox asked him to come with the cock and the hen to see her off.

They went on and met a duck on the road. The duck, too, was frightened and ran away. The fox said to the other birds, "Tell the duck not to be frightened, because I'm going on a pilgrimage. And take her along with you to see me off."

So they went on and came to a secret spot where they stopped. The fox said, "Good-bye to you, but please, hen, confess your sins so that I can pray for you, too." The hen said, "I haven't sinned. I only lay eggs at my master's house and go out and eat grass." "Oh, then you're full of sin," said the fox. "For one egg you disturb your mistress's peace with your ka-ka-ka. As you're full of sin, I sentence you to death." With that, she killed the hen and hid her in a corner.

When the cock saw the hen killed, he trembled with fear, but then reflected that he could not be in fault as he did not lay eggs. The fox turned to him and said, "Confess your sins so that I can pray for you, too." The cock said, "I don't lay eggs and so I have no sins." "You're quite wrong," said the fox. "You're even more sinful than the hen. In the middle of the night you crow ki-ki-ki so that the children wake and cry and their mothers get up and beat them. Since you are a sinner, you are sentenced to death like the hen." And the fox killed the cock and hid him in a corner.

After that she questioned the turkey. He replied, "I neither lay eggs nor crow at night." "You," said the fox, "are a bigger sinner even than they were. When your master buys another cock, you peck him on the head and won't leave him alone." In this way, the fox sentenced the turkey also to death and killed him.

Last of all, she called the duck and questioned her as she had done the others. The duck replied, saying, "When I lay eggs, I don't make myself heard at all. I don't quarrel with my friends, and at night I sleep quietly." "Oh no," said the fox, "You're more sinful than the others. Although your master gives you water in a clean plate or bowl, you go and put your beak into dirty puddles." In this way she sentenced the duck like the others and killed her.

And so the hungry fox found food by her cunning for a whole week.

[told by Stavre Xhimitiku of Berat]

32

How the Baldhead Married the King's Daughter

Once upon a time there as a woman who had a baldheaded son. One day he said to his mother, "The king must give me his daughter in marriage. We have nothing to eat and he has a lot of money." The old woman went to the king and gave him this message. The king said, "Old woman, your son is a baldhead. However, go and tell him to get the priest from the church and bring him here." The mother went back to her son and gave him this message, saying, "Go and get the priest in the church and take him to the king. Then the king will give you his daughter." Her son said, "Alright, I will fetch the priest."

He made a jacket with bells on it, went to the priest's church, and climbed onto the roof. With the priest underneath him, he shook the bells. "God, what is that?" exclaimed the priest. The baldhead said, "It is no good resisting. I am St. Michael and I am going to take your soul away. You have lived long enough. You are a hundred years old." "Oh no, I am very young," protested the priest. "Well, come out and let me see whether you are a hundred years old or not." The priest came out of the church and the baldhead climbed down from the roof. "It's true," he said. "You are young, you are not old. Have you got any money on you?" "Yes, I have," said the priest. "Well, take what you have and follow me. I'll take you to God. He wants to see you." What could the priest do, so he followed the man.

In the morning, the king's servants opened the door of the palace and saw the priest tied to it. "What are you doing there, priest?" they asked. "St. Michael brought me here," he said. "Devil take him!" said the servants. "It must have been the baldhead." They untied the priest and brought him to the king.

"Who brought you here, priest?" asked the king. "St. Michael did," said the priest. "It was the baldhead, my dear priest," explained the king. He released him and he went back to his church.

The baldhead's mother again went to the king and said to him, "The baldhead brought you the priest." "He took a lot of money from him," replied the king. "He did," countered the old woman, "but the coins were rusty and he just wanted to wash off the rust. Now he wants to marry your daughter." The king said, "Well, let him come and steal the wheat in my granary." "I will tell him," said the old woman.

The king set a number of guards in the granary with orders to kill the baldhead, should they see him near it. At night, the baldhead set out and went to the granary. He opened the backdoor and saw at once that there were numerous guards there and that he could not get in. So he shut the door, dug a tunnel under the ground outside, and so got under the granary. He bored a hole in the floor, stole all the wheat, and went away.

When it dawned the following day, the king asked if the baldhead had come that night. They replied, "No! How could he come?" "Well, take a look at the granary," said the king. The granary had been emptied, there was nothing inside. "He has stolen my wheat! Where were you?" said the king to his guards. "What sort of watch did you keep?" Then they looked around and they found the tunnel. "The devil got under the granary!" exclaimed the king.

The baldhead's mother went to the king a third time. "My son sent me to ask you to get your daughter ready," she told him. "Where has he taken the wheat he stole from me?" asked the king. "He has it at home, " she said. "He is winnowing it because it was rather dusty." "Go and tell him to come and see me," said the king. So his mother went home and told him that the king was asking for him. The baldhead then went to see the king.

He went straight to him. "Are you the baldhead who stole the priest from the church?" asked the king. "I am," replied the baldhead. "And who stole my wheat?" "I did." "I am going to execute you, you devil," exclaimed the king. Then he said to his soldiers, "Keep the

34

baldhead with you and don't let him out. And go and ask the priest to come here." They called the priest and he came.

The king said to him, "Priest, I have caught the baldhead. I have him here. We mean to kill him." "Let's both kill him," said the priest. "Let's both have the crime on our conscience, you as well as I." So they placed the baldhead in a sack and took him down to a river to drown him.

The king then said to the priest, "Don't let's kill him tonight. It is best for many people to come and all take the sin on their conscience. He has stolen all over the place." So they left the baldhead on the river bank for the night.

During the night, a rich merchant who had thirty or forty packhorses laden with merchandise came by. When the baldhead heard them coming, he began to shout inside the sack, "I don't want to, I don't want to!" The merchant came up and stopped by the sack. "What is this? Who are you in the sack?" he said. "The king has asked me to marry his daughter and I don't want to," said the baldhead. "Why don't you want to marry her, you devil?" said the merchant. "Where can I take her to live? I am a poor man," replied the baldhead. "Let him give her to me!" proposed the merchant. "Well, if you want her, let me out of the sack," said the baldhead. The merchant untied the sack and let the baldhead out. "Now you get in in my place," said the baldhead. After tying the mouth of the sack firmly, he left the merchant lying on the bank in the sack. "When the king comes tomorrow, shout 'I want her, I want her!'" he said. Then he took the horses and went away.

Next morning, the king, accompanied by a great crowd of people, came to the river bank. The merchant inside the sack shouted, "I want her, I want her!" As the men came up, the king said, "Who do you want?" "The king's daughter," said the merchant. "Take this fool and fling him into the water and drown him," said the king. His servant picked up the merchant and flung him into the water.

The baldhead led the horses all round the town and sold the merchandise, sugar to some people and coffee to others. They said to him, "Baldhead, the king drowned you!" "May his hand wither who threw me into the water where he did." "What do you mean?" "He

35

threw me into the water near the bank, and that's where I found these horses. Had he only thrown me into the middle of the stream, I should have found diamonds."

The king heard that the baldhead had escaped and, sending for him, said, "Baldhead, I drowned you!" "Oh, Your Majesty, if you had only thrown me farther into the water, I should have grown richer than you." "What do you mean?" asked the king. "In the middle of the river there are diamonds, but by the bank where you threw me, there was nothing but horses," replied the baldhead.

"Come and show me the place," said the king. "Come on then," replied the baldhead. He took the priest and the king and led them, let's say, along the bank of the river Shkumbin. "In the deep water over there you will find diamonds," he stated. The king and the priest gathered themselves up and jumped into the water. And they were both drowned.

The baldhead then returned home and married the princess.

[told at Shëngjin in the district of Elbasan]

The Maiden with the Foolish Husband

Once upon a time there was a rich man who had a son for whom he wanted to find a wife. But the son would not consent to be married.

One day, the young man went for a walk through town. On the outskirts of the town he saw a girl in the courtyard of a poor house. She rushed into the house at once to hide and keep him from seeing her. He asked who the house belonged to and was told that it belonged to a sweeper. Then he went home.

There, he said to his father, "If you really want me to get married, I should like to marry the sweeper's daughter in such-and-such a place." His father replied, "That girl is only fit to be our servant." "That's not so," protested the young man. "I've property enough of my own, and I want that girl because I saw what sort of person she is." His father did not go against his wish, and the young people were married.

The father was a wealthy merchant. A year after the wedding, he had to go to Istanbul to buy goods in the shops there. His son said, "Do let me go this year." "All right, you go," replied the father. So the young man took three servants with him and went to Istanbul.

When they got there, they went to a hotel and ordered coffee. As they waited, his servant asked him, "How did you come to marry the sweeper's daughter?" "Why, what business is it of yours?" he replied. He then called again to the hotelkeeper to bring coffee. Now this man had heard the servant asking him how he had come to marry the sweeper's daughter and, when he brought the coffee, he asked them where they were from. "We are natives of Elbasan," they replied. "Ah, Elbasan is a very fine town." he remarked. "Oh, have you been there?" they inquired. "Yes, I have," he replied. "What did you do there? Where did you stop?" they asked. "I stayed with a sweeper who had a pretty daughter," he answered. The young man exclaimed, "You are lying!"

37

"I am not lying, why should I lie?" he said. "Well, if you really did stop there, I will be your servant," said the young man. "What proof do you want me to bring you?" asked the hotelkeeper. "A dress she has worn," said the young man. "I know her clothes."

The hotelkeeper set out and hastened to Elbasan. In the street, he asked where such-and-such a person's house was, and was shown the sweeper's house. Close by, there was a poor man's house with only an old woman in it. He went and knocked on the door, and said, "Can you take me in for tonight? I am a stranger here." "All right, come in," said the old woman. So he followed her into the house.

After a little while, he said to the old woman, "Can you take me to the house of the local Agha?" "Yes, I can," she said, "I can show you the door." "I don't want to be seen to the door," said the fellow, "I'll get into a box and then I want you to carry it into the house on your back. If anybody asks you what you are doing, you will say that you have been invited out tonight and that you have certain things in the box which you want to leave with the Agha. You are afraid the things will be stolen if you leave them at home."

So the old woman carried the man in the box on her back to the Agha's house. "What do you want, old woman?" his servants asked her. "I want to leave this box in the bride's room," said the old woman. "All right, leave it there," they said and the old woman left it in the bride's room and went home.

After supper, everyone in the Agha's house went to his room to sleep. After the bride came to hers and fell asleep, the hotelkeeper opened the box and came out. He went to the clothes chest belonging to the bride and, opening it, took out all her clothes, and again closed the chest. Then he got into his own box once more.

Early in the morning, the old woman arrived, lifted the box onto her back, and left the Agha's house. When she reached home, the hotelkeeper came out of the box. He gave her a good tip and, taking the clothes with him, went straight back to Istanbul.

There he found the young man and called to him to come and see his wife's clothes. He spread them all out and the bridegroom saw the very clothes which he had given to his wife. "How I have been fooled! To think I married that girl!" he exclaimed. And so, the hotelkeeper was able to keep the young man in Istanbul as his servant.

The young man then telegraphed to his father, bidding him to kill the wife he had left at home. "Because of her," he wrote, "I have to stay here as a servant."

The wife heard that he had sent word to kill her. His father, the wealthy merchant, however, could not bring himself to slay her. So she said to him, "If you love your son and me, give me some money, and I will put things right." "How much do you want?" he asked. "About five hundred naps," she replied. The merchant pulled out his purse and gave her the money for which she asked.

She next sent word to a tailor to come and see her. When he arrived, she asked if he knew how to make men's clothes well. "Yes, my lady, I can cut them as well as you could wish," said the tailor. "No prince must have clothes so fine," said the young wife. "Very well, my lady, we shall make them as you please," he promised. When they were ready, the clothes were brought to her. She looked at them and liked them, and paid the tailor as much money as he asked.

She then put on the clothes and made herself look like a man. So dressed, she went out into town, where she found four or five fine young men. "Are you willing to come and be my servants for any wages that you care to name?" she asked. "I can give you two or three naps a month," she added. They accepted her offer and she dressed them up nicely in new clothes, and then said, "Now, follow me." She then took them with her and went to Istanbul.

There she and her servants stopped at a hotel, where she asked which hotelkeeper had hired a man from Elbasan as a servant. They showed her the hotel and, accompanied by her young men, she went there. The hotelkeeper greeted the rich man, as he thought, with servants behind him, saying, "Welcome, your lordship!" After drinking coffee, she and her servants rose to go. But first, she drew out ten naps from her purse and gave them to the hotelkeeper, as the price of the coffee. The hotelkeeper was amazed when he saw so much money. "Who is this? A prince?" he wondered.

The young wife visited him again the following day. She sat down on a chair and the hotelkeeper rejoiced. "Make some coffee," she ordered. "Yes, my lord," he replied. When he brought the coffee to her, she said, "Do sit down and have a talk with me. I am bored and want someone to talk to."

The hotelkeeper sat down and talked with her for a little while. At length she said, "You are a fine fellow. Do come and stay the night with me and let us go on talking." "Yes, my lord, I will," replied the hotelkeeper. Before she went to her hotel, she again drew out her purse and paid him ten naps for the coffee.

In the evening the hotelkeeper went to her hotel and soon they began to drink raki. "We're going to drink tonight!" she said. "What is your name?" she asked. "My name is Ali," he replied. "And your family name?" she asked. "They call me Ali Shejtani (the Devil)," he answered. "That is a poor name, but never mind. Long life to you," she said. He got very drunk, in fact as drunk as a lord. She then said to her servants, "Undress this fellow." They uncovered his shoulders and, after heating an iron ring in the fire, branded him on both shoulders. Then they dressed him again.

When dawn came, the hotelkeeper got up and said, "Hello, you there! I am off to open the hotel." "All right, go," she replied.

When it was full day, she went with her servants to the authorities to lodge a complaint. She said, "I used to have a stupid servant that I brought up, but he has run away." "Who is this person?" they asked. "He is called Ali Shejtani," she said. In response, they sent a gendarme to fetch Ali Shejtani. When he arrived, the authorities said to him, "Why did you leave your master here?" "He was never my master and I was never his servant," he protested. "He was my servant," she insisted, "my faithful servant. I have many of them, not only one. And he is branded. If he has not been my servant, he will not carry my mark on his shoulders. If he has been my servant, then you will see that he has been branded." The authorities undressed him and saw the branding. "Why do you lie, you scoundrel?" they shouted. "Throw him into prison and summon all of his people." They brought all his people,

40

including his wife and servant, to the authorities. Then they said to the girl visitor, "Here they all are. Take them with you."

She made ready in all haste and left for home the next day. Gendarmes walked in front of the party and behind it, because it was feared that Ali Shejtani's people would run away. When they drew near to her native town, she told the gendarmes to take Ali Shejtani's people to such-and-such a house. Then, followed by her servants, she herself went on ahead.

She went straight home and said to her father-in-law, "Come out and welcome your stupid son!" "Why, has he come back?" asked the father. "Yes, he has," she replied.

The gendarmes brought up the whole party and all sat down with only the gendarmes standing. She said to her husband, "You stupid fellow, why did you go to Istanbul and chatter about me? Your father sent you there to buy merchandise and not to make a scandal like this, letting Ali Shejtani come and steal the clothes in my clothes chest."

She then ordered her servants to give Ali Shejtani a sound beating. "I'm the sweeper's daughter. Whenever were you in my house?" she asked. "Anyway, I now know how much brains my husband has," she added.

After giving a sound beating to Ali Shejtani, they sent him back to Istanbul together with his wife. And so, the sweeper's daughter rescued her foolish husband from him.

[told at Shëngjin in the district of Elbasan]

41

The King's Two Children Who Were Thrown into the Sea

I will tell you a story, a nice but a rare story of the good old days, of things that came to pass.

The King of Persia was a bachelor. In his kingdom there was a town, a little town. In a house near the town, three sisters worked day and night to earn their bread.

One night, the King ordered officers and soldiers to go out to guard the town because it had been learned that some of his enemies meant to throw bombs at the Royal Palace. As it was very cold, a major, who was the King's close friend, hid behind the corner of the house where the three girls were working. The three girls did not know he was behind the kitchen.

The three sisters, all of whom were of marriageable age, were talking. The eldest one said, "Sisters, should the King marry me, I would feed his whole army with one oven of bread." The second one turned and said, "Should he marry me, with one reel of thread I would sew clothes for his whole army." The youngest one said, "Should be marry me, I would not be able to do such things, but I would promise, with God's help, to bear him two children at the same time, a son and a daughter, the boy with a star on his forehead and the girl with a moon on her breast.

The major heard what they said and went to this friend, the King, and told him what he had heard. "In such and such a street, at such and such a number, I went and hid when Your Majesty had ordered us to go out into the town. In the house where I hid, there are three sisters. I heard the first one saying that, should the King marry her, she would be able to feed all the army for a day with one oven of bread." He then proceeded to tell him all the other things he had heard.

The major then said to the King, "It would be a good thing if they all did what they said. If I were in your place, Your Majesty, I should marry them just to see if these things prove right or not." The King thought it over and then sent a go-between to see them.

When the go-between questioned them, the eldest girl said: "What I said is the truth." "But would you like to be a queen?" "Of course!" So the King married her and gave a wedding party, at which I, too, was present. How we enjoyed ourselves! We played and danced so much that my feet ache even to-day.

When he had been married to her for a week, the King said to his wife, "Well, wife, what now? Produce the oven of bread!" "Are you in your senses, husband? How could it be possible, King, to feed your whole army with one oven of bread?" "All right," the King replied, "but that was the condition on which I married you." "I can't do it," his wife said. "Then you will be my servant at my court," the King replied, and took the second sister to wife.

When he had spent ten days with her, he said to her, "Wife, I married you because of what you said – that you would sew clothes for my whole army with one reel of thread." "How is it possible, Your Majesty, for one reel of thread to be enough for your whole army? It is not possible." "You will then do as your sister does, be a servant," the King replied.

He then married the youngest sister. "Mistress," he said to her, "I married you on condition that you do what you said you would do." "So help me God and so God grant it, I hope to succeed," she replied.

When the King had lived with her for two months, he went away to fight because a neighbour had declared war on him. Before starting out, he said to his wife, "Mistress, I'm going away. The man who brings me the good news that my wife has done what she said she would do, will get a good present." Nine months later, the lady gave birth to two children as she had said. But her sisters were jealous of her. Why should they not have children like she did? Just see what they did to her.

On the same day, a bitch had given birth to two puppies. Her sisters took her two babies, put them in a box, and flung them into the sea. Then they put the puppies in the babies' place. And they spread rumours that the queen had given birth to two puppies. Instead of good news, they took bad news to the King. "Your wife has given birth to two puppies," they said.

The King was very unhappy and issued a decree that his wife should be severely punished for not doing what she promised. "Take her," he commanded his men, "wrap her in a bull's hide, and hang her at the palace door. A sentry is to be stationed there to see that whoever goes out or comes in spits on her. My order is not to be disobeyed." And naturally, the King's order had to be carried out.

Now we shall learn what happened to the babies. When they were thrown into the sea, the waves pushed them along and carried them far out to sea where there was a little island, with a palace in the middle of it. And whose was this palace? Saint Nicholas's, may he give us his blessing, for he is the patron of both fresh and salt water. What did God feed the saint on? A fig tree. It bore four figs each day, one for lunch and one for supper for Saint Nicholas and his wife. But one day the fig tree bore eight figs. When Saint Nicholas's wife saw them, she was surprised, the fig tree never having had so many figs before. Why so on that day? Because food for the babies was included. When the old woman got up, she went to the shore, and what did she see? A box being washed ashore by the sea waves. When the box came nearer, she heard two voices. The babies were crying in the closed box.

The old woman, hastening to Saint Nicholas, said, "Old man, old man, the sea waves have cast up a box in which you can hear babies' voices." Saint Nicholas got up at once and went to the shore. And what did he see? The babies were really crying. Driven forward by a big wave, the box came ashore. Saint Nicholas caught and opened it, and in it were two children of indescribable beauty.

The old woman took them, washed them, changed their clothes, and attended to them like a real mother. But they needed to be fed as well as tended. They cried and touched the old woman's breast. Saint Nicholas thought for a little while, then had the idea of praying to God for help. A wild goat came in reply.

The goat was as fond of the babies as if they had been her own kids. She used to come and lick them while Saint Nicholas put her teats in their mouths and they sucked. They were well looked after. Saint Nicholas baptised them, naming the boy Constantine and the girl Illyria.

The babies grew. As much as a baby should grow in a year, they grew in a day, and in 25 days they grew to be 25 years old. Saint Nicholas taught them philosophy, and they learned a great deal. Very few are those who study so much nowadays. In this way, they finished their schooling in five days, going through elementary school, secondary school, university and a college of philosophy, that is to say, there was no higher learning to be had by either the boy or the girl.

When they had lived about ten years with their adopted father and mother, the time of martyrdom came for the saint and the time to die for his wife or, as they say rather, the time for both to pass away. The saint summoned the boy and the girl. "My dear children," he said, "it is with great grief that I say this to you, but God's commands are not to be ignored. I am now to pass away and you must look after yourselves. Stay here! Whenever you are bored, you can go to the seashore. Here is my horse's bridle. If you need help, put the bridle in the water. Then a horse will come and attend to anything you need. Do you understand?" "Yes," they replied. "Here, boy, take this book. When you are in distress or great danger, read this book and you will escape from the danger. Now good-bye." The saint and his wife kissed them both, with tears in their eyes. The boy and girl wept after they had gone. For besides them, they had known no other parents.

When they had been there two or three years longer, the girl felt bored and said to her brother, "Dear brother, please, please listen to your darling sister. Let's go to the seashore. I'm very bored." "Now listen, sister," he replied, "our parents left us here, and here we must remain." "All right, brother, but I'm bored here." "Well then, put the horse's bridle into the water and let's ask the horse to see what it will say."

They put the horse's bridle into the water, whereupon Fig-Bali appeared. "What's the matter, dear masters?" it asked. "What indeed?" the young man replied. "We only want to go out into the sea. What do you say?" "As you please, though I would say you are all right here. But do as you please." "No, no, we want to go far out to sea," the boy and girl cried. "All right," it replied. "Then one of you get on the saddle and the other on the pillion." The girl mounted on the saddle and the boy rode pillion. From the seashore to their native town it was a five or six days' journey, but the horse did it in two hours.

He took them to their native town but they had no idea they had been born there and thought they had been born on the island. The horse went away and they rented a small house, but did not have a penny piece of money.

However, the young man and the girl had put on saintly raiment, the like of which there was none in this world. You could not look at their clothes because they dazzled your eyes. After they had settled down, the young man went into the town. As he passed along the royal avenue, he came on the dwelling of the King and his ministers. The young man went in and was greeted respectfully by everyone. They entertained him, but they dared not question him because he was more beautiful, wiser and better dressed than they were. However, the King plucked up his courage enough to say, "Where are you from?" "I am the King of Greenland," the young man replied. As soon as the King's eyes fell on him, he liked him as much as a son, though he did not know that it was his son. And so they began to get acquainted.

The King said, "Constantine, shall we play cards for a little?" "I don't know how to play," said the young man. "Come on, let's play," said the King. "All right, let's play. Only don't be angry but I've no money." "I'll give you some," the King said. He put his hand into his pocket, drew out 100 naps [Napoleons], and said, "Either you win them from me or I take them back from you." However, no matter with whom he played, the King always won back his money. As the proverb says, "Where money's meant to enter, it enters by the chimney." But when the King played with the young man, he lost and Constantine won all the money. The King felt a little angry. They played a second game. The young man did not dare to say he could not play, for he did not deserve the money. They played a third game and the King again lost, so that the young man won 200 naps in one day.

46

At midday, the young man bought the food he needed and went back to his sister. "Good morning, sister." "Good morning, brother. Where have you been?" "At the royal restaurant. I played cards with the King and won 200 naps." "I'd give my life for you! But how could you play without having any money at all?" "Sister, we are very lucky."

They played for one, two and three days, and the King always lost. But as time went on, the King's affection for the young man increased. One day he went home in a very thoughtful mood. The first wife he had married, the young man's aunt we should say, asked him why he was so downcast. "Nothing's the matter with me," he replied. "Perhaps another King has declared war on you?" "No." "Well, why are you so worried?" "I've found such a handsome young man and I'm so sorry for him that I cannot get him out of my mind." She knew in her heart that she was not free from guilt. "Why did you not question him?" "I did," said the King. "Where is he from?" "Greenland." "Why has he come?" "I did not ask him." "Has he come alone or is there someone with him?" "I did not ask him." "Well, do."

The next day the two men met again. "Constantine, who did you come here with?" "My sister." "Where is your house?" "On the outskirts of the town." The King came home in the evening and found his wife waiting for him. "Hey," said the first wife in the presence of the second one, "did you meet that young man?" "I did." "What relatives has he got?" "Only his sister." Then they were terrified. "What shall we do?" they exclaimed to each other. "Do you know what we should do? We should send an old woman to the girl to do away with the young man."

The next day, they sent an old woman to her. They gave a gold coin to the old woman. Some old women are as cunning as foxes. This one went to the girl and began to flatter her very much. "Good morning, pretty girl." "Welcome, auntie." "How are you, girlie?" "All right, auntie. Please come in. Let me give you a cup of coffee." The old woman went in and was astounded by her beauty. She began to talk cunningly. "What a pretty girl you are! What a lovely one! But how can you stand living here alone?" "What can I do?" the girl replied. "I will teach you what to do," said the old woman. "What?" asked the girl.

"The best thing for you, daughter, is to have a Bilbil Gjyzar. It's a nightingale that sings beautiful songs. I believe you would never be bored if you had one." "Where are these nightingales?" "Your brother knows, and when he comes home to-night, you must cry. When he asks why you are crying, tell him it's because you cannot stay alone here. When he asks what you want, you his dear sister, say you want a Bilbil Gjyzar. When he asks where it is, say 'you know.'"

And so it happened as the old woman said.

"In that case," said the young man, "put the horse's bridle in the water." Some minutes later, Fig-Bali appeared. "What is it, masters?" "We want a Bilbil Gjyzar." "A Bilbil Gjyzar is very hard to catch. They live between two mountains which open and close every five minutes and so catching the birds is very dangerous." "No matter how dangerous, we mean to go." "Then take a basket with you and let's be off."

It was a three months' voyage but Fig-Bali did it in three days. When they arrived near the mountains, the horse said to its master, "As the mountains opens, I will dash forward, but you must not turn your eyes either this way or that, you must keep them fixed on my head. The fairies will call to you, but you must not move your eyes from my head. When we sink to our knees in the middle of the nightingales, fill your basket with the birds, but don't turn your head around, else the fairies may seize you."

The mountain opened, the horse rushed in, and he caught the nightingales. The fairies called from the back, "Wait, young man, let us give you some better ones," but the young man paid no attention to what they said. They returned home, very thin in the face because they had suffered a lot.

A week later, Constantine returned to the royal restaurant. The King had been worried about him a good deal and, on seeing him, asked where he had been these days. "I was ill," Constantine replied. He did not tell him the truth.

The girl was very glad when she saw the nightingales. They poured forth sad and happy songs, enough to make a man's heart flutter like a leaf.

48

Every evening, when the King went back to this palace, his first two wives asked him if the young man had returned. On the days when he had not done so, the King would say, "No." But this night, he said, "He's come back, but he looks very sickly. He's been ill." "Bad luck for us that he's returned alive," said the two to each other. "What else can we do to destroy him?" One said, "Let's send the old woman again to tell the girl to ask him to fetch the Earthly Beauty."

The old woman knew her business. The next morning, she got up and went to the girl and, as before, asked her if she was satisfied with the nightingales. "Very much so." "But they'll bore you soon." "If they bore me, what can I do?" "Here is what you can do. You must find a friend." "Oh, auntie, where are there friends to be found for me?" "Of course there are, daughter!" "Where?" "There's the Earthly Beauty. She'd make a fine friend for you." "Where is she?" "Your brother knows. When he returns home in the evening, cry as before and he will bring her to you as he did the nightingales."

The brother returned in the evening to find his sister weeping. "What are you crying for, sister?" "How can I not cry? You brought me some wretched nightingales that bother me the whole day." "What else do you want?" "A friend." "Sister, where can friends be found that are fit for you?" "Why not? There is the Earthly Beauty, she'd make a friend." "Where is she to be found?" "You know, brother!"

He then put the horse's bridle in the water. The horse appeared and asked him, "What's up, what's up, master?" "My sister is asking for the moon! Can I find the moon in the snow?" "No, you can't," said Fig-Bali. "What is your sister asking for?" "The Earthly Beauty." "That's bad because we will be killed there. Many go there, but none have ever come back alive." "Well, let's go and see, come what may, whatever fate has in store for us." "All right," said the horse, "but it's a six months' journey." "Even if it lasts twelve months, we shall go!" "Get ready then." "I am ready," said the young man.

They set off, but I don't know how many days it took them. I only learned that they got there. The Earthly Beauty had come out onto the palace balcony and was talking with her maids. She had sat down on the lap of one, who pretended to delouse her. The servant, seeing how good-looking the young man was, felt very sorry. Without her meaning to cry, tears rolled down her cheeks and fell onto the face of the Earthly Beauty. The Earthly Beauty sprang up at once. "What's happened? Is it raining?" "No," replied the maid, "a very handsome young man has come by, as beautiful as a star. I implore you, mistress, not to kill him at once." "Oh, you whore of a servant, what do I care if he is handsome!"

The young man came nearer, but the girl on her balcony did not stir. He called out, "Come down, you beautiful creature. It's for you I left my home, six or seven months' journey away" "Ha, ha! Such a lot of men like you I've seen! May you turn to marble up to the horse's knees!" And he did. "Come down, now," said the young man. "I'll never give you up." "May you turn to marble up to the horse's belly!" "Now, come down, I say," repeated the young man. "Such a lot of men I've seen like you. May you turn to marble up to the horse's back!"

Only the horse's head was then left and the young man had only half of himself not yet turned into marble. The horse cried out, "Don't speak to her anymore. She is destroying us. But where is the book your father gave you? Read it. Otherwise we'll lose our lives." The young man took out the book at once and read it. Immediately all the marble dissolved.

The horse then jumped onto the balcony. The young man seized the Earthly Beauty by the hair, put her on the horse's saddle and himself rode pillion behind her. They set off on the return journey. This time they did it faster, returning in two weeks. He took the Earthly Beauty home and there, at the sight of her, the nightingales began to sing. And another strange thing occurred, too! When the two girls saw each other, they were surprised.

The King had been greatly worried about Constantine. But two weeks later, they met again at the same restaurant. How glad the King was when he saw Constantine! If you only knew how glad, dear reader! I who witnessed his joy don't know how to describe it. The King asked where he had been. "I've been ill," he replied. "If you were ill, why didn't you tell me so that I could send you my physician?" "Excuse me,

Your Majesty, I did not think of it." "You weren't wise, Constantine."
"I wasn't," Constantine replied, but he did not tell the truth to the King.

After they had amused themselves all day long, the King went
home happy in the evening. "Why are you so happy?" the maid, his
wife, asked him. "Because I met Constantine to-day. He was very weak
because he'd been ill for two weeks." "We're done for!" said the two
sisters. "What shall we do now?" "There's nothing we can do now.
However, let's ask the King to invite them to call on us. Then we'll
manage to poison them. Otherwise there's nothing we can do."

When the King came home in the evening, they said to him,
"How is it, King, that you've never invited Constantine and his relatives
to call sometime on us?" "I've been wrong not to invite him," said the
King. "I'll do so to-morrow. It's a holiday." "You certainly must as you
are so fond of each other."

The next day, they met the young man. The King said to him,
"Dear Constantine, I have made a great mistake." "How's that?" "I'm
so fond of you, Constantine, more than I can tell you. I care for you as
though you were my own son and not a stranger. Yet I've never once
invited you to call on us." "Oh, never mind," said Constantine, "you've
entertained me here in the restaurant. We needn't go to your house."
"No, you must come to my house. To-morrow without fail, take your
sister after church, and bring her to my house. I'll be at church. Keep
near to me."

In the evening, Constantine went home and said to his sister
and his wife, "To-morrow, we're invited to the King's. After church.
What do you say? Shall we go or not?" The girl said, "Don't let's go."
The Earthly Beauty said, "Let's go. He is a King, he has invited us, and
why shouldn't we go? Are you in your senses?"

The next day, the young man got up to go, taking his sister and
his wife, both with nightingales on their shoulders. Up to that day
neither woman had seen the light of day at all. They were white as this
sheet of paper or as milk and red as a rose in May, in short, they were
the Earthly Beauties. The nightingales sang. They were all beautiful,
the young man like a star, so beautiful that I can hardly describe him.
I'm happy to have seen him! They went to church, the saintliest of the

saintly. All the people were amazed. The priests forgot they were at church. When the service was over, they went out. The people jostled each other, trying to get nearer to them to see their beauty and the nightingales.

They then went to visit the King, who gave them the best of drinks and foods. But I forgot to tell you at this stage that when they came in through the palace door, the mother of the young man and of the girl was still alive and hanging at the palace gate. As they tried to pass through, the King said to them, "Spit on that woman! She's the third wife I married who gave me a false promise. She said she would bear me a son and a daughter together, the son with a star on his forehead and the daughter with a moon on her breast. Instead of doing what I just told you, she bore two puppies. Go for her!" "No," said the Earthly Beauty, "God sent the puppies, too!" It's not good to think so little of anyone. How many years has she been here?" "Twelve or thirteen." The Earthly Beauty knew quite well that her companions were the son and daughter.

When the poor mother saw them, she recognised them because of their birthmarks, but she could not believe that her hostile sisters could do such a thing to her. The Earthly Beauty said, "We won't spit on her." The King seemed a little affronted, but she insisted, "Are we to do as we please? Since we're left free to choose, this is what we want."

As they left for home, they said to the King that it was his turn to visit them. "We shall see what we shall see," said the King. "You must come to-morrow. We shall expect you. You must come without fail," they replied.

The King and his ministers started out and what was it they saw when they got there? Although the young man's dwelling was smaller, it was ten times more beautifully arranged than the King's palace. And what else did they see? All the foods and the drinks and everything else that was necessary came at a word, without anybody moving from his place. They ate, drank, sang with the nightingales, and left for home,

The King then invited them to lunch. The poor sisters were terrified. When the young man and the girl went to the King's, the

52

sisters drank a little. Then they set the table and poisoned the first dishes. But the Bilbil Gjyzar knew what they were plotting over in the corner for, being a bird, it had gone into the kitchen and seen what they were doing. When they began to eat, the nightingale stopped them, saying, "Master, don't eat that food, it will poison you." Immediately, the young man stopped everybody from eating, saying, "All the food has been poisoned." The King grew angry and said, "How can it be poisoned?" "If you care to test it, find a cat and give it the food. Then we'll see." The King acted on the suggestion, and the cat died. Then the King was much worried, but was calmed by the others. They ate the rest of the food and set off for home.

The Earthly Beauty then said to the King, "Next Sunday, you and your army must have lunch with me." "All right," the King agreed. Two or three days beforehand, the King ordered all his bakers and cooks to prepare the food at his expense, saying, "Constantine has invited us over."

But the Earthly Beauty sent a message to the King to ask what he was doing. "Take away all these people. I knew what I was doing when I invited you. So please send them all away! But don't kill those poor men or you'll come to harm." The King did not want to send them away, so the Earthly Beauty cried out, "Oh God, let a stick beat the men working over there!" The stick began invisibly to beat the bakers; it took vengeance according to Lek's Kanun. The men were in a fix, went to the King and complained that an invisible stick was beating them. The King was convinced and thus commanded, "Stop working."

Sunday came. The King got up in rather a bad temper. "Since she will not accept my help, let's see how Constantine will fête us to-day," he said, and he took with him nearly 10,000 people.

Near the town there was a wide plain. As soon as the Earthly Beauty said, "Let a large tent be put up!" it was done. And so it happened with the table and its leaves for 10,000 persons. They received their guests with great honour, with bands, orchestras and the nightingales. The tables were all set alike for King and soldiers. The King's and the soldiers' food and drink were alike. They ate and drank the best of foods, all of which came without being prepared by anyone.

One of the ministers liked the golden spoon with which he ate, and hid it in his boot. The Earthly Beauty saw him. When lunch was over, she demanded roll call for the spoons so that the one hidden by the minister would respond. "Spoons, are you all here?" "No, no, mistress, I'm not here." "Minister, you've hidden my spoon. Come out!" With this, the spoon emerged from the boot.

The King again invited them over for lunch. The Earthly Beauty said, "We'll come but on condition that things are done as we say. Do you agree to this?" "Yes, I do," said the King.

So one day they went to the King's palace to amuse themselves. The girl said before the parliament, "Do you still stick to your word, King?" "In all circumstances, yes!" "Well then, summon the two wives you married first." He called them in and they came. "Now, King, give orders that the woman you hung at the gate should wash herself and then dress in her best clothes." The King said, "That is not possible here." "Keep your promise!" said the parliament. They washed, dressed and fed her; and then brought her in.

"Now," said the girl, "tell us what happened to you with these sisters." She told them what had happened. "But, ladies, how could this woman bear two puppies?" she asked the sisters. "No, she didn't," they said. "How was it then?" "It was like this. Our sister here did as she had said and we were jealous of her and substituted two puppies for her babies." "Well, what did you do with the babies?" "We threw them into the sea." "Did you hear that, Your Majesty?" "I do, I have sinned against her." The mother of the young man and the girl began to cry with joy, and seeing them cry, we cried also.

"Come along, King, don't you cry, but rejoice! These are your children," said the Earthly Beauty. "They've now learned that you are their parents. Get up, young man, and kiss your father's hand and take off your hat." The young man rose and kissed his father's hand. With his right hand he lifted his father's hand to his lips and with this left he took off his cap. The star appeared, for it had been hidden under his cap, where it could not be seen. That is why, when we greet someone respectfully, we take off our hats, because of this custom. "You get up, too, girl!" said the Earthly Beauty. The girl did so. "Kiss your mother's and your father's hands, as your brother did." The girl put her hand on her bosom, undid it, and the moon appeared. That is why it is the custom for women to place their hands on their hearts.

And then all the people present greeted them respectfully one by one. The Earthly Beauty kept her word, as she had always done up to that time.

I am Constantine's bride. I too rose with my hand on my heart and kissed the hands of my father-in-law and my mother-in-law as well as those of the people there.

But listen, reader, there was someone who did not cry for happiness. The trial came of the Queen's sisters. The Queen got up, told her story, and concluded saying, "Although my sisters dug my grave and those of my children, I forgive them."

Then there was great merriment. They began the wedding celebrations. How splendid they were! I, too, who am telling you this tale, was there. But I have told you no story, I have only made fun of you.

How the Couple Got Rid of Three Priests

Once upon a time, there were three priests who fell in love with the same woman, as she reported to her husband. "These priests annoy me," she said. "Well," said her husband, "invite them over for supper one night and when they come, I'll take care of them." She invited them over as he had proposed.

When the evening came, one of the priests arrived before the others. She stuffed him at once into a big vat of cheese. Then the second one came and she stuffed him into the vat with the first one. Lastly, the third priest arrived, and she stuffed him into the vat, too, along with the others.

Then she went back into the house and sat down by the fireside. "Where are the priests? Inside?" asked her husband. "All three are inside," she replied. She then put a big pot full of water on the fire and boiled it. Quietly she took it to the cheese vat and emptied the boiling water over the priests and scalded them to death.

Then husband and wife pulled them out of the vat and placed them, dead as they were, in a row. The husband put one of them over his back and lugged him to the door of Simon's mill, where he set him down. He then knocked on the door. "Who is there?" asked Simon. "Open the door, open the door!" he cried and went and hid as Simon opened the door. The dead priest, who had been placed against the door in the standing position, slumped to the ground. Simon flung him over his shoulder and carried him down to the river Shkumbin, where he flung him into the water. And that was the end of the priest.

Simon went back to his mill. The husband then placed another priest at his door, knocked on it and shouted, "Open the door, Simon, open the door!" "Who is there?" Simon responded as he went and opened the door for a second time. Again the priest slumped to the

56

ground. "Oh, you devil, you followed me home!" exclaimed Simon. He threw the second priest over his shoulder and carried him down to the river and flung him in.

Simon went back to the mill again and shut the door. The husband then brought the third priest and, after placing him against the door, knocked. "Simon, Simon," he called, "Come out, come out! Where have you been?" Simon approached and, when he opened the door again, the third priest crashed to the ground. "Oh, you devil, are you going to keep at this all night?" said Simon. This time, he fetched his rifle, then flung the priest over his shoulder, and went and threw him into the river. Then he hid in ambush, waiting for the priest to come out of the river.

An unfortunate priest was coming down from Shpat. As he began to wade through the water at the ford, Simon shouted to him, "Where are you going? Where are you going?" "Home," replied the priest. "I have carried you all night on my shoulder. Three times I have had you. Enough is enough!" shouted Simon. Raising his rifle, he fired at him and killed him. And that was the fourth priest who died that night.

[told at Shëngjin in the district of Elbasan]

The Merchant and his Love

Once upon a time, there was a rich merchant who had peasants working for him in the village. One day he took a servant with him and went to see one of his peasants. The man slaughtered a ram in his honour. While they were eating, the merchant pulled off the kidneys and the tail and gave them to his servant, saying, "Take these to my love." The servant went home, but cast the meat to the dog.

His mistress saw him. "What did you throw to the dog? What was that you brought home?" she asked. "Master gave me the tail and the kidneys of a ram and told me to take them to his love, and I did." "Why?" she said, "is the dog your master's love?" "How do I know?" said the servant. "That's what he told me."

When the merchant got home, his wife asked him, "Who did you send the meat to?" "To you," he replied. "But the servant threw it to the dog. Oh, oh!" she wailed. Then she grew angry with her husband and, putting on her cloak, she left him and went back to her father's house.

"You drove my wife away, you devil!" the merchant said to his servant. "Never mind, I'll get her back for you. Give me about five piasters," said the servant. With the money in his pocket, he set off for her father's house.

First of all, he went to the houses of the neighbours. "Have you any eggs?" he asked. Those who had, produced them and he bought them. His former mistress came out and, recognising him, said to a woman neighbour, "Ask him why he is buying those eggs." The woman asked the servant, who said to her, "My master is going to get married." The woman donned her cloak in great haste and ran as fast as she could back to her husband's house. "You scoundrel, I hear you are getting

58

married!" she shouted at her husband. "Well," he replied, "if you had not come home, I should have."

[told at Shëngjin in the district of Elbasan]

How the Thief's Son Recompensed the King

Once upon a time, there was a rich man who had a son. The father closed his shop in the evening, came home, ate supper, and then went out to steal. His son did not like this. "Why should you steal?" he asked. "You have a lot of stuff in your shop and you also have a lot of money." But the man enjoyed stealing, even a cup, and after thieving he always ate with good humour.

One night his son said to him, "I'll take you to-night to a place where you can load yourself up with gold. But you must swear not to steal anymore." "All right," said the man. "Well, follow me," said the son and led him to the King's treasury. They soon climbed the wall with the help of nails and got into the upper room. "Go on in," he said to the father. Inside there were piles of money as big as haystacks. "Take what you want. Load yourself with as much as you can carry," said the son. They each loaded themselves, climbed down by the nails and ran away.

When they got home, the son said to the father, "Well, are you satisfied now?" "Oh, yes, I am," replied the father. "I am full of money. I don't want anymore."

The next day, the father went and opened his shop and in the evening he returned home. He ate his fill and then began to put his sandals on. "Why are you putting your sandals on?" asked the son. "Am I to leave all that money there?" he said. "I simply must go and steal it." "But," said the son, "you swore that you would not go stealing again." "I simply must go," he said, and go he did.

He climbed the wall to the window, but underneath the window the King had placed a barrel of tar. The man climbed up and then, thinking he would land on the floor as he had done the previous night, he jumped down. But he fell into the tar up to his neck and he couldn't get out again.

A little later, his son followed in search of him. When he reached the window, he lit a match and saw his father in the tar. "Is that you, father?" he asked. "Yes, it is," replied his father. "For heaven's sake, come and help me out!" But it was impossible to pull him out. Seeing this, his son drew his knife and cut off his father's head.

In the morning, the King's men went to see the Treasury and noticed blood on the surface of the tar. They dragged out the dead man and found the severed head.

The King issued orders that the head should be put on a pole and taken to the market place. "Watch the people," he said. "The dead man's relatives will come to mourn him. See that you catch them."

Hearing of these events, the young man's mother said, "I must go to mourn your father." The young man replied, "You will ruin me." "I must go," she said, paying no attention to his warning. So he filled a sack with earthenware pots and asked her to carry them on her back. "Fall down near the body," he said, "and break the pots." Then scream and cry, saying, "Oh, my pots, oh my pots! What a thing to happen to me!"

The woman went to the market place, fell down, broke the pots, and screamed, "Oh my pots! What a thing to happen to me!" The gendarmes said, "Go away, you devil, with your broken pots!" They thought she was weeping over the pots.

They left the man's head on the pole for three days and three nights, but they saw no one else coming to cry over it. The King had paid them their money for nothing and could not find the culprits.

Then the Council of the Ministers said to the King, "Send a camel to market for sale. No one except the man who stole your treasure will have enough money to buy it." The King found a camel-boy, gave him a camel and said, "Take this camel to the market place and sell it." "Camel for sale! Who wants to buy a camel?" shouted the boy. He went all around the town, but no one asked about the camel. No one wanted to buy it.

Then the young man whose father had stolen the King's treasure saw the camel. He said to his mother, "Put on your best clothes and go to the camel-boy and ask him what he wants for the camel.

Laugh and joke with him and, behind his back, I'll steal the camel." The woman went up to the camel-boy and asked him for what he would sell the camel. "One hundred Napoleons," said he. The woman walked in front and the camel-boy followed, with the woman laughing and joking. Her son came up behind the camel-boy's back, slipped off the halter, stole the camel and took it home. His mother walked on ahead with the camel-boy, then turned around, and left him. He looked back at the camel, but there was no camel to be seen. He was leading the halter only. He turned back to find the animal but it was lost and could not be seen anywhere. He then went and told the King that they had stolen his camel. "Are you blind?" asked the King. "How could they steal it from you?" "Well, they did and I saw nobody and nothing," he replied.

The young man killed the camel and smoked the meat, for a camel's flesh is edible. An old woman went to the King and said, "I can find your camel." "If you do so," said the King, "I'll give you a dinner of meat and *pilaf*." The old woman went around the town asking at every door for camel meat, saying, "My son is ill, he is dying, and he longs for camel meat." At last she came to the young man's door. "Have you by any chance some camel meat?" she asked his mother. "My son is dying and longs for camel meat." "I do have some," said the young man's mother. "Let me give you a little." She went and produced a huge piece of meat. "Here you are," she said. The old woman took the meat and left the house.

The young man was just coming in. "What is this meat, old woman?" he asked. "Some camel meat for my son," she replied. "A blessing on your mother for giving it to me!" "She has not given you much. Come back and let me give you a bigger piece," he said. He made the old woman turn back, led her down to the cellar and killed her. Then he took her head, stuck it on a pole and during the night took it to the King's palace and put it in front of the King.

Early next morning the King saw the old woman's head there. "She found the camel!" he said. He then sent out the town crier to proclaim, "Let the man who stole my treasure and the camel and who cut off the old woman's head come and see me. I have pardoned him." The young man went to see the King. "I'm the man," he said. "My

62

father stole your treasure, I cut off his head and then I stole the camel and cut off the old woman's head." "All very well," said the King, "but now all the other Kings are making fun of me. What am I to say to them?" "Give me a ship full of rings, necklaces and women's clothes," said the young man. The King gave him a ship full of these things.

The young man set sail and landed in, let's say Russia. There he had the town crier cry, "A ship full of all sorts of women's things has arrived. Whoever wants to come and choose something should come and do so."

All the King's womenfolk and all those belonging to the generals and the nobles heard the news and were excited. A good twenty of them gathered together and went down to the ship. "Choose anything you like, ladies," said the young man. "Here you have whatever you want." As they were busy looking at the things, he got the ship underway and set sail with the women still on board. He took them to the King whom he had robbed. "Here are the other King's women," he proclaimed. "Now you can send him word that if your money was stolen, his women were stolen."

[told at Shëngjin in the district of Elbasan]

63

The Two Friends and the Bear

There were once two hunters who had become dear and true friends. A rich neighbour, a furrier, said to them, "If you can kill a wild animal, I'll give you a lot of money, because I want the skin."

Fully armed, the two friends went out to the mountains and the hills to shoot wild animals.

Before long, a bear came out of a cave. It had grown very hungry, and when it saw the two men, it rushed at them, with its eyes as bright as sparks. When they saw this alarming wild beast, they were terrified. One had time to catch hold of a branch on a tall tree and climb to the top, but the other in his fright had no time for this and lay down on the ground. He did not move, because he had heard that a bear, however hungry it may be, will not eat a dead man.

So when the bear came up, he did not move or breathe, but remained as still as a corpse. The bear walked right round him and smelt him, but seeing he was lifeless, left him and went back to its cave.

The man who had climbed to the top of the tree came down, his blood frozen with fear. He went up to his friend and said, "Whew! How brave you are, not to be afraid of a bear!" After a short silence, he said to his friend, "I say, mate, what did the bear say when he whispered in your year?" The other replied, "The friend who deserted you, turned out to be a false friend." The first one hung his head and gave no reply.

The moral is that an ally is known in time of danger, and a friend in the hour of difficulty.

[told by Mehmet Gjavori]

64

The Foundling

Once there was a gentleman who went travelling round the world. When he was on his way back and was near his home, he was overtaken by night and could not reach his native town as he had hoped. He went instead to a village where a peasant took him in for the night. "Welcome, Sir!" said the peasant, who was alone with his wife in the house.

That very night, God granted the peasant a son. "You bring good luck, Sir. God has granted me a son," he said. "I am very glad. Long life to him!" responded the gentleman, rejoicing in turn. The two of them had supper and went to bed.

The gentleman dreamt a dream in which he heard a voice saying to him, "Your property will be enjoyed by the boy who was born to-night." He awoke with a start. "What was that dream? What did it mean?" he asked himself. He again went to sleep and again dreamt a dream in which the same voice said to him, "Your property will be enjoyed by the boy who was born to-night." He again awoke, but this time he could not fall asleep again and kept pondering about his dream until morning.

When the peasant awoke at dawn, the gentleman said to him, "Will you sell this boy of yours to me?" "Oh, no, sir, I cannot. A human being is not for sale," replied the peasant. "But you're poor," said the gentleman. "God will give you another boy and I will give you a lot of money for this one. I'll give whatever you ask." "Let me ask my wife," said the peasant. He went to ask her and she said, "Let's sell the boy to him, husband." The gentleman paid 200 Napoleons and so bought the boy.

He mounted his horse and, putting the little boy in front of him, rode away. The path led them through a rocky stretch of mountain.

There, the gentleman picked up the boy and threw him down onto the rocks to kill him.

A deer happened to be there, for it was only a little way from where her fawns were. When she heard the boy crying, she went up to him, caught him up in her mouth, and carried him to her own home. There she reared him along with her own fawns.

Some hunters, who had gone hunting, came and found the baby. The deer ran away, taking her fawns but leaving the baby behind. It began to cry and the hunters heard it. "What's this weeping?" they asked. Then they went up to the deer's home and found the baby. "It's a human being!" one said. "I'll take it with me," said the other. He had no children of his own and was glad to have this baby. The hunter reared the boy to manhood and called him "Foundling."

The man worked as a servant in a hotel, where the gentleman came to stay. One day, the gentleman said, "What's this name Foundling? Why do you call the boy that?" "Because I found him on a river bank up in the mountains."

The gentleman understood that the boy was the very baby that he had thrown away. In fear he said to the hotelkeeper, "Please let your Foundling take a letter to my home." "Why, of course, send him," replied the hotelkeeper. The gentleman then wrote a letter in which he said, "Kill the young man who brings you this letter." Foundling took the letter and set off for the gentleman's home.

Now the gentleman had children of his own at home, a son and a daughter old enough to marry. The son met Foundling as he approached. "Where are you going?" he asked him. "I'm taking this letter to a gentleman," responded Foundling. "Let me see it," said the young man, and taking the letter, he opened it. "Kill the young man who brings this letter," it read. He destroyed this letter and wrote it differently: "The master has given orders that when this young man comes, you should at once celebrate his marriage with his daughter," just as if his father had written it so. The young man went on to the gentleman's house and was immediately married to the girl. He remained in the house as the gentleman's son-in-law. When the gentleman came home some time afterwards, he found the young man

66

there. "What have you done?" he said to his son. "You yourself gave the order," his son replied. "I never gave such an order," the gentleman said. "My orders were that he was to be killed. However, it doesn't matter. I'll fix him."

In the fold outside he had some sheep. "To-morrow," he said to his wife, "wake Foundling early. I want him to go and fetch a ram. I want one to be slaughtered for us to eat." He had ordered his shepherds to kill the person who went to fetch the ram. But his wife did not wake Foundling up. She was sorry to disturb his sleep. Instead, she woke up her son. "Get up, son," she said, "and go and fetch a ram."

Her son got up, mounted a horse, and went to fetch the ram. When he came near the fold, the shepherds turned their rifles on him and killed him.

The gentleman, who was still in his own room, awoke. "Did you wake Foundling and send him to fetch the ram?" he asked his wife.

"No, it was our son that I woke," she replied. "Oh dear, what a thing you have done! What a murder!" he exclaimed. He mounted his horse and galloped off to see if his son was still alive.

The shepherds saw the horse coming towards them at full gallop. "Master is coming to kill us," they said to each other. In their fear, the snatched up their rifles and killed him. And there was the master dead and gone.

Foundling remained in the gentleman's house and succeeded to his father-in-law's estate.

This is a true story, some people say, but I am not sure.

[told at Shëngjin in the district of Elbasan]

67

The Aga Who Understood the Speech of Animals

Once there was and once there wasn't. Once there was an Aga and his wife who were very rich.

A *hizr* came to them one night. After he had eaten and drunk his fill, he said to the master of the house, "What would you like me to give you?" "I don't want anything," the Aga said, "except to understand the speech of all the animals so as to know what they say." "Very well, you shall have this power," said the *hizr*.

When the man got up in the morning, he found that he understood the speech of all the animals. He understood everything they said.

He then said to his wife, "Let's go and see the cattle fold in the mountains," "Yes, let's," said the wife. So they made ready and started for the cattle fold. It happened that they had a mare and a colt in the stable at home. The wife mounted the mare and the husband mounted the colt to go and see the cattle fold.

As they were on their way, the colt said to its mother, "Oh, mother, I'm tired." The mare replied, "Son, there are only two of you. What about me who am four? The woman on my back is pregnant and so am I. She with her baby and I with my foal make four." As the husband understood what the two horses were saying, he said to his wife, "Get off the mare and let me get on." His wife got off the mare and he got off the colt. The wife then mounted the colt and he got on the mare." As such, they were both three - the mare with her foal and the husband, and the colt with the woman and her baby.

When they reached the cattle fold, the shepherds came out to meet them. "How splendid that the master is coming with his wife!" they cried. Husband and wife stayed in the fold that night.

"Oh," said the big old dog to the other dogs, "Master has come to-night. Don't go to sleep at all, but keep watch and bark all night. To-morrow I'll reward you with milk." Their master understood all that was said. The dogs did not sleep the whole night but barked and barked and kept watch.

When the shepherds got up in the morning, they began to milk the sheep. They milked all of them and filled a big boiler with milk ready for boiling. The old dog went up to the boiler and, raising its leg, peed into the milk. The shepherds rushed forward to catch and kill him because he had dirtied the milk, but their master cried, "Don't touch the dog! Give all the milk to the dogs." The shepherds poured all the milk into the dishes out of which the dogs usually ate. In great content the dogs drank the milk and had their fill. The old dog said to the others, "You see now that I kept my word and got milk for all of you."

The shepherds ran to get a kid to kill for lunch for their master. They caught a good one, but it bleated. Its mother heard it and called out, "What's the matter, sonny?" "The shepherds are going to kill me," said the kid, "because Master has come." "I wish to God that Master's child may be killed just as you are being killed!" said the mother. In haste, the Aga called out, "Let the kid go. Catch a lamb instead!" The shepherds caught a lamb and, like the kid, it bleated. Its mother said, "What's the matter, sonny?" "The shepherds are going to kill me," said the lamb, "because Master has come." "It doesn't matter," said the mother, "we are all to sacrifice ourselves for the Master." They then slaughtered the lamb, roasted it and ate it together.

Then the wife said to her husband, "Why did you let the kid go and take the lamb?" "What about it, wife?" he replied. "You are going to tell me why," she insisted. He did not want to tell her for he knew that if he did, he would die. "It's nothing, wife," he said. But she insisted again. "Either you tell me or it's over between us," she cried. "All right, I'll tell you but I shall die," he replied. "I don't mind your dying, only tell me," she said. So he invited all his friends over one night and gave them a good dinner, and then said, "I'm going to die to-morrow."

The dogs did not eat their supper, they mourned for their Aga who was going to die. Then a cock flew down from his perch and

69

crowed ki-ri-ki and enjoyed himself calling ko-ko-ko to his hens. He then went to the dogs' dish and began to eat the food that the dogs would not eat in their mourning.

The old dog said to the cock, "Get away, cock, or I'll eat you. Don't you know that Master is going to die? You should not come and eat my food and sing and crow like that." The cock replied, ""What is that? Why should the Aga die? He is not ill. He is as healthy as a pig."

"Ah," said the dog, "God has given him the gift of understanding our language, but if he reveals it, he dies. He's now going to tell his wife about it and he'll die." The cock replied, "Why, can't he manage one woman? Look at me. I have twelve hens. I pick up a grain of maize and I fool all the twelve. I pretend to want to give them the maize, but in the end I eat it myself. Master cannot manage one woman! What would he do if he had twelve, like me? If I had only one, I would beat her every day."

The Aga overheard this and went straight to his wife and gave her a sound beating. "This is for the kid," whack! "And this is for the lamb," whack! And so he was saved from death by the cock.

The tale for Jatesh.

Health to us.

[told at Shëngjin in the district of Elbasan]

How the King's Youngest Son Found the Bilbil Gjyzar

Once long ago there lived a King who was very rich. He was so rich that his wealth could not be estimated or even imagined.

He had three sons, and loved the youngest more than the others. One day he thought of building a big church in which he himself and the people of the capital could worship. When he had decided to build it, he urgently bade his sons to summon masons from the four corners of the Kingdom, to build the sacred building.

The masons were collected and began to work. A long time afterwards, they finished the building, making it very beautiful. No church could be more attractive.

Some days later, it was to be consecrated. The King invited bishops and priests, and such a crowd gathered that there was no room to throw an apple. The church was lit with candles made from good wax and with lamps of olive oil presented by the congregation.

When the congregation was finished, all the people left the church.

The King's sons asked them as they went out, "What is the church like?" They replied, "There isn't a prettier or finer church anywhere. Far though we've travelled, some of us more, some of us less, we've not seen another church as beautiful as this one."

One of the men turned to the King's sons and said, "Brothers, the church could really not be more beautiful, but it has one defect." The King's sons inquired, "What is that? Please tell us." He replied, "It wants a Bilbil Gjyzar (bird of paradise). If this bird was put in a cage and hung above the screen and was to sing well, there would be nothing more amiss with the church."

The King's sons went to the King and said, "One of the men at the church has told us that there's something wanting in the church, a

Bilbil Gjyzar." The King was angry and said to his three sons, "Go away as fast as your feet can carry you, and don't come here again until you bring me a Bilbil Gjyzar."

The King's sons thought and thought, and decided to go off to find the bird. After walking for a day along a straight road, they came to three roads. They stopped to think and then said to each other that each should take a different road, and on finding a Bilbil Gjyzar, the finder, whoever he might be, should turn back and go to the King to give him the Bilbil Gjyzar.

So they set off, the eldest taking the road to the right, the second one the middle road, and the youngest the road to the left.

After the eldest had travelled for some days, he reached a town where he searched as much as he could to find a Bilbil Gjyzar. But he could not, and so he felt ashamed to return home to his father. His money also was done, so he hired himself out as an apprentice to a baker for nothing but his food and drink.

The second son also travelled some days and reached a town where he searched for a Bilbil Gjyzar and, failing to find one, lost hope. When his money was nearly finished, he went as an apprentice to a cook, who engaged him for nothing but his food and drink.

New let's see what the youngest son did. After he had travelled for a day and some hours into the night, he came on a forest, where midnight overtook him. In the middle of the forest, an ugly old woman appeared to him, short and squat with eyes gleaming like fire. She was a witch. She held a bundle of lighted pine shivers, the flames from which reached right to the top of the trees in the forest. The boy was afraid, but the old woman went up to him and said, "Don't be afraid, boy. I won't touch you. Come with me and do as I tell you. If you don't, you are done for."

The ugly old witch took him with her to her house. After she had given him food and drink, she said, "I'll hide you in a pannier, but don't make a sound, because I have forty sons. They are devils, for I mated with a *kulshedra*, and they can't be seen but are only heard. I fear that they'll eat you if they see you. When once I've secured their promise not to touch you, I'll take you out of the pannier. If they've given their word, they won't touch you." So saying, the old woman hid him in a pannier.

After some minutes, the forty sons of the old woman arrived. When the entered, they said, "There is the smell of a human being here. Speak! Have you hidden a human being or not?" The old woman said, "No." But they insisted, saying, "There's no doubt there's a human being hidden here." At once they said to their servant Sharko, for that was his name, "Sharko, quick, look in all the corners of the house and as soon as you find the human being who is hidden, bring him to us."

At once the old woman flung her arms round the necks of her sons and said, "Yes, I have hidden a boy here. He is very handsome and seems to be a King's son. Give me your word that you will not hurt him or do anything bad to him."

Her sons said, "Old woman, we give you our word not to hurt him or even to lay a finger on him, and we'll do nothing bad to him. Let him out, and we'll make him our foster-brother." The old woman rose at once and let the stranger boy out.

As soon as they saw him, they embraced him and said, "Whatever trouble you have, tell us. We'll settle it, don't be afraid. Come to-night with us; we're going to enjoy ourselves on the balcony we've made at the top of the poplars in the very middle of the thick part of the forest, where all the bands of the world play."

When they went there, they took with them not only the King's son, but also Sharko, their servant. He could not be seen, only when he spoke was his voice heard. They stayed the whole night enjoying themselves among the poplar tops. Next evening they did the same thing, and so it went on for six or seven days.

The King's son was enjoying himself, but he wanted to find a Bilbil Gjyzar. He kept thinking and worrying.

One day, the old woman's sons, seeing him worrying and unhappy, felt very sorry for him, brother as they had made him. They said to him, "What are you worried about? Why are you so cast down? What's your trouble? Tell us. We're able to do whatever you want done, whether it be above the earth, under the earth, in the sea, or at the very bottom of the sea, and even if it's in the sky, still we'll manage it for you!"

The King's son took courage and said, "Brothers, I am a King's son. My father built a very big and beautiful church. They told us that his church must have a Bilbil Gjyzar to sing in it. So my father the King sent us, his three sons, me and my two brothers, to find a Bilbil Gjyzar. I came here and now I don't know what to do, or where to go. And to go back without finding a Bilbil Gjyzar, I can't. So I beg you to tell me where to look for the bird, and how to look for it and catch it so that I may go home to my father all joy and please my father, too, with the embellishment and beautifying of the church."

The forty sons of the old woman called to Sharko to come and bring a winged horse with him, a horse that could fly and save the life of the man on its back.

The horse arrived by itself, as it seemed, for Sharko could not be seen. The devils mounted the King's son on it and gave him bread and food and some of the water which they were wont to drink, for the devils drank water and chose it where it was best.

The King's son set off as soon as he mounted the winged horse, and Sharko followed him, tracking him wherever he went. After a four or five days' journey, they came to a very big river. Besides being wide and deep, it flowed with a very strong current, for its source was on a high mountain, the summit of which could not be seen because it went up into the sky. The roar of the water was loud enough to frighten a man away from sitting on the bank, let alone from trying to cross it. The water was as black as tar, pitch-black, worse than tar, and it was hot and burning like hellfire. The King's son wondered how he could get across and how it was possible for the horse to cross, for the water was so hot that its steam could not be endured and as soon as a person went near it, he could not breathe.

Sharko who knew all about everything without asking anybody, saw that the King's son was worrying and said, "Why are you worrying and troubling and hesitating, King's son? Haven't you got me alive and with you? Or don't you realise that that's why I am following in your footsteps, that I've been sent by my masters to guard you?"

"No," said the King's son, "but I was taken aback when I saw this river so big and with water so hot that we can never cross. So I ask you, Sharko, my helper and protector in the difficulties which confront me, how shall we get across this river?"

Sharko answered, "Don't be afraid! Sit tight on your horse, and remember that the horse you're on is winged. I will call out to the horse in a booming voice, but don't be alarmed. Do you hear me or not? "All right," said the King's son, "I won't be at all frightened, so call out!" Then Sharko called to the horse in a voice so loud and terrible that it was impossible not to feel frightened. It was like the devil's voice. But the King's son was not in the least frightened, since he knew that Sharko was his defender and would save him from danger.

The winged horse flew very high above the river, and crossed safely, and won the other side. Sharko was with him, for Sharko had got up on the crupper.

After he crossed the river, the King's son was delighted, for on the other side of the river there was a plain more beautiful than tongue can tell. The mind cannot grasp the majesty of that plain, adorned with all sorts of beautiful flowers and fruit trees, the fruits of which were good to eat, very sweet, and good to look at. There were numbers of flying birds, all very beautiful. Streams flowed through the meadows which were full of fresh grass. So much beauty was in that plain that one might say it was paradise and there is no other paradise.

After the King's son and Sharko had stopped and rested a little, they ate some of the sweet fruits, drank clear, clean water, and the horse grazed on the fresh grass. Then the King's son said to Sharko, "Sharko, now that we've eaten and drunk, tell me, where is the bird I'm looking for?" Sharko turned round and said to him, "Boy, to find a Bilbil Gjyzar, you'll have a bad time for a long while to come. But I will give you a goose's feather. When you're in danger, put this in the fire and in a moment I shall be with you. Now mount, fly up into the sky, and act according to circumstances. Only I tell you, don't sleep with the very pretty girls you'll find up there. If you sleep with them, boy, I don't know how to say it, you'll be lost altogether, and I can do nothing more for you. So be on your guard against them, for they are very beautiful, very sweet of speech, and their faces are like the fifteen-day-old moon. I don't know how to put it. In appearance they are like angels in the sky. But they have human customs, and if they see a male human being, they at once attract him with the love they offer and the beautiful songs they sing. There is no man who can hold out and not be corrupted. Not only because you're a boy, but also because you're handsome, I charge you strongly to resist them and not give in, to be as hard as stone and to be cold."

After the King's son had flown through the air for a long time, night overtook him. Then he saw in the distance a gleam of light high up in the sky. The nearer it came, the bigger it grew. After a little it came quite close, and what should he see? A very big palace. The horse came down to the very threshold of the gate, which was of gold and inlaid with diamonds.

The King's son dismounted, and entered the courtyard. The horse flew away, returned to earth, and joined Sharko.

At once the prettiest girls in the world surrounded the King's son and said, "Welcome, King's son, who are looking for a Bilbil Gjyzar for the church of the King, your father, who built it away down on earth. Come and let's enjoy ourselves, let's drink sweet wine to calm both body and soul, and let's delight our hearts. There isn't a Bilbil Gjyzar here, but we'll tell you where there is one, so that you can catch it and take it to the place you want."

The King's son answered, saying, "Thank you very much." Then they took the lad and led him up into the palace, which was all built of diamonds and sparkled like a mirror, blinding you when the sun's rays fell on it, and the most beautiful of the girls came up to him, and set food before him, all sorts of good dishes, and he ate. After supper they brought him sweets and good wine to drink, and said to him, "Drink, it's good for you." But the King's son answered, saying, "As for drink, I can't take it; that's the order I have from my father." They begged him very hard to drink but he would not.

They wanted him to drink wine and to get drunk so that they could come when he was asleep, lie by his side and enjoy themselves.

To cut a long story short... he held out manfully and controlled himself until dawn broke and it was light.

After it dawned and was full daylight, they took him out into the courtyard of the palace. In the middle there was a fountain with four spouts pouring water into it. There they kept him an hour, and when they gave him coffee, the cup was gold set with diamonds. After he had drunk the coffee, the King's son bethought him of the goose feather and said to the prettiest girls in the world, "Have you got a Bilbil Gjyzar or not?" They replied, "There isn't one here, but there is in the third palace above the one in which you are to-day. So you must go still higher, but don't forget us. And when you are on your way back, come here again so that we can greet you when you go from heaven to earth."

The lad blew on the goose feather. At once the winged horse came, he mounted it, and flew up to the second palace. And in this palace, he suffered what he had suffered in the first palace.

After that, he climbed to the third palace. As soon as he arrived, he was surrounded by the prettiest girls in the world, like sirens. Their figures were as stately as a cypress, their noses were like candles, their eyes were as big as cups, their eyebrows were as black as carbonised paper, their teeth were like ivory, their skin was as clear as crystal, and their hair was like gold thread.

They asked him where he came from. He told them all he had endured and suffered, and begged them hard to give him a Bilbil Gjyzar which he had so long been suffering to find but could not catch.

When it grew dark, they took him by the hand and led him up into the palace, and set him down on the ottoman. This was strewn with very valuable rugs, such as are found in no palace owned by any of the many kings of the world on whom the sun rises and sets. When the King's son sat down, they set good food before him to eat along with them. And he ate. They also gave him some of the finest fruits and brought him very sweet and delicious drink.

The most beautiful of them went up to him and bade him drink. But the lad did not drink according to the orders he had. Next they all came round him and bade and begged him to drink and sleep with them. Otherwise they could not give him the Bilbil Gjyzar he was seeking.

77

And so, the King's son found himself in a difficulty. He turned his eyes towards the most beautiful among them and bade her come to him. And she came and sat on his knee. At once she took the glass to give him the drink which they themselves drank.

But he whispered in her ear, "I am very troubled this evening, and I am very tired in body and still more so in mind. I give you my word that to-morrow evening I will drink as much as you please, and we will sleep together. But to-night protect me from the others and keep them from annoying me in my sleep, because I need to sleep undisturbed."

When the lad said this to her, she believed him and promised to protect him while he slept, and keep the other pretty girls from annoying him. So he lay down to sleep and she sat beside him and guarded him the whole night. At times, she cried over him and kissed him.

Every time that her teardrops fell on his face, the lad awoke from sleep, but she wiped away the tears and it did not show that she was crying. The lad understood that she had fallen very much in love with him, pretended to awake from sleep, and said to her, "Don't you bother in the least. To-morrow evening your wish and mine shall be fulfilled, but not to-night because, as I told you, I am tired." And he begged her to sleep, too.

It was close on dawn, not far from the time when the sun would come up. The pretty girl was fast asleep. The lad got up quietly and kissed her on the forehead, whereupon she awoke from sleep and day broke.

When it became daylight, the pretty girl said to him, "Come, let's go into the courtyard to drink coffee beside the fountain with water as bright as gold."

So the two went hand in hand into the courtyard. And when they sat down, servants brought them coffee and milk to drink. As they sat drinking the coffee, a Bilbil Gjyzar appeared.

It flew three times round the fountain and lighted on the pretty girl's shoulder. At once the King's son caught it and rose to go. But the pretty girl said to him, "Why do you get up? Stay here! Now that your aim is accomplished, stay some days to enjoy yourself and then go. The

King's son said, "I will stay some days here. I have not forgotten the promise I gave you. But I want something valuable from you, and you shall give it to me now. And I beg you not to disappoint me, because I did not disappoint you and gave you my promise."

The pretty girl thought a little and got up and went to the room where she slept. There she took a fish-bone and came and gave it to the lad. She also gave him a small bottle containing a medicine and said to him, "Both these things are valuable, when they are mixed."

As soon as the King's son received these gifts, he thought of the goose feather. At once he blew on it, and the winged horse appeared. He mounted it and flew away.

The pretty girl began to cry and said aloud, "By the tears which I shed for you, may God not torment you! But may your brothers torment you! When you are in danger, think of me, and take the fish-bone. Wet it in the bottle and when you are blind, rub your eyes with it."

So the King's son, with the Bilbil Gjyzar in his hand, mounted the winged horse and arrived flying at the second palace. But though the pretty girls there came out to meet him, he would not listen. He also dismounted at the first palace, and would not hear of stopping there. Instead, he sank straight down to the riverside.

When he landed, he met Sharko. Sharko jumped up behind him on the horse and they flew across the hot river and came to the other side. Some days after they got to the other side, they reached the old woman's palace, where he was met and greeted by her sons, his foster-brothers. After stopping some days there, he went away, going straight to the three roads, where he had separated from his brothers.

When he reached the end of his own road, he stopped to think a little. As he thought, he decided to go and look for his other brothers, so that the three could go joyfully to their father, the King, who was waiting for them.

So he started along the right-hand road and as he went, he came to a town. There he went to the bakery to buy some bread. At once he was astounded when he saw his brother selling bread. And so he told him with great joy that he had found a Bilbil Gjyzar and told him all he had been through. In the same way, his brother told him all he had been through, and next day they started off as soon as they had bought bread and food.

After travelling some days, they reached the end of this road and took the left-hand road. At the end of it, they reached a very beautiful town. When they reached it, being tired, they went to an eating-house to eat some food and to drink a glass of wine each. But what should they see? The man bringing the food was their brother. They flung themselves on him, embraced him and greeted him with tears running down their cheeks. All three sat down beside each other. They ate and drank and told each other their adventures.

After eating and drinking well, they spent the night there. Next morning, they got up betimes and started for home

As they travelled along, the two brothers who had not found a Bilbil Gjyzar began to think and ask themselves, "How did the young brother find it, and we not?" So they came up with an evil idea. They talked with each other of killing their brother, taking the Bilbil Gjyzar from him and carrying it to their father, while saying that their brother had died on the way.

After they had this evil idea and decided to carry it out, they seized their brother, gave him such a beating that he was blinded, and left him alone in the forest. They then took the Bilbil Gjyzar with them and fled, leaving their brother there blind.

They themselves went to their father and gave him the Bilbil Gjyzar. Their father, the King, was on the one hand very much pleased at getting the bird, but on the other extremely sad at the death of his son. So they took the Bilbil Gjyzar to the church where they put it in a cage. But the bird would not sing at all. Many people collected, stayed there, and looked at it. In vain, it would not sing. The King was astonished, "What's ado here?" he said to himself. "Why doesn't the bird sing?" And so the matter remained.

Out in the forest, the King's son, blinded by the trouble that had come on him, said in his own mind, "What was I doing, wretched man, to be faithless to that pretty girl and not to grant her wish? She loved me. She shed tears like rain over me all night and she guarded me. I did

80

not grant her wish." Suddenly he bethought him of the fish-bone and the bottle of medicine which she had given him, and also of her words, "When you are in trouble, rub your eyes with it." He took the fish-bone, dipped it in the bottle, and rubbed his eyes. An amazing thing occurred. At once he could see again.

But he did not have the Bilbil Gjyzar. His brothers had taken it from him. He blew on the goose feather and at once Sharko came with the winged horse. "What do you want?" he asked. "I don't know where I am, but I want to mount the horse and get home quickly," he replied. "All right," said Sharko. And so he mounted the horse and in a little arrived at his father's, where he told everything that had happened to him. His father, the King, embraced him and kissed him on the brow, which done, he summoned his two other sons, stood them in the courtyard and let loose his lions and tigers to tear them to pieces.

After a little the King died. This son was chosen as King, and the Bilbil Gjyzar sang most beautifully as it had done ever since his eyes had their sight restored.

As soon as he became King, he mounted the winged horse, went to the third palace, and took the pretty girl for his bride, saying, "There is nobody who could be faithless to you, but I was forced to be so till I got the Bilbil Gjyzar." And so they both lived very happily.

The tale is for Godolesh.

Health to us.

[told by Peter Xhufo of Elbasan]

The Cowherd Who Married the Earthly Beauty

Once there was a cowherd who herded all the village cows. A heifer would not graze. "Why does my heifer not graze? The other cows come home full fed," said the lady who owned it.

She made food for the cowherd to take with him and said to him, "When you eat it, think of the heifer." So when he began to eat, he remembered the animal. At once he rose to his feet and counted the cows. He found that the lady's heifer was not there and went to look for it. He eventually found it in a hole in the ground. When he peered into the hole, he saw the Earthly Beauty. "Why do you keep my heifer from eating?" he asked and went away.

After some time, the young man married the Earthly Beauty and took her home to his cottage in the village. When they reached it, he said to her, "I have neither clothes nor a place in which to sleep." She replied, "Don't worry." At once some rugs appeared and then a whole palace.

"I haven't any food to eat," said the cowherd. "Don't worry," said the Earthly Beauty. Immediately a dining-table with all sorts of food was set before them. As soon as they had eaten the food, they lay down to sleep.

Now there was a very rich bey in their village. When his servants saw the cowherd's cottage turned into a palace, they rubbed their eyes, thinking they were not seeing properly. They called to the bey, "Come out for a moment, bey, and look at something." He replied, "Plague on you!"

When the servants called the bey again, he came out. "Look at the cowherd's cottage," they said. He rubbed his eyes, then ordered the servants to go and bring the cowherd to him. The Earthly Beauty, who

82

had just come to the window, heard them and went and woke the cowherd, saying, "The bey wants you.

The cowherd got up and went to the bey, who said to him, "I want a little bunch of grapes from which the whole people shall eat and leave some over." The cowherd went back to his palace and began to think. The Earthly Beauty asked why he was thinking. He replied, "The bey has asked me for a little bunch of grapes from which the whole people shall eat and leave some over." The Earthly Beauty said, "Off you go to the place where you found me and bid my mother give you a bunch of grapes from the little vineyard." The cowherd went to the place and got a bunch of grapes from the vineyard indicated by the Earthly Beauty.

As the cowherd took the grapes, he said to himself, "How can this little bunch satisfy the hunger of the whole population and leave something over?" When he got home with the grapes, the Earthly Beauty said, "Bring the grapes and let's eat. Afterwards, you can take them to the bey." The cowherd asked, "How can we eat them? What am I to take afterwards to the bey?" She replied, "Bring them and let's eat. Some will be left over." They took the grapes, ate until they were satisfied, and then the cowherd took what was left to the bey. The bey ate until he was satisfied, the whole population then ate, and some were left over.

When the bey saw that the grapes were not coming to an end, he said to the cowherd, "Find my father for me." "Where am I to find him?" the cowherd replied. "If you don't, I'll hang you," said the bey. The cowherd went home and began thinking and said to the Earthly Beauty, "The bey has asked me to find his father, but his father died before I was born." She replied, "Off you go to my mother, who is where you went before, and ask her for the little white horse." He went there, got the horse, and came back home with it.

The bey next gave him a letter for his father. He went home and the Earthly Beauty said to him, "His father's grave is where the horse will stop." He mounted the horse, set off, and rode to a certain spot, where he knocked on the ground. The ground opened up and the cowherd and the horse rode down into the lower world.

83

There they saw many people. The cowherd asked where so-and-so was. "A little lower down," they replied, "among the thorns which are pricking his hands." When he found the father, he said, "Here's a letter for you. Your son gave it to me for you." The father took the letter and on the blank page wrote, "Son, do not do wicked things or when you come down here, you'll pay for them. Break up all your estates and give the land away, keeping only what you need for yourself. I behaved like you, and now the thorns here prick my hands."

The cowherd took the letter from him and returned to the upper world, where he carried the letter to the bey. When the bey read it, he said, "Please pardon my shortcomings and go home and stay there in peace." And he promised the cowherd many estates. The cowherd took his departure and went home. He lived to be old and had children.

[told by Selman Ali, a teacher from Vashtëmia in the district of Korça]

Necessity

One fine day a father said to his son, "Son, go out and bring a horse-load of firewood." "I don't know how to load the horse, father," the son replied. "Son," said the father, "go and call Necessity to teach you."

The son went to the forest with his horse and called out, "Necessity!" once, twice, thrice. Necessity wasn't there.

The son waited and waited for her to come. It was growing dark and nearly night. What did he do? He took his axe and cut a stick with forked ends on which he hung the loop of the pack-rope. Then he laid the pieces of firewood one by one on the rope and tied them together. The other side he loaded in the same way, and went home. There he said to his father, "You tricked me, father. Necessity wasn't there." "Well, how did you load the horse, son?" "This way, father," he answered, "I cut a stick and hung the loop of the pack-rope on it and loaded the horse, first on one side and then on the other." "Well, son, that's Necessity."

[told by Qazim Kosma Tullumi of Bujaras in the district of Elbasan]

The Three Suitors and their Magic Tricks

A King had a very beautiful daughter, a girl as beautiful as the Earthly Beauties. When she reached marriageable age, her father wanted to find a man who should be her equal to marry her. He sent word all over his kingdom that the young men were all to come to his palace, so that his daughter could marry whoever she liked best. So all the young men gathered and lined up in front of the palace. The girl then appeared with a golden apple in her hand to give to the young man she liked best.

Surprisingly the girl liked three young men and did not know which to take and which to leave. The King was in a fix so he summoned the assembly. There it was agreed to send the three young men abroad and to give the princess to whichever should make the most money or should best learn queer tricks.

The King took a large sum of money and divided it equally between the three young men, giving one as much as the other. Then each left for the place he fancied. One went to England, another to Russia and the third to Constantinople.

The one who went to England visited all the towns of England. In one town he found two men quarrelling with each other about a carpet. One said, "I'm going to have it!" and the other said the same. Our young man intervened, saying, "Stop! Let me settle the row. What's the matter? Why don't you cut the carpet in two and stop quarrelling?" They said, "It's no good cutting it in two. If it is cut like that, it will lose its value. If you sit on it as it is and say you want to go to Constantinople or elsewhere, you are there in an hour." "Oh!" said the boy, "then I'll settle the business this way. Let it belong to the one that I give it to." "Yes," they both said with one voice. As soon as the young man got it, he at once sat down on it and said he wanted to go to

86

Constantinople, where in truth he found himself within an hour. The two men were left with their mouths open; they had thought him a nice person. He was nice in fact, but a man rather looks after his own interests, even by unfair means.

The young man who went to Russia became great friends with the captain when crossing the Black Sea in a ship. One day the captain took a mirror out of his chest. It was the special quality of this mirror that if you wanted to see anyone you had in your mind, you could at once see him in it, however far away he was, wherever he was, and whatever he was doing.

The captain wanted to see what his wife who was at home, was doing. She was pretty and he was worried because he had married her for love. Unfortunately he saw her sleeping in his bed with another man. In his despair, he let the mirror fall and threw himself into the sea and was drowned.

As a friend of the captain who had taught him the trick of the mirror, the young man took it and returned to Constantinople.

The third young man, who had gone straight to Constantinople, was wandering through the Turkish capital when he noticed a dervish who had in front of him a bottle of water with a strange virtue. If it was poured over a dead man before an hour had passed, he would revive. The young man questioned the dervish, who told him the truth. The young man looked to see that there was no one in the offing and killed the dervish. He took the bottle from him and found himself with the two others in Constantinople, where they had promised to meet.

When they met again, they talked about what each had acquired. When they heard what each had learned, they set to work.

"Sir," said two of them to the owner of the mirror, "won't you look to see what the princess is doing and what has happened to her?" The moment he looked, he said, "She had died this very minute!"

The second man – the owner of the carpet – took the two others with him on the carpet and in a twinkling they found themselves in front of the princess.

The third, who had the water of life, sprinkled water on her and she came back to life.

Which of the three, I wonder, got the princess? Without each other nothing could have been done, and one of them married her, but which one, I wonder? And why? By what right? If the reader is kind, he will tell us.

[told by Gjergj Simota of Grapsh in southern Albania]

The Maiden Who Married a Snake

Once there were an old man and woman who had no children. The old woman prayed to God to grant them even a snake, and God promised one to her.

Some days after the snake was born, it began to shriek loudly. Its parents sent to fetch some priests and hodjas, who read passages of scripture over it. An older hodja found in the Koran that the time had come for the snake to be married. "You are to go to so-and-so and ask him for his daughter's hand for the snake," he said to the father. The snake then stopped shrieking.

The snake's father said, "A man will never give his daughter to a snake. Such a thing has never happened." But the father himself went to ask for the girl.

The girl's father said, "If you will pave my road with gold and shade it with apple and pear trees on both sides, I will give you my daughter." The snake's father returned home in the evening.

The snake climbed immediately onto its father's lap and said, "Did that man promise to give me his daughter?" The father replied, "We are not able to accept her, the way he promised her." "What did he ask?" said the snake. "He said we must pave the road between his door and ours with gold." The snake said to its father, "Take a bag and fill it with earth from the garden. Walk towards his house, spilling the earth behind you as you go. Then take a pear and an apple tree and plant them one after another in the middle of the road. And don't look back. When you reach the door of his house, turn round and then look back."

The snake's father called on the girl's father and said, "I've come again. Look at the road," he added. "Have they done it well or not?"

"It has been written that I am to give my daughter to your snake!" her father exclaimed, adding, "However, you must bring me a wedding party of 100 persons on horseback and the snake as well." The wedding party arrived and entered the house, where they ate and drank.

After supper, the girl's father said to the leader of the wedding party, "Will you give me the snake to-night? I'd like to put him to sleep by himself in a room." The head guest replied, "I can't give him to you," for he was afraid that the man would murder the snake. The girl's father said, "I guarantee that to-morrow morning I'll give him back to you safe and sound as an apple."

The girl's father took the snake and put it in a room with his daughter for the night. "Look! This is your husband," he said to his daughter. "Take him away, father!" the girl begged. But her father replied, "It is fated that he shall marry you." And he locked her into the room.

During the night the snake took off its skin and hung it up on a nail. And he looked the most beautiful man that ever there was. He said to his wife, "For to-night you are my sister, not my wife." He added, "Look after my skin for me. See that no one touches it if you want to keep me alive." He made her promise this, and in the morning he woke up, took down the skin and put it on.

In the morning, the girl's father went to the room and found the snake again coiled like a snake. "Were you frightened last night?" he asked his daughter. "No, I wasn't frightened. Don't worry about me," she replied. The snake had said to its wife, "During the day I'll remain a snake, but during the night I'll be a young man."

The girl's father took back the snake safe and sound as an apple to the wedding party. They went away and held a wedding feast at home.

In the evening, the bride went to sleep with the snake. One fine night, the snake's mother talked with her daughter-in-law and the girl's mother, and said, "The snake is very dangerous for a young wife and for us old women." The bride replied, "Don't worry about me. During the day he is a snake, but at night he is a young man. I would not change him for all the young men of our clan in this district."

90

The girl's mother was very glad. She went and looked at the lock in the door, then made a wax impression of the key and made another key exactly like it. Next night she went and opened the door, and was delighted when she saw the young man sleeping with his bride. She also saw where he had his skin. "I'll take and burn it!" she said. She took it away and immediately put it in the fire. When his skin was burned, the snake awoke.

"You've killed me!" he cried out to his wife. "Did I not tell you to look after my skin, or I'd be done for?"

And then they gave me this cap.

[told by Simon Nue of Ungrej in the district of Mirdita]

Cinderella

A man once had a wife and a daughter, but his wife died and he married another woman. He also owned a cow.

As the girl grew up, her step-mother made her take work with her when she went out to take the cow to pasture. She gave her wool, saying, "Spin this wool for me." The girl, little as she was, cried and cried because she could not do the work. But the cow said, "Don't cry. I'll do your work." It span the wool and the girl took it home in the evening.

The step-mother then said, "I want more wool done to-morrow." The girl cried again as she could not do more. Again the cow said, "Why are you crying? I'll do the work for you." And again it span the wool for her.

The step-mother realised, however, that the girl couldn't do this work herself, and sent a daughter of her own with the girl to tend to the cow, saying, "See who does the work for her."

Her own daughter, like the stupid girl she was, fell asleep. The cow came and did the girl's work, and in the evening they all went home. The mother asked her daughter what she had seen and the daughter replied that she had fallen asleep and seen nothing.

Next day the step-mother sent another of her daughters, the middle one. She also fell asleep. In the evening, when they all went home, the mother asked her second daughter what had happened, and she said, "I also fell asleep."

The following day the step-mother sent her youngest daughter, for she had three. This daughter was sly. She lay down as if to sleep, but instead of falling asleep she stayed awake. Her step-sister thought she was asleep and called the cow, which came and did her work.

In the evening the sly daughter got home before the cow and said to her mother, "Her cow-mother span the wool for her."

The step-mother then pretended to be ill. She rolled pastry, baked it, and spread it on the ground. Then she flung a rug over it and lay down groaning. When her husband came home, she said, "I'm very ill." "Let me lift you up a little," said he. As he lifted her up, the pastry which was under her crackled. "Oh my bones!" she cried.

"What do you want to eat?" her husband asked. "I couldn't eat anything," she said, "except a piece of meat from the cow-mother." "Why from her?" he asked. "We have young animals – calves, lambs… Why from her? She's old." "If I don't eat a bit of her, I may die," she replied. And the husband, afraid that his wife would die, agreed to kill the cow.

The orphan girl went in tears to the cow. "What are you crying for?" asked the cow. "Father's going to kill you," said the girl. "Well, what about it? Let him kill me," the cow replied. "But don't you eat my meat," it added. "Instead, gather my bones and put them into two holes."

The step-mother got better as soon as they killed the cow. Sometime afterwards, a wedding was being held in the village. The step-mother said to the girl, "You stay at home because I'm going with my daughters to the wedding." The girl stayed at home and her step-mother went to the wedding.

The girl said to herself, "Suppose I take a peep at the bones of the cow!" She opened one hole and found a set of beautiful clothes and beautiful shoes inside it. She put them on and became like a grand lady. "Now," she said, "I'll go to the wedding. Nobody will know me." And she went to the wedding.

Because of the fine clothes she had on, they put her in the corner. Her step-mother was left by the door. After they had supper, the step-mother left to go home. The girl left by another door and ran home. There she took off her clothes and put them back in the hole. When her step-mother arrived, she found her in the house. "Oh, girl," said the step-mother, "a beautiful, a lovely woman came to the wedding. She wore fine clothes like a lady." "Oh step-mother," said the girl, "If I'd only been there to see her!"

The next night came. The step-mother said to her, "You stay here. I'm going to the wedding again." "I'm coming, too," said the girl to herself. "You can't do anything to me with your tricks."

With this, the step-mother left for the wedding. The girl opened the other hole, and found inside a different set of clothes that were even finer than the others. And so, she went to the wedding again. Oh, she was like a grand lady!

They put her in the corner, they had supper, and her step-mother then left to go home. The girl also left in a great hurry. There happened to be a muddy place on the way, and one of her shoes came off and stuck in the mud. In her haste she left the shoe there and ran on home. There she took off her clothes and put them back in the hole.

By a queer accident a gentleman was out shooting with his servants, and found the girl's shoe, which was of gold. He said, "Collect the villagers, for I'll marry the girl that the shoe fits."

The gentleman went from door to door looking for such a girl, but the shoe did not fit anyone, for it was the girl's size.

He then went to the girl's door and asked her step-mother how many daughters she had. "Three," she replied. She brought her daughters out, and the young man tried the shoe on them, but it did not fit them.

The dog cried out, "She's behind the pack-saddle." The young man said to the step-mother, "Have you other daughters? "No, I haven't," she replied.

Then the cock cried out, "She's behind the pack-saddle." The young man rushed over to the saddle and found the girl there. He tried on the shoe and found it was exactly right. "I'll marry you," he said. "On such and such a day I'll come to fetch you."

But the step-mother gave him her own daughter instead. She put the daughter in the coach and sent her to the bridegroom. However, he recognised her, sent her back to her mother, and fetched the orphan girl.

After he had been married to her for two or three months, she said, "I want to go and see my father." During the visit, her step-mother blinded her and flung her out by the wayside. Two little birds then came

94

by. She caught them, rubbed one on each eye, and once more was able to see.

Her step-mother had meanwhile sent her other daughter to the bridegroom, who did not recognise her this time, for she was, and she wasn't, like his wife.

The orphan girl wandered off to a poor man's cottage and stayed there for some days. She said to the poor man, "Go to such-and-such a gentleman's house and get a horse that has only three days to live."

The poor man went to the house and asked for a horse that had only three days to live. The gentleman did not have horses enough. "I'll give you a good horse," he said. "No," returned the poor man, "I want a horse that has only three days to live." The servants then brought out the gentleman's own horse, and the poor man took it stumbling home to his cottage. The girl put her hand on its shoulder and it grew finer than the rest of the gentleman's horses. "Take it back to the gentleman," she said. "I don't want it anymore."

The poor man took it back to the gentleman, saying, "There's the horse. We don't want it anymore." But the horse had a gold saddle. The young man saw the horse and recognised it as his. "Why is the horse like this? Who made it like this?" he asked the poor man.

The poor man told him the truth. "I found a girl in a hedge. She sent me to fetch the horse and she made it like this."

The gentleman mounted the horse, and took with him another sick horse as well. He went to the poor man's cottage and found his real wife. She at once put her hand on the second horse, and made it better than the first one.

They mounted the horses and went back to their own house. He killed the other wife he had there, and killed her mother and also her two sisters in their house.

The end.

[told by Xhafë Kuqi of Kuqan in the district of Elbasan]

The Three Dervishes and the Judge

Once upon a time there were three dervishes, who used to go out to the villages to beg. Once they set out to go to town with their horse. They stopped at night outside the town and unloaded their horse and let it loose to graze.

In the morning they got up and went to find the horse but somebody had stolen it. Said one of them, "The man who has stolen our horse is a tall man." Said the second one, "If the man who has stolen our horse is a tall man, he has yellow whiskers." Said the third dervish, "If the man who has stolen our horse is a tall man with yellow whiskers, then his name is Deli Ymer. Let's go into town and find him."

They found a tall man with yellow whiskers and said to him, "What's your name, sir?" "Deli Ymer," he said. "Very well, we want our horse back," they demanded. "What horse do you want from me? Get away with you!" he exclaimed.

The dervishes then took up the matter with the judge. "Deli Ymer has stolen our horse," they complained. The judge gave them some gendarmes, who had orders to bring Deli Ymer to him.

When Deli Ymer stood before him, the judge said, "Why did you steal their horse?" "Why, I know nothing about it," he replied. The judge then said to the dervishes, "Have you any evidence that this man stole your horse? Has anyone else seen him steal it?" "No, we just know that he has stolen it," they said. "Then you must have imagined this," said the judge. "If you say so," they replied.

The judge had a wooden chest in the room. He pointed to it and said to the dervishes, "What have I got inside this chest?" Said the first dervish, "There is something round in it." Said the second dervish, "If it is round, it is yellow." Said the third dervish, "If it is round and

96

yellow, its name is an orange. Open the chest and let's see it." The judge opened the chest, and there was an orange inside.

The judge then turned to the robber and said, "Go and bring the horse at once." Deli Ymer went away and soon came back with the horse. The fact that he had stolen the horse was proven.

The judge then said to the dervishes, "To-night you must be my guests." And they went to his house. The judge had a lamb slaughtered in their honour and roasted and prepared it for their supper. After it was served, he said, "Eat and be merry. I'm now going to bed." So saying, the judge bade them good night and left the room

But he stayed behind the door and spied on them, listening to what they were saying. One dervish took the meat and cut it. "Oh, this is dog's meat," he exclaimed. The second dervish said, "This bread is from a grave." The third dervish said, "This judge is a bastard." Then they began to eat the meat and the bread.

Next day, when the judge awoke, he called in his tenant farmer. "What kind of lamb was this you brought me yesterday?" he asked him. "Its mother died and I had it suckled by a bitch. It was brought up on dog's milk," said the peasant. "What about the maize you brought me?" "It grew in a graveyard," said the peasant. "It grew so well that I brought it for you." "Now you may go," said the judge, dismissing him.

The judge then went to his mother and said, "Tell me the truth. Am I my father's son?" "Your father could not have children and I married another man," she replied.

In this way, the judge found out that dervishes were good people.

[told in Shëngjin in the district of Elbasan]

Bald Maria

There was what there was. Once there were six brothers, who had a mother and a little sister that they loved as much as their own lives. They were noble, that is to say, they were of high rank and the name of their family was known far and wide because of their ability and bravery.

But since they had fallen very low financially speaking, and no one looked at them anymore, they decided to emigrate so as to grow rich again and have their fame spread abroad as before.

So the six brothers, after getting their mother's blessing and kissing their beloved sister on the mouth, went to seek their fortune in the East.

After a long and very difficult journey they came to a very large kingdom, and there they presented themselves directly to the King and were made pashas. From that time on, they sent their mother a lot of money, and they always reminded her to love and look after their sister, Lulesha. She had now grown and become one of the cleverest and most beautiful girls in the village.

By her good behaviour, this girl had won the respect of all the other girls who loved her with all their hearts. Often when they gathered at the fountain, these girls would say to one another, "How unlucky that girl must be, not to know what fraternal love is!"

One day, having understood that they were talking about her, Lulesha turned to them and said: "What is the matter with you, girls? Why do you tease me? If I have no brothers, that is God's doing." "No, Lulesha, don't say that. You have brothers. They are abroad, but your mother doesn't tell you, because she is afraid that you will leave her." "Is it really so?" said the girl in amazement. "Yes, it is so," they replied. "If you want her to tell you, go home crying, and when she asks you,

'What's the matter?' say, 'I want to suck your breast through the crack in the door.' And when she gives it to you, squeeze her breast and say, 'Have I brothers or not?' She will then tell you the truth."

And indeed, after doing what her friends said, the girl discovered that she had six brothers, who were pashas in such-and-such a kingdom.

So one day, Lulesha set off to find her brothers. She was accompanied by a greyhound and a maid-servant, who was white-skinned but black-hearted. When they had almost arrived, this maid, who was called Bald Maria, broke the greyhound's legs with stones and flung it into a torrent. She then made Lulesha get off the mare and take off her fine clothes. She put the fine clothes on and forced Lulesha to put on her clothes. Then with Lulesha riding on the donkey and Bald Maria on the mare, they continued their journey.

Some hours later, they arrived at the house of Lulesha's brothers. When Bald Maria told them she was their sister, they were much delighted and took her upstairs into the palace. Lulesha, said by Bald Maria to be her maid, was sent to another room, a downstairs one, where the other servants were. And afterwards they sent her out to herd the cows.

Although Lulesha had never in all her life seen how cows were herded, she did not despair in the least. For on the one hand she knew that the truth would come out and on the other hand she was not herding other people's cows, but her brothers'.

In fact it was not long before the eldest brother asked her one day to have a look at his head, because it was itching. Not to disappoint him, she began to look at it behind him, but facing the other brothers. Presently she saw a crow flying in front of the window, and called out to it:

"Crow, oh, crow, oh,
Greet my mother, oh,
Tell her Lule, Lulesha
Is sent to herd the cows,
And Maria of the bald head

Has mounted the throne,
Tears, oh, tears, oh."

"What is that you say?" said her youngest brother, who was facing her and saw that she was crying:

"I say nothing, nothing,
A cloud came laden with rain,
It caught you, it caught me,
It caught the babies in the cradle,
It caught the lambs in the fold,
It caught the mares and foals,
It caught the birds and partridges."

From this, they understood that Lulesha the Beloved was really their sister and that they had made a mistake in putting Bald Maria on the throne. They took her down quickly and said to her, "Which do you want, lying little sister? To be tied to the tail of a maddened horse, or to be cut to pieces with a sword?" She chose the former, and was torn to bits as she was dragged over sharp rocks.

[told by Hasan M. Maleshova]

The Old Woman and her Three Daughters

Once long ago there was an old woman who had three daughters.

One fine day, the Devil sent a marriage-broker to her to say, "Can you give me your eldest daughter for a bey?" But it was not for a bey, it was for the Devil. The old woman replied, "Oh, tell the young man that I haven't a trousseau for her." "That doesn't matter," replied the broker. "The bey will buy one for her. So make the girl ready."

The old woman made her ready and the Devil married her. In the evening he said to her, "How are my feet? Are they hot or cold?" The bride replied, "They're cold, husband." For the Devil always has cold feet.

The Devil again asked, "How are my feet? Are they hot or cold?" She replied, "Cold." The Devil then asked, "What do you mean? How are my feet cold?" She simply said, "Look, your feet are cold." The devil then seized her and hanged her. The old woman's daughter thus gave up the ghost and died.

The Devil again sent the marriage-broker to the old woman to get her second daughter, saying to her, "I've found a better family than the first one. Get your daughter ready by evening because we're coming to fetch her."

In the evening they came and fetched her. Next day, the Devil went to the bazaar. A little afterwards, a turtle-dove came by and said to the girl, "*Guguftoo, guguftoo*, bring me two sultana raisins and I'll tell you your fortune." The girl remembered what had happened and said, "Enough! My sister is dead, but I'll give you your sultanas alright." She picked up a stone, threw it at the dove's leg and broke it.

The Devil came home in the evening, and they had supper. Afterwards, the Devil said to her, "Rub my feet a little. I'm tired." She

101

was rubbing his feet when he asked, "How are my feet? Cold or hot?" "Cold," she answered. "How are they cold, woman?" the Devil asked again. "They are cold," she repeated. The Devil seized her and hanged her, too, and put the bodies of the two dead sisters together.

The Devil again sent the marriage-broker to the old woman to get her youngest daughter, saying, "Another man, who is richer still, wants to marry your daughter. So get her ready, because we're coming to fetch her." In this way, the Devil married the third daughter, too.

The day after the wedding, a turtle-dove came to the third daughter and said, "*Guguftoo, guguftoo*, bring me two sultana raisins and I'll tell you your fortune." The girl said, "Not two, I'll give you a whole handful, if you only give me good fortune. I'm sad when I think of my sisters being hanged."

The turtle-dove said, "When your husband says to you, 'How are my feet? Hot or cold?' say, 'hot.' He is the Devil. Do you see that candlestick there? There are twelve rooms in it. Say to it, 'Let the candlestick open, let it open and let it let me in.' It will open and when it does, go into the twelfth room."

A little later, the Devil came home, meat in hand, and called out, "Wife, wife." She was not there, she was in the twelfth room of the candlestick. He flung the meat on the floor where the jackdaws ate it.

The Devil then picked up the candlestick and took it to the bazaar to sell it. A bey fancied it and bought it. When he did so, the Devil burst as soon as he went home.

The bey put the candlestick in his bedroom and slept there night after night. Just about the very time he had bought the candlestick, he had also got married. The maids said to him, "Come, bey, your bride is waiting." But he slept in his room with the candlestick.

After sleeping the first night with it, he got up in the morning and found a gold coin by his head, another by his hands, and a third by his feet. He wondered who had put them there.

The girl was used to being in the candlestick, but she came out of it once every 24 hours to eat. Every night when she came out and had eaten, she kissed the bey on his head, hands and feet, and put a gold coin, as we said above, at each place she kissed. Then she said to the candlestick, "Let the candlestick open, let it open and let it let me in."

The fourth night the bey meant to keep watch, but sleep seized him. The girl did as before. The fifth night the bey managed to keep awake and did not fall asleep. The girl began to do all that she was used to doing, but in vain. The bey seized her by the hand and said, "What are you? A human being or a devil?" "A human being," she replied. "What do you want here?" he asked. She told him how she had suffered with the Devil and how her sisters had suffered. The bey said, "Come here again to-morrow."

Next day she came out of the candlestick, but in vain. The maids saw her. She tried to flee back into the candlestick, saying, "Let it open, let it open, and let it let me in," but her clothes stuck in the door and the maids pulled and pulled at them until they dragged her out. They then took her golden clothes from her, dressed her in rags, and set her down outside by the lavatory door.

The girl later ran away and went to a poor old woman and said to her, "Mother, let me come in." The old woman answered, saying, "Daughter, I've nothing for you to eat." The girl replied, "If you eat dirt, I'll eat dirt. I'm going to be your daughter." "All right, then," said the old woman, "come in."

When the bey came home, he did not find the girl and when he saw the door of the candlestick open, he knew that they had taken her away. He pretended to be ill and asked for a little food from all the people in the town. This the maids brought to him, only they forgot one old woman. They said to the bey, "There's a poor old woman left but she can't cook anything." "All right," he replied, "tell the old woman that the bey said, 'What will you cook? Dirt? Then dirt I'll eat.'" And the maids went and repeated his words to the old woman.

The girl made a pastry with nettles, and put her ring into it and the old woman took it to the bey. He looked at it and found the ring, and said to the maids, "There's a girl in that old woman's house. Tell her that the bey wants her for his bride. And tell the old woman to make her ready."

So they spread costly velvet on the streets and fetched the girl to be his bride. The bey sent his first bride away, saying to her, "You wanted to kill my wife, and now you've come to a bad end yourself." He also brought the old woman home to live to his house.

[told by Fridherik Caku of Elbasan]

The Three Angels and the Girl

Once there were a wife and a husband who had no children. One day, as they were going to a village, they met three Angels. The woman went up to them and exchanged greetings with them. They asked her whether she had children or not, and she replied that she hadn't. "We'll give you medicine to make God give you a child," they said. "If it's girl, it's yours; if it's a boy, it's mine," she said in reply.

At the end of the year, a girl was born to the woman as the three Angels had said. The child went to school and made fair progress in both manners and lessons. At the end of twelve years the three Angels met the girl one day in the street as she was coming out of school. "Girl!" they called. "What do you want, ladies?" she replied. "Who do you belong to?" "So-and-so." "Is your mother alive?" "Yes, she is, ladies." "Tell your mother to remember what we said to her." But the girl forgot to tell her.

The Angels tied a thread on her finger so that she should not forget, but the same thing happened a second time. Then the Angels filled the bosom of her dress with walnuts to keep her from forgetting what they said. In the evening, when she went home, she said to her mother, "Mother, three woman told me you had made an agreement with them when you had no children. And they filled my bosom with walnuts to keep me from forgetting what they said." The mother replied, "Don't heed them, daughter."

Another day the Angels appeared to the girl and spoke of what they had said to her. She went home to come to an understanding with her mother. This time the mother said, "It shall be as they wish."

The girl went to the three Angels and they all set off for their village. On the way, one Angel said, "We'll give her a trade." The second said, "We'll eat her," and the third said, "We'll cook her with

105

rice." The first repeated, "We'll give her a trade." So they continued for a long way, arguing all the time till the one who said they would give her a trade, won the day. So they taught the girl all sorts of things. When she laughed, she made roses; when she cried, she made pearls; when she washed, she made gold. When she had learned all this, she went home to her mother.

She stayed there for some time. After a year she became engaged to a King who was from the same quarter of the town. After a year he married her and when he brought motorcars and a bridal party to fetch her, there were women enough in the wedding party to fill the cars.

When the bride left to go to the King's palace, her way led along the seashore. Her maid said, "Shall we stop the car for a little?" and it was stopped. Maid and bride got out, but the maid was evil-hearted and pushed the bride into the sea. Then she herself dressed up as the bride and went to the King.

At the end of a week, the King learned that when his bride laughed, she made roses, and when she cried, pearls, and when she washed, gold. But she could not do any of these things and at the end of three months he wanted to send her away.

A poplar tree grew at the seashore where the maid had pushed the bride in. As soon as the evil-hearted maid heard about it, she ordered it to be cut down and said, "Don't leave a single chip of wood there, but bring them all here." As she bade them, the servants collected all the chips and brought them to her.

On the way to the palace, a chip fell down on the ground. When a poor old woman was going to work in her garden, she found it on the road and picked it up, meaning to burn it. She took it home and put it on a shelf and in the morning went to work as she did every day.

When she came home at supper time, she found all the work of the house done. In great joy, she laughed and wondered at this.

One, two, and up to three days this happened. The fourth day, the old woman watched through the key hole, and what did she see? A beautiful bride who shone like the sun. At once the old woman opened the door and went in. The girl immediately wanted to hide, but the old

106

woman said to her, "Bless me, girl, where are you from?" The girl did not want to tell her.

After three days the old woman made her like her own daughter. The girl said, "If you love me, don't tell anybody."

The old woman went across the gardens to the houses of the beys and sold roses in mid-winter. The beys wondered at this.

One day she went to the palace of the King where the maid was. The maid asked her where she found the roses in the middle of winter. "I have a wild rose-tree," she said to the maid.

Another day, she had some pearls and went to sell them to the maid, who had ordered them. "Where did you find these pearls, old woman?" she asked. The old woman laughed, saying, "I had them in my time." The maid said, "Old woman, tell me God's truth and I'll give you as much money as you want." But the old woman would not listen and set off home.

That night the old woman was sad when she went home. Next day she went again to the palace and it was supper time before she came home. Next day, she went to the maid who said, "Now, old woman, you must tell me." The old woman told her what she had seen and heard. As she told her, the bride slowly died. When the old woman came home in the evening, she found her in the throes of death and said, "What's the matter, daughter?" "May you wither body and soul!" the bride replied, adding, "Cover my grave with molten gold."

When the old woman went to the maid, she had said, "I found the bride I have at home in a chip of wood which your servants had let fall." The maid seized her servants and beat them for what they had done. She went immediately afterwards to catch the dove at the foot of the poplar tree and while the bride was in the throes of death, she cut off its head. She took its heart and hung it on the crook over the fire.

The old woman buried the bride with full honours and covered her grave with molten gold and diamonds. She inscribed on the outside of the mausoleum, "Repent if you enter, and repent if you do not."

A little angel ran round and round the grave. The King, having gone out hunting, was quick to notice the new-made grave. He took the boy that was running round it and led him home. The boy wept and pointed at the crook where the bird's heart was hanging. Then he tried to catch it with his nails, and at last they gave it to him.

They took him to the grave where they had found him, and what should they see there? The woman had got up. The King took her in his car home to his palace where he married her as his first bride, whose place the maid had taken.

She told him all that the maid and the old woman had done. The King cut off the old woman's head and chopped up the maid into little bits, and hung the bits up on the walls like pig's flesh.

[told by Josif Kostandin Todja of Elbasan]

The Luck of a Lad

There was once a poor young man, who had been left nothing by his father except a cat and a dog.

One day the young man took the dog and the cat with him, and started off to seek his fortune. On the way he came on some ants and bottleflies, which had found a dead animal and were quarrelling about it. The ants said, "We'll take the meat, because we're smaller." "No," said the bottleflies, "We'll have the meat and you will take the bones."

As they quarrelled, the young man got in between them, took the meat and gave it to the ants, and gave the bones to the bottleflies. The two sides were very pleased. Then the ants turned to the young man and said, "See! We'll give you a wing feather for this good turn you've done us, and whenever you're in any difficulty, warm it in the fire, and we'll come at once to do what you want."

The young man put the feather in his pocket and resumed his journey. Again on the way, he met an old man, who asked him, "Where are you going, my boy?" "I've set off to kill the King of the Jinns and get his ring. If I have it, I shall be able all my life to get everything I need." "But do you know how to kill him?" "No," answered the young man. Then the old man said to him, "If you find him asleep, don't kill him. But if you find him awake, then kill him."

The young man left him, and after some time reached the King of the Jinns. When he saw that he was awake, he killed him, and after taking his ring, went away.

At this time there lived a King, who had a very beautiful daughter. He had issued a proclamation, saying, "Whoever wants to marry my daughter must build a gold ship in the middle of the sea, sort the different goods in the store, and make himself a better palace than mine is."

109

When the young man heard of this, he embarked on a ship and after some time crossed the sea and came to the place where this King lived.

There, unknown as he was, he went to an innkeeper, and sent him to the King to say, "A young man has come, who wants to marry your daughter."

The innkeeper went to the King and told him what the young man had said. "Yes," said the King, "he may have her, if he fulfils the conditions I have proclaimed."

The innkeeper told the young man what the King had said.

Next day, the young man got up early and went to the seashore. There, thanks to the orders he gave to the ring, a gold ship was created in the middle of the sea.

From the seashore the young man set off for the store to sort the different grains, such as wheat, maize, barley, rice, oats, hemp, etc. which were all mixed up. When he got there, he went into the store and warmed the wing that the ants had given him. Without loss of time they came. When all had collected, the young man said, "You big ones, sort out the big grains, and you little ones, sort out the little grains." So the ants began to sort them with cries and the extraordinary noises that ants make. In an hour they had sorted them all out and divided them into separate heaps.

When the King got up from sleep, he climbed the highest tower in the palace, cast his eyes towards the seashore, and was astonished enough when he saw the gold ship sparkling in the middle of the sea. Then he left the tower and went to the store. When he saw that the grains were all divided into separate heaps, he said, "Let the young man come and take my daughter. He's a fine fellow, but he must build himself a better palace than mine is."

Before the young man was married to the girl, the King gave her orders, saying, "My daughter, see if you can trick him and take the ring from him. If you can get it, bring it to me."

The young man married the girl and took her to his own country, where he had built his palace. After a considerable time had passed, the girl began to worry a great deal. When the young man saw

110

her like this, he said to her, "Why are you worrying and growing thin?" She replied, "I'm worrying because I want to know how you do all these wonderful things." As the young man was sorry for her, he told her in full about his experience, and in the end he told her also about the ring.

The girl, having it in her mind to take it from him, kept watch one night till he fell asleep. She then took the ring from his mouth and carried it to her father. When the young man got up from sleep, he saw that he didn't have it anymore in his mouth. At once it occurred to him that his wife had taken it from him. And so he began to rack his brains about how to get it back.

As he worried, the cat and the dog came to him and said, "What's the matter? What are you worrying about?" "Don't ask me!" said the young man. "A great misfortune has befallen me." "Tell us what the matter is," they insisted. "My wife has stolen my ring and given it to her father." "Don't worry about that," said the cat, "we will bring it back to you."

The two set off and went to the seashore. There the cat got on the dog's back and the dog, swimming in the sea, carried her to the farther shore, where the King lived.

The cat then, losing no time, went to the King's palace and, roaming this way and that, found a jar of pepper. She rubbed her tail in it and went into the King's room through a hole. He was sleeping at the time, and she put her tail in his mouth. As the pepper burned him, he coughed and spat out the ring. The cat caught it and, joining the dog, took the way she had come.

As they travelled across the sea, the dog said to the cat, "You've carried the ring long enough. Give it to me to carry for a little." "No," said the cat, "you'll let it fall into the sea." "Give it to me," said the dog, "or I'll drown you." "Oh don't!" said the cat. "Give it to me," said the dog again, and he made as though to drown her. The cat, seeing herself in danger, gave the ring to the dog, who dropped it into the sea soon after.

As soon as the ring fell into the sea, the dog stopped and said to the cat, "The ring's fallen into the sea. Turn round, perhaps we'll find it on the shore." "Didn't I tell you," said the cat, "that you'd lose it?"

111

They turned round, and came out of the sea once more onto the shore. As the cat prowled along the seashore, she saw that two fishes had found the ring and were playing with it. She went quietly up and flinging herself between them, said, "Give me the ring, or I'll eat you."

The fishes, to save their lives, gave it to her. The cat took the ring and, together with the dog, carried it to her master, and he won back the King's daughter.

[told by Thomas Prifti of Bubullima in the district of Lushnja]

The Treachery of a Merchant and the Charity of an Old Woman

There was once a very rich man, who wanted to start a big business and for that reason went to Constantinople to buy goods, taking with him a large sum of money.

When he arrived in Constantinople, his pocket felt heavy with the large amount of money he had, and he thought of leaving the money somewhere. In the end he left it with a merchant he did not know, and the merchant took charge of it.

Next morning the man went to the merchant to get his money, because he was going to shop, but when he asked for it, the man pretended to be ignorant of the affair and not to know him. "You've left no money here. Just try to remember where you did leave it!" he said. "Oh, sir, I remember quite well, it was here I left it," he said. "Sir, this town is called Constantinople, and you've lost your way. You haven't found the place where you left the money," the merchant answered. "I left it here, and don't split my ears any longer," said the man. To this the merchant replied, saying, "Well, have you any receipt or witness to show that you left the money here?" "I am my own receipt and witness," the man replied. The merchant then said to him, "Since you've neither receipt nor witness, hop it!"

The man saw that it was not possible to get his money by force. So he begged the merchant to give him half of it. But again the merchant would not listen and said to him, "Go away, or you'll catch it!"

The man went away in great despair, beating his head with his fists. And he went to the corner of the wall where he stood in sorrow. While he stood there, an old woman with a basket in her hand arrived. As soon as she saw him, she asked him, "What are you sad and worried about?" He told her in full all that had happened to him. As soon as she

113

grasped what was the matter, she said, "Don't worry! I'll get your money back for you, if you tell me where it is."

After the man told her, she went to the merchant and said, "Mr. Merchant, isn't it possible for Your Honour and me to join forces? I'm left alone. Two years ago to-day my son came home from America, bringing a lot of money and valuable objects. But unluckily he did not live to enjoy them. It's not safe for me to live alone with all the property he left me. I've talked with many people, and they have praised Your Honour as an honourable man."

The merchant was delighted and replied, "Done, madam!" The old woman then said to him, "Send four or five servants to fetch the money, and seven or eight carts to fetch the other things, and two or three porters to load them."

The merchant said, "Stop a moment, woman. Don't be in a hurry." He ordered coffee and the two drank it together. After the old woman had drunk hers, she said to the merchant, "I'm going home to get some things ready." The merchant in his great joy went out into the street and called in the man and gave him his money. He was afraid that the old woman might hear about it and change her mind about himself.

When the man received his money, he said, "Eternal damnation to your soul!" But the merchant paid no attention and made no reply.

As the old woman had bidden him do, the merchant sent seven carts and six men to take her things. But what should they see when they reached her house? She was baking bread with thorns for firewood and half her house was thatched, and half was in ruins.

The men saw there was nothing to be done. They turned away and went back to the merchant and said to him, "The old woman tricked you." He replied, "How could she possibly trick me?" And then he went himself to her house and said, "Where is your house and your property?" She answered, saying, "Over there, where that white house is. But don't trouble to go and take the things." "Why not?" the merchant replied. "Go away," she said. "You're bad-hearted and nearly kept the stranger's money."

114

The merchant bowed his head and went away sad and sorrowful, beating his head with his fists and saying, "Whatever made me give the money back to the stranger?"

When he went home in the evening, he remained sad. His children sat round him as always, but he did not speak to them. His wife, seeing him unhappy, said, "What's the matter, husband?" "Leave me alone, wife," he answered, but then he told her what had happened from beginning to end.

When she heard it all, she said, "Calm yourself and don't worry. I'll get the money from him to-morrow."

Next day the merchant's wife put on ragged clothes, and along with her husband went to the bazaar, where her husband pointed out the stranger to her. He was in a café. The wife went into the café, saying "How d'ye do, sir?" and sat down beside the stranger. They began to talk.

After a time the wife asked him, "Where are you from, sir?" "From Albania," he replied. "Oh, you've cured my homesickness," said the woman. "That's my country, too. But I am married here, and for seventeen years I have not been home to see my parents. Isn't it possible for you to take me with you when you go to Albania, and to make me your wife, as it were, so that we shan't have any bothers?"

The man liked the idea, and they went to the *cadi* to get married. After the ceremony, they went to stay in a hotel. After a little, the man went out again to the bazaar, bidding the woman take good care of his things. Her opportunity had come. She stole the money, and went home.

When the man came back to the hotel, he was astonished to find nobody there, and he soon understood the treachery of the woman. Very sad, he went to the old woman and told her what had happened. She was surprised and said, "I'll get the money back for you once more, but don't you show your face here again, or you'll be done for altogether. To-morrow morning, take a basket of loaves and go to that woman's house. Her son will come out. Seize him and run away. If anyone follows you, go to the *cadi*, and he will decide the question."

The man did everything that the old woman told him. When he came to the woman's house, crying the hot loaves he had, her son came out to buy a loaf. The man dropped the basket, seized the child and ran away.

The merchant and his wife soon understood what was ado and they went to the man to get the child. But he said, "What boy are you looking for? This child is mine."

Then they all went to the *cadi* to get him to decide the matter. The stranger told the *cadi* that the woman was his wife and that he wanted to divorce her. The *cadi* said, "As you, sir, are to separate from your wife, you will take the boy, and you will give money to her." "No, no," answered the woman, "I don't want money, I want the boy." Then he gave her the boy, and got back his money from her. He gave a present to the old woman and, in the morning, he was no longer to be seen.

[told by Jan Bocova, from near Fier]

The Treachery of a Merchant and the Charity of an Old Woman

There was once a very rich man, who wanted to start a big business and for that reason went to Constantinople to buy goods, taking with him a large sum of money.

When he arrived in Constantinople, his pocket felt heavy with the large amount of money he had, and he thought of leaving the money somewhere. In the end he left it with a merchant he did not know, and the merchant took charge of it.

Next morning the man went to the merchant to get his money, because he was going to shop, but when he asked for it, the man pretended to be ignorant of the affair and not to know him. "You've left no money here. Just try to remember where you did leave it!" he said. "Oh, sir, I remember quite well, it was here I left it," he said. "Sir, this town is called Constantinople, and you've lost your way. You haven't found the place where you left the money," the merchant answered. "I left it here, and don't split my ears any longer," said the man. To this the merchant replied, saying, "Well, have you any receipt or witness to show that you left the money here?" "I am my own receipt and witness," the man replied. The merchant then said to him, "Since you've neither receipt nor witness, hop it!"

The man saw that it was not possible to get his money by force. So he begged the merchant to give him half of it. But again the merchant would not listen and said to him, "Go away, or you'll catch it!"

The man went away in great despair, beating his head with his fists. And he went to the corner of the wall where he stood in sorrow. While he stood there, an old woman with a basket in her hand arrived. As soon as she saw him, she asked him, "What are you sad and worried about?" He told her in full all that had happened to him. As soon as she

117

grasped what was the matter, she said, "Don't worry! I'll get your money back for you, if you tell me where it is."

After the man told her, she went to the merchant and said, "Mr. Merchant, isn't it possible for Your Honour and me to join forces? I'm left alone. Two years ago to-day my son came home from America, bringing a lot of money and valuable objects. But unluckily he did not live to enjoy them. It's not safe for me to live alone with all the property he left me. I've talked with many people, and they have praised Your Honour as an honourable man."

The merchant was delighted and replied, "Done, madam!" The old woman then said to him, "Send four or five servants to fetch the money, and seven or eight carts to fetch the other things, and two or three porters to load them."

The merchant said, "Stop a moment, woman. Don't be in a hurry." He ordered coffee and the two drank it together. After the old woman had drunk hers, she said to the merchant, "I'm going home to get some things ready." The merchant in his great joy went out into the street and called in the man and gave him his money. He was afraid that the old woman might hear about it and change her mind about himself.

When the man received his money, he said, "Eternal damnation to your soul!" But the merchant paid no attention and made no reply.

As the old woman had bidden him do, the merchant sent seven carts and six men to take her things. But what should they see when they reached her house? She was baking bread with thorns for firewood and half her house was thatched, and half was in ruins.

The men saw there was nothing to be done. They turned away and went back to the merchant and said to him, "The old woman tricked you." He replied, "How could she possibly trick me?" And then he went himself to her house and said, "Where is your house and your property?" She answered, saying, "Over there, where that white house is. But don't trouble to go and take the things." "Why not?" the merchant replied. "Go away," she said. "You're bad-hearted and nearly kept the stranger's money."

The merchant bowed his head and went away sad and sorrowful, beating his head with his fists and saying, "Whatever made me give the money back to the stranger?"

When he went home in the evening, he remained sad. His children sat round him as always, but he did not speak to them. His wife, seeing him unhappy, said, "What's the matter, husband?" "Leave me alone, wife," he answered, but then he told her what had happened from beginning to end.

When she heard it all, she said, "Calm yourself and don't worry. I'll get the money from him to-morrow."

Next day the merchant's wife put on ragged clothes, and along with her husband went to the bazaar, where her husband pointed out the stranger to her. He was in a café. The wife went into the café, saying "How d'ye do, sir?" and sat down beside the stranger. They began to talk.

After a time the wife asked him, "Where are you from, sir?" "From Albania," he replied. "Oh, you've cured my homesickness," said the woman. "That's my country, too. But I am married here, and for seventeen years I have not been home to see my parents. Isn't it possible for you to take me with you when you go to Albania, and to make me your wife, as it were, so that we shan't have any bothers?"

The man liked the idea, and they went to the *cadi* to get married. After the ceremony, they went to stay in a hotel. After a little, the man went out again to the bazaar, bidding the woman take good care of his things. Her opportunity had come. She stole the money, and went home.

When the man came back to the hotel, he was astonished to find nobody there, and he soon understood the treachery of the woman. Very sad, he went to the old woman and told her what had happened. She was surprised and said, "I'll get the money back for you once more, but don't you show your face here again, or you'll be done for altogether. To-morrow morning, take a basket of loaves and go to that woman's house. Her son will come out. Seize him and run away. If anyone follows you, go to the *cadi*, and he will decide the question."

The man did everything that the old woman told him. When he came to the woman's house, crying the hot loaves he had, her son came

119

out to buy a loaf. The man dropped the basket, seized the child and ran away.

The merchant and his wife soon understood what was ado and they went to the man to get the child. But he said, "What boy are you looking for? This child is mine."

Then they all went to the *cadi* to get him to decide the matter. The stranger told the *cadi* that the woman was his wife and that he wanted to divorce her. The *cadi* said, "As you, sir, are to separate from your wife, you will take the boy, and you will give money to her." "No, no," answered the woman, "I don't want money, I want the boy." Then he gave her the boy, and got back his money from her. He gave a present to the old woman and, in the morning, he was no longer to be seen.

[told by Jan Bocova, from near Fier]

The Kalagjystan

There were once a King and a Vezir who each had a son. One day when these boys were playing ball, they hit an old woman who was drawing water at the fountain and they broke her water-pots. She turned to them with the exclamation, "Ah, boys, it doesn't do to curse you, because you are royal children, but I say to you, 'May you fall in love with the Kalagjystan!'" When the boys heard her say this, they left the ball lying on the ground and began to talk about the Kalagjystan. "Oh, whoever can she be?" they wondered.

When the boys went home, the King's son asked his father to give him two saddle-bags full of gold Napoleons so that he could go and find the Kalagjystan. As soon as he got them, he started off and travelled far. He stopped at a house in a certain village and asked, "Where is the Kalagjystan?" The mistress of the house, who had brought the Kalagjystan into the world as the midwife, said, "She lives far away, and can only be found in a big house, where she is surrounded by three battalions of soldiers, three battalions of lions and three battalions of jackdaws. To get her, you must clear away all the droppings of the jackdaws, all the dung of the lions and all the slops of the soldiers."

After she had told him this, the King's son gave her most of his money, keeping only a little for himself, and took his leave. On and on he went and found the house he wanted. He began to scrape away the droppings of the jackdaws, the dung of the lions and the slops of the soldiers, and little by little he got into the courtyard. In the evening he went right inside and talked with the girl.

She at once said to him, "I am engaged, and in a week I shall be married. Stay till I am getting married. Stay, and when I am being married, they will take me to my mother's grave to pray because I am getting married that day. When we go there, you come, too, and there we'll change clothes, and you will become the bride in my stead."

At the end of the week the wedding began. After dressing this bride, they mounted her on a horse and took her to her mother's grave. She went inside it, together with the King's son. It was like a locked room. They changed clothes, and the King's son became the bride.

When he appeared dressed in the bride's clothes, the bridegroom's people took him amid great joy and led him home. The Kalagjystan remained behind in the grave.

After eating the wedding supper in the evening, they put the bride to sleep with the eldest sister of the bridegroom. During the night, he told her all about the business, and said to her, "You come, too, with me, because I'm going to fetch the Kalagjystan, who is in her mother's grave. I'll give you to the Vezir's son." The bridegroom's sister made up her mind to go with him. They got up and each laid a burned coat on either side of a brazier with live embers, and hastened off to the grave.

In the morning, the people in the bridegroom's house began to play music because the bride was about to come out of her room. But since she did not appear, they broke down the door and went inside. And what did they see? The two, bride and bridegroom's sister, seemed to have been burned to death, so they began to cry and lament their deaths.

Meanwhile the King's son and the eldest sister of the bridegroom had taken the Kalagjystan out of her mother's grave and escaped with her to his home, where he and the Vezir's son were married to the two girls.

[told by Spiro Poppa]

The Donkey That Dropped Money

Once there was an old man who had a donkey that dropped money, but the man himself put the coins in the donkey's backside.

As the donkey went along the road, the coins dropped out. When they did so one day, they were seen by two butchers. "Oh, old man," they cried, "What are you doing? You're losing your money." "My donkey drops money," he said. "How much do you want for the donkey?" "Five Napoleons. The donkey drops that much."

"What does it need, old man, to make it drop money?" they asked. He replied, "A boiler of wheat and a boiler of water. Then it drops money. Then it produces money."

They shut the donkey up and closed the door. When they went to open the door, the door was blocked. The donkey had blocked it. "The donkey has filled the stable with gold coins and that's why it does not let the door open," they said in great joy. They took off the roof of the house and found their way in. The donkey was dead.

"The old man has cheated us! Let's go and kill him this minute," they exclaimed.

They went to the old man's house. He kept two hares that he used as servants. He received his visitors well, gave them food, and gave them meat. He could not ask his wife for food, for she was in the field.

He said, "The hares are my servants and I send them to my wife with bread and food." "Eh, give us one, old man." "I'd like to, only I need them for myself," he replied. "How much do you want?" they asked. "Three Napoleons per hare."

They paid the money and went home with a hare. There they let it go, but the hare ran away into the woods.

123

They went off once more to kill the old man, exclaiming, "The old man has cheated us again!"

This time the old man had tied a gut full of blood round his wife's neck. When the butchers came, he quarrelled with the old woman and stabbed her. She fell to the ground gurgling, and blood flowed from her. The old man took his flute, for he had a flute, and played on it. He wanted to bring the old woman back to life. He played and played on the flute, and the old woman came back to life.

The butchers said to him, "You'll give us the flute. We have some badly behaved women at home. We want the flute. First we'll kill them and then we'll bring them back to life with the flute. That will teach them a lesson." They bought the flute for two Napoleons.

When they went home, the older one quarrelled with this wife, killed her, and played on the flute. He played and played, but she did not come back to life.

The younger one said, "You can't have known how to play on the flute. I'll kill my wife." He killed his wife, too, and afterwards played and played on the flute, but she did not come back to life. Both of their wives were dead.

Once more they went to the old man to kill him. When they arrived, the old man's wife was crying. "Why are you crying, woman?" they asked. "The old man is dead," she replied. The old man had buried himself alive in a grave, taking with him an iron nail he had sharpened.

"Where is his grave? We'll go and dirty it." The elder one sat down on the grave and, immediately, the old man stabbed him with the nail. "Devil alive, devil dead!" the man exclaimed as he rose hastily from the grave.

The younger man said, "Some thorn or other pricked him!" In his turn he sat down, and the old man stabbed him, too. "Devil alive, devil dead!" the man exclaimed as he rose hastily from the grave.

They then went home, and the old man came back to life.

The end.

[told by Jon Apostol Dede of Nezhar in the Shpat region of the district of Elbasan]

The Wife Who Would Not Work

A woman had married seven husbands, and all seven divorced her because she would not work.

Another man's wife died and he said to his foster-brother, "I'll marry so-and-so." The foster-brother said, "She won't work. Seven husbands have married her and divorced her. What do you want her for? Is it for her beauty or her work?" "Her work," he replied. "She won't work," his foster-brother insisted.

The man sent for the woman and married her. He gave special orders to his household that they were all to do as he said.

When they got up in the morning, everybody went to work. This man's wife did not go. When dinner-time came, the husband set the table, and the whole household sat down round it. The husband asked one of the head workers what work he had done. "I did this and I did that," he replied. The husband gave him a big portion of food.

He asked the next man what he had done. He had done two or three jobs, and the husband gave him two portions of food.

The husband questioned them all, and gave them food according to the work each had done. He then asked his own wife, "What work have you done?" "I've done no work at all," she replied. "Oh, you are the best of them all! Now I've got a good wife. I must put cushions under my wife's feet. Everybody else puts them under the head." And he did not give her a scrap of food.

Supper-time came. Again he questioned the whole household and gave them food according to the work they had done. Again he questioned his wife. She had not worked, and he gave her no food.

Morning came. As soon as this man's wife rose, she let the calves out into the meadow and brought in an armful of wood. She piled

126

the wood in a corner and went to the fountain for water. She swept the house and did a great deal of work by dinner-time.

Her husband gathered the whole household and questioned them and gave them food according to the work they had done. Again he questioned his wife. "I got up in the morning, I let the calves out into the meadow, and I brought in an armful of wood. I went for water, and I swept the house," she replied, mentioning also all the other work she had done.

"Ah!" said the husband. "I wanted you just as a wife for myself, and you've behaved like the others. You've put me under an obligation. To-day I must give you two portions of food." She ate the food.

Day by day the wife worked, she never was idle. And one day her father came to see her.

She saw him some way off, and went to meet him. "Father," she said, "pick that log up and carry it to our house. My husband won't give you any food if you don't work."

Her father guessed the trick her husband had played on his daughter. To keep her from seeing through it, he picked up the log and carried it on his shoulder to the house.

When his son-in-law saw him, he exclaimed, "Father-in-law, what are you doing?" "Oh," he replied, "I want some food, I can't do without food, and so I must work." "Oh," the husband replied, "you've put me under an obligation. I thought you came for a quiet chat with me to-night. I'll give you two portions of food."

In this way the husband made his wife work, and they had children.

[told by Xhafë Kuqi of Kuqan in the district of Elbasan]

The Black Ram and the Twelve Meadows

Once there were a husband and a wife, who were rich, but had neither son nor daughter.

The husband said to his wife, "We've neither son nor daughter, let's invite people over." He began to invite and entertain friends night after night and ran through all his money. He even sold his house.

The woman became pregnant. When her time came, she had nobody at hand except her husband. He said to her, "Who is your neighbour, so that I can go and call her?" She told him about them all, and he set off to go to them.

He knocked at the first door he came to. The woman was asleep, because it was night. When he knocked at the door a second time, she got up and said, "Who are you?" He replied, "For God's sake, neighbour, come! My wife's going to have a baby." But she answered, "Go away, idiot. You've waked me up."

He went to the next neighbour, and she said the same as the first one. He went away and said to his wife, "I'll turn midwife to you." Directly he had said that, three angels came, bringing a cradle and other things needed, and seeming to the couple like their neighbours. The wife said, "Thank goodness you've come." A daughter was born to her.

The angels said to her, "When you wash the baby, don't throw away the water at once, but keep it till the next day." And one said, "When she cries, may she spout ivory." And the second said, "When she laughs, may she spout roses." And the third said, "When she takes hold of something and washes it, let the thing turn to solid gold and silver."

Then they went away. When the couple got up in the morning, they found that the water in which the baby had been washed, had turned to solid gold and silver. The husband and the wife were

128

astonished at the way it had solidified, and he took a piece to sell and buy a little paraffin, because they had none.

He thought the bit would bring three or four piasters, and went with it to a gentleman, who was a money-changer. He said, "How much shall I sell this for?" When the gentleman said, "twenty Napoleons," the man jokingly replied "forty," and by going on joking, raised the price to one hundred Napoleons. The money-changer gave them to him, and when the man saw the one hundred Napoleons, he was astonished and took the money home. He sold the whole tubful and became more of a gentleman than he had been, and bought a house.

When the girl cried, she spouted ivory. When she laughed, she spouted roses, and when she picked up anything, it turned to solid gold and silver.

When the girl grew up, the King's son heard that when she cried, she spouted ivory, and roses when she laughed, and that when she touched anything and washed it, it turned to solid gold and silver. The Prince said to the man that he wanted his daughter. The man said, "No, sir. You are a Prince, and my daughter is not good enough for you, a Prince."

The Prince said again that he wanted her. "All right, sir, then I'll give her to you," said the man. And he made her ready and put her into a carriage along with a maid.

This maid had a daughter, whom she took with her in the carriage. The man's daughter took all sorts of things with her. She always ate when travelling, and when she ate, she always needed water. So she said to the maid, "Go and fetch me some water." But the maid replied, "Wait a little. We're far from water." And on and on they went. The girl said, "Do go for water, maid, do go!" "Wait, wait," said the maid. When they came to water, a lake was close by and the girl said, "Do go, maid, and get some water. There it is!"

The maid said, "Let me put out one of your eyes. Then I'll give you water." The girl said, "But how could I go to my husband like that?" The maid said, "If you want water…" The girl was dying of thirst and said to the maid, "All right, then, put out my eye." The maid put it out and gave her a glass of water.

129

On and on they went. The girl again wanted water and said, "Give me a little water, maid." The maid replied, "Let me put out your other eye." And the girl said, "How can I go quite blind to my husband?" The maid replied, "If you want water..." "Go on, then, put it out," said the girl. The maid put out her eye, stripped her of her clothes, and threw her into the sea. She dressed up her own daughter in the clothes she took from the girl, to make the King marry her.

When the maid's daughter went to the King's palace, his son gave her his stock to hold and turn to solid gold and silver. But she could not make it do so.

The Prince was not pleased at marrying her. When he made her cry, she did not pour out ivory, and when he made her laugh, she did not pour out roses.

In the place where the real bride had fallen, there was a beautiful and slender cypress tree. When the King's horses went to drink water, they shied away from the cypress, and would not drink.

One fine day, the Prince said to his groom, "Why are those horses getting thin?" "I don't know," he replied. Again the Prince said, "Tell me why they are growing thin." The servant told him, saying, "There's a tall, beautiful cypress tree that frightens the horses when they see it, and so they won't drink." The Prince said, "I'll go myself and have a look at it," and go he did.

The girl, who was very beautiful, had been staying night and day by the cypress tree, and the servants brought her food. It happened that the Prince had a journey to make and the maid learned that the girl was at the cypress tree. She went to bed ill. When the Prince's father said to her, "What's the matter?" she replied that she was ill. "What's the matter?" "I've a fever, and I shan't get well unless you cut down that cypress tree to make a bed for me." The King sent his servants out to cut down the tree. They did so and made a bed for her, and she recovered.

When the servants had cut down the cypress tree, some chips of wood were left at the foot of the tree. An old woman went to pick them up, and gathered them all. The girl's soul happened to be in one chip which she picked up. The old woman took them home, put them on a stone slab, and went away.

The girl came out of the chip of wood, swept out the house, lit the fire and cooked the food. When the old woman came home, the girl went back into the chip of wood.

The old woman said in astonishment, "Who has swept the house for me and baked and cooked?" She went to a neighbour and said, "A blessing on you, neighbour, for doing my housework and cooking and baking for me!" But the neighbour said, "Oh, old woman, who's done the work for you? Tell me, and lucky be it. You've got somebody in your house."

The old woman went home and again left the house, but this time, only to hide behind the door. The girl, coming out of the chip of wood, went to fetch firewood. "Bless me!" exclaimed the old woman. The girl said, "Don't cry, old woman. Somebody may hear you."

When the girl grasped a thing, it turned to solid gold and silver. She said to the old woman, "Here's gold and silver. Go to the palace gate and cry, 'Who wants gold and silver?' And don't sell it for money, but only for a goat's eye." The old woman went to the palace gate and cried, "Who wants gold and silver? Who wants gold and silver?"

The maid went to the gate to buy some gold and silver, and said to the old woman, "How much money do you want for this, old woman?" "I don't want money for it, I want a goat's eye," the old woman said. "Dearie me! Where can I find a goat's eye?" said the maid. "If you want gold and silver..." the old woman replied.

"Oh, mother, you've got that bitch's eye," said the maid's daughter. "True, daughter," said the maid. And she called out to the old woman, "Come over here, old woman, come over here! Here's the goat's eye." In return for it the old woman gave her gold and silver.

When the old woman took the eye home to the girl, the girl put it back in its place and saw with one eye. The maid showed the Prince the gold and silver, but he took no pleasure in being married to her.

Whenever the girl, who lived at the old woman's house, cried, she spouted ivory. One day she said to the old woman, "Go to the palace gate and cry, 'Who wants ivory?' And don't sell it for money, but only

131

for a goat's eye. And don't tell anybody that I am here." The old woman went to the palace gate and called out, "Who wants ivory? Who wants ivory?"

The maid heard her, went out to the gate, and said, "Old woman, how much will you sell it for?" "I won't sell it for money, but only for a goat's eye," she replied. "Oh, old woman, where can I find a goat's eye?" said the maid. The old woman said, "If you want the ivory…"

"Mother, we have that bitch's other eye," said the maid's daughter. "Come over here, old woman, come over here. Here's the goat's eye," said the maid. In return, the old woman gave her the ivory and went away.

She gave the eye to the girl, who put it back in its place and saw with both eyes.

When this girl laughed, she spouted roses. One day she said to the old woman, "Here, old woman, sell these roses for money at the palace gate and don't tell anybody that I am here." The old woman went to the palace gate, calling out, "Who wants roses?"

The maid heard her and went to the gate and said, "Old woman, come over here, come over here. Who have you got in your house?" "Nobody," said the old woman. "Confess! I'll give you a sieveful of money," the maid insisted. The old woman then confessed, saying, "I have a girl there. When she cries, she spouts ivory; when she laughs, she spouts roses; and when she touches anything, it turns to gold and silver."

The maid said to her, "Old woman, go and say to her, 'Where do you keep your soul?'" The old woman obediently went and said, "Darling, where do you keep your soul?" "Why do you ask, old woman? You have told about me!" replied the girl. "Oh no, daughter, who could I tell about you?" said the old woman. "You've told! Go and say, 'There is a black ram in the twelve meadows. If you kill this ram, a dove appears. If you cut off the dove's head, two diamonds will appear. If you hang these two diamonds on the crook over the fire, my soul will depart.'"

The girl then added, "When I die, lay me by the seashore." "All right," said the old woman.

She went and said to the maid, "In the twelve meadows there is a black ram. If you kill that ram, a dove appears. If you cut off the dove's head, two diamonds will appear. If you hang the two diamonds on the crook over the fire, her soul will depart."

The maid said to her servants, "In the twelve meadows there is a black ram. If you kill this ram, a dove appears. If you cut off the dove's head, two diamonds will appear. Bring these diamonds to me."

In the twelve meadows, the servants killed the black ram and the dove appeared. They cut off the dove's head and the two diamonds appeared. The servants brought the two diamonds to the maid, who hung them on the crook over the fire. The girl's soul departed, and the old woman carried her out to the seashore.

On the seashore, a beautiful mausoleum sprang up. When the King's horses came to drink water there, they shied away from the mausoleum and would not drink. When the King's son said to his servant, "Why are these horse getting thin?" the servant said, "They don't drink water because there is a mausoleum there. They are afraid of it and won't drink."

The Prince went there himself and saw there was a girl inside the mausoleum. He sat there day and night and wept. From his tears, the girl became pregnant, and bore him a son.

The child was born able to talk and he said, "Mother, look at father. Father, look at mother. Mother, look at father. Father, look at mother." The man took the boy home to his palace and said to the woman, "Don't let a sound from him be heard. If you do, I'll kill you."

The child approached the diamonds and cried out. The women said, "Pooh, he doesn't know anything," and they gave him the diamonds. As soon as he got them, he hurried off to his mother and put the two stones in her nostrils. She sneezed and said, "Oh, how long I've slept!" He said, "You haven't slept, you've been dead." The King's son took her, dressed her in his own fur-coat, and sent her to his palace.

He gave her a melon. It turned to solid gold and silver. He said, "This will be my wife."

Then he said to the maid's daughter, "Which do you prefer? Three knife-thrusts in your liver or three stallions?" She replied, "Three stallions, to go back to my father and mother. But give that bitch you've now married three knife-thrusts in the liver."

She got the three stallions, and went back to her father and mother with one leg and one hand.

[told by Hamit Skilje of Elbasan]

The Three Dogs

Once there were an old man and woman, who had a son and a daughter. It wasn't long, however, before the old man's wife died, and he married again.

The boy and girl did not get on with their step-mother. The boy said, "Sister, rather than be disgraced every day, let's run away somewhere." The boy took his sister and went to a great forest.

They worked there and built a house. They also got a few sheep together. One spring a bear came to the boy and said, "Hi, shepherd!" "What is it, Mr. Bear?" he asked. "Please give me a lamb. My children are dying." The shepherd said, "Come and choose one for yourself." "No, no. Give me one yourself," the bear returned. The boy chose a lamb and gave it to the bear. "Would you like a cub from me?" the bear asked. "Yes, give me one," said the shepherd. So the bear gave him a cub.

To cut the story short, the wolf also asked him for a lamb, and he gave it to him. The fox, too, asked him for a lamb, and he gave it to her. The wolf and the fox each gave him a cub.

The boy took the cubs and put them in the fowl-house and fed them well. They grew up as his dogs and became very strong, and the shepherd took them everywhere with him. One day a robber set out and went to the boy's house. There he found the girl, this boy's sister, and said to her, "I want to make you my wife." "All right," said the girl. "I want you for my husband." But she added, "What are we to do with my brother? He has three dogs which all the men in the Kingdom can do nothing against, let alone us." The robber replied, "When your brother comes home to-night, say to him, 'Brother, leave the dogs to me to-morrow. I'm bored.' He will leave them with you. You put them in the fowl-house, and I'll go and kill them." "Very well," said the girl, "I'll do that."

The brother came home, he had been on the mountain with the sheep. After they had had supper, his sister said, "Brother, leave the dogs with me to-morrow. I'm very bored." The boy said, "All right."

The next day the girl shut up the dogs in the fowl-house as soon as her brother went away to the mountain. The robber went up to the boy on the mountain to kill him without any more ado. "Please let me say just one word. May I play once on my flute?" the boy asked. "Yes," said the robber. The young man played on the flute the tunes that called the dogs.

The fox heard him and said to the wolf, "To arms, men. They're killing our master!" The bear at once jumped up and clove the door of the fowl-house in two, and they rushed to their master's help. He cried to them, "Turn him over, bear, but don't kill him." The bear caught the robber, and the boy picked up his rifle and said, "What had I done to you that you wanted to kill me?"

The robber said, "I wanted to kill you because of that sister of yours that I talked of marriage to." Then the boy said to the bear, "Cut off his head!" The bear, following his master's order, cut off the robber's head.

At once the shepherd drove his sheep home and said, "Sister, I won't touch you, but it was for your sake that I left home and came here, not to let our step-mother torment us. And you try to kill me? Oh!"

He then said to his sister, "You go that way, and I'll go this. And don't let me see you here again." The girl took the road he said and ended up in the capital, where she went as servant to the King. The boy also ended up there, but he went farther from the road and went to an old woman's house.

By good luck the King was having one of his daughters, his eldest one, married. A *kulshedra*, however, had seized the place where the water was, and it was the *kulshedra*'s custom not to let the water flow unless she ate one of the daughters of whoever was celebrating a marriage. The King could not but send his youngest daughter to the *kulshedra*. That day they told the young man about it, saying, "We have

136

a *kulshedra*, and this is what she does to us, this and goodness knows what else." The boy took his three dogs to the girl who had been sent for the *kulshedra* to eat. "Never mind about me. This is my fate. But why have you come here, sir?" asked the girl. "Where you die, I'll die, too," said the boy.

Then they saw the *kulshedra* coming and saying, "Hu, hu, hu, instead of one they're two!" The boy made signs to the three dogs, and they caught the *kulshedra* and tore her to pieces.

When they had done so, this boy cut out her twelve tongues, for she had twelve heads. The girl then gave him a handkerchief, as a sort of engagement token, and the boy gave her a ring from his finger, and he went away.

After a little, one of the King's servants went to see what had happened that so much water was coming, and what did he see? The *kulshedra* dead and the girl alive. The King's servant, an *arap*, struck the *kulshedra* and cut off her twelve heads and went away. He then said to the girl, "Don't tell, or I'll kill you dead." The *arap* went to the King and announced, "I've killed the *kulshedra*." Then the King gave him as reward the girl that the *kulshedra* would have eaten, and those very days he was to marry her to the servant.

The girl, however, said to the King, "Since it was my luck to be saved, invite to dinner at my wedding not only the people of this town, but also the dogs." "All right," said the King to his daughter.

Not to make a long story of it, the King really invited the dogs, too. The messengers took invitations to the whole town, but not to the boy or the old woman. From mouth to mouth it was passed round that they were not invited, and later the King sent to invite them. The young man got up with the old woman and the dogs, and they all went to the wedding.

When they went to the palace, the King said to the young man, "If it's possible, put the dogs in the fowl-house. The women are frightened." "I'll put the wolf and the fox in the fowl-house, Your Majesty, but not the bear." "All right," said the King.

Well, it was not long before food appeared. Instead of his napkin, the young man put on his plate the handkerchief which the princess had given him and which had her name on it. As soon as the King saw it, he said, "Where did you find that handkerchief, sir?" The young man told him how it had happened.

He then went and called the *arap* and said to the young man, "Here's the man who killed the *kulshedra*." The young man said, "As he killed the *kulshedra*, open the twelve heads and see if they have tongues or not. If they do, let me be punished according to the law. But if the heads haven't got tongues, then I want the *arap* to be killed." "All right," said the King.

When they opened the *kulshedra*'s heads, they found no tongues at all. Then the young man took out the twelve tongues and showed them to the company. When the King and his ministers saw this evidence, they hanged the *arap*. And they gave the princess to this young man according to the proofs they saw.

That night, when the young man was about to go to his bride, his sister, who was a servant of the King's, put poison on three splinters and laid them in her brother's bed. When her brother was shut up with his bride, he lay down to sleep, and the three splinters went into his back, so that he died on the instant. When the princess saw he had died, she informed her father, who took the young man, but found no place in which to put him. His sister said, "Bury him seven countries away." For the dogs would find him dead and raise the devil.

The King found two men and sent them with the dead man, and they buried him. As soon as they had buried him, the fox smelt him and said to its companions, "Get up and break in the door of the fowl-house. Our master is dead and they've buried him." When they heard this, they got up, got out, and spread out, saying, "Let's meet in that high forest." Indeed, it wasn't long before they met. The others said to the wolf, "Open your eye, friend, and see if you can see any newly dug ground and tell us." The wolf looked very carefully all round and said to his friends, "The ground's newly dug in only one place." And so they went to the grave, and the fox said, "Here he is. Uncover him, bear, slowly."

The bear fell to and uncovered him and took him out. The others said to the wolf, "Look and see of what he died." When the wolf had studied him, he said, "His death came from poisoning by three splinters in the back." So they sucked out all the poison, and the man came back to life and said, "I've slept a fine long time!" "All right, all right," said the dogs. And they took him up and put him on the bear's back. The wolf took the fox, and so they went to the King.

The King then began the wedding celebrations again, firing cannon shots and doing other things.

When the young man found that his sister had poisoned him, he told the bear, which made mincemeat of her. In the end, the young man had heirs by the princess.

[told by Mehmet Myslim Starova of Dunica in the district of Pogradec]

The Old Man and the King
(version 1)

In the olden days, a certain King used to go travelling to see if there were any brainy persons in the world or not. He used to take his Prime Minister with him and also other companions.

He once found an old man at work and said to him, "Good luck to your work, old man!" "Good luck to you, sir!" the old man replied.

"Why didn't you work when you were young, but struggle along now in your old age?" the King asked. "I did work," said the old man, "I did work, but it was for other people I worked, not for myself." The King wrote these words down.

The King next asked, "How are you with the far-off?" "I was far off, and I've come near," the old man replied.

"How are you with the pair?" the King asked. "I had a pair, now I've three," the old man said.

"If you had a goose, could you pluck it?" "I could," the old man replied, "but who will bring me one?"

When the King went home to his palace, he summoned the Prime Minister and the colleagues who had accompanied him. He said, "Within ninety-one days I want an explanation to the words the old man said! If you can't explain them, I'll cut off your heads."

The Prime Minister and his colleagues tried hard for many days, but they could not find an explanation to give to the King.

Then they took their riches with them and went to beg the old man for help. "How much do you want for the explanation of something you said to the King?" they asked. But he replied, "Go and mind your own business. I have my own troubles."

After a hard bargain they fixed the price to be paid to him for the explanation of only one phrase.

140

They said, "When the King asked you why you had not worked early but woke up late, you said you had worked but for other people. What does that mean? We want to know."

"The King didn't ask about the work I had done. He was asking about my sons, saying, 'Where are your sons?' I replied that I had worked for other people because I had no sons but only daughters, who are married and gone to strangers, while I am left alone."

They put another question to him. "We want to know why the King asked you how you are with the far-off." The old man said, "Go and break your necks. We bargained for one phrase only, not for the whole lot." Again they pleaded with him and bargained for the second phrase.

He said, "When the King asked me how I was with the far-off, he was asking about my eyes, whether I could see or not. I answered, 'When I was young, I saw far away. Now that I am old, I see only what is near my feet.'"

Again they pleaded with him and asked him why the King said, "How are you with the pair?" and he replied, "I had a pair, and now I have three." Again they bargained about that phrase and the old man consented to explain it also.

He said, "The King asked me how my legs were. I said, 'I had two and now I have three.' I am old and my legs can't carry me, so I've got a stick and become three-legged."

"Please tell us what the goose you are to pluck is." He replied, "If I explain that, you must give me all the riches you have."

The men had no more money, it was all finished, so they gave him their horses and the clothes they were wearing, saying, "Explain the remark."

"You are the geese I have plucked," he said. "I've taken your riches from you, and you'll go on foot now back to the King."

When they went back to the King and gave him the explanations, he pressed them to say where they had found them. For a little they would not tell him. Then out of fear they said to the King, "We went to see the old man, and he gave us the explanations himself."

141

Then the King said, "There really are clever people in the woods, but you must look for them!"

[told by Tahir Jorgji Baduri of Shelcan in the Shpat region in the district of Elbasan]

The Old Man and the King
(version 2)

Once there was a King who wanted to go and talk to an old farmer.

Before the King set out to talk to him, he found twelve men to take with him and he said to them, "You must be able to explain the meaning of all that I say to the old man." He took the twelve men along with him and went to talk to the old man.

When the King reached him, he found him in a field ploughing with a wooden plough. He said to him, "How are you for distance, old man?" "I've come nearer," said the old man. "How are you with the two?" the King asked. "I'm with three now." "How many houses have you burned?" the King asked. "Two," said the old man. "'I've one left, but I've nothing to burn it with." In the evening, the King said to the old man, "If I give you these twelve geese, don't leave a feather on them."

When the King had finished talking to the old man, he turned to the twelve men he had brought with him and said, "Exactly what I said to the old man is what you must be able to explain. I give you three days in which to do it. If you can't, you shall all die."

The twelve men were in great trouble, because they did not know what the words said by the King to the old man meant. As they thought them over, it occurred to them to go and consult the old man. They set off and went to him. "Please, old man," they said, "We throw ourselves at your feet and implore you to tell us the meaning of what the King said to you. He has said that if we can't find it out within three days, we must all die."

The old man replied angrily, "Don't make my head ache. I am busy and I haven't time to waste with you." Again they pleaded with

143

him, saying, "For God's sake, old man, tell us. If you don't explain what the King said to you, you'll ruin us." For the third time they pleaded with the old man. Then he said, "Pay me each twelve medjids and then I'll tell you." Without a murmur they each gave him twelve medjids.

When he had been paid the money, he said to the twelve men, "Now tell me what you want to know." They said, "What's the meaning of the words 'How are you for distance? I've come nearer.' The old man replied, "The words, 'How are you for distance? I've come nearer' mean that when I was young, I had long sight, and now that I'm old, I have short sight."

"What about the words, 'How are you with the two? I'm with three now.'" "The words, 'How are you with the two? I'm with three now' mean that when I was young, I walked with my two legs, and now that I am old, I've taken a stick and got three legs."

"What about the words, 'I've burned two houses and have another left to burn, but I've nothing to burn it with?'" "These words mean that I had two daughters, both of whom got married and that now I have a third one old enough to be married, but I've no money to marry her with." "But what about the words, 'If I give you these twelve geese, don't leave a feather on them?'" "These words mean that you twelve men are twelve geese and that I am to empty your pockets. Go away now."

[told by Shaqe Zadrima Gera, a teacher from Fier]

144

The King

A King had three sons. He also had an apple-tree which bore three apples every year but somebody always ate the apples and the King did not know who ate them.

The eldest son of the King said to him, "Father, let me go to-night to guard the apple-tree." And he went. But he fell asleep and a *kulshedra* came and ate an apple, and when he got up, there were only two apples.

The second son said to his father, "Father, I'll go to-night to guard the apple-tree." He went there, but fell asleep and when he awoke, only one apple was left. He went home and told his father that somebody had eaten another apple.

Then the youngest son, who was a Baldhead, went to keep watch. He dug a hole, fenced it with Christ's thorn, and lay down to sleep. But the thorns pricked him and he did not sleep soundly. When the *kulshedra* came by, he woke up and struck her and wounded her so that she went away.

He called to his brothers, who came and along with him followed her tracks. They thus found where her lair was.

The two elder brothers said to the Baldhead, "Go on in." And he went in. There he saw the Earthly Beauties fetching water. "How is the *kulshedra*?" he asked them. "Ill," they replied. The Baldhead went farther in and cut off the *kulshedra*'s head.

The Baldhead then said to the Earthly Beauties, "Will you come with me, or will you stay here?" They said, "We'll come with you."

The Baldhead shook the rope as a signal to his brothers and sent up the oldest Earthly Beauty, who sat down on the ground. He shook the rope again and sent up the second Earthly Beauty, who also sat

145

down on the ground. The Baldhead then tied the rope round the youngest one and shook it, and she got out of the *kulshedra*'s lair.

The two elder brothers said, "Let the Baldhead have the most beautiful one!" And with that they left him in the pit and went away with the three Earthly Beauties.

The Baldhead went into a room where he found a wild mare, which said to him, "Oh, son of man, it is forty years since I've seen the light of day." He got up on her back and she flew away with him to his home town.

In the town the Baldhead engaged himself to a tailor who had forty apprentices. The eldest son of the King came one day and said to the tailor, "Make me a suit of clothes without cutting them with scissors, without sewing them with needles, and let them be strong enough to stand up by themselves. If you don't, I'll cut off your head."

The new little apprentice said to the tailor, "What did he say to you?" "If I don't make him a suit of clothes, he'll cut off my head," the tailor replied. The little apprentice said, "I'll make them for you. But I want three okes of wine and three roast lambs." And the tailor gave him both wine and lambs. He clapped his hands and the mare appeared. They ate and drank. The Baldhead then said to the mare, "Go and get the clothes for the eldest prince, dye them gold, and bring them here." The mare dipped them in gold and brought them to the little apprentice. He hung them up and said to the tailor, "Come and see the clothes. They are ready."

The prince, the eldest one, came in the morning and saw the clothes. The tailor asked him for 1,500 Napoleons. The eldest prince paid the money and said, "Let the little apprentice bring the clothes to my palace." The little apprentice did not want to go with them, but the prince gave him a Napoleon as a tip and so he took the clothes to the palace. The Earthly Beauties were sitting in the kiosk and when they saw the Baldhead, they laughed. He left the clothes at the foot of the stairs.

The King's second son came and said, "I want a suit of clothes that scissors have not cut or needles sewn, and that will stand up by themselves."

146

The Baldhead said to the tailor, "I will make the clothes for you but I want six okes of wine and six roast lambs." He clapped his hands and the mare came again. They ate and drank, and he said to the mare, "Go and bring the second prince's clothes, dye them gold, and bring them here."

When the mare brought the clothes, the Baldhead hung them up and said to the tailor, "Let him come a little later." And the tailor ordered him to ask the prince to pay 5,000 Napoleons.

The King's second son came there, paid the money, and said, "Let the little apprentice bring the clothes to me." The little apprentice cried. But the prince gave him two Napoleons as a tip, so he took the clothes home to him. The Earthly Beauties were sitting in the kiosk and when they saw the Baldhead, they were overjoyed. The Baldhead threw the clothes down in the kiosk and hastened away.

The youngest son of the King now came to the tailor's and said, "I want a suit of clothes that scissors have not cut or needles sewn, and that will stand up by themselves." He had been adopted as a brother by the two elder princes after the Baldhead was left in the pit.

The Baldhead said to the tailor, "I want nine okes of wine and nine roast lambs." The Baldhead clapped his hands and the mare appeared. They ate and drank. The Baldhead then said to the mare, "Go and get the clothes for the youngest prince, keep them two hours in gold dye, and bring them here." The mare brought them.

The Baldhead hung them up outside, and said to the tailor, "Come late to-morrow." The tailor looked at the clothes and the Baldhead said, "Ask him for 10,000 Napoleons."

The King's youngest son came by, saw the clothes, and paid the money and said, "Let the little apprentice take them to my palace." The little apprentice did not want to do so. But after the youngest prince had given him three Napoleons, he took the clothes and went with them to the prince's. The Earthly Beauties were sitting in the kiosk and they laughed when they saw the Baldhead. He flung the clothes down on the stairs and hastened away to the tailor.

The eldest son of the King was getting married to the eldest Earthly Beauty in a distant palace. The Baldhead took the mare,

147

changed his clothes, got on the mare's back, and flew away across the sky to the palace. When they saw him arrive, they were astonished. He went into the palace immediately, broke the window and went into the room where the music was, and found his father had gone blind. The Baldhead took a little medicine from the mare, and cured the King's eyes, and then said to him, "I am your son." The two embraced and kissed each other, the Baldhead saying again, "I am your son." They sent away the third brother they had adopted and he went to his own home.

The Baldhead then said to the King, "Who cured your eyes? I did, didn't I?" Thereafter he lived a happy life with his brothers and his father.

[told by Josif Sqapi of Elbasan]

148

The Gheg and the Tosk

Once long ago a Gheg and a Tosk became foster-brothers and loved each other very much. And what did they say to each other?

"What job shall we take so as to earn our bread?" said the Gheg to the Tosk. The Tosk replied, "We must really find a job so as to get food." The Gheg said, "Can we get some onion seed to sow? When the onions grow, we can eat all we want ourselves and sell the rest to get the things that we must buy with money." "Let's get the seed," replied the Tosk.

They found some onion seed, sowed it, and the onions grew and put forth long leaves. The Tosk and the Gheg began to eat the tender leaves.

After some days, the Gheg said to the Tosk, "Oh Tosk, shall we divide the onions into two parts, each taking his proper share?" "All right," said the Tosk, "let's divide them."

"Which do you want?" the Gheg said to the Tosk. "The tails or the tops?"

The Tosk said to the Gheg, "You take whatever you want."

What did the Gheg say? "I want the tails," he said. "Take them," said the Tosk. So the Gheg took the leaves of the onions, and the Tosk the bulbs.

After the Gheg had taken the onion leaves, they withered and crumbled into dust and fell to pieces. The Tosk had all the onion bulbs.

The Gheg saw that the Tosk's onions were still all there. "You cheated me, Tosk," he said.

What next did the Gheg say to the Tosk? "Shall we sow wheat?" he asked. "Let's," said the Tosk. And so they sowed wheat.

The wheat sprouted and grew tall and became ready for harvesting.

149

The Gheg said to the Tosk, "Shall we divide the wheat in two now, before we reap it?" "Let's," replied the Tosk. "Which do you want? The tops or the tails?"

"You cheated me once," the Gheg responded. "You gave me tails and kept the bulbs. Now I'll take the roots of the wheat and you can take the tops." The Tosk took the tops of the wheat, and the Gheg took the roots.

The Tosk took the wheat, threshed it, and turned it into money. The Gheg took the roots, which rotted.

The end.

[told my Shaip Efendi Hoxha of Mbreshtan in the district of Berat]

The Aeroplane

Once there were a husband and a wife who had one son. The man was very rich but his son was extravagant and spent a lot of money.

His father often said to him, "Don't behave like this. You'll be reduced to poverty." When his father grew old and was round about eighty or ninety years of age, he filled a large bag with gold coins and put it up on the rafter. He then tied a rope to the bag and let it hang down like the noose of a hangman's rope. He took his son by the hand and said to him, "Come, your father will show you something." And he led him into the room with the rope. "When you're penniless," he said, "don't go out to beg, for that's a disgrace. But come and place your head in this noose and hang yourself." With that, his father died.

Each night the young man took home a dozen or so of his friends and they ate and drank together. Little by little he sold all his property and was left penniless. "I'll go and hang myself," he said, "What my father said has come true." He went to the room with the hangman's rope, placed his head in the noose, and hanged himself. The bag of hoarded money was pulled down by his weight, and he fell to the floor, bag and all. In great delight, he explained, "How glad I am about what my father left me!"

Next day he went to the bazaar, but he had given up his former friends. In the bazaar he hired about ten masons. "You must build me a fine house," he said to them. "All right, we'll come and do it," they replied. They soon began to build a house for him as he wished.

One of the masons took ten boards and began to work on them apart from his friends. The young man said to him, "Mason, you're working for nothing. Your friends receive money for what they do. You only play with these boards." "I am making something," the mason replied. "If you like it, you shall pay me for it. If you don't like it, I shall keep it for myself." The mason made an aeroplane (Aeroplanes were already planned then. I heard this story fifty years ago).

The mason got into the aeroplane and said to the young man, "Look, young man!" He flew off in the plane. How high it rose into the air. In fact it rose until it was lost to sight. In astonishment, the young man exclaimed, "God, what is this?" The mason flew the plane down, straight towards the young man's house. "Do you like it, young man? Would you like to have it? I'll sell it to you for the price of your house," he said. "You must teach me how to fly it," replied the young man. The mason taught the young man to fly the plane and was rewarded amply for it.

One day the young man got into the plane and piloted it high up into the air. At last he landed on a field in another kingdom. The people there were surprised when they saw the plane and said, "What can this be, an ogress?" Then they saw the plane landing on the field and there they saw the young man also.

Word went round that the young man had arrived with a bed for they did not recognise it as a plane. And all the town went to see the flying bed. A princess also went to see it and said, "What is this wonderful thing? What is it, young man?" "I take people for rides in it, my lady," he replied. "They give me tips." "I should like a ride," said the princess, "but see that you don't let me fall out." "Oh no, my lady, I won't let you fall out. I shall be in the plane myself." The princess got in and the plane took off. And so the young man carried the princess off.

When it began to grow dark, he could not see well enough to go farther. He could not find the way and landed together with the princess on the seashore.

As they felt cold, they wanted a fire. The young man saw one burning on a mountain, but the sea lay between them and it. "Stay here," he said to the princess. "I'll go with the aeroplane and fetch some firebrands." So he got into the plane and went to fetch the firebrands.

He took some firebrands and, after placing them in the plane, he got in to fly back to the princess. But the plane caught fire and was

152

destroyed, leaving the young man on the farther shore and the princess all by herself on the nearer shore.

Next day, several people came to fish in the sea and saw the girl on the seashore. They went to take her, but quarrelled with each other about her. "I'll take her," said one. "I'll take her," said another. A man came by riding on a horse and found them arguing. "Why are you quarrelling?" he asked. "We found this girl on the seashore and now we're quarrelling about her," they replied. "One says, 'I'll take her,' and another says, 'I'll take her.'" The rider said to them, "Go and catch some fish and I'll ask the girl which of you she prefers." They went off to fish, but in the meantime the rider seized the girl, mounted her on his horse, and turned back with her the way he had come.

The princess said to this gentleman, "Let's change clothes. Everybody knows me." She took his clothes, put them on, and became like a boy. They went to a certain place to get some food. There the princess said to the gentleman, "Do you know what to do? Go to that village over there and fetch some bread." The man set out for the village by the mountain. While he was away, she mounted his horse and rode away.

After some time, she reached a big town which was the capital of the kingdom and contained the King's residence. Now the King had died that very day and it was the custom in that country that when the King died, the first person to enter the town after his death should be proclaimed King. The princess entered the town riding on the gentleman's horse and they welcomed her with cries of, "Come in, sir! Come in, sir!" They did not know she was a girl because she was wearing the man's clothes, and they proclaimed her King.

She ruled for a month and then said to her servants, "Find me several good masons." When they were found and sent to her, she gave them orders, saying, "You're to build a fountain in front of my palace. If you make a really nice fountain, I shall reward you generously." The masons built the fountain to suit her taste.

The King then ordered a suit of clothes to be made to fit a girl, such as she really was. She put on this feminine attire and called the masons in again and said, "Do you see what I'm like?" "We do," they

153

said. "You are to make a picture of me in this attire on the fountain," she said. "Yes, Your Majesty," they said and made the picture. She paid the masons for their work and they went away.

The King placed a guard to keep watch over the fountain. "You are to imprison anyone whose face changes when he goes to drink at the fountain," she gave orders. The fishermen who wanted to seize her arrived. Their faces showed surprise at the fountain because the girl's picture was like her and they were led off to prison by the guards. After that, the gentleman who carried her off on his horse arrived and his face, too, betrayed surprise and he was arrested by the guards. After him, the young man arrived. He drank some water and, on seeing the princess' picture, he fell down. He felt very sorry but the guards took him also and imprisoned him.

They then informed the King that they had seized five persons and had arrested them. "Bring the three fishermen here before me," the King gave orders. The guards brought them before the King at once. "Why did your face change when you drank at the fountain?" the King asked. "Majesty, we found a girl by the seashore. We wanted to take her but there were three of us there and we quarrelled about her. A great fellow came and carried her off," they replied. "She wasn't a fish for you to seize, she was a human being," the King replied. He beat them and then let them go.

The King called in the gentleman who had carried her off on the horse. She beat him, too, like the predecessors and this man also went away. "Bring in the young man," the King commanded. They brought him to the King, who said, "Why did you drink water at the fountain and fall down?" "I had no reason," replied the young man, "I was in a bad mood." "Either tell me the truth or I'll cut off your head," the King said. He then told his story to the King. "Majesty," he said, "I had an aeroplane. I took a princess for a ride in it and night overtook us on the way and I had to land the plane on the seashore. There we felt cold and wanted a fire. I went in the plane and flew to a mountain to fetch some fire. There I took some firebrands and put them in the aeroplane, but the aeroplane was burned and I was left on one shore and

154

the princess on the other. When I saw how much the picture on the fountain resembled the girl, I felt very sad."

"Would you know her if you saw her?" asked the King. "Yes," he said. "Well, stay here," the King replied. The King went into another room and put on the women's clothes which he had just had made. Then he called in the young man. When he went in to see the King, he saw this girl. "Is it really you?" he asked. "Do you recognise me?" she asked. "Why, yes. I recognised you as soon as I saw you. What became of the King?" he asked. "I came here and became King," she replied. "Now I shall make you King," she added. Then they were married. He ruled as King and she was his Queen.

[told at Shëngjin in the district of Elbasan]

The Priest and the Baldhead

Once there was an old man who had three sons. They lived in a very poor way so the father sent the eldest son away to find work. The son went to a village, where he became servant to a rich priest on condition that he should work for a year and that if either he or the priest repented the bargain within a year, he should get a good beating from the other with a stick.

The young man took up his work. One day the priest gave him a pair of oxen and bade him graze them in a meadow which was surrounded by a wall and had no door or other opening through which he could drive the oxen in. He thought hard, but could not discover how to get them into the meadow and in the evening he brought them home hungry. The priest scolded him well for not grazing them. The young man repented his bargain and, as arranged, the priest beat him with a stick. Without having earned anything, he went home sadly.

The second son said, "I'll go and be servant with the priest, and I'll revenge my brother." He went and became the priest's servant on the same terms as his eldest brother. But he, too, could not do the work the priest told him to do. He repented his bargain. The priest beat him, and he went home sad and penniless.

The youngest son, a Baldhead, jumped up and said, "I'll go and be servant to the priest, and I'll manage to revenge my two brothers."

He went to the priest and was engaged on the same terms as the others. He asked the priest for work and was given the oxen to graze in the meadow surrounded by a wall. He went to the place and when he saw there was no way of driving in the oxen, he took out his knife, cut them into pieces, and flung the pieces into the meadow. Then he went home and said to the priest, "I put the oxen into the meadow. They ate a great deal of grass, swelled up, and were so clearly going to die that I

156

killed them." The priest went to the meadow and found the dead oxen. "What have you done? A great deal of damage," he said to the boy. "Have you repented," asked the boy. "No," said the priest.

The young man said to him, "Give me something else to do!" The priest sent him with the sheep, bidding him graze them well. The Baldhead did graze them well, as the priest had told him to do, but soon he began to think of finding a way to annoy his master. One day he saw a flute-maker and said to him, "Can you make a flute for me so that the sheep will dance when I play it?" The man then made a very good flute, as ordered.

When the young man went to the field, he played the flute and the sheep danced the whole day. He continued this for a long time, until the sheep grew very thin. When the priest noticed that they had grown thin, he went one day to the field and hid in a bush to see how the shepherd pastured them. As soon as the shepherd reached the field, he began to play on his flute, and the sheep began to dance. At the beautiful notes of his flute, the priest himself began to dance in the bush. His clothes got torn and his face scratched till it bled. He went to the shepherd and said, "Why do you make my sheep suffer like this?" The young man said, "Have you repented, priest?" "No," shouted the priest and went home.

"How can we get rid of him?" said the priest to his wife. "Don't try," she said. "It seems to me he'll have to beat you."

When the shepherd brought the sheep home, the priest said to him, "To-night we're going to a party. When we go out, take the light and show us the way." When the time came for the priest to go out, the shepherd set light to the stables and called out, "Is it lighting enough for you or not, priest?" The priest went into the house and said, "You've played a nasty trick on me, Baldhead." The young man said, "Have you repented?" The priest said, "No."

So the priest and his wife talked together and said, "To-night we must all go and sleep on the bridge over the river. You shall sleep between the shepherd and me. In the middle of the night, after we've fallen asleep, I'll prick you, wife. You give the Baldhead a push, and he'll fall into the river and be drowned."

157

But the Baldhead overheard what they were saying. In the evening the priest said to him, "To-night we're going to sleep on the bridge over the river." "Very good," said the Baldhead. They set out and went to the river. After they had fallen sound asleep, the young man, knowing their evil thoughts, got up and lay down between the priest and his wife. About midnight the priest pricked his wife as he thought to make her push the young man into the river. But the young man gave the priest's wife a push, and she fell into the river.

The priest said, "Oh, what have we done to the Baldhead?" The young man said, "What have we done to the priest's wife?" The priest cried out, "You're still here, Baldhead?" "I am. Have you repented?" "I have. I can't help myself." "Give me a year's wages and let me give you three lashes on your back. Then I'll go," said the Baldhead. The priest did what he said. The young man got his wages, gave the priest three lashes, and proudly and bravely marched home.

[told by Banush Demiri, a teacher from Braçanj in the district of Devoll]

The Boy and the Kulshedra

Once there was an old man who went every day to the bazaar to sell a donkey-load of wood so as to feed his family.

He had been married for a long time, but unluckily God had not given him a single child. For this reason he decided one day to go to town and get his fortune read by a fortune-teller.

As he walked along with this idea in his head, a *kulshedra* appeared to him and said, "What's the matter that you're so sad, poor man?" From the shame he felt, the peasant did not tell her, but pretended to be deaf, attaching no importance to her words.

On his way home, the *kulshedra* again appeared to him and asked him the same question as before. The peasant then turned to her and said, "How can I help being sad? It's ten or twelve years since I married, and Almighty God has not given me a single child. For that reason I left home to-day with the intention of getting my fortune read by a fortune-teller in town. But I did not find him at home, and so I'm going home again and I am sad."

The *kulshedra* turned to him and said, "I'll give you a son, but only if you promise that, when he becomes fifteen years old, you will give him to me."

The unfortunate peasant, longing for a child, accepted the *kulshedra*'s proposal. She then took out an apple and gave it to the peasant, saying, "Eat half yourself and let your wife eat the other half."

When the peasant got the apple, with complete faith he gave half of it to his wife and ate the other half himself. And in fact God gave him a son that year. The boy was reared very carefully by his parents and at the age of fifteen became competent to go and sell wood in his father's place.

159

One fine day, the *kulshedra* appeared to him and, on learning whose son he was, said, "Dear boy, tell your father to keep the promise he gave."

When the boy went home, he forgot to give his father the *kulshedra*'s message. This went on for some days. Every day the *kulshedra* appeared to him on his way, and she asked him if he had given his father the message or not. At long last, to make him remember what she said, she put some hazelnuts into the bosom of his shirt, so that when he undressed and saw them, he would remember her instructions.

In fact in the evening, when he was undressing to go to bed, the hazelnuts fell out and he remembered what the *kulshedra* had said. At once he told his father. When the latter heard the message this son had brought, his eyes filled with tears. At the sight of them, the boy felt uneasy and wanted to know their meaning. So, embracing his father, he said to him, "What's the matter, father, that you are crying?"

At first, his father did not want to tell him, but when he saw that his son insisted, he explained, "Dear boy, the *kulshedra* wants you. You belong to her." And just as we have related above, he told him what had happened when he met the *kulshedra* for the second time.

The boy responded, "Dear father, please don't be in the least unhappy about this. As things are so and I cannot live here anymore, I beg you very much to buy me a good horse and to give me leave to go my way. I'll go to another country where the *kulshedra* cannot possibly find me."

The father approved of this idea, and next day, after buying him a good horse, the boy set off with the blessing of his father. As soon as he separated from his father, the *kulshedra* saw him from a distance and rushed after him to catch him.

The boy, flying like lightning from the *kulshedra*, came upon Mr Saturday and told him about the danger approaching him. Mr Saturday gave him two puppies to protect him from it, saying, "These are your saviours from this danger." The boy took them and again set off at top speed.

After a few hours, the Goddess Friday appeared to him. He told this goddess of his trouble, as he had done to Mr Saturday, and she gave him two needles, saying, "Putting their points together makes a bridge." After he got the needles, he set off again.

A few hours later, he came to a very big river – so big that even the horse could not ford it. The boy then remembered what the Goddess Friday had said, and put the points of the two needles together. At once a bridge appeared, over which he crossed to the other side. As the *kulshedra* arrived at the river, she was pulled up short and could not cross.

Dusk that night overtook the boy near the house of the head shepherd, and in that house he spent the night.

Next morning he asked the head shepherd to take him into his service. The head shepherd agreed and next day sent him with some sheep. Whenever he went with them, he left his dogs at home.

One day it happened that the *kulshedra* crossed the river and tracked down the boy.

Another day, as the boy was herding his sheep on a green plain where there were also many poplar trees, he saw the *kulshedra* in the distance coming straight towards him. At once he trembled with fear and, since he had nowhere else to hide, he climbed the poplar.

As soon as the *kulshedra* came, she gnawed the foot of the poplar with her teeth. But before the tree was felled, the top of another poplar bent down to the boy. As she was gnawing the second one, a third one bent down, and so on and so on.

The dogs he had left at home sensed that their master was in danger, so they broke loose from the stable, rushed off to find the boy, and there tore the *kulshedra* to pieces.

So the boy escaped from the *kulshedra* and joyfully returned to his parents.

[told by Abdurrahim Ostreni from Dibra]

The Man with No Children

A man was in despair because he had no children. One day a dervish came to beg and said to him, "I see you're in despair." After the man had given him some food, he told him the reason for his despair. The dervish then said, "I'll make you have three children. Only, when they're twenty years old, I must have them."

The man agreed, and a year later he had a son. So in the course of three years he had three sons. When they were getting on for twenty years of age, he kept worrying because the dervish would take them from him.

The eldest son asked what he was worrying about. When he told them, they said, "To keep the dervish from getting us, we'll go away."

The three sons went away and as they travelled, came to a place where there were two roads. They asked a man where they led. The man explained, saying, "One takes you where you can never come back, and the other where you can."

The youngest son, afraid of the dervish, said, "I'll take the road from which you cannot return," and he left the others there.

After a long journey in great heat, he heard a hissing noise, which was none other than the hiss of a serpent. As the boy was extremely clever, he recognised it and seized a big brick which he held in front of his breast to protect himself from the serpent. When the serpent saw him, it attacked with great force. But it struck the brick and fell to the ground dead.

After travelling still farther, the boy entered a forest where he found some robbers. After they had searched him, they found nothing on him. Then they took him with them to their house, where their chief was.

It was their chief's custom to welcome everybody that came with coffee and food, etc., but only on condition that the visitor should say, "I do" every time that he said, "Do you want more coffee or food?" Otherwise he was killed by the chief.

This would have been the fate of this boy, too, if one of the robbers, the one who showed him the way, had not been kind.

When he went to their house, the chief made coffee for him. When he had drunk it, the chief asked him if he wanted more or not. "I do," he replied. And so it went on till the coffee was finished. He played the same game with the food. In this way, the boy escaped the danger.

When the kind robber saw him off, he gave him a knife he had, saying, "Tell the knife about everything you need, and it will bring it to you."

After he parted from the robber, the boy continued his journey and went to an inn, beside which was the King's palace. When he went to the inn, he was all dirty and in rags. He asked the innkeeper for a place to sit and sleep in. But the innkeeper would not take him in at first because he was poor. At last he gave him a room, but not till the boy had paid for it.

When the boy went into the room, he put on a good suit and went downstairs. When the innkeeper saw him, he was astonished and said, "Yes, sir?"

The boy asked the innkeeper to go to the King and bid him give his daughter in marriage to the boy. "If the King," he continued, "asks you, 'What sort of man is it who wants my daughter?' say it's a dirty creature, all in rags."

The innkeeper went to the King and told him what the boy had said. The king then sent 500 soldiers to kill the boy. As soon as the soldiers arrived to kill him, the boy called the knife. The knife replied, "Sir?" "Kill all the soldiers, leaving only one," said the boy. The knife killed them all except one.

The one who escaped informed the King of what had happened. The King then sent 2,000 soldiers. Again the knife killed them, leaving only one, that's to say, the one he left before. He did the same with 10,000 to 15,000 soldiers.

163

At last the King went himself and asked the innkeeper which was the man. The innkeeper told him, and the King went up to him and said, "You want my daughter?" "Yes," said the boy, "I want her."

The King then said to him, "If you want my daughter, I want you within twenty-four hours to build a palace in the sea so that when I get up in the morning, it will hurt my eyes because it will sparkle so." Since there was a sea close to the King's palace, the boy ordered the knife to build a palace in the sea, such as there was nowhere else in the world, so fine that it should sparkle like the sun's rays. The knife built it directly the boy bade him.

When the King got up in the morning and went out on his balcony, his eyes were hurt by the sparkle of the palace. He was pretty surprised, and said, "That dirty creature's got my daughter!"

In the same way, the King bade the boy spread the road with velvet, and the boy, by means of this knife, spread the road from his own house up to the King's palace.

When the boy had done all this, the King gave him his daughter in marriage. But the girl had orders from her father to find out what the boy did all these things with. The girl by her talk persuaded the boy to let her see the knife.

One night, after letting her husband fall asleep, the girl stole the knife and ran away. By its means she destroyed the palace and sent the boy beyond the sea.

The boy understood who had played him this trick. There was a forest where he found himself and, as he walked through it, he found an apple tree which had very large apples. He plucked one and ate it, whereupon two horns grew out of his head.

He went farther on and came across another apple tree. He ate an apple from it also. As soon as he had eaten the second apple, he found that his horns had fallen off.

He then filled two bags with apples, one with the first sort and the second with the other. He cut a thick oak stick and with its help jumped across the sea. He went to the innkeeper and told him how he was to act now.

He took a basket, put the first sort of apples into it, and went to the King's gate. As soon as the King's daughters saw the apples, they went and bought them. But as they ate them, horns grew out of all their heads.

With the doctors called in by the King, it was impossible to get rid of the horns. Then the boy said, "I'll get rid of them, if all the knives are collected in the King's courtyard." The King gave the necessary orders, and all the knives, with the magic knife among them, were collected.

When the boy found his knife among the others, he gave each of the King's people one of the second apples. In this way he got rid of the horns of all the King's family.

In the end the King, understanding who the boy was, again gave him his daughter to wife, and the two lived happily afterwards.

[told by Thanas Bocova of Fier]

Honesty and Dishonesty

There were once two neighbours, both poor but good workers, and they always worked together. When work was stopped for a time in their district, they went to work in distant places.

One accepted a small wage because he wanted people to give it whole-heartedly. The other was always dear. Besides, he was also crooked.

At last each earned a certain sum of money and set off for home. On the way, the one who had earned most money, said to his companion, "I'm lucky to earn a lot of money, and I'll try to buy everything I need. But though you worked with me, you couldn't fill your pockets as I did." "You're quite wrong there," his companion returned. "However little a man has, God increases it if he works honestly, and his little becomes a spring that never fails." "Honesty's not good at all," said the one with a lot of money. "Dishonesty beats honesty. That's plain. Because I was dishonest, I earned all that money – so much that people may call me a famous rich man, and rich men are always luckier than poor men. So dishonesty is better than honesty."

"What do you say, poor man?" replied the partisan of honesty. "What you say isn't possible. Believe men, honesty's better than dishonesty."

"Oh, you don't want to believe what I say," returned the partisan of dishonesty. "Ask other people, and they'll tell you what I do."

After disputing a little longer, they made a pact that the one who won, should put out the other's eyes.

As they went on, they came across an old man with greying hair and green clothes. He was Satan. Not knowing this, they asked him which was better, honesty or dishonesty? The old man told them with a

166

smile that dishonesty was better, and expressed surprise that they didn't know this.

But they had arranged for three tests, so they had to ask two more people.

On the way, they asked another man, but he was actually the same person, i.e. Satan, who had met them the first time. They did not recognise him. And he again answered as he had done the first time. Dishonesty thus gained a second supporter.

They continued their journey. But Satan again appeared to them and, when the travellers questioned him, he gave the same answer for the third time.

"What I said turned out right," said the partisan of dishonesty. "And as we arranged, I'm going to put out your eyes." "All right," said the honest one. "Only leave me as I am till we reach that big tree."

When they reached it, the honest man's eyes were put out, and he was left alone at the foot of the big tree. The dishonest man set off joyfully for home. When he arrived, his neighbour's wife asked him what had become of her husband. He told her all that had passed between them.

When it grew dark, the blind man crept into a hollow in the tree. That place happened to be a nest of Devils, - the roadless ones. In the evening they came home but they did not see the blind man because he was deep in the hollow.

After they had sat still a little, the old Devil bade the others tell him all that they had done that day. In turn they told their devilries. One said that he had wounded the King's daughter. The old Devil was delighted at this, and praised him.

Afterwards the old Devil began to tell of the strange quarrel that he himself had provoked between the honest and the dishonest man. The little devils were much delighted and asked him how the King's daughter and the blind man could be healed.

The old Devil said that for both, it was a very easy matter. The blind man would see if he washed his face with the muddy water in which the Devils washed. And the wounds of the King's daughter would heal if she burned a leaf from the tree in which they lived and

167

smeared the ashes on her wounds. The blind man listened carefully to all that they said.

As soon as it dawned, the Devils disappeared and the blind man crept slowly out of the hollow of the tree, washed his face with the mud, and could see again.

Then he took some leaves from the tree and set off to the King's palace to cure the princess.

When he reached the palace, he saw that a great many doctors had gathered to cure the King's daughter, but not one was able to do so. Then he went closer in order to get leave to go in. But they did not wish to admit him.

He begged very hard and at last they let him enter. When he went in, he did all that he had heard from the Devils, and the King's daughter soon grew well. They all praised him and were surprised at what he had done. The King rewarded him by giving him his own horse and its saddle-bags filled with gold.

Then the honest man mounted the horse and set off for home. When he entered his house, his wife did not recognise him or even think of him because she thought of her husband as blind. She received him as a guest. He made himself known to her and told her what had happened to him. His wife then was very glad that honesty had saved him.

It was not long before his neighbours also came to congratulate him. Along with them came his companion also. He was astonished that his eyes had healed and he had grown rich enough to buy so good a riding horse.

He asked him how things had gone with him and the honest man told him. The dishonest man grew very excited and begged the honest man to come and put out his eyes, as the dishonest man had put out his - all below the same tree as before.

The honest man said it was a bad business and he could not do it. But since the dishonest man kept on pleading with him, he accompanied him to the tree. There he showed him how it had happened. Then he put out his eyes and returned home.

168

In the evening the Devils gathered. This evening the old Devil was very cross because he had heard that the blind man and the King's daughter were healed. So he pressed all the others to confess if they had revealed the way to get better.

As he beat one of them, it happened that they saw the blind man in the hollow of the tree and, thinking that he had revealed the way for those two to get better, they tore him to pieces.

This folk story tells us that we must be honest.

[told by Aleks Dani of Lushnja]

The Seven Sons and the Missing Princess

Once upon a time there was a King, who found a louse. He caught it and shut it up and always fed it. The louse grew and grew until it was as big as a kid. The King then killed it and skinned it. He then asked his town-crier to proclaim that, "The King has a skin. The man who is able to say what kind of skin it is shall marry the princess."

Everybody went to the palace and was shown the skin by the King, but no one could identify it. The Devil went to the palace and looked at the skin. "Can you identify it?" the King asked him. "It's like a louse's skin," said the Devil. "It is a louse's skin," said the King. "You've identified it correctly." The King gave his daughter to the Devil and the wedding took place. The Devil stayed about two days in the house. Then he took the princess and went to the sea, and the princess was lost.

The King kept looking for her but she was nowhere to be found. The King then ordered the town-crier to announce in the market that no one was to sing or laugh at all but everybody was to mourn the loss of the princess. After the proclamation had been made, the King ordered his gendarmes and soldiers to prevent anyone from singing or laughing in the streets.

An old woman who was kneading bread in her home sang over her work and was heard by the gendarmes. "What are you doing, old woman?" they said to her. "I am not doing anything. I am merely kneading my bread," she replied. "But you're singing," they said. "Yes, I am," she replied. "But don't you know that the King's daughter is lost?" they asked. "What do I care?" said she. "I've seven sons and each of them has a special trick. They'll find the King's daughter." "Come along then with us," said the gendarmes. And they took the old woman to the King.

170

They said to the King, "We found this old woman singing." "Why were you singing, old woman," he asked her. "Don't you know that my daughter is lost?" "What do I care if your daughter is lost?" said the old woman. "I have seven sons who'll find her." "Should they find her," said he, "your sons and you will eat meat and rice with me." "All right, I will go at once to find them," said the old woman.

When she went home, the old woman took a handkerchief like a shirt, found some red and some white thread as well as other colours, and pretended to sew. Her eldest son came home. "What are you sewing, mother?" he asked. "I'm embroidering a shirt with flowers," she replied. "Who is it for, mother?" he asked. "You tell me first what your special trick is, then I'll tell you who I want the shirt for." "My trick," said the young man, "is that I listen to what goes on under and above the ground." "It's for you, my son, that I'm preparing this embroidered shirt," she said. The young man entered the house.

Soon afterwards, the second son came home, and he, too, said, "What are you sewing, mother?" "I'm embroidering a shirt with flowers," she replied. "Who is it for, mother?" he asked. "You tell me first what your special trick is," she said, "then I'll tell you who I want the shirt for." "My trick," said the second young man, "is that I stick my finger into a wall and bring out water." "It's for you, my son, that I'm preparing this embroidered shirt," she said.

The third son next came home and he said what his brothers had said and she replied as before. "My trick," said the third one, "is that I can steal from you and strip you bare without you spotting me." "It's for you," said his mother, "that I'm preparing this embroidered shirt."

The fourth son arrive, and he said to his mother, "My trick is that I strike the ground with my fist and build a castle in which I shut myself up." "It's for you," said his mother, "that I'm preparing this embroidered shirt."

The fifth son came home and said to his mother, "My special trick is that I strike the sea with my fist and make a field there." "It's for you, my son, that I'm preparing this embroidered shirt," said his mother.

The sixth son arrived and said to his mother, "I've a special trick. I can hit the Devil with my bow and arrows and blind him." "It's for you, my son, that I'm preparing this embroidered shirt," said his mother.

When the youngest son came home, he said to his mother, "My special trick is that when a mountains falls down, I can catch it in my hand." "It's for you," said his mother, "that I'm preparing this embroidered shirt."

The old woman laid down the shirt she was sewing and entered the room where her sons were. "My sons, the princess is lost and I want you to find her," she said to them. "Mother, it's late to-night, but we'll go and fetch her to-morrow," the eldest son replied.

When dawn came, the old woman again said to her sons, "Find the princess!" "Come, brothers, let's go and find the princess and bring her home to mother," the young men said.

They walked along the seashore. The eldest one who listened to what went on under and above the ground paid close attention. "Brothers, she is at the bottom of the sea!" he suddenly exclaimed. Then he said to the brother who could strike the sea with his fist and make it into a field, "Smite the sea! Make it into a plain!" And this brother smote the sea and made it into a plain. Then the fourth brother struck the plain with his fist and immediately built a castle. The brothers passed by the palace and saw that the princess and the Devil were in it. The eldest brother said to the sixth one, "Shoot him with your bow and arrow!" The sixth brother shot an arrow and blinded the Devil.

The brothers went into the palace and took the princess out of it and brought her to their mother. They said to the old woman, "Here's the princess, mother." "God prosper you, my sons," replied the old woman.

The old woman took the princess to the King. "Here she is, King. Here is your daughter," she said. "Old woman, take your sons and come and live comfortably with me in my palace," said the King. "My children support ten countries with their tricks," the old woman replied.

172

In his joy at getting back his daughter, the King gave a party and invited me, too. How we did enjoy it!

The Boy Who Had a Knife

Once there was a man who had a son and was very poor. A rich merchant said to him one day, "Sell your boy to me. I'll give you whatever money you ask." The poor man said, "Give what you please. I'll make you a present of the boy." The merchant, who was very rich, took the boy home with him and made him his servant.

He said to him one day, "Kill that old buffalo, cut her up, take out the tripe, and wash it in clean water." When the boy had done all this, the merchant seized him and popped him into the buffalo's tripe. He then sewed him up in it with a needle and thread.

He next said to the boy, "Two big eagles will come and take you, tripe and all, to the top of that mountain over there. When you arrive there, tear the tripe open and shout, 'Uha-a-a!'"

Everything took place as the merchant said. The eagles came, picked up the boy, tripe and all, and carried him to the top of the mountain. The boy tore the tripe open, shouted, 'Uha-a-a!' and the eagles flew away.

A dervish had died there, leaving in trust to the earth first his mirror, secondly his knife, thirdly his handkerchief and fourthly his cap.

The boy rose to his feet and took first the knife, secondly the mirror, thirdly the handkerchief and fourthly the cap which the holy dervish had left in trust to the earth.

The merchant had said to the boy, "When you're coming back, don't open the knife on the way, and when you come back, hand over the three other things to me for safekeeping."

All the same, the boy opened the knife on the way back. Two large *araps* stepped out of it and said, "Where do you wish us to go for you? What errand do you wish to send us on?" The boy said, "Go and

174

catch the big merchant, cut him up and throw the bits right into the middle of the Black Sea."

When the boy went home, he could not find the merchant anywhere. The boy again opened the knife, and again the two *araps* stepped out of it. "What do you want of us?" they said. The boy said, "Take me on your backs and carry me through the air to Elbasan, just like an aeroplane." The *araps* took him on their backs and carried him to Elbasan.

There he lodged with an innkeeper. Our poor boy had no money at all on him, so he opened the knife and said to the *araps*, "Go and bring bread and food." Only the boy could see the *araps*, ordinary people could not, for the *araps* were like ghosts. They stole the bread and food and brought them to the boy.

The boy and the innkeeper became foster-brothers. The boy fell in love with the daughter of the King of Durrës, and said to his foster-brother, the innkeeper, "Go to the King and bid him give me his daughter, and for nothing."

The innkeeper went to the King and said, "A certain boy has come to my inn and wants your daughter. What do you say? Will you give her to him or not?"

The King said, "If he builds houses and shops all along the road from Elbasan to Durrës, then I'll give him my daughter."

The innkeeper set forth from Durrës and again went to the boy in the inn at Elbasan and said to him, "If you build houses and shops from here to Durrës, the King will give you his daughter."

The boy got up in the morning and placed the mirror in the sun's rays. There was magic in the mirror, and in a twinkling it built the houses and shops from Elbasan to Durrës. The King made up his mind to give his daughter to the boy, because he was a wonder-worker.

The next day, they began the wedding celebrations, and the boy went to the King's palace with his foster-brother, the innkeeper, and many other friends. They took the King's daughter and brought her home to Elbasan.

The bridegroom said to the King, "Please come to my party to-morrow evening." The King and his friends went.

The bridegroom and guests sat in the men's room in the palace. The servants who waited on them were the two *araps* from the knife. The King and his friends could not see the *araps* at all because they were invisible. They brought *raki* and set the table. The guests looked on, but could see nothing. Appetisers, bread, food, meat, sweets, everything there is they set on the table. The guests ate, but could not see who served them. Next, the *araps* took away the bread and food and table. Still the guests could not see what kind of people they were who served them.

The King was very much worried. "He's a great wonder-worker, my son-in-law," he said, "but he will devour me, he will devour me!" His son-in-law really was a great wonder-worker.

The next day the King and his friends set out and went home. By the bridegroom's leave, he took his daughter with him.

The King said to his son-in-law, "Take your friends and come to the return dinner-party at my house to-morrow evening." The boy and his friends went to the old man's.

The King said to his daughter, "Daughter, what magic did my son-in-law use to give me that dinner when I couldn't see a thing?"

His daughter was tricked. She said to her father, the King, "My husband's power lies in his knife. The knife has two *araps* in it, and so you couldn't see anything."

The King gave his son-in-law and his friends a great welcome when they came to the return dinner-party, and he made his son-in-law drunk with *raki*. He then stole the knife from him as he lay drunk.

The King went into another room in the palace and opened the knife. In a moment, the two *araps* stood before him.

They said to the King, "Where do you wish to send us?" "Take my son-in-law and carry him to the very middle of the Black Sea," the King replied. The *araps* took him and carried him to a flat place in the very middle of the Black Sea.

When the bridegroom woke up in the middle of the flat place, he wept tears of sorrow.

A holy dervish came by, "Hallo, my son, why are you sitting here?" he said. "The King has stolen my knife and I'm lost in the middle of the sea," the bridegroom replied.

The holy dervish said, "I am about to die. When I die, you are to dig me a big grave, and I'll send you right to Elbasan." The boy dug the dervish's grave.

The dervish wrote a letter and then died. The boy buried him in the grave he had dug and took his letter, which lifted him high up like an aeroplane and carried him to the innkeeper's at Elbasan.

As the boy was sweating, he took the first dervish's handkerchief and wiped his face. The handkerchief was filled with gold coins and Napoleons – there was magic in it.

They all ate their fill at the innkeeper's. Then the boy took the dervish's cap and put it on his head. It was very full of magic, making a man vanish so that other people could not see him at all.

The boy set forth to go to the King's palace, where his wife was. As he had the dervish's cap on his head, people did not see him, nor did the King. The boy stretched out his hand and took back his knife from the King.

The boy went to the door and opened the knife. At once, the two *araps* stood before him.

"What do you want of us, boy?" they asked. "Take the King," he said, "cut him into little bits and throw him into the very middle of the Black Sea."

The boy stayed on there. He went to fetch his father and mother because they were poor and he put them in a motor-car and brought them to the palace. He himself ascended the King's throne, and that's all. There's no more.

[told by Kodhel Dede of Nezhar in the Shpat region of the district of Elbasan]

177

The King with Nine Daughters

Once there lived a King in a certain country. He had nine daughters and not a single son. The next time his wife was pregnant, he said to her, "If you have a girl this time, I'll kill both you and the midwife."

One day the Queen, being angry, told the midwives what the King had said. They replied, "If it's a boy, it's all right. And if it's a girl, we'll tell people it's a boy."

In fact, they did what they said when a girl was born. There was great joy over the birth, for the King and everybody else thought that a son had been born.

Month and years passed, and the boy went on growing. When he reached the age of nine years, his father wanted to circumcise him, as he was his only son. But his wife begged him to leave him alone for two years more. The two years passed, and again the father wanted his son to be circumcised. But this time the boy himself begged his father to leave him alone for two years more, and the father granted his wish.

All the same, this time also passed, and the King prepared for the festal occasion. Three or four days before the circumcision was to take place, he began the rejoicings. And the day that the circumcision was to be done, they chose a fine horse for the boy and loaded it with all sorts of beautiful and costly gifts. When the time came for the boy to mount the horse, he asked leave from his father to take another horse, as this one was rather high. Attended by a servant, he went to the stable to choose one. He left the servant at the door and went in where the horses were, weeping because there was nothing now for him to do but find a little horse called *dërdyl*, which is a Jinn breed. As he walked through the stable, he heard the voice of a little horse, which said to him, "Take me, prince. I'll make things all right for you." So the boy

178

took his horse and, after wiping away his tears with a handkerchief, led the animal to the door and gave it to his servant. He himself went to see his mother, because he did not know if he would ever return.

They covered the horse with all sorts of trappings and ornaments, mounted the boy, and took him riding, according to custom, three times round the house. On the way, the horse, at a lash of the whip, flew off with him. All the merrymaking and rejoicing which were taking place were turned to grief and sorrow. The whole house was painted black as a sign of mourning.

The *dërdyl*, alone with the boy, stopped on a high mountain. There, another King lived. The *dërdyl* said that when the caravan of horses came, the boy should mingle with them and stay with the King as servant, and when he needed anything, he should burn one of the *dërdyl*'s hairs.

The boy did as the *dërdyl* said. When he went into the palace, he begged the people there to take him on as servant. At first they wanted to drive him away, but in the end an old woman who cooked and baked kept him to help her.

The King of this place was changed every year because one of the big giants came and ate out his heart. Now the time was coming for the King to die, and two or three days beforehand the palace was painted black. The day that the giant was coming to eat out his heart, the King took a drug to make him like a dead person, so that he should not feel the giant eating him.

Before the appointed time came, the boy set light to a hair, and at once the *dërdyl* appeared. The boy told him that he had it in mind to kill the giant, and asked him to teach him what to do for that purpose.

The *dërdyl* gave him his own sword, and told him to stay behind the door in the King's room, and when the giant came, to strike his head, but only once. And if the giant said, "Hit me once more," he was to say, "I was born only once." In this way the boy killed the giant and cut off one of his ears to have it as a sign to show the King.

Many persons went to the King, who saw when he awoke, that he was alive. There was great rejoicing, and everybody was given a

179

present of money. All those who went to the King said, "I killed the giant."

At last, the boy went, token in hand, and proved that he had really killed the giant. Then the King said to him, "What do you want from me? You've done me a service that's beyond price." The boy said, "I want your youngest daughter, the one who was dressed in her best when the others were in mourning for you." The King said, "I'll give you another one, whichever you want, only not this one. She is against me."

The boy understood that this princess had had a Jinn for a father and said to himself, "I'll get on with this job. I don't want anything to come of it except that I should earn the hatred of the Jinns and get them to curse me, so that I may get changed and become a male." And he insisted that he wanted no other girl but this one.

The King sent to ask her if she was willing to be married to this boy. She said, "I'll think it over this evening."

In the evening, at the sixth hour, a pigeon came into her room and became a very handsome young man. The other boy saw him through the cracks of the door and heard all that was said, among other things what concerned himself. The pigeon, on hearing what the girl reported, bade her say next day, "The man who marries me must fetch the mirror which is at the giant's head."

When the boy heard this, he went to his room and fell asleep.

Next day, they gave him the answer that he knew would be given. He set light to another hair, and the *dërdyl* came. He told him what he had in mind, and asked him what to do to get the mirror. The *dërdyl* bade him go during the hot hours, because the giant was then asleep. If he had his eyes open, he was asleep, and if he had them closed, he was awake. The *dërdyl* also gave the boy power to run away quickly.

The boy went to the giant and in fact found him asleep and took the mirror he had at his head. The giant at once awoke and gave a very loud cry to make the boy turn his head so that he could suck him in with his breath. But the boy knew not to turn his head, for the *dërdyl* had told him not to do so. At last he arrived back at the King's palace and gave the mirror to the servants to take to the girl.

180

The girl was rather cross when she saw the mirror, which he had taken from a place where men died, for the giants ate them as soon as they drew near.

When the pigeon-boy came at the time arranged, she showed him the mirror which the other boy had taken. The pigeon-boy was astonished at this escape without being eaten by the giant. And he said he must also get the golden ball which was at another giant's.

The boy was eavesdropping and heard what the pigeon bade the girl say to him next day. He then went away to sleep. When he woke next morning, he again received his answer. The King, as before, advised him not to go to the giant's. But the boy, helped by the *dërdyl*, was determined to go.

He set light to another hair and the *dërdyl* came at once. He said to it, "To-day she has asked me to fetch the golden ball belonging to another giant." As before, the *dërdyl* told him what to do and gave him another hair.

The boy, finding the giant asleep, seized his golden ball and brought it to the girl.

This time she was in even greater despair and when the pigeon came in the evening, she told him about it. The pigeon, too, was angry and said, "This boy has power like ours, it seems. Tell him to fetch a pear and an apple tree from the giant's garden and to pull both trees up by the roots." After he told her this, the pigeon said, "If he does this, you shall be his!" The boy heard all this, and then went to bed.

Next morning they again brought the boy his answer. He burned another of the *dërdyl*'s hairs, and when the *dërdyl* came, he asked it what he must do to get the trees.

The *dërdyl* gave him a sheepskin mat and a bonnet. With these he became like a ghost and could not be seen.

The pigeon, together with the girl, went into the garden to see him uproot the trees. The whole garden was surrounded with soldiers who had orders to shoot the boy when he arrived. These two sat down to eat some food.

The boy came immediately, riding on the sheepskin mat, uprooted the trees, and sat down and ate with the pigeon and the girl.

181

But he remained invisible. The soldiers fired, but could see nothing. The pigeon understood that the boy was eating with them, because the food kept getting less. So he bade his servants take the food away and said to the girl, "Be his!" Along with these words, he cursed the boy, saying, "If you are a boy, become a girl, and if you are a girl, become a boy!" And indeed, the boy became a boy, and next day the wedding took place and he married the girl.

After staying some time there, they asked leave from the King to go to the boy's home. And the King gave them leave. The joy when his parents saw their son was great and indescribable. There were festivities and merrymaking for a whole week. The boy told his father and mother, as also his wife, what he had gone through until he won her hand.

[told by Halit Miraku]

The King and the Boy

Once there were a King and a Queen with an only son whom they dearly loved.

One night, a man appeared in a dream to the King and said to him, "Take seven hodjas and seven rams of sacrifice, and send your son to the place where the mountains open and close, but forbid him to pick up anything from the ground."

The King was persuaded. He found the hodjas and the rams, and sent them with his son to the place indicated in the dream.

As soon as the party reached the place, they slaughtered the rams and went in between the mountains. The hodjas went first and the boy after them. As they came out, the boy was persuaded and picked up three diamonds along with a box. As soon as he picked them up, the mountains closed and trapped the boy inside all by himself.

When the boy was left alone, he saw in the distance a hole as small as the point of a needle, and set off to look at it.

The nearer he came, the bigger it grew. When he went close to it, the hole which had seemed in the distance like the point of a needle, became as big as a window. He crawled through it and ran away to a town, where he became a hotel-keeper's servant.

One day, while with the hotel-keeper, he made up his mind to give the diamonds to the hotel-keeper. When the latter got them, he built a big house for the boy, and said to him, "This is your house, and you can live here without doing any work."

The boy decided one night to open the box that he had taken from the place where the mountains open and close. But he said to himself, "Let me have supper first and then I'll open it." After supper, he lit twelve candles and opened the box. At once, twelve *peris* came out and said to the boy, "Do you give us leave or not?" He answered,

183

"Yes." As soon as they heard him give permission, they set their music going and sat up all night. In the morning, when it was light, they disappeared, leaving a handful of gold on each candlestick.

Close to the boy's house there was the King's palace. The King's daughter, who had been upstairs, had heard this music, and said to her father, "I want the box which that boy has – that boy the hotel-keeper built that house for. Last night he opened the box and twelve *peris* came out of it, and after getting leave from him, they began to play music."

The father, not to disappoint his daughter, asked the boy for the box. But he said, "I want it for myself." After much pleading from the King, he made up his mind to give him the box, and the King took it home with him.

He invited all his own friends to come and spend the evening, and after supper they began to open the box.

But when they opened it, out came twelve *araps*, each with a club in his hand, and they said, "Do you give us leave?" The King said, "Yes." Then they began to beat the King with their clubs, and they sat up all night beating him and his friends. When it was light, the boy came and shut the box, and the *araps* vanished. After the boy got the box, he went away to the house where he lived.

Some days later, he decided to go to his own home, where he was born.

So he set out and, two weeks later, reached his home, where he was welcomed joyfully by his own people.

One evening some days later, he opened the box in the presence of the whole household. Out of it came the twelve *peris*, as they had done before, and they played music all night. When it was light, they left on each candlestick a heap of gold.

[told by Hilmi Dakli of Elbasan]

Charity Rewarded

In a certain town there was once an old woman who had one son. They were very poor and owned nothing except a donkey.

Day by day the son went to the forest with the donkey, loaded it with wood, and drove it to market, where he sold the wood for three grosh. With this money he bought food. So he went on, all to get food.

One day he had sold his wood, and was returning home when he saw some boys killing a cat. He stopped and said to them that he would give them a grosh if they did not kill her. When they said, "We won't kill her," he took out one of the grosh he had received for his wood and gave it to them. Then he took the cat and went on his way.

Farther on, he saw some other boys who were killing a dog. He tricked them by giving them his two remaining grosh and took the dog with him.

When he reached home, he told his mother how he had rescued the dog and the cat. The mother was very glad to find she had so kind a son. That night the poor things were left without food, as the son had given the boys the money he had got for his wood.

As they were left that night without food, the son got up betimes in the morning and went and cut a donkey-load of wood, and sold it. With this money he bought food and went home.

Next day he again went for wood. On the way he saw a big hedge burning, with a serpent inside it. As soon as the serpent saw him, it begged him to snatch it from the fire.

When the young man heard this, he went up to the hedge and snatched away the serpent. Then the serpent made him its blood-brother, and said they must go to its parents.

When the young man agreed, the two set off, and went to where the serpent's parents were. Before arriving, the serpent said to its new

185

brother, "When my father asks you what reward you want, ask him for the ring that he keeps in his mouth."

When the serpents saw the young man, they darted at him to bite him. But the young serpent hastened towards them and said, "Don't touch him. He saved my life!" And it told them its story. Then they were very glad and showed him attention enough.

The serpent's father said, "What present do you want now from me?" As bidden, the young man said, "I want the ring you have in your mouth." The serpent took it out, gave it to him and said, "Whatever you want, you may have with this ring, if you just lick it with your tongue."

When the young man got the ring, he bade the serpents good-bye and set off for his little house, which was opposite the palace of the King of that country.

When he went home, he told his mother all that had happened to him. About midnight he licked the ring, wishing to have a palace built there, a much better palace than the King's one and finished before it was light.

When the King saw this building in the morning, he was astonished at its beauty, and even more at its being built in one night.

As soon as the young man got up, he told his mother to go to the King to ask for his daughter for him. The mother went and said to the King, "I want your daughter for my son." When the King heard this, he said very angrily, "Your son who was a wood-cutter till yesterday, wants to-day to marry my daughter! It's not possible." The old woman returned home and said to her son, "It's not possible."

Although the King had said, "Nothing doing!" the young man sent his mother to him a second time. This time the King shouted, "If you come again, I'll roast you in the oven." Again the old woman returned home and told her son what the King had said.

After a third visit, the King, at the end of his patience, told his servants to take "the wretched old woman" and roast her in the oven. As he bade them, the servants roasted her.

The young man waited for a time for his mother, but to no purpose, for the servants had burned her to ashes. Then he realised they had roasted her. He set off for the oven and revived his mother by licking the ring. Afterwards he returned home along with her.

Next day he again sent her to the King, who was astonished at her resuscitation and said to himself, "That young man is very clever. He has done two wonderful things – built his house in one night and resuscitated his mother after she was burned to ashes in the oven. I'll tell him about some other things as well. If he does them also, then I'll give him my daughter." So he said to the old woman, "I'll give your son my daughter if he carpets the road from your palace to mine with velvet. Besides that, when he fetches the bride, he must bring one hundred men all riding white horses." And he fixed the wedding day for two weeks later. The old woman returned home joyfully and told her son what the King had said.

When the day appointed drew near, the young man licked the ring to get the road carpeted with velvet and also to obtain one hundred of the best white horses. When they were ready, they went and fetched the King's daughter. The King was amazed at what he had done, and according to his promise, gave him the princess.

Some time later, the bride asked her husband what he had that worked these wonders. At first, her husband would not tell her. But since she pleaded very hard, he told her about the ring and the art of making it work wonders.

One fine night, she stole the ring from him and ran away to the King. She gave it to him and told him the trick of using it. As soon as he got possession of it, he licked it so as to go far away, together with his son-in-law's palace, while leaving the young man and his mother behind. In the morning the young man woke to find himself back with his mother in his old hut.

The poor man kept thinking about the faithlessness which his wife had shown him. Seeing their master was in trouble, the dog and the cat said to him, "What are you worrying about?" He told them what his wife had done. Then the cat and the dog promised to find the ring and told him he was not to worry.

187

So the two animals set off, and after many journeys found the palace. But it was impossible to take the ring from the King because he kept it in his nostril.

Just at the time they arrived, a mouse in the palace was getting married. The cat caught him. The other mice begged her to let him go on the plea that he was being married. The cat said she would if they would get the ring that the King had in his nostril.

One of the mice then rubbed red pepper on its tail, went to the bed on which the King was sleeping, and flicked his nose with its tail. As the pepper burned him, the King sneezed, and the ring dropped out. But he did not awake. The mouse seized the ring and took it to the cat.

The cat took the ring, let go the bridegroom and joined the dog. Together the two set off fast and joyfully. On the way they came to a sea. The dog said to the cat, "Put the ring into your mouth and jump on my back. But don't talk on the way or the ring will fall out." The cat went so far and then began to talk. The ring fell out of her mouth and dropped into the sea.

When they got to the farther shore, the cat told the dog she had let the ring fall. But he was not to despair because she would find it again.

And in fact, when hunting on the seashore, the cat caught a blind fish. Near it there were other fish also, and these begged the cat to let the blind one go. The cat said, "I will, if you find this ring that I let drop into the sea."

The fish hunted here and there, and then saw some little fish playing with the ring. They took it from them and brought it to the cat. She let go the blind fish and took the ring.

Then she and the dog went off and handed the ring to their master. He licked it to have his old palace back, with his wife and all in it. Afterwards he killed her.

So the charity that he once did to the dog and the cat was rewarded.

[told by Harun Sefa of Lushnja]

The Three Sisters

Once upon a time there were three sisters, the eldest of whom was called Mara, the second Agja, and the third Beta.

One day their mother was ill and asked Mara for a glass of water. The girl replied, "I haven't time to get it. I'm weaving." The mother cursed her, saying, "Weave and weave, and never reach the end!"

The mother called her second daughter, Agja, and asked her for a little water. She, too, answered, "I can't get it, mother. I'm singing." The mother cursed her also, saying, "Sing and sing until you burst!"

At last she called Beta, the youngest girl, and said, "Beta, Beta, do bring me a little water!" Beta hastened to bring it to her. The mother blessed her, saying, "Child, may you be light for the dead and death for the living."

Mara is thus like the spider which weaves and weaves and never succeeds in attaching its web. Agja is like the cicada which sings and sings and then bursts. So any child that does not obey its mother, comes to grief.

Beta is sweet and good as the bee, whose wax is used to make a candle when the living die and again when the dead are commemorated.

[told by Marije Mazja, a teacher from Shkodra]

The King with Three Daughters

Once upon a time there was a King, who had no son but only three daughters, and he wondered what to do with these and to whom to bequeath the kingdom. To his misfortune, a royal servant came at that time and brought him a letter. When he opened it, he saw that another King had declared war on him. So he assembled all his senators and ministers to talk over this war and how he should face it.

Since it was necessary for him to go in person to the war and he had no near relative to leave as regent, he was obliged to leave one of the heads of his Parliament. So he chose the one he wished, put his army in order the following day, and went off to the war.

When he went to the war, he left his daughters in the palace. In those times they had a custom of spinning white wool with a distaff. So the day that the King left, his daughters went out into the garden and, according to the custom of the period, began to spin, sitting on chairs.

The first day, the eldest girl's spindle fell to the ground and she made signs to the minister to give it to her. He wanted to kiss her and said he would then give her the spindle. And she promised to let him do it. The second day, the second girl's spindle fell to the ground and the same thing happened to her as to the first one. The third day, the youngest girl's distaff fell, and she asked the minister to give it to her. He asked her to let him kiss her first. With a voice of despair she replied, "I'm not like my sisters. I am different."

Her sisters were now afraid that she would tell their father when he returned from the war what happened with the minister. So they looked for a chance to do away with her.

One day it was very hot, and she asked her sisters for a drink of water. They at once handed her a water-pot, but it contained a young serpent as well as water. After she had drunk the water, her stomach

190

began before very long to swell day by day. Her sisters asked her why she was so swollen. She replied that she did not know. "Have you gone wrong?" She gave the same answer.

One day they shut her up in a deep cellar where the only food they gave her was dry bread and a little water. After a long time had passed, the people heard that the King was coming home in triumph from the war and went out to welcome him. The girl who had been imprisoned by her sisters was very glad to be going to see her father and to be freed from the burden her sisters had put on her.

The King arrived, entered the palace, inquired how they had been, and then asked for the youngest girl. She asked leave to see him for a little. But her elder sisters said to their father, "She has gone wrong and disgraced us." And the King ordered her to be killed.

On the flat space in front of the palace she prayed to God, saying, "Oh God, since I am guiltless, send a tapeworm on my father, and until I come back, let him find no rest for his soul." The servants put her in front of them and marched her out to a forest to kill her. But she begged them to leave her alive, saying she would not return again to her father's home, and she swore this to them.

The servants left her there and went to the King, saying they had carried out his orders.

After the girl separated from the servants, she hid in a wood. Rain, or rather sleet, was falling. When night overtook her, she fell into a deep hole and could not get out and began to cry in the dark. Unexpectedly some dogs barked in the distance, and shepherds who had sheepfolds close by, approached her. They went up to the hole and looked in, and found the girl. They took her to their huts and saw that she did not have a very pretty face and was pregnant. They asked her about herself, but she and they could not understand each other well, because they had different languages.

The next morning, the shepherds milked the sheep and boiled the milk on the fire, and she sat warming herself by the fire, when she felt sick. In a moment she vomited up serpents! A shepherd saw her and held her head till all the serpents had been brought up. Then he said to

191

her, "Would you like to marry my son?" She agreed, and she was married to the son.

Later on, she felt sorry for her father, and begged her father-in-law to give her leave to go along with his son to see him.

When her father-in-law gave her leave to go, she took her husband and went to where her father lived. After they reached the town, they went to the palace gate and went inside. They had learned that the King had tapeworms and wanted people to tell him fairy tales to pass the time away. This shepherd lad went with his wife to see him. When he went up to the bed, the King bade him tell any folktale he knew. The shepherd said, "I don't know any, but my wife does." She said, "I do know stories, but don't let any of the people here leave the room."

Then, holding the King's hand, she told her story, and each time she spoke, she said, "Fall, tapeworms, fall!" Then they began to fall till they all fell.

After she had saved the King from them, he understood that she was his daughter. He ordered the minister and his other daughters to be killed, and he nominated the shepherd as King. And from that time, no more is known about them, but if they haven't died, they may still be alive.

What I knew, I have told. But I've lied even more.

[told by Jorgji Aleksi, a teacher from Niça in the district of Pogradec]

Fear

Once a peasant had a donkey, with which he did the work of the house. After a time, seeing that the donkey had grown old and could no longer carry the load it had carried before, he and his wife planned to sell it and to buy a younger one. As the peasant talked over the matter with his wife, the donkey, being close to them, heard what they said and planned to leave its master and to go to the town and become a clarinet-player.

Next day the donkey got up before dawn and went away from its master. As it walked along, it noticed a cock following it. The donkey asked where it was going. The cock replied that it had run away from home because its master had ordered his wife to kill it as a friend was coming over that night. "When I heard the danger I was in, I plucked up courage enough to leave home in order to save my life." The donkey replied, "You've had the same experience as I've had!" And it told its story to the cock.

Then it turned to the cock and said, "I've thought of going to the town to become a clarinet-player. By joining me, you can become a good singer."

They joined forces and set out for the town. When they had gone on a little, they met a cat, which was running very fast. When the donkey saw the cat like that, it said, "What's happened to you to make you run so fast?" The cat replied, "I had a narrow escape from my mistress! She was cutting up the meat for supper, when I stole a piece and started to run off to eat it in a secret hole. Then what should I see? She was coming after me with a meat-chopper in her hand to cut off my head. I escaped with nothing more than a great fright."

In his capacity of leader, the donkey now spoke. He said to the cat, "We've had the same experience as you. Now we've planned to go

193

into the town. I'll become a clarinet-player, the cock will become a singer, and you, if you join us, will undoubtedly become a good tambourine-player."

After the cat had agreed to this plan, the three of them set forth. After they had gone a short distance, they met a dog, which was running about aimlessly. The donkey asked where it was going. It replied, "I've left home because my master planned to tie me up in a forest so that the wolves could eat me as I've grown old and can't hunt any longer."

The donkey then said to the dog, "We've been through the same thing. We've planned to go to the town. There I'll become a clarinet-player, the cock a singer, the cat a tambourine-player, and if you join us, you can become a violinist."

When the four united, they continued on their way to the town. They passed that night in a forest. According to its custom, the cock flew up to the top of a tree. The cat climbed the tree to a place just below the cock. The dog climbed to a place below the cat. The donkey, unable to climb, remained at the foot of the tree.

After a time, the donkey thought of the danger that might come to him from wolves. So he said, "Friends, we're not right here. Look, cock, as you are highest up and see if you can see a light anywhere in a house so that we can go there for to-night?" The cock looked this way and that, and said, "I see a light close at hand." The donkey replied, "We must go there, then."

The four, as they were, set off. But the house to which they were going belonged to robbers. After reflecting a little, the donkey said to the others, "I've found how to drive away the robbers. I'll go up to the window of the house. You, dog, climb on my back. You, cat, climb on the dog, and the cock on the cat. Then we'll all shout together. The robbers will be afraid, thinking it's evil spirits. They will run away and so the house will be ours for to-night."

In truth, after they had made use of this device, the robbers ran away, leaving all their belongings behind. The cat settled down by the hearth, the dog in the kennel, the donkey in the stable and the cock on the handle of the plough.

194

The thieves who had been frightened by them hid in the forest. After a time their leader said, "Which of us is brave enough to go and find out exactly what happened to us to-night?" The youngest said, "I'll go." He picked up his rifle and set off for the house.

When he got inside it, he was obliged to light a lamp to see what there was in it. Instead of picking up a live coal from the fire to light the lamp, he tried to pick up the cat's eyes, thinking they were coals over the fire, for in fact a cat's eyes glow like fire during the night.

The cat sprang at his eyes. The robber in terror ran to get out of the kitchen. But the dog which was in the kennel, dug his teeth into his thigh. When the donkey, which was in the stable, saw the robber making for it, it kicked him in the ribs. As the robber ran out of the courtyard gate, the cock began to crow. The robber, running at an unheard-of speed, reached his companions out of breath.

After a little, when he had got his breath again, he began to tell his companions the tragic story of what he had been through in the house.

"When I went into the kitchen," he said, "that awful witch flung herself at my eyes to kill me. After I escaped from her, the butcher stuck a knife in my thigh. When I was getting out of the stable, a dervish laid into my back with a club. After I got past all these dangers and was outside the door, their chief shouted, "Hold him, men, hold him!""

The thief's fear had thus turned the cat into a witch, the dog into a butcher, the donkey into a dervish, and the cock's crow into an order from their chief, "Hold him, hold him!"

[told by Mustafa Delimeta, a teacher from Elbasan]

195

The Cock and the Cat

Once upon a time there were an old man and an old woman who owned a cock and a cat, but nothing else. After some time, they separated. The cock fell to the old man, and the cat to the old woman.

The old man sent the cock abroad. On its way the cock came on some wasps, a vixen and a wolf. All three went with the cock, saying, "We'll come with you." The cock said, "I'm afraid you'll get tired." But they said, "No, we shan't."

They set out together and after a time complained that they were tired. "Get under my feathers," said the cock. They got in under his feathers. Then they went to a village, where an *aga* was having a wedding.

The cock jumped on the roof of his house and crowed ki-kiu-ki-i-i. The *aga*'s children climbed on the roof and caught him and took him into the house. The wasps which were under his feathers attacked the children and stung them. The children said, "Let's put him with the other cocks so that they'll kill him," and they did this. The vixen which was under the cock's feathers ate all the fowls! Then the *aga*'s children put the cock in the stable with the horses. But the wolf which was under the cock's feathers devoured the horses.

The children then put the cock into a treasure-house full of gold coins. The cock ate gold till he could eat no more, and then pretended to be dead. The *aga*'s children threw him outside, thinking that he was really dead. As soon as they had gone away, the cock went joyfully off to his own house.

When the old man saw the cock, he spread a carpet and stood him on it. Then he took a silver cane and beat him. As the blows fell, the gold coins came tumbling out. So the cock came out the winner, and the old man became rich. The cat did not go to seek her fortune, and so both the old woman and the cat remained poor and suffered.

[told by Demir Koçi]

The Half-Cock

Once there were two old people, a man and a woman, who owned nothing except one cock.

The old man said to the woman, "Shall we kill the cock for supper to-night?" "Let's kill it," she said, "but I won't eat my half. I want to send it to seek its fortune. You can eat your half."

They killed the cock and cut it in two. The old woman said to her half, "Off you go, half-cock, to seek your fortune." And it set out.

It came to a torrent. "Where are you going, half-cock?" said the torrent. "To seek my fortune," the half-cock replied. "Shall I come with you? If you have trouble, so have I. They dam me up and want to send me another way." "Come on then, but see you don't get tired."

They went on and on. "I'm tired," said the torrent. "Get inside me then," said the half-cock.

They walked and walked. They came on a hare, which said, "Where are you going, half-cock?" "To seek my fortune," the half-cock replied. "Shall I come with you? Whatever you may have, I have trouble. All day they hunt me with hounds, and all night they set snares for me." "Come along then, but mind you don't get tired."

They walked and walked. "I'm tired, half-cock," said the hare. "Get inside me then," said the half-cock.

As they went along, they met a ram. "Where are you going, half-cock?" said the ram. "To seek my fortune," the half-cock replied. "Shall I come with you? Whatever you may have, I have trouble. I am the oldest of the rams and when some festival comes, my master says, 'Let's eat the old ram.'" "Come along then, for you're in trouble, too. But see you don't get tired."

They walked and walked. "I'm tired, half-cock," said the ram. "Get inside me then," said the half-cock.

On they went and met a wolf. "Where are you going, half-cock?" asked the wolf. "To seek my fortune," the half-cock replied. "Will you give me some bits of that ram's flesh?" "Open your mouth and shut your eyes. Then I'll come and put them in your mouth," the half-cock replied. To the ram it said, "Take a run and butt the wolf to see if you can kill it." The ram took a run, hit the wolf and killed it dead. They then skinned it and took the skin with them.

Night overtook them on their way. They found refuge in a cave of thieves, and as they approached the entrance, they called out, "Oh master of the house!" "Welcome in," he replied. The half-cock left the wolf's skin behind the door, and they went in.

As soon as he was inside, the half-cock jumped on the tie-beams and crowed, "Ki-ki-ki! May I do to you three what I did to the one behind the door?"

One of them went out to see what the half-cock had left behind the door. When he saw the skin, he did not tell his companions, but ran away.

Then the second one said, "What's taken away our friend?" He went out to see where the man had gone. He saw the wolf's skin behind the door and, in his turn, ran away without telling his companion.

The third man went out to see what had happened to them. But an old man got up and bolted the door behind him. The half-cock called out, "Oh, where are you, comrades? They're catching me!"

The half-cock flew up on the couples and pecked the old man's head, the hare ran between his legs, the ram butted him with his head and his horns, and a donkey kicked up his heels and kicked him. The half-cock escaped, left the house and ran away.

It went to a peasant house, flew up on the couples, and crowed, "Ki-ki-ki! May I hold the King's daughter in my arms!" They caught it and put it alive, feathers and all, into the oven in their rage at its crowing like that.

As soon as it was put into the oven, it released the torrent it had taken with it. The torrent put out the fire, and the half-cock came out of the oven.

199

It flew up on the couples, and crowed, "Ki-ki-ki! May I hold the King's daughter in my arms!" They said, "What shall we do with it? Shall we let it loose in the stable of the wild horses so that they can kill it?" They let it loose in the stable. But the half-cock let out the wolf against the wild horses, and the wolf ate the wild horses. The half-cock escaped and went to the King.

It called out to the King's assistant, "Will you come out to see me for a moment, or shall I go over there?" "Come over here," said the assistant, and the half-cock went over.

"What have you come to say?" asked the King. "I've come to seek my fortune," the half-cock replied. The King said to his assistant, "Catch it and put it in the safe to eat as much money as it wants until it gasps, because then it will die. After that, throw it out among the bushes."

After the half-cock had eaten its fill of money, it pretended to die. The King's assistant threw it out among the bushes. But it revived and went home.

There it flew up on the couples and crowed, "Ki-ki-ki!" The old woman said to her husband, "Spread the carpet, man, because the half-cock's come back from seeking its fortune." The old man spread the carpet, and the half-cock vomited the money from the couples. The old woman gathered the money, and kept it for herself. The old man was terribly annoyed because he had eaten his half of the cock.

[told by Marka Zef Ndoj of Laç in the district of Kurbin]

200

The Half-Cock and the Cat

Once an old man and woman had a cock which crowed very prettily, and also a cat.

One fine day, this old couple had a longing for meat. So they killed the crowing cock for supper. The old man ate the half which fell to his share, but the old woman kept hers for the next day.

In the morning, as soon as it was light, the old woman saw that the half-cock she had left uneaten, had revived and was crowing in the yard. She was very much surprised at this miracle.

As soon as the half-cock saw the old woman, it went up to her and said, "I'm going to treat you as my mother, and now I'm off to wander in search of a fortune."

The half-cock set off, and went to seek its fortune. On the way it met a wolf, which said, "Where are you going, half-cock?" "I'm off to seek my fortune," the half-cock answered. "Will you take me with you?" asked the wolf. "I will," said the half-cock. "Only I'm afraid that you can't walk as well as I can." "Oh, you're wrong," said the wolf, "you who have only one leg, can't walk better than I can!" "All right," returned the half-cock, "get inside me then."

So the half-cock put the wolf into its inside, and continued on its way. Farther on, it came on a vixen and a river. After talking with them as it had done with the wolf, it put them both into its inside, and went into a King's courtyard, where it began to crow, saying, "I want the King's daughter."

The King, hearing it crow like this, was angry and ordered his servants to catch the half-cock and put it among the horses, to get trodden on. The half-cock, seeing itself in danger, took out the wolf as soon as the servants went away. The wolf at once killed all the horses that were there.

201

The King then ordered his servants to put the half-cock among the other cocks, so that they should kill it. There the half-cock took out the fox, which killed all the cocks.

Then the King, seeing that even here the half-cock came to no harm, ordered his servants to put it into a hot oven and burn it up. But here the half-cock took out the river, which cooled the oven. So the half-cock escaped from this danger, too.

At last, the King bade them take it to the money-chest, to kill itself eating money. The half-cock, seeing that the purpose for which it had left home was achieved, began to eat Napoleons until it had eaten its fill. At last it kept only one Napoleon in its mouth, and pretended to be dead, as though it had been killed by eating so much gold.

The King's servants, seeing it had died, flung it in a corner outside the yard.

The half-cock got up and went home to the old woman. It bade her hang it up by the leg, head downwards, and beat it with a stick. The old woman did this, and as she hit it, it disgorged the Napoleons which it had eaten in the King's money-chest. In this way, it filled the old woman's pockets with money.

The cat, seeing the half-cock bring home all this money, said to the old woman that it, too, would go and seek its fortune. And it set off. But it did nothing except go out to the roads and hedges, where it ate all the serpents, frogs and lizards it could find until it was quite full. Then it came home and told the old woman to tie it up, head downwards, and to beat it with a stick, as the half-cock had been beaten.

The old woman beat it and the cat disgorged all the creatures it had eaten in the hedges and the roads. It filled the old woman's house with serpents, which almost took the poor old woman's life.

So the half-cock was able to bring good things to the old woman, but not so the cat.

[told by Kristo Vide of Verria in the district of Fier]

The Young Man Who Had a Wicked Uncle

Once upon a time, there was a King who had a brother who died and left a son. After the death the King evicted his nephew from his property. When the nephew learned this, he took his mother and went away, saying, "My uncle has seized my property. Come, let's go away."

They took with them their pet lion and tiger and went to pass the night in a cottage which they found in a forest. They went into the cottage and began to talk. Now the cottage belonged to forty robbers, who heard the voices of the mother and son as they talked. The chief of the robbers said to one of his men, "Step inside and see what sort of people there are there." The man went in. "Hello," he said. "Welcome, come in," the young man replied.

The young man had pleasant manners and kept the robber talking in the cottage so that he did not go out to tell his friends who was there. At last they all went in. "Hello," they said. "Welcome," replied the mother and son. After talking for some time to the young man, the robbers rose to leave. They said to the young man, "This cottage belongs to us but we give it to you and we shan't come here anymore ourselves." The young man thanked them and they took leave of him and went away.

The young man was fond of shooting and often took his double-barrelled gun and went to the forest. Near the cottage, an *arap* was hidden in a tree. The thieves did not know that he was there. One day, when the young man had gone shooting, the *arap* climbed down from the tree and said to the young man's mother, "Let's kill your son and live together." "All right, let's kill him," she replied. "When your son comes home," said the *arap*, "pretend to be ill and say, 'I feel like eating a watermelon, only you must fetch it from the Giants' melon field.' The Giant will kill the boy."

When the young man returned from shooting, he knocked on the door and heard his mother groaning inside. "Oh, oh, how ill I am!" she said. "Son, I want a watermelon from the Giants' melon field." "Why not have it?" he said. "I'll go and get it."

The young man made ready and, taking his lion and tiger with him, went to where the Giants lived. He found the melon field, picked two or three melons, and put them in his saddle-bags. The Giants saw him and rushed out to kill him. But with the help of his lion and tiger, he killed them all.

The Giants had a cottage in a corner of the melon field. They had hidden in the cottage the daughter of the King of India, whom they had kidnapped. The young man went to the cottage and, finding her, said, "What are you doing here?" "Brother, the Giants kidnapped me," she replied. "Whose daughter are you? Who's your father?" he asked. "My father is the King of India," she replied. "Come along, let's leave this place" he said. He led her out and mounted her on the tiger and himself mounted the lion, and in this way he took her to her father, the King of India.

The King was delighted to see his daughter and said to the young man, "Where did you find her, young man?" "The Giants had kidnapped her," the young man replied. "I went to the place where they lived and took her away." "Since she was lost to me, I'll give her to you in marriage," said the King. But the young man replied, "No. That cannot be. I must go for I have something to do. But I have a brother and we may arrange to marry her to him if God wills." The young man then went away from India.

He went to find his mother in the house in the forest. When he knocked on the door, his mother came out, moaning, "ah, ah, ah," as she opened the door. "I've brought you some melons, mother," the young man said. She cut one open and ate it.

She then said, "I am dying. But I've had a dream and I want a medicine for the heart which has been prepared by the daughter of the

King of Baghdad." "Why not have it, mother? I'll go and get it," he replied. Again he made ready and went away.

On his way, he came upon an *arap*, who called out to him, "Where are you going? I don't allow a bird to pass this place as it flies through the air. I won't let you pass either." The young man shouted at him, "What do you think you're doing? Don't put difficulties in my way. I'm going to pass along the road." The *arap* seized a club and hurled it at the young man. The young man caught it and hit him with it. The *arap* sank into the ground up to his knees, such was the force of the blow struck by the young man with the club. The *arap* then hit the young man again, and once more the young man hit him. He now sank into the ground up to his waist. The young man rushed at him on his lion to cut his head off. But he said, "Please don't kill me. You're my brother." "How can you make me your brother so soon? You wanted to kill me a minute ago," the young man replied. He then caught the *arap* by the hair and pulled him out of the ground. The *arap* embraced him, saying, "You're my brother. Tell me where you're going." "To see the daughter of the King of Baghdad. My mother is very ill," the young man replied. "For Heaven's sake, brother, don't go there. She will kill you. Go back home. Your mother is not telling you the truth," the *arap* implored. "I cannot go back. I must go there," the young man replied. He took his leave of the *arap* and went to the King of Baghdad.

He went to the King's office and said, "I have a mother who is ill and I have been told that Your Majesty has a medicine for the heart. "Ah, my son," said the King, "this medicine is prepared by my daughter. If you fight with her, she will kill you. Stay here and I'll go myself and look for the medicine." The King went to his daughter, moaning and clutching his heart with his hand. "What's the matter with you, father?" said his daughter. "Quick, a little medicine, I am dying!" he cried. "I'll not give it to you without a fight. I'll not give it to you without a struggle," she replied. The King went back to the young man.

"Go away, my son," he said. "I asked for the medicine for myself and she would not give it to me. Go away for she will kill you." "It doesn't matter. Let her come as she pleases," said the young man. So people went to the girl and told her that a young man who wanted a

205

medicine had come. She made ready to appear. She had a strong horse, a wicked horse, and with it alone she could kill a man. Mounted on her horse, she came out. The young man mounted his lion and advanced to meet her.

The girl said to him, "Strike, young man!" "I won't. I haven't come to kill people. I've come only to get a medicine that will heal them. You may strike me, you may kill me, but I'll not stir," the young man replied. The lion said to the young man, "Don't strike the girl, but look out for her horse. It will rise on its hind legs to kill us. I'll get under its belly and then you must cut off its legs." The girl shouted to her horse, which lifted its fore legs straight up into the air. The lion got under its belly at once. The young man struck it with his sword and cut off its legs. The girl was thrown over the horse's head because it collapsed when its legs were cut off.

The young man dismounted and caught the princess by her hair. Her father, the King, called out, "Kill her, my son! She has committed many crimes. She has killed many people." "I won't kill her," the young man said. The princess caught him by the arm and said, "Come with me. Let's go to my father."

They rose to their feet and went together to the King. She kissed her father's hand and said, "If you regard me as your child, here's my husband. I did not want to kill people. I was only searching for my husband. There are many possible husbands, but I wanted a man who could thrash me." She took the young man with her, saying, "Come and let me give you a medicine." She prepared some and gave it to him and said, "Leave your lion and tiger here with me. I'll give you my lion and tiger in their place. If anybody kills you, my animals will let me know." The young man took her animals and went away.

He went straight to the *arap* he had found on the road. As soon as the *arap* saw him, he embraced him and was so delighted to see him. "How did you manage to save yourself from her?" he asked. "Just as I did from you," the young man replied. Bidding him good-bye, he went to find his mother. He went straight to the cottage in the woods and knocked on the door. His mother opened the door and came out. "See, mother, I've brought you the medicine," he said. She took it out of his

206

hand and said, "I am a little better. To-day I swept out the house and on the rafters I found a piece of netting wire." "Why bother about it? We don't need it," said her son. "Let me tie your hands with the wire. Let's see if you're strong enough to break it, my son," she said. "All right, tie them," he replied. She then tied his hands and said, "Now try to break the wire. Let's see if you are strong enough." The young man tried to break the wire.

Two threads broke and made his hands bleed. "Ah, mother, I am so strong that I've broken several threads of the wire, only my hands are bleeding," the young man said.

The *arap* came down from the rafters and plucked out his eyes. He then took him and threw him into a well outside. The lion and the tiger broke their chains and ran away and told the lady that the young man had been killed. Later on, some wayfarers, with a caravan, came to the well. They looked for water but could find none except in this well. "Come along," they said, "let's tie a rope round one of us and drop him in to bring up some water." They tied a rope round one of the party and dropped him into the well. But he did not find any water, there was none in the well. But he found the young man. "What do you want here?" he asked. "An enemy of mine threw me into the well. Help me out, won't you?" said the young man.

When they saw him, they exclaimed, "What are you? Who are you?" "Ah, brothers, an enemy of mine tied my hands together, blinded me and threw me into the well. Now drop in a rope and pull out your friend." As he said, they drew out their friend.

"Follow me. Let me lead you to water," he said. They followed the young man and found water quite close.

"Where will you stay now, young man?" they asked. "If you will be so kind, take me with you," he replied. "If my enemy finds me, he'll kill me." The wayfarers put him on a horse and led him straight to the door of the princess.

It was now the ninth day since the young man had been killed. The princess had prepared pots and pans full of all sorts of food which she was distributing to the poor in commemoration of the young man who had been killed. She said to her servants, "Have we given food to everyone?" "Yes, we have," they replied, "but there is a blind man at the door." The princess filled two big trays with food and ordered her servants to carry them to the blind man. The servants did so. "Here you are. This food is for you to eat," they said to the young man. "Why? What's this for?" he asked. "The King's son-in-law has died," they replied. "God rest his soul," he returned. "He's alive, but rest for the soul is a good thing. Never mind." He ate two spoonfuls of the food and drawing his ring from his finger, hid it in the food he left. "Here, take this food to your lady herself," he said.

They took the food to their lady. "Why hasn't he eaten?" she asked. "He did eat some," they replied, "then told us to take the food to our lady." The lady took the tray and poured out its contents. There she saw the ring among the food. She picked it up and recognized it. "His ring!" she exclaimed. Then she turned to her servants and said, "Bring in the blind man at once!" The servants went out and brought him in to their lady's room at once.

The lady went to a bathroom and after heating it, led the blind man into it. She washed and cleaned him. She prepared her medicine and healed his eyes and made them see better than they had ever done before.

As soon as he opened his eyes, he saw her. "I'll go once more to my mother," he said. "Don't," she replied, "she will not care. Don't go to her. She will kill you." "No matter. I am sorry for her. Let her kill me," he said. He took the lion and the tiger with him and went straight to find the *arap* on the road.

As soon as he saw the young man, the *arap* was so delighted that he jumped for joy. "Oh brother, are you alive?" he said. "Who's going to kill me, you silly?" the young man replied. He continued on his way to his mother. He reached her house and knocked at the door. She opened the door and let the young man enter. "How do you do, mother? Are you better?" he asked. "I'm better, my son," she replied. The young man then said to her, "When my father died, the King, my uncle, seized my property and you and I came to this cottage here. You fell ill and you wanted melons from the Giants who would kill me. But it was the Giants who were killed. Then you sent me to fetch a medicine for the heart, so that either the *arap* on the road or the princess with the medicine would kill me. But it was they who were done for. When you tied my hands together with a piece of wire netting, who was the man who jumped down from the rafters?" The young man then killed his mother. He called out to the *arap* who was on the rafters. Terrified, the *arap* fell down, and was killed by the young man.

The young man then got up and went to find the *arap* on the road. "*Arap*, do you consider me your brother?" he asked. "I do, most sincerely," said the *arap*. "Then follow me," said the young man.

Along with the *arap* he went to his cottage. "This is my house. You must go and get my wife," he said. The *arap* said, "I'll go and get your wife. You will go to the King of Baghdad and find my wife. I shall go to the King of India and find your wife. We must go at the same time and return here at the same time." Then off they went.

The *arap* went to the King of India and took the young man's wife on his arms. The young man went to the King of Baghdad and fetched the *arap*'s wife. In this way they each brought the other's wife to the cottage. The young man's uncle, the King, learned what they had done. People said to the King, "Your nephew, your dead brother's son, has married two beautiful women." "I'll take them for myself. I'll not let them escape me," the King replied. He then raised an army of soldiers to go and capture the women.

Our young man learned of this and said to the *arap*, "*Arap*, guard the women well. I must go somewhere." "Go, brother, and don't worry. No one can take the women from me," the *arap* replied. The young man went straight to his uncle, the King, disguised as a wretched Baldhead so that no one at the King's should recognise him.

"Why is the King raising this army?" he asked the King's servants. "He's going to fetch two women, his nephew's wives," the servants replied. "His nephew has a dangerous *arap* who kills soldiers." "But I can overcome the *arap*," said the young man. The servants went to the King and told him this. The King ordered the young man to be brought to him. When he arrived, the King said to him, "Can you overcome that *arap*?" "I can," he replied. "Then come to-morrow and let me send you with the army," said the King.

209

Next morning the army and the young man set out. When they drew near the cottage, the *arap* came out and struck the soldiers with his club.

The young man dashed forward and caught the *arap*. The officers then ordered the soldiers to advance and kill the *arap*. But the young man let go the *arap*, who killed about 500 of the soldiers, he was so strong. The young man and the rest of the soldiers then returned to the King.

"Didn't you catch him, young man?" the King asked. "I did, but the soldiers took him from me," the young man replied. The soldiers made a report, saying, "The *arap* killed 500 of us because the young man let him go." The King next day commanded that his soldiers should not go near the *arap*. "Let this fellow catch him and bring him here," he ordered.

Next day, the army and the young man again set out. Again they tried to find the *arap*, and again the young man caught him. This time he said to the soldiers, "Go away. I'll bring him myself to the King." "We'll take the women," they said. "No, don't. As I am going to bring in the *arap*, I'll take the women, too," said the young man.

They took the *arap* to the King, the young man leading the way. He conducted the *arap* to the King's office. The nobles, about ten persons altogether, were with the King. When the *arap* was brought in, they closed the door. The young man said to the King, "What shall we do with him? Shall we slay him or shall we hang him?" The King was afraid to answer. "Do you smoke?" the young man said to the *arap*. "I do," replied the *arap*. The servants filled a huge pipe with three or four okes of tobacco for him, and brought a huge firebrand to light the pipe because the *arap* was colossal in size. The *arap* at once began to smoke the pipe, filling the room with smoke so that no one could see his neighbour.

The *arap* rose and caught the King. With one gulp he swallowed him. Then the young man rose and opened the door to let out the smoke. When it cleared, the room was light again. The young man could not see the King and said to the *arap*, "What has happened to the King?" "He went out of the room, he went away somewhere,"

210

the *arap* replied. "But he did not go out of the door," said the young man. "How could he go out? I was near the door all the time." The young man struck the *arap* on the shoulders with his fists. "Produce the King!" he ordered. The *arap* brought up the King, who fell to the ground.

"*Arap*, how dare you eat my uncle? He's my father's brother," the young man exclaimed. The King bent his head in shame. "Uncle," the young man continued, "you took my property from me before and you want to take my wives from me now." The *arap* then twisted the King's head and killed him. Now he recognised that the wretched young Baldhead was his brother. So delighted was he to see him that, in his joy, his eyes opened as wide as a window.

"Come on, *arap*, go and fetch our wives," he said. The *arap* made for the door with a rush and hastened out of the palace. He went to the cottage, flung one woman over one shoulder and the other over the other shoulder and carried them home to his brother. They then gave a great party and celebrated their weddings in splendid style.

Burzylok and Mysynok

Once there was a King and his wife, who had no children.

The King was about to go to war and said to his wife, "If I find no children when I return from the war, I shall cut off your head."

The Queen sat pondering these words and did not know what to do. As she sat lost in thought at the window, she noticed two persons passing outside. One of them said to the other to ask her why she looked so worried. She replied, "When my husband went to the war, he said to me, 'If I find no children when I return from the war, I shall cut off your head.' So what am I to do?"

"You must find the King of the Fish and eat it," they said. "Then perhaps you will have children." The Queen instructed all the fisherman to catch the King of the Fish, but they could not find it.

When the two men returned, they asked her about the King of the Fish. "They could not find it," she replied. "Let her find it at the mill wheel, but don't let her name the baby till we come," said one of them to his companions. The Queen again gave instructions and the fish was found. When it was brought to her, she gave it to her servant to cook. The servant cut it open and threw away the guts. A little dog and a mare happened to be near. They smelt the fish guts and became pregnant. While cooking the fish, the cook tasted it to see how it was and she, too, became pregnant. When she took in the cooked fish, the Queen ate it and became pregnant. The King returned from the war and was delighted to find his wife in this condition.

When their time came, the dog had two puppies, the mare had two foals, the servant had a boy, and the Queen had a son, too. A week later the King issued a large number of invitations to a party at which the two children were to get their names. They had dined and were talking about the names when the Queen appeared and said, "Have a

212

good time, but other people will be deciding on the names." The King went up to the Queen and said, "You are not in your senses to talk like this!" But she would not withdraw what she had said.

Three days later, the two men who had told her about the King of the Fish came to the palace. The Queen came to greet them, then ushered them in and said to the King, "These are the men who are going to name the children." When they entered, the men lifted the two babies, the servant's and the Queen's. They named the King's child Burzylok and the servant's child Mysynok.

The boys grew as much in one day as they should have done in one year. Mysynok was the elder, having been born a little before the other, so the King consulted him more than he did Burzylok.

After they had finished their education in their own kingdom, they asked the King's leave to go and pursue their studies in another country. Before they left, they asked him to give them each an iron club weighing 500 okes. The King gave them each a puppy, a colt, the club they had requested, and saddlebags filled with gold.

Both boys set out with a puppy, a horse and a club each. When they had gone some way, they halted for their midday rest and both fell asleep. Two roads met there.

When Mysynok woke, he saw an inscription on a tree which said the two brother must not travel by the same road. However, he made light of it. When Burzylok woke, he read the inscription and said, "According to what that says, we have to part. I will give you this ring and if it ever hurts your finger, you will know that I am in danger and must hasten to my help." Mysynok made his finger bleed and dropped three drops of blood on his brother, saying, "When this blood begins to fade, I shall be in danger."

When they parted, Mysynok went to a town but he left his dog and horse outside the town and took only the bridle with him. He found employment in an inn where he had to clean the stables. When Burzylok was near the town, he made for a cottage which stood a little apart. He dismounted, unsaddled the horse, removed its bridle and the saddlebags, and entered the cottage. There he found an old woman. He asked her for a glass of water, but she had no water to give him. There

213

was only one fountain in the town and a monster had seized it. That self-same day the monster was to eat the King's only daughter. Burzylok could stand his thirst no longer and asked the old woman to go and fetch water. She obediently picked up her water-jar. As she came near the fountain, the monster called out, "I am expecting the King's daughter and he sends me an old woman?" In terror the old woman replied, "Burzylok sent me. He is thirsty." The monster laughed, "Ha, ha!" and Burzylok came out and the monster let her take water.

Burzylok had hardly finished drinking the water when he heard the band coming with the King's daughter. The people turned back and the princess moved forward to the fountain and sat down there.

Seeing the girl at the fountain, Burzylok went up to her and said, "Delouse me a little and let me sleep, but wake me up when the monster arrives."

As soon as Burzylok fell asleep, the monster appeared. In her terror the girl burst into tears, and her tears fell on the young man's cheek.

The young man woke up. The monster said playfully, "Every other day I've had one person to eat, but to-day the King has sent me two." Burzylok snatched up his club and hit the monster so hard that it sank into the ground up to its knees. It struck at him with its own club which weighed 300 okes, but the young man caught the club with his hand. He then struck it two or three times and drove it so deep into the ground that only its head was left visible.

The young man went up to it and cut off the tips of its tongues. He pretended he hadn't a handkerchief so the King's daughter gave him hers and also a ring from her finger. When the young man turned round to tie the tips of the monster's tongues with the handkerchief, she smeared her hand with the monster's blood and pressed it on the young man's shoulder. The young man went away.

As the girl returned alone to town, she met a blacksmith who was going to fetch water with which to cool his iron. As soon as he heard that the monster had been killed, the blacksmith drew out his knife and said, "Will you say that I killed the monster? Or shall I cut

214

your throat?" The girl was frightened and said she would say he had killed the monster.

Together they went to the palace, where everyone admired their bravery, but the girl remained deep in thought. The King said to her, "Since my daughter was good as dead, the blacksmith has the right to marry her." The girl reflected a little and then said to her father, "If I am to be married, I should like three days in which to look at all the people in this town. When the three days are over, I shall marry." The King issued orders that for three days the whole population was to pass by the palace. And so it was done.

The young man heard the royal order and asked the old woman to go and buy two okes of flour. When she brought this to him, he kneaded a loaf, put in the ring he had got from the King's daughter with congratulations on her escape. The old woman passed with the loaf in front of the palace but the gendarmes would not allow her to enter so that she was forced to return. As she did so, the King's daughter saw her and called her over. She gave her the loaf. The King's daughter broke it in half and found the ring. When the old woman went away, the King's daughter gave her handsome presents, but pretended not to know about the young man.

On her third day of grace, the King's daughter noticed a second person coming out of the old woman's cottage and ordered the police to go and look. She added if there was anyone there, he was to be sent to her. When the police went, they found the young man and asked him to pass in front of the palace. He replied, "I will not come unless the King himself comes to ask me." They sent many other messengers to bid him come, but he would not go. Not to disappoint his daughter, the King went in person to the cottage. The young man received him on a gold saddle and with coffee in a gold cup. The King was surprised.

The young man found the bridle and the horse came. Then he and the King went together to the palace, where he was received with great respect and found everybody talking about the girl's marriage to the blacksmith. After the young man sat down, the girl came behind him and showed her father the print of her hand which she had made on his shoulder with the monster's blood.

While the Council was discussing this, the young man said, "As officials you must be able to say what the distinguishing features of a man are." They replied, "The head is the only distinguishing feature of a man." The young man drew out the handkerchief containing the tongue tips of the monster. The blacksmith saw he was proved a liar. One by one he threw away the cushions on which he was leaning and hastened through the door. They caught him outside and killed him.

The young man stayed with the King, who wanted him to marry his daughter. The young man said to the girl, "I cannot get married. I have an elder brother and cannot get married before he does."

Mysynok was longing to see his brother. He mounted his horse which smelt the right direction to take, and brought him to the royal palace. Three days later, he married the King's daughter.

After the wedding, Burzylok went to another country and found his way to the capital. On entering the city, he bought a sheep's tripe, put it on his head, and went into the royal garden. It happened that a few days earlier, the garden boy who used to take flowers every day to the King's three daughters, had died, and his gardener was looking for another to take his place. When Burzylok appeared, the gardener said, "Would you care to be hired, young man?" Burzylok only replied, "Berlim." The gardener said to himself, "This dumb man would do very well for sending flowers to the King's daughters."

The gardener sent three bouquets of flowers to the girls every day. The eldest two joked with the young man, but the youngest one did not bother him. When Easter was approaching, the King ordered handsome clothes for the young man so that he should look like a prince. The young man did not get the clothes when they were brought, but the gardener put them under his pillow on Easter Eve. When the time came to go to church, the King's eldest daughter did not go. All the men about the King except the young man went. Knowing they were all going to church, he pretended to be sound asleep so as to avoid going. He then raised his head and looked all round but could not see any light besides the garden lamp. He drew out the horse's bridle, shook it, and the horse came.

216

He said to the horse, "Flying high in the air, you must carry me three times round the garden and three times past the palace window." The horse did this. Then the young man dismounted and told the horse to stamp on all the flower, and this the horse did. The King's daughter, who was in her room but had no light, saw everything.

When the gardener arrived, he saw the state the garden was in. He went to the young man, who was still asleep, to beat him, but the King's daughter called, "I will kill you if you beat him." The young man got up and went to the garden to pick flowers. Wherever he trod, flowers grew. In this way he made three bouquets and took them to the girls.

During Easter, a prince came and asked for the hand of the eldest princess. The King gave her to him. So it was with the second princess, too. When it came to the turn of the youngest daughter, she refused the prince's offer. For she said, "I am going to marry Berlim."

The prince to whom the King would not give his youngest daughter, declared war on the King. The King informed his two sons-in-law and asked them to help him. They came each with a large force. Berlim, who had continued to live in his cottage, asked his wife to go to the King and get a horse, which should be the weakest and worst one available. When it was brought, he put his saddlebags on it. Then together with the King and his sons-in-law, he set off to the war. On the outskirts of the town, he put this horse into a ditch, where he left it. He then drew out the bridle of his own horse and shook it. His own horse, his dog and his club all came to him.

He then went off to the war, flying through the air on his horse. The enemy had penetrated a distance of six days' journey into the King's territory. Berlim asked the King for his sabre and dashed ahead. In six hours he reconquered the occupied territory and penetrated a distance of six days' journey into the enemy's territory. He wounded his own finger slightly and asked the King for his handkerchief to bandage it. The King gave him the handkerchief, thinking it was a saint who was helping him.

On their return from the war, Berlim flew ahead of them again, while the others prayed that they would be successful and get rid of

217

Berlim. When Berlim came to where his sorry nag was, he dismounted from his own and got on the bad one. He then entered the town with the others and rode with them to the palace. He went to his cottage and put a feed in the nose-bag of the horse, but it died.

Sometime later, the King became blind and tried to find a medicine to restore his sight. He instructed his sons-in-law to find one. They filled their saddlebags with gold and set out on their quest. Berlim sent his wife to ask the King for a horse. The King sent him one, a very bad one, as he asked. Berlim loaded it with ashes and set out to look for the medicine. On the outskirts of the town he abandoned the horse in a mud-hole. He then drew out the bridle of his own horse and shook it. His horse came at once. "Where can such a medicine be found?" he asked the horse. "It is very difficult to get here," the horse replied.

He mounted his horse and in succession crossed a wooden bridge, an iron bridge and a copper bridge. He then drew near a huge rock, where he dismounted. "Plait my tail to make the rock open up," said the horse. And this was done and the rock opened up.

When Berlim got into the rock, he saw a fountain beside which the Earthly Beauty was sleeping, while a huge snake kept watch over her. Berlim filled his water-bottle at the fountain and withdrew. As he was about to mount his horse, he sighed and the horse would not let him mount. "Why do you sigh?" it asked. "I wanted to kiss the Earthly Beauty," he replied. The horse told him to plait its mane and then go and kiss her without any fear at all. He did so and then he and his horse returned to the wooden bridge. There, he opened a druggist's shop with goat's milk.

The two sons-in-law arrived. "This is medicine for the blind," he informed them. "How much do two bottles of it cost," they inquired. "I won't sell it for money. I'll sell it only for the right to brand your flesh with my horse's shoe," he replied. To avoid going back to the King without any medicine, they agreed to let him brand their thighs. The horse shoe had three nails in it.

When the sons-in-law left, Berlim left, too. But he reached the mud-hold before they did, where he had abandoned the King's horse. He pulled the animal on to dry ground and drew out a bottle which he

218

was filling with mud when the others arrived. They said to him, "We've been there and back. But you stayed here. You miserable creature!" Berlim went to his cottage and disposed of his horse as he had done of its predecessor.

The two sons-in-law went with their medicine to the King. When they put it on his eyes, but these ached more than ever. Berlim then gave his wife the bottle of medicine as well as the handkerchief from the war to take to the King. "Here is the medicine Berlim gave me for you," she said. "Go away," shouted the King. "It was worry about you that brought me to this." After much pleading, she was allowed to put one drop on each eye. She also gave him the handkerchief to rub them with. When he rubbed them, his eyes saw again. The King then understood what sort of a man Berlim was.

The King gave a party to celebrate the recovery of his eyesight and invited Berlim as well as the others to attend. Berlim sent his wife to say to the other guests, "Berlim will come to the party if you give it to him in writing that things will be done as he says." To avoid breaking with him, they all agreed to his condition and he went to the party.

When they were talking about the medicine, he revealed to them, "No one else cured the King. I did. I deceived you. I branded you with my horse's shoe." According to the written promise they had given, he ordered the two sons-in-law to undress. All the guests were convinced that Berlim had managed it.

The eldest son-in-law said, "I went to find the Earthly Beauty. I went on until I had crossed the wooden bridge. Then I returned because I did not know the way any farther." The second son-in-law had had the same experience. But Berlim had gone on and on until he crossed the wooden bridge, the iron bridge and the copper bridge.

When Berlim was crossing the copper bridge, he saw a young man throwing an apple into the air. This fell on Berlim's head. The young man then threw himself into Berlim's lap and kissed him. They entered the courtyard together.

Two or three days later, Berlim felt bored staying there and wished to go out shooting. He fetched his rifle which hung on the wall and started out. The Earthly Beauty said to him, "Don't go over the mountain. There is a monster there which may eat you." But he went over the mountain, shot a partridge and began to roast it on the spot where he had killed it.

While he was roasting it, he saw an old woman up in a tree who was trembling with cold. "What is the matter with you?" he asked her. "I'm frozen, but I'm afraid to come down. Your horse and dog may bite me. But here is a hair to throw to them." Without guessing there was anything wrong, Berlim caught the hair and flung it at his horse and dog. The old woman came down from the tree and took out a frog. She put this on a spit and beat the partridge, crying, "Yours drips, mine doesn't!" Infuriated, Berlim got up to kill her but, before he could, she stuck a pitchfork into his head and he died. The horse and the dog stood as still as if they were tethered. They did not stir and the monster buried them in the mountain.

The ring on Mysynok's finger grew tight. He mounted his horse and set off, with his dog behind him. He went to one after another of the places where Burzylok had been and at length, arrived at the house where the Earthly Beauty lived. On the morning after his arrival he got up and took down his rifle to go shooting. The Earthly Beauty warned him as she had done Burzylok. He shot a bird as Burzylok had done, and the same old woman said to him what she had said to Burzylok, but instead of throwing her hair to his horse and dog, he flung it into the fire. The monster thought she could treat him as she had done the other, but with the help of his horse and dog, he overcame her. She then showed him where people were buried. The dog went and pulled the pitchfork out of Burzylok's head. The horse and the dog were besmattered with blood.

"Oh, oh! How I have slept!" cried Burzylok as he woke up. Mysynok showed him his finger, which was nearly falling off his hand, and together they went back to the Earthly Beauty.

Some days later, Mysynok took his own wife and Burzylok's, and they all came here. One day Mysynok said, "I'm going to see my parents." He went to the town where they lived and what did he find? The people of the town had been eaten by a monster, for Mysynok's mother had turned into a monster because she had worried about him

220

so much. She alone was left. He went to the palace and entered. A woman came forward to greet him, and asked him various questions until she went off to prepare coffee. She bade him play the drum until she returned.

There was a mouse living in a hole in the wall. It said to Mysynok, "Let me play on the drum and you sneak away. If you don't, death may come to you." Mysynok followed the mouse's advice and ran away.

The monster had really gone off to sharpen her teeth. When she returned, she could not find Mysynok. There was only a mouse playing the drum. She ran after Mysynok to eat him, but she could not catch up with him. When he reached the door of the house where the Earthly Beauty lived, he flung himself on the ground, pretending to be dead. There, he turned into a stone as big as a mill wheel and completely blocked the way. To lift the stone, forty ovens full of bread and forty barrels of wine were promised, and then the stone was removed from the road.

The two brothers and their wives established families on that spot and perhaps their issue live there to this day.

A Virtuous Girl

A girl had nobody except her old father and mother. The old man took his son with him and went abroad. When he bade his daughter good-bye, he bade her not open the door at night, and he asked her neighbour to look after her and to see to her when she needed anything.

Sometime later, the neighbour went to the girl and said he wished to marry her. But the girl would not accept him. No matter how hard he tried, the neighbour could not persuade her, and in despair he wrote a letter to her father, saying that she was behaving very badly.

The girl's father sent his son home to kill her and to bring back her finger as proof that he had done it. The girl's brother bade his father good-bye in his foreign home, and arrived some days later at the old home.

When he arrived, it was midnight. With the object of finding out about his sister's misbehaviour, he went to the house and knocked on the door. His sister did not open it, but said, "To-morrow you may come. I don't open the door at night. My father ordered me not to." So her brother slept outside.

When dawn came, he was admitted. When the girl saw it was her brother, she kissed him with emotion. After staying with her for some days, he could not see any signs of misbehaviour in her. At last he said to her, "I've been sent by father to kill you." She replied, "You must do as father told you. You must not disobey him."

The brother was sorry to kill his sister since he saw that she was innocent, but to carry out his father's orders he took her to a distant cave. There he cut off her finger and went away, leaving her alone. He went back to his father, taking the severed finger with him, and told him that he had done what he was told to do.

The girl lived like a wild animal in the cave. One day a rich man, who had gone hunting, found her and took her home with him. After some time, liking her manners and her beauty, he married her. A year later she had a son.

One day she remembered the cave where she had lived so long and in which she had found refuge. She asked her husband to give her leave to go and visit it. He bade her take her son and a servant and go to the cave.

When they were near the cave, a wicked idea entered the servant's head. He asked her to be his wife; otherwise he would kill her son. The poor girl decided to have her son killed and not to give in to the servant's wickedness. Better lose her life than be called an unchaste woman. The servant then killed the child. The woman fainted, lay like a dead creature. The servant took the murdered child and went to his master and said, "Your wife has gone raving man! She's killed the child and run away. She's taken to the mountains." His master was sad at the child's murder.

After the woman came to, she straightened herself and went to the cave, where she found a shepherd tending sheep. She bought his clothes, dressed in them and went to a town, where she engaged herself as servant in a hotel for no pay but her food and drink and a room to herself to sleep in.

Shortly afterwards, her husband came to that very hotel with the wicked servant. Her father also came with her brother and the neighbour who had wanted to marry her. All five gathered round one table, and she, dressed in boy's clothes, served them. They did not know who she was. But she knew them all.

Her husband said to her, "Servant, can you tell us a story?" She replied, "Yes, sir. I know a very good story. But before I tell it, you must surrender your weapons so that Master can lock them up. It doesn't do for you to keep them with you here." They all agreed with what she said, and handed over their weapons. She began to tell what had happened to her, and all five of them, listening to her in astonishment, looked one at the other. At last she showed where her

223

finger had been cut off, and introduced herself as the person she really was.

Then her husband flung himself on the servant to kill him, and her father and brother flung themselves on the neighbour. But to no purpose, for they had no weapons. The girl got in between them and separated them. She then took her husband and went home, where she had previously lived.

[told by Aziz Mulla, a teacher from Mezhgoran in the district of Tepelena]

The Faithful Daughter

Once upon a time, there was a bey who had a son and a daughter. He made ready to go to America with his son and said, "Son, who shall we leave the girl with?" "Who's your most faithful friend, father?" said his son. "The teacher, I think," replied the bey. "Well, why not leave her in his charge," said the son. The bey called the teacher and said to him, "We wish to leave the girl in your charge. We'll leave as much money with you as she is likely to need. Don't let her want for food and drink or for clothes until I come back." Then the bey and his son went away to America.

After fifteen years passed, the teacher said to the girl, "Will you marry me?" "Don't dare mention such a thing to me again. I'll not disgrace my father," the girl replied.

Since she would not listen to him, the teacher shut her up in a room and wrote to her father, saying, "Your daughter has been trying to get married, but I've shut her up in a room to wait until you come home, sir."

The father sent his son home, saying, "Son, go and kill my daughter because she has disgraced me. I don't want to see her again."

The son went straight to the teacher's house. "Where have you shut up my sister?" he asked. "In such-and-such a place," said the teacher, and he took the young man to the place. The young man knocked on the door. "Who's knocking on the door?" asked the girl. "It's me, your brother," said the young man. "I don't believe you're my brother," the girl replied. "Put your head in at the window and let me look at you with my own eyes." He put his head in at the window and she recognised him as her brother. She opened the door and he went in.

"Sister, why did you disgrace us?" he said. "Brother, I did not disgrace you. I'll never disgrace myself and my father," the girl replied.

225

"Why did the teacher shut you up?" he asked. "Because he wanted to marry me and I refused," she replied.

"By my father's orders I have to kill you," said her brother. "If I am innocent before God, I shall not die. If I am guilty before God, then I'll kill myself with my own hands," she replied. "Follow me! We're going away," he replied.

They climbed a high mountain and on the top, her brother ran away and hid. The girl began to cry. Another bey's son had gone hunting, and his hounds found the girl and began to bark. The hunter went to see what they had found. "Why are you crying, girl?" he asked. "Because my brother has abandoned me," she replied. "Follow me," he said, and they went home together to his house.

He talked things over with his father, saying, "I found a girl alone on the top of the mountain. What do you think I should do? Shall I marry her?" "If you wish, marry her," his father replied. The young man went to the girl and asked her to marry him. "Since you saved my life, I'll marry you," she replied. So he married her and in the course of time, God gave her a son. The bey who had gone to America now returned home. He had become a pasha.

The young man's father went to see his son and his daughter. "Son, let your wife get ready. We're going to call on the pasha who has come back from America," he said. He prepared the coach and put the young wife and her son into it, and also a servant. "Go on by yourselves. I'll follow you. I am rather busy at present," he ordered them, and left them to travel alone.

On their way they came to a big forest through which the road led. What did the servant now do? "Will you marry me? If you don't, I'll kill your son," he said to the young wife. "You may kill my son, but I'll not marry you," she replied. He killed the little boy, seized its mother by force and entered the forest.

There she ran away as fast as she could and he could not catch her. She went up to a mountain and, finding a shepherd, called out, "Brother!" "What's the matter, lady?" he replied. "I want you to give me your clothes and I'll give you mine," she said. She was dressed in women's clothes of course. When the shepherd agreed to the exchange,

226

she gave him her clothes which he put on, and she took his clothes and put them on.

Then she said, "Show me the house of the pasha who has come back from America." "I don't know where it is," he replied, "but I know where a bey lives who found a girl on the mountain." "All right, then, take me there," she said.

Led by the shepherd, she went to her husband's house and knocked on the door. The servant came out to see who was there. When he went inside again, the bey said, "Who is it?" "A shepherd," replied the servant. The young wife carried a staff in her hand and was dressed in the shepherd's clothes. "What does he say?" the bey asked. "He asked me to tell you to send him to herd the sheep," the servant replied. "Let him go with them!" said the bey. And so the girl who was dressed as a shepherd went to herd the sheep.

She sang a great deal and had a beautiful voice. When she had been there for four or five months, the bey wanted to marry her husband to another woman and gave a wedding party. He invited the pasha from America to come to the party. The pasha, with his son and the teacher, set out and came to the party. There was much singing and dancing. The bey's son said to him, "Father, let's call in the shepherd to sing to us. He sings beautifully." "Go and fetch him," said the bey, and the young man did so.

The pasha sat in the corner over there, the teacher sat here in the middle, and close by was the husband, with the servant in the background. "Good evening," said the girl. "Welcome, shepherd. We want a song from you," said the bey. "I'll give you a song," the young wife replied. "I'll sing a story for you. This is how it goes. Once upon a time there was a bey, who had a daughter. He put her into the care of a teacher and went away abroad. The teacher fell in love with the girl and wanted to marry her, but she refused him. He then sent a letter to her father, saying that she had lost her honour. His son came home, took her away and abandoned her on the top of a mountain. What did the girl do then? She married the son of another bey, and God gave her a son. Her father, now a pasha, came back from America. The bey wanted to go with his daughter-in-law and her son to visit the pasha. What was

227

done by the servant that he sent to accompany her instead of himself? He killed the little boy and tried to marry her. But she ran away at top speed. She was found by a shepherd and changed clothes with him and became a shepherd herself. She herded the sheep of the bey who was her father-in-law. This bey gave a wedding party for his son, for whom he had found another wife. Turn round and question me. Here's my father, this is the teacher, this is my husband, and here is the servant who killed my boy."

What did the pasha do? He caught the teacher, put him in the oven and roasted him alive. He caught the servant, put him in the oven, and roasted him, too. Last of all, he caught his daughter, led her to the door of the oven and was about to thrust her into it, when she said, "Father, after all the misfortunes that I've suffered, do you still not trust me? Step aside. I'll get into the oven myself." She got into the oven. But the oven immediately cooled. Just as she got in it, so she came out of it again. The bey's son sent away his new wife and married his first one again.

Sword

Once upon a time there was an old woman, who had a son. The boy fell ill and after a time the old woman lost him.

She lamented every day for him, sitting on a sofa, but tearlessly, because she did not really grieve for him. One day a well-known old man passed and turned in to comfort her in her lamentations, according to the custom. When he saw that she was not shedding tears, he said, "If you mourn for your son with tears, collect them in a cup and drink them. Then you'll soon forget your son."

The next day the old woman mourned with tears for her son, collected them in a cup and drank them as the old man had said. After some time, she found herself pregnant and, in her joy, she forgot her dead son. When her time came, she gave birth to a boy. In her joy she not only forgot the son who had died but she also forgot to baptise the baby and to give it a name. It grew big and began to go out with other boys, but had no name. For that reason the other boys called it 'Nameless.'

One day when the boy was climbing over the rafters of the house, he found a sword. He took it, girt it on and went out to his friends.

When they saw him wearing the sword, they cried out, "Sword has come, Sword has come." And so from that day, the name Sword stuck to him.

When he grew up, he said to his mother, "I'm going to go abroad to make money and to look after you because you're old now." "All right, son," she said. So one day he set out and went away. When he was at a distance, he encountered an old man. After greeting him he asked him which road to take, for three roads met at the place where the old man sat.

229

The old man said to him, "One of these roads goes and returns, the second goes but does not return, and the third goes as it comes." The boy took the road that went but did not return.

He went on and on for many days, for about half the way. In the middle of the road he came across an *arap* who did not want to let him go any farther. The boy hit him once with his sword and turned his head round so that his face looked backwards. "Please," said the *arap*, "turn my head round as it was. Then I'll let you continue along the road." "If you give me your word that you'll let me pass and not only me, but also every other person who comes here, I'll turn your head round the way it was," the boy replied. The *arap* promised that he would not molest anyone.

The boy set out once more and went on and on, till he came to a forest. In that forest there was a huge palace belonging to the Earthly Beauty, who was guarded by forty fairies. On seeing the palace, the boy turned and went straight towards it and into it, for at that time the fairies weren't there. They had gone shooting.

When they returned, they saw the Earthly Beauty sitting on the balcony with Sword. They wanted to dash at him and kill him, but since they saw the young man looked brave and wore a sword, none of them dared to confront him

The young man's name, Sword, was well known because he had done many brave deeds when on his way from his own house to the Earthly Beauty's palace. Among other thing, he had saved two brothers from a pack of wolves. The brothers had made him their foster-brother, and before separating, each had dipped his handkerchief in the wolf's blood as a souvenir.

That is why they were all afraid of him and when the Earthly Beauty came down hastily from the balcony and said to the fairies that this was Sword, the fairies approached one by one and did obeisance to him. After staying a little, they bade him good-bye and lumbered downstairs to their rooms. Sword kept only one upstairs with him, the eldest.

When they went downstairs, they began their work. They put a boiler with forty handles and full of meat on the fire to boil. When the

230

food was ready, they tried to lift it off the fire, but since the boiler had forty handles and there were only thirty-nine of them, they could not lift it off. They began to dispute with each other so loudly that they were heard upstairs.

"What is the matter with them?" said Sword to the fairy he had kept with him. "Why are they quarrelling?" "They need one more," he said, "to lift off the boiler from the fire. It has forty handles and they are only thirty-nine." Sword rushed downstairs and, taking hold of the boiler by himself, lifted it off and set it on the ground. They were astonished at his feat and spread the news of it.

The King of the country heard about it and sent Half-Man, a brave man, with five hundred men to kill Sword, because he had engaged the Earthly Beauty for his own son. Half-Man had only one eye, one ear and one hand, but was a really brave man. He went with the five hundred men, seized Sword and cut him to pieces.

They wanted to carry off the Earthly Beauty, but she would not go, saying, "Tell the King I'll not come till I've buried this man." Next day, after she and the fairies had buried him and made a big gravestone on which they wrote his name, she went away to the King.

When she arrived, the King wanted to marry her off and have a great wedding, but she said, "I will not marry till the forty days of mourning are up."

As soon as Half-Man had killed Sword, the handkerchiefs which had been dipped in the wolf's blood by the two brothers who had adopted Sword as their foster-brother, began to drip blood. Seeing this, they said that undoubtedly something had happened to their brother Sword, and at once they took their rifles and went out to look for him.

They went along the road where the *arap* was. They asked him if anyone with a sword had gone along the toad. He said, "Such-and-such a one has gone," and he related what had passed between the two of them. They both took the road which Sword had taken, and when they neared the palace, they turned towards it. But before they reached it, they found the grave by the wayside, and when they saw his name written on it, they knew he had been killed. They began to dig open the grave. When they had finished, they took out the pieces of flesh, laid

231

them in order on the ground, and made him as he had been. They looked for his sword, because they knew that his soul would not come back without it. But Half-Man had thrown it into the sea, because he knew that if it was found, the young man would come alive again.

As they did not find his sword in the grave, the two men went to the palace to ask who had killed him in order to find the sword. But they found nobody in the palace, everybody had gone. They looked this way and that, but could not find the sword. They went out of the palace and walked along the seashore looking. After looking all day, they at last found where it had been cast up on the shore by the waves. They snatched it up and went back to the grave where their dead foster-brother lay.

They laid the sword by his side, and instantly their foster-brother came back to life and saw the two of them sitting by his side. He asked them how and where they heard about him, how they were and where they found the sword, and they in their turn asked him how he was killed and who did it. Sword said to them, "Now you may go away and attend to your own affairs. I don't need you any longer. I won't die again."

So they both went away and he set out for the King's palace to get the Earthly Beauty and to kill Half-Man and to avenge himself. When he was near the palace, he saw the Earthly Beauty at the window looking out and crying. When Sword came up and spoke to her, she was astonished to see him, because it had never struck her that her lover could come back to life.

Sword then asked her where Half-Man was, and if he was there, to ask where he had his soul. Half-Man said first that he had put it in the fire. The second time he said, "I have it in the rafters." Finally he said, "I have hidden it in the belly of a sow. It is like a live dove, and the sow is over there on the mountain."

The Earthly Beauty went to Sword and told him all this. This third time, Sword believed the story and set off for the mountain. On reaching it, he killed numerous boars and sows. He cut open all those he killed to find the dove, Half-Man's soul. Since he could not find it anywhere, he thought to himself that Half-Man had lied to the Earthly Beauty.

He set out again for the palace and the Earthly Beauty. On the way, he came across a shepherd with his sheep. After greeting the shepherd, he asked him if there were pigs in that place. The shepherd replied, "I know of only a solitary sow in this place," and he showed him her wallowing pit. Full of joy, Sword climbed over to the pit and cut her to pieces with his sword. Then he cut her open, found the live dove, put it in his bosom, and went back to the town where the King's palace was.

There he dressed as a vendor of medicines and walked through the streets. He went to the King's palace, calling, "I'm a pedlar, I have medicines." The King heard him and called him in to cure Half-Man, who had taken to his bed ill when the dove was caught. Since Sword had kept the dove alive in his bosom, Half-Man hadn't died, but was in his last agony.

When Sword went in, they took him to the room where Half-Man lay at his last gasp. Sword then ordered them all to go outside and to leave the two of them alone. When they were alone, Sword said, "Look at your soul in my bosom, Half-Man. Your life is just so long." With these words, he killed the dove in front of him. Along with the dove, Half-Man hung his head and died.

As soon as Half-Man died, Sword took out the sword he wore under his clothes and attacked first the King and then the others in turn. He killed and slew them all except the fairies and the Earthly Beauty. The latter he again made his wife. As he came out victorious over them all, they made him King and the Earthly Beauty Queen. In this way, they lived a happy life, and we a happier one.

[told by Foto Rumbo]

233

The Girl Who Lost her Necklace

Once there were a brother and a sister, who had no parents. They both herded pigs in the forest. The brother played on the flute and his sister danced.

Once a King went to that forest and said to the boy, "Please bring me a cup of water." The boy replied, "I haven't got any water, but I'll ask my sister. She may have some." The boy went to his sister and said, "The King wants a cup of water. Is there any or not?" The girl replied, "I haven't any water, but let's fill a cup with milk for him." She sent this to the King.

As a reward, the King gave the girl a gold necklace and hung it round her neck, saying, "If you lose this necklace, I will curse you. Go to your grave wearing this!"

As the brother and sister walked home, a great darkness and storm came on. The storm was over before the brother and sister reached their house. At once they remembered the necklace which the girl had round her neck.

Unfortunately she had lost it. They at once turned back to look for it. After walking a long way, they came across a fairy who said to them, "Welcome, travellers," repeating the words three times. The boy and the girl could not see him because he was very little and the grass hid him.

As soon as the two heard the voice, they said wonderingly, "Who is calling us like this?" The fairy stretched out his little hand and caught their hands, saying, "Welcome." They said, "How are you? Well? Strong and healthy?" The fairy asked where they were going. They told him what had happened and why they were going where they were. He said, "If you go farther on, you'll see a man who's smaller than I am. The grass covers him and he can't be seen. When you go there, be careful not to tread on him."

234

The two set out again and reached the second fairy. He, too, said, "Welcome, travellers," as the first had. After he said this, they went on a little farther and found a third fairy, who was even smaller than the others. They told him what had happened and he said, "Go to the priest's house," for he knew everything.

The two set out to go to the priest. They knocked on his door and the priest opened it, asking, "What do you want?" They told him what had happened to them. The priest explained to them, "The fairies have taken your necklace. To get it, you must go round this well three times. After you've done so, the fairies will come out to eat you. Say to them, 'We've heard that this is a holy night for you and so we've come to amuse ourselves among you.' When the fairies hear this, they will be glad and so will not eat you. When you go in, you'll see that on that night, they put on display everything they have stolen. When you dance, you'll see your necklace. When you see it, stamp your feet, saying, 'Death to the witches, death to the evil-doer who took our necklace!' After you say this, all the fairies will fall on their faces and die."

They left the priest and went three times round the well. When they had done so, the fairies came out to eat them, so they said what the priest had told them to say. When the fairies heard this, they were very glad and took them to the place where they were going to play and where they had set out all the things that they had stolen.

After they had sat for a little, the fairies set them to dance together. As they were dancing, they came close to the necklace. On finishing the dance, they shouted, "Death to the witches, death to the evil-doer who took our necklace!" All the fairies fell on their faces and died.

The boy said, "Sister, there's our necklace." The sister replied, "Don't let us take only our necklace. Let's take the carpet and all the things on it." They took the things home and grew rich. For all these things were valuable.

[told by Olga Zallari of Përmet]

Astafa

There was what there was. Once upon a time, there was a certain Astafa. This man was a sort of vagabond, who always wanted to get something for nothing.

In the town where he lived, there was a very rich man who had been ill for a long time. When Astafa heard of his illness, he planned to play him a trick, and every day asked how he was. At last, the man died and paid for his sins. When Astafa heard of his death, he was very glad. See what passed through his mind.

The night that the man died, Astafa got up at midnight, put on some shabby clothes, hung some bells round him, took also some iron chains, and went to the dead man's house. He climbed quietly onto its roof, and pretended to be the Archangel Gabriel.

Inside the house were the dead man's three sons, their mother, and some of his cousins, who were all holding a wake for the dead man. He had died late in the day, and they did not bury him in the evening but, according to custom, left him lying for one night in the house.

On the roof, Astafa made his bells jingle, rattled his chains, and with a frightening voice cried out, "I owe Astafa 2,000 piastres and two cows. Give them to him as soon as possible. My soul cannot rest."

When the three sons and the others heard this terrible voice, they fell with their faces to the ground in fear, and one said to the others in a low voice, "It seems to be Gabriel with Father's soul." They discussed what sort of debt it was.

The great fright given them that night made them at last decide to pay the debt to Astafa next day without fail. Astafa played the same game several times, shouting from the roof of the dead man's house before climbing noiselessly down and going back to his own house. In those days, people were afraid to go out at midnight, especially when they were waking a dead person, so nobody saw Astafa.

The next day the three sons buried their father with great pomp. But when they thought that Gabriel might perhaps come in the evening, they had no peace of mind and wanted to find Astafa. Luckily for them, Astafa passed their shop two days later, and said, "Good morning."

They stood up, saying, "Welcome. Won't you come in and sit down for a little?"

Astafa said he hadn't time. The three men, however, begged him to come in, saying, "Please come in for two minutes, Mr Astafa, and have a cup of coffee." Astafa stopped with a careless air as though he knew nothing, and said, "Well, I will sit down for a little, not to disappoint you." The moment he sat down, they gave him their tobacco box and ordered coffee for him.

As they talked, they spoke of an account he had had with their father. Mr Astafa, do tell us about it, please. Did you by any change have an account with our father?" Wrinkling his brow, Astafa said, "How is the old man?" "Oh, he died some days ago, but by word of mouth he asked us to pay the debt he owed you." When Astafa heard that the old man had died, he pretended to be sorry, and exclaimed, "You don't say so? I am so sorry. What a man he was! God rest his soul. Ah, ah, such men are rare. You can't find such men anymore."

Again the sons asked him how much the old man owed him. Astafa responded, "Don't mention it now. Never mind the debt now. You are full of sorrow, and I am stupefied by the bad news, though he was only a friend to me, and not a father as he was to you in every sense of the term."

The sons would not leave the matter alone, and he saw that they were very anxious. Finally he said, "He owed me 2,000 piastres and two very good cows."

The sons at once counted out 2,000 piastres and then went to the market, where they bought two cows and handed them over to Astafa, asking him to pardon the old man.

He pulled his cap off his head, saying, "I pardon him, I pardon him a hundred times. And all honour to you, his sons, who did not leave this debt unpaid as a burden on the old man's soul."

Astafa led away the cows and put the money in his pocket, rejoicing in somebody else's property.

[told by Urania A. Thanassi of Elbasan (the wife of a peasant)]

The King's Daughter Who Married a Bear

In the old days, Kings used to keep wild beasts in a secret place.

One day, the daughter of a certain King went to the place where the wild beasts were shut up, and opened the door. A bear suddenly flung himself on her, caught her and carried her off to a forest, where he put her in a big hole, or rather a cave.

The bear married the King's daughter and every day brought her fruit and ever so many other things to eat. Nine months later, a son was born to the bear's bride. She had nothing in which to wrap up the child and said to the bear, "Go and see if you can find a sheep. I need a sheepskin to wrap the child in. It will die like this." The bear went out and caught a sheep, and brought its skin to his bride.

When the boy was ten years old, he said one day to his mother, "Why do we live shut up in this cave, mother?" "Oh son, don't you see the big stone that the bear has put in front of the door? We haven't the strength to move it." "Oh! I can move it by myself," said the boy. And he went to move the stone, which weighed more than two hundred kilos.

When his mother saw him moving it, she called out, "Don't, don't. Afterwards you can't put it back as it was, and when the bear comes back, he'll kill us, he'll make mincemeat of us."

Boy: "But, mother, why do we stop shut up in this prison?"

Mother: "We've nowhere to go, son. If the bear saw we had gone out, he'd murder us."

Boy: "Don't be in the least afraid of the bear. Come on, let's go out. How's this happened? Here am I almost ten years old and I don't know what there is outside."

Mother: "Son, stop here to-day, and when your father comes home in the evening, say, 'Father, shall we have a try at throwing each

239

other?' And if he says yes, wrestle and see if you can throw him. Tomorrow we'll leave this hole."

In the evening the bear came home. After supper the boy said to him, "Father, shall we have a try at throwing each other?" The bear answered yes. The boy wrestled with his father and threw him. The bear was very angry and wanted to bite the boy with his teeth. The poor mother saved the boy by her entreaties to the bear.

The next day the boy again said to his mother, "Mother, let's go out. We've stayed long enough in this dark hole!"

Mother: "Yes, let's go, boy. But if the bear sees us outside, he'll stone us to death."

Boy: "Don't worry, mother. I'm equal to catching the bear's stones with my hands."

So the boy removed the stone from the door and they went outside.

When the boy saw the beauties of nature, he almost went mad. Mother and son set out without knowing where they were going. When they were rejoicing happily at their deliverance by God from the cave, the bear saw them from a distance and rushed towards them with lightning speed. The poor mother's knees shook under her, and she said to her son, "Son! I'm so frightened that my feet won't carry me. The bear has caught us."

Boy: "Don't be frightened, mother. So long as I am alive, I won't let the bear come near us."

As mother and son were talking, the bear flung two stones at them. But the boy, quick as a greyhound, caught one in his hand and flung it back at the bear's breast, knocking the breath out of him. He caught the second stone and threw it back at the bear, hitting him in the middle of the forehead and knocking him senseless.

Seeing that the bear could not get up for two hours or so, because he was senseless, the boy took his mother on his back and they set off again in the direction they had first taken. The mother hadn't a drop of blood left in her body; she was so frightened that the bear would kill the boy that she had no strength to walk on her own feet. After some time, the boy grew tired, carrying his mother pickaback.

Three days later they arrived at the King's palace. They entered the city at night, because both mother and son were naked.

When they knocked on the King's door, the porter came out and asked who they were. "I am the daughter of the King that the bear carried off," said the mother. The porter went and told the King. The King said to the porter, "Go and look. If she has a birthmark on her left shoulder, she is really my daughter." The porter went out and saw that she did have a birthmark on her left shoulder, and he took her inside.

But the boy was afraid to go in, because he was like a wild creature and had never set eyes on a human being. His mother begged him hard to come in, but it was not possible to make him enter. The King also went out to fetch him, but when the boy glared at him with his murderous eyes, the King nearly died of fear and went back inside without saying a word.

King: "Daughter, why did you bring that boy here?"

Daughter: "You're wrong about him, father. He's really as quiet as a lamb. But he has never set eyes on a human being, and has grown kind of wild."

King: "Oh, he may never have set eyes on a human being, but he frightens one to death."

His mother went out once more and said, "Come in, boy. Come, don't break my heart." In her distress she began to cry.

The boy, seeing tears on his mother's cheeks, entered the King's palace. His mother took him and dressed him in clothes, shoes and other things. Next day the King sent him, the bear's son, to school along with his own son.

The boy, who was like a wild creature, looked at the walls of the schoolroom and at the pictures which hung there. The teacher said, "Don't look about you, but listen to what I am saying." The teacher repeated this to him several times, but the boy did not listen. The teacher lost his temper at the boy's disobedience and tried to teach him to listen to what he was saying. He gave the bear's son one slap. The boy, using the strength which God had given him, dug his nails into the teacher's face, and threw him dead on the ground.

241

The news went to the King that the bear's son had killed the teacher. The King said to his daughter, "Oh, daughter, God's praise on you. Why did you bring that boy here? Do you see what he has done?"

Daughter: "I don't care if he killed the teacher."

King: "But I'm afraid that some night he may kill me, too."

Daughter: "No, father. He hasn't gone mad so as to kill you."

The King called a royal council and asked, "How are we to get rid of this boy? If we don't kill him, he'll land us in greater trouble."

Council: "If we collected forty donkeys and gave them to him to take to the forest and load with firewood, wild beasts would eat him there. In that forest there are a great many wild beasts, and so you wouldn't be his murderer, you whose grandson he is."

King: "Excellent! We'll send him there."

The bear's son had become great friends with the King's son, who was called Jemal. Jemal said to him, "Don't go where father wants to send you. There are a great many wild beasts there and they'll eat you."

The bear's son replied, "Don't worry, Jemal. You'll see me back here in the evening." And he went to the forest for firewood.

As soon as the bear's son reached the forest, he began to tear up trees by the roots, he was so strong. But when he went to fetch the donkeys, he did not find a single one. The wolves had eaten them. He returned home without any firewood.

King: "Where are the donkeys?"

The bear's son: "The wolves ate them."

"Oh dear me, I'm in for trouble with this boy," said the King to himself.

Jemal: "Oh, you've come back! You managed to escape."

The bear's son: "Oh idiot, wild beasts can't do anything to me."

Jemal: "You haven't seen all our rooms and houses yet, have you?"

The bear's son: "No, I haven't. Come on, let's have a look at them."

What should he see? All sorts of ornaments and beautiful things. Jemal didn't have the key to one room, because the picture of the Earthly Beauty was in it. The bear's son asked him why he hadn't brought the key to that room.

Jemal: "Oh, I'm not allowed to see a picture which is in this room, stupid."

The bear's son: "Where is the key?"

Jemal: "Father has it."

The bear's son rushed to the King and said, "Will you give me the key to that room?"

"Come and take it out of my pocket," said the King, turning his head away in terror because he could not look the bear's son in the face.

The boy took the key and went and opened the room which contained the picture of the Earthly Beauty. He said to Jemal, "You silly, are you afraid of this bit of paper?" And he tore the picture to pieces.

The King was very angry when he heard that the bear's son had torn up the picture of the Earthly Beauty, and for the second time he summoned a royal council. When it met, the King said, "What are we now to do with this boy?" "Let's send him to fetch the Earthly Beauty as he's torn up her picture." replied the councillors. "Excellent!" said the King. "He'll come to grief there."

They summoned the bear's son and said to him, "You have to go and fetch the Earthly Beauty." "All right, I'll go, only I don't know the way," he replied. Then the council and the King wondered how they could find a man who knew geography and could be given to the bear's son as a guide, for the Earthly Beauty lived very far away. As the council and the King were thinking about this, the bear's son cut in, saying, "I'll take Jemal, the King's son."

The King: "Yes, take Jemal. He knows those roads."

The bear's son: "Jemal, get ready. We're off to-morrow to fetch the Earthly Beauty."

Jemal: "Oh stupid, you've gone out of your mind."

The bear's son: "Why?"

Jemal: "Up to now, who knows how many thousands of people have gone to fetch her, and they haven't been able either to do it or to come back. How can you manage to fetch her?"

243

The bear's son: "God's faith, Jemal, don't be in the least afraid. We'll fetch her."

Jemal: "All very good, you ass, but I can't come. I'm convinced we'll never come back."

The bear's son: "You come with me. By God, I'll bring you back as sound as a bell."

With this argument, the bear's son persuaded Jemal to come with him.

"Listen, then," said Jemal to the bear's son. "The teacher told me at school all the history of the Earthly Beauty. First of all, she will come out to us and pour boiling water over us. What will you do?" "I'll catch you from behind and with the fleetness of foot which God has given me I'll get behind the Earthly Beauty. In her surprise she will be frightened and will run away," replied the bear's son.

Jemal: "Splendid! But then she will belch forth flames from her mouth and burn us. What will you do?"

The bear's son: "Oh, I'll throw stones at her."

Jemal: "But when she lets loose small flies at us which will bite us, what will you do?"

The bear's son: "Oh stupid, don't speak like that. If anyone hears us, he will poke fun at us, and you've gone through school. For the flies we'll take a woman's handkerchief and cover our faces."

Jemal: "All right, then. Now let's be off. God give our task a happy ending."

They set off and got through all the dangers of the journey without once having to run for it. As they went along, the bear's son asked Jemal, "Are you tired?" "No." "Come on, all the same. Jump on my back."

After some days they reached the house of the Earthly Beauty. When they went in, they found many people there. The bear's son asked what they were doing. "Nothing," a man replied. "The Earthly Beauty has caught us and now she won't let us go." "Where is the Earthly Beauty? We have never seen her," said the bear's son. "There's an old woman upstairs there. Maybe she knows. When we came here, we found that old woman," said the men.

The boy climbed the stairs and sought out the old woman. "Granny, where is the Earthly Beauty?" he asked. "Sons, I've never set eyes on her. I only hear her when she comes and opens the door of this room, and leaves a sheepskin outside the door. Stand here behind the door and watch. If you can take the sheepskin from her when she comes, then you've got her, too."

The bear's son: "All right. I'll keep watch. But what does she do in that room?" At a guess, she combs her hair and paints her face and makes herself up." "Thank you, granny," said the bear's son.

The bear's son watched out for the Earthly Beauty. She came and left the sheepskin outside. The bear's son seized it and went inside. The Earthly Beauty said, "I am yours. I am in your hands and in God's."

The bear's son: "Don't worry. I won't harm you. But what good is this sheepskin to you?" "I fly with it and no one can see me," replied the Earthly Beauty. "Splendid, come on, let's go on it," said the bear's son. The three of them got on it - the bear's son, the Earthly Beauty and Jemal.

They travelled about five hours, when the bear's son said to the sheepskin, "Land now!" The sheepskin landed.

The bear's son: "You stop here for a little. I'll go to the King and hear if he's talking about us."

The King had summoned the council and had learned that the bear's son had got the Earthly Beauty and was on his way back.

King: "Oh dear, what shall we do now?" he said to the council.

Council: "Let's take some glasses and fill them with sherbet. Let's put poison into one of them and give it to the bear's son."

King: "Excellent! We'll do just that."

They had no idea that the bear's son was in the room with them, invisible in the sheepskin. The bear's son mounted the sheepskin and went to the place where he had left the two others. The sheepskin flew like an aeroplane. When he reached the place, he found only Jemal. "Jemal, where is the Earthly Beauty?" "Oh, what a misfortune to fall on us!" Jemal answered. "What is it? Tell me?" said the bear's son. "I fell half asleep and she ran away. I don't know where," said Jemal.

The bear's son mounted the sheepskin, saying, "Take me where the Earthly Beauty is!" The sheepskin took them to a beautiful room, in which the Earthly Beauty, a man called Wrestler, and a girl who was Wrestler's sister and pretty enough, were playing."

They were playing with an iron ball, like the one with which children play.

The bear's son bunched himself up in the corner of the room, but those who were playing could not see him.

Wrestler's sister passed the ball to the Earthly Beauty. But the bear's son put out his hand and caught it, and struck Wrestler hard with it. So hard that he sent it right through Wrestler's body like a rifle bullet. But Wrestler did not feel it, he was so strong.

Wrestler said to the Earthly Beauty, "Don't hit me so hard. You knock the breath out of me." He did not know who had hit him.

In the same way, the bear's son hit Wrestler several times and at last killed him.

The bear's son took the two girls and Jemal and went to the King. The King and the council went out to meet them, and when they came near, wanted to give them sherbet. But the bear's son knew very well that there was poison in his glass. He seized the poisoned glass and poured it down the treacherous King's throat.

[told by Ibrahim Riza, a teacher from Bicaj]

246

The Shoes of the King's Daughters

Once in very far-off times there lived a King, who was surrounded with every blessing and luxury. He tried to use the power which our blessed Lord had bestowed on him for the good of his people. He won unnumbered prayers from his people and was daily more exalted in their estimation and more powerful.

But since God, amid all the magnificence which He may bestow upon a man, is sure to omit something in order to demonstrate His own omnipotence and to keep the man from straying from the path which leads to goodness and justice, so with the King. Amid all the wealth which God had bestowed on him, He had never given him a son, to whom he should one day leave his name and power, and through whom the renown of his countless riches should never be lost.

Well, the bitter thought that sometimes wounded the King's heart as he reflected that his mouth was condemned not to call "Son!" began to leave him as he looked on his twelve young daughters who, fair as the flowers of spring, grew taller every day. His greatest care was given to their education in both knowledge and good conduct and in the manners required of a princess who might one day become a mother and the mistress of a house.

One portion of the royal palace was set aside expressly for this purpose, and the girls were compelled to present themselves every morning before the King. Beautifully dressed and shod, they had one after the other to curtsey to him and to kiss his hand.

The father use to stroke each girl's hair lightly as if to caress her, while he studied their behaviour to see how it was. He rejoiced inwardly as he reflected on the coming of a time when the girls would be married to Kings or princes, whose power embraced the broadest lands and splendid wealth, and he himself would be surrounded by sons

247

and daughters, boys and girls – he whose heart had often been so sore for the want of one of those sons that the last days of his life were approaching, one might say, before their time.

The hours passed, the days and years passed, and it happened that at one of the appearances of his daughters, the King's eye fell precisely on their shoes. Seeing that they were very old, he at once ordered the stewards of the palace to bring as many pairs of shoes as there were princesses in the palace.

A few moments later, the stewards informed their master that his order had been carried out. But when the girls were lined up before him next day, the King was much surprised to see what dirty shoes they had on.

It happened as was seen. Although the King noticed everything about the shoes, he did not say a word and gave no sign of annoyance except by giving a fresh order. He ordered new shoes for the princesses but commanded that they should be delivered to him. The unfortunate father, very concerned about his daughters, waited impatiently for the dawn. Trying sometimes to calm his mind and to sweep away the doubts massing in his heart, he sought a few moments' rest in sleep.

At the same time, his daughters, richly dressed in silk, wandered secretly in the stillness of the night among flower-beds, weaving garlands of flowers for remembrance.

The night passed and dawn came. A little later, the daughters began as always to cross to the far side of the palace, where a now broken-hearted father awaited them, a father whose grievous wounds they pitilessly tried to worsen every day.

Without delay, the scene of the past days was repeated on their appearance before the King. Stiff with surprise and reflecting on the violence which had probably been done to his daughters, he was in despair. In the midst of this despair he gave orders that a large number of servants and guards should watch closely the movements of the girls.

Although the King himself tried to discover something by means of the shoes which he changed every day, and although he left nothing undone, all his efforts were in vain. A short time later, he was forced to issue an almost amazing order, one might say, to all his kingdom.

"Whoever," so ran the royal proclamation, "proves able to solve the mystery of the shoes of the daughters of the overlord of all these realms, shall be heir to the throne after the King's death, and shall also be given to wife whichever of the daughters of the King he may desire."

From all the kingdom, which included very broad lands, came sons of princes and rich men, each in the hope that he might one day secure the reins of power, the wealth untold, and along with these, the fairest girl within the royal home.

It seemed an easy matter to them when they began to delve into the secrets of the palace. But the King's clever daughters found ways of exhausting their brains within a few hours. All in their turn came bringing a thousand happy thoughts for the future, and within the appointed time left full of despair.

While the old man sat sadly reflecting on the disaster which had come on him in his palace, all sorts of people came and went. As they could not bring anything to light, they almost forced the King to give an order to stop them from coming. But so long as he cherished a hope that one of the many persons in his great kingdom would appear to unearth the amazing secret of the shoes, he was held back from issuing the order.

Outside the royal palace, in a corner of the capital, there lived an only son. Being much interested in the disaster with which his King had met, he wandered up and down, asking about the events within the royal palace, questioning in particular those who had managed to gain admittance. Whenever he happened on a chance of unravelling the secret of the shoes, he travelled through cities, cherishing the hope that somewhere in the great kingdom, in some corner or field, the truth would appear, the truth which he had set out to track down.

In his many travels he met with the ripe, the wise and the learned, with the young and the old, with men who sought to find a method of sorting the tangled threads of the ball of wool of this life. He also met fortune-tellers who unveiled the machinations of the mind with one piercing look. The young man remembered the advice he got from these, thinking that one day it might profit him, but hoping still more that it might save the King from disaster and bring happy days to one whom everyone desired to be fortunate.

A pretty long time, as we may say, had passed since the young man began to wander from town to town. During his travels he had once occasion to enter a thick forest in which there was a great danger of being torn to pieces by wild beasts. Although he had an iron will and unexampled courage, luck nevertheless could not have guided him through those paths so full of difficulty, if God had not sent him an old woman, not only to show him the forest path he had lost, but also to solve the problem which had cost him so much trouble.

When the old woman came in sight, the young man quickened his steps, and on reaching her, greeted her in the usual manner by saying, "Well met," and stopped in front of her.

"Which is the road to take, my old woman, to get out of this forest?" he asked.

"And, nice boy," said the old woman, "what business has brought you here? I think no human foot except my own has ever trodden this spot."

The young man told her all he had suffered in the course of his journeys and also the purpose for which he had endured so much. The old woman, who knew all about the troubles of the time, was sorry for the misfortune that had befallen the unfortunate King. Seeing that the young man, who was still really young, had stopped in front of her, she took a crystal ball out of the belt she wore round her waist. Putting the ball into his hands, she said, "Listen, son, I'll tell you what steps to take to discover what deed lies hidden in the shoes of the daughters of the royal family. By taking these steps without loss of time you will manage to relieve the mind of that old man who, surrounded to-day by daughters, is bent double by all these troubles. You must hasten to the King's palace and the very first night, when you happen to be received by the daughters of the King, you will be careful to keep ever in mind that you must not indulge too much in those drinks which are expressly offered in order to fuddle the minds of guests as well as to destroy the

250

traces of the deeds done by the daughters of the King. To avoid such a danger, you will hang round your neck a vessel into which you will pour all the liquids you are offered. Then, without allowing them to discover anything, you must pretend to be the worse for liquor and ask for a place in which to lie down. Meanwhile you will be easily able to observe their every movement from that place. In the crystal ball you have the means of making your body invisible and of being able, undisturbed by anybody, to see the comings and goings of the King's daughters outside their home – at a distance of who knows how much."

"This is the only path which can lead you to the end of your quest. There is no other way to get out of this forest except by turning back at once to the place I have indicated."

All this said, the old woman disappeared in an instant. She was lost and no more to be seen. The young man remained alone, petrified at the sight of the great number of trees, all as high as heaven itself.

The sun had reached the West, and its last rays were touching the windows of the room in which sat the King in the depths of despair, reflecting on the desperate difficulty in which he found himself. In the midst of these gloomy thoughts came a light knock on the door by which the servants let their lord know they had business with him.

Now the King heard no other sounds than those that hummed in his brain and oppressed his heart. So for days he neither ate nor drank and, growing thin and tottering like an old man, he showed signs that the end of his life had come. Late on this particular evening, thinking that somebody might be waiting outside, he ordered him in a faint voice to enter. The door opened and a servant entered.

"Your Majesty, an unknown young man has presented himself," he announced. Leaving a letter for the King on the table, he cut short his message and left the room. The King opened the letter and saw that, in accordance with the proclamation made throughout his kingdom, an inhabitant of more distant parts sought to share the sovereign's grief. And though the King, not having seen such guests for some time, was astonished, he at once ordered his servants to admit the new arrival. As it was rather dark, the servants took the visitor to the part of the palace in which the princesses lived and had been locked up

251

a long time before. When the princesses saw one of the men whom their father had sometimes sent previously to keep them company, they were surprised. And since the guest would cause them a little trouble in their secret pleasures, they made no delay and in a few moments spread the table, as was their custom. Round it began to tinkle sweet words and joyous laughter, sprung involuntarily from the cups of golden liquor that they offered rather than from their hearts, which were far from being pure.

The princesses did not drink anything and the young man for his part did not drink the liquor which he accepted, but slipped it secretly into the vessel which he had hung round his neck. At last, after fulfilling all the conditions which he had been given in the middle of the forest by the old woman, he asked for a place in which to lie down. He lay down there and, after removing the wet vessel from his neck, began to snore. With that the princesses, thinking that he, too, would suffer the same fate as the others, began to make their own preparations.

Each of them, working with remarkable speed, and making as little noise as the wings of a fly, began in the darkness of the night to dress all in silk and gold and put on the new shoes which the King left by their beds every evening through the intermediary of servants, and then they began, still without making a sound, to go out.

The young man, keeping awake and watching from the opposite side of the room what they were doing, got up from his bed. Scrambling to his feet, he took out the crystal ball and holding it in front of him, rendering himself invisible to all, he followed the princesses on tiptoe.

As he followed their tracks along the secret roads of the palace, he found himself brought out through some narrow turning to a hole in a rock. On opening an old door which was hardly noticeable in the rock, he passed inside, together with the princesses. A flower-garden, astonishingly beautiful, appeared before his eyes. While the princesses ran with all speed from flower to flower, each picking a bunch more beautiful than the other, the young man made no sound. When the princesses, flowers in hand, ran farther on, he followed them.

As the rays of the moon fell gently in that peaceful hour and spread over the leaves of the trees, they covered these with a silver sheen. In his great surprise at this, the young man thought that the leaves were really silver and that the fruit on the trees was really made of gold.

If it had not been that duty called him to unravel the problem of all the deeds which lay hidden behind the shoes, the princesses would have vanished from his sight whilst he stood watching the beauties of that night. But reflecting that it was for them that he had imposed this burden on himself, he ran after them to catch them up. He happened to overtake them at the edge of a forest where the water of a lake lapped noiselessly against banks that were green with fresh spikes of grass.

Just under the banks, he saw twelve boats drawn up side by side and in them twelve young men dressed and shod in garments all of gold. When the twelve princesses approached, the young men gave them each a hand and helped them into the boats.

All was ready. All in a row the oars slid into the water and the sound of them, creating a harmonious tinkle, spread an air of gaiety over the lake. And if the young man had not hurried to jump into one of the boats, he would not have seen so clearly the games and joys in which, entirely undisturbed, the princesses indulged in those secret places that were so far from their father's palace.

The little boats, completely covered with velvet, clove the water of the lake, while the young men and the princesses reclined in them and talked, and our clever, daring young man listened to all that was said, especially by those who were near him. He even smiled when he heard the regret which the princesses expressed both for the guest they had had that night, and also for the trouble they had had until they had managed to addle the pate of the ragamuffin.

Passing from one subject of talk to another, they eventually managed to reach the farther shore of the lake. The boats stopped and the princesses, supported by the young princes, stepped ashore. Each handing over her bunch of flowers to her escort, they started to walk along the shore of the lake.

A road which might easily distress a person led over some jagged rocks to a point where the top of a tower suddenly appeared. The

253

lights in the tower looked at first sight like sparks but on a nearer approach they appeared everywhere, one after the other, revealing the decorations for a festival which was being celebrated that night in the gigantic building.

Now our young man, following in the wake of one of the princesses, managed to see and even to take part in the festival which, with dances, music and amusements of the most magnificent type, was held for some hours at night within the castle.

Only the dawn, which slowly approached to change the whole face of the world, had power to cut short the desires and boundless appetites of the princesses. Rising hastily, they climbed the rocky path along the shore of the lake and were flung into the boats. Without uttering a word, they separated from the twelve princes at the place where they had met.

The whispered words in their final good-byes made it evident that they would meet again on the coming night. So our young man, hearing what they said, understood the cheating of the princesses very well. They ran from the lake and hastened towards their father's palace, which they had so disgraced with their unseemly conduct.

When, some minutes later, they reached the door in the rock which led to the secret paths into the palace, the invisible young man, who had accompanied them in all their wanderings, went ahead. Keeping always in front of them, he reached the room from which they had all started a few hours earlier.

Shortly afterwards, the princesses, finding themselves in the room where the young man was lying, made one jesting remark after another, without raising their voices, about the cleverness of their guest and then, their heads being swollen, they boasted about the trick which no living man had been able to find out. Finally, they laid down to rest the bodies which they had so wearied up till then.

What was seen that night in the deceitful acts of those girls was repeated the second night also.

For the third and last night, the tracks of the invisible young man followed those of the princesses again. When they were sitting all in a row in the decorated boats on the shore of the lake, just as they started off across the lake, our young man secretly seized the bunch of flowers which one princess had tied together with very great care. With a swing of his arm he flung it on the fresh grass which was close by.

When the journey across the water ended, the princess and prince followed with quick steps the beaten track which led to the castle of the dances. Our young man, bringing up the rear, saw lying on the shore the white gloves of the young prince who had forgotten them in a corner of the boat.

At once he hid them. As he caught up to the pair with whom he had come across the lake, he heard the lament uttered by the princess for the flowers which had been left behind on the shore where they had stopped. Since it was rather a long way to go back and they would return later, they decided not to lose time looking for them.

After they returned, our young man was no longer with these two, and so he was not able to hear what was said between them.

And since he had come to hear what they said only in order to achieve his end, he did not bother more about them, but on landing on the other shore he hastened to pick up the bunch of flowers which he had flung on the grass. Walking hastily all the time through the forest, he also broke off a branch of the trees which had silver leaves and with a bundle of such thing, tired and worn out, he reached his bed with difficulty.

Sure of all that had happened up to the last moment, he next day presented himself to the King, aged before his time by misfortune. Unveiling in all its detail the deceitful conduct of the princesses, which so secretly affected their shoes, he finally showed the tokens, which he had gathered in the places where they had walked.

The old man remained in open-minded astonishment at what the young man said and, turning over those scenes in his mind, could not at first believe all that was said. But looking again at the evidence which he held in his hand, he rose to his feet and immediately ordered the servants to bring the princesses to him.

When the princesses, with fear in their hearts, presented themselves to their father before the usual time, he was no longer gentle and sweet as before, but with a frown on his face he began to question them, speaking of all that had happened during the three nights.

The princesses, in complete panic, defended themselves by denying all that had happened and said that all this was only the imagination and fanciful fabrication by a sick man's brain to degrade the daughters of the mightiest sovereign who ever ruled over wide dominions.

But the King, who now understood the matter very well, cut short their words and showed them the twig from the forest which had silver leaves. When they saw the evidence connected with the dances on the nights when they went on their expedition, they bent their heads and when they saw in their father's hand the bunch of flowers which they themselves had carefully tied together in the flower garden, they saw through the trick which the clever young man had played on them.

The gloves of the young prince, which the King showed them, destroyed their last hope. As the truth had come out, the twelve princesses fell on their faces before their father, confessing perforce the sin they had committed. One after the other, they begged his pardon for it.

Then the King clapped the young man on the back for the manliness, bravery and skill which he had shown. Indicating that he might have any of the princesses that he wished for his wife, he proclaimed him through all his kingdom as heir to the throne and, with it, all the countless possessions which he owned.

As the clever young man was really rather old, he chose the oldest princess. She, now knowing very well his qualities, accepted him with great joy. Before many days had passed, a very magnificent wedding was celebrated. For a month on end the whole palace resounded with songs and dances and constant shots of "Long live the King! Long live the Heir Apparent!"

[told by Tevfik Gjyli, a teacher in Halikej]

256

Noah's Ark

In former days, snakes used to walk on feet. This was in the time of Noah. When the flood took place, Noah made an ark and took into it all male and female animals, one specimen of each. It rained so much that the whole world was flooded.

The ark floated on the water, with Noah and his animals safely inside it. When the rain stopped, Noah sent a magpie to see if the water had subsided. The magpie flew away and searched everywhere, but could see nothing except water. Next day, Noah sent forth a dove. It flew away and found the tip of a tree sticking out above the ebbing water. It broke off a twig and carried it to Noah, who was very pleased to have this proof that the flood was receding.

A mouse then went and, gnawing the side of the ark, made a hole through which water began to leak. A snake went and curled itself up in the hole, stopping it and preventing the water from coming in. The water sank and the world became as it had been before.

Noah let out the animals one by one from the ark and said to the snake, "What present would you like me to give you? You save me from the flood by stopping the leak that was letting in the water." "I'd like the sweetest blood to drink," replied the snake. Then Noah said to the humble-bee, "Go and test the blood of all the animals. Find out which has the sweetest blood so that we can give it to the snake."

The humble-bee went and tested the blood of every living creature, and found that man's blood was the sweetest of all. "Whose blood is the sweetest?" the swallow asked the humble-bee. "Man's," the humble-bee replied. "Just let me look a moment at your tongue," said the swallow. The humble-bee put out its tongue and the swallow clipped it off with its tail, which is like a pair of scissors.

The humble-bee went to make its report to Noah, but could not do so because it could not speak any more and could only hum. "Speak! What is the matter with you?" cried Noah. But the humble-bee only hummed in reply; it could not speak.

"Frog's blood is the sweetest," said the swallow. Noah then said to the snake, "To get the sweetest blood, go and eat frogs." But the snake replied, "I won't. You have cheated me!" It then addressed the swallow, saying, "When you have babies, I won't leave them to grow up. I'll eat them for what you've done to me." The swallow replied, "You can't harm me, for I will build my nest where it is under man's protection."

The Boastful Mouse

They tell of a mouse which thought itself superior to all the other animals and boasted of its numerous relatives, and especially of its clever sons.

When the time came for its eldest son to marry, the boastful mouse decided not to seek a wife for its son among the daughters of other animals, but to ask for the Moon's daughter, the Moon being one of the finest of the heavenly bodies, making the dark night shine.

The mouse went to the Moon and said, "Mrs. Moon! I have a very clever son. I don't fancy finding a wife for him among the daughters of the beasts of the earth, and they're of poor stock as well. I decided to come and ask your Ladyship to give me your daughter for my son, who is handsome and fair like your daughter. Besides, it's fitting to make a match between our two families. Just as your Ladyship is the finest of the heavenly bodies, so I'm the finest of the animals."

With a laughing face, the Moon replied, "You've been imagining things. I am not better than the other heavenly bodies. The Sun is superior to me. He quenches my light when he rises, so that nobody sees me at all during the day. Your Lordship should make a match with the Sun."

The boastful mouse went joyfully to the Sun to ask him for his daughter, and said to him what it had said to the Moon. With a smiling face, the Sun said to it, "You've made a mistake. I'm no greater than the other heavenly bodies. The Cloud is greater than I am. She often covers me, so that on an overcast day nobody sees me. Your Lordship must make a match with the Cloud.

The boastful mouse went joyfully to the Cloud to ask her for her daughter, and said to her what it had said to the Moon and the Sun. The Cloud replied gently, saying, "In this you're mistaken. I'm not of better family than the others are. The Wind is greater than I am. When he blows with force, he chases me off and doesn't let me stop in the sky. Your Lordship must make a match with the Wind, who is greater than I am."

The mouse went joyfully to the Wind and asked him for his daughter, and said to him what it had said to the others. The Wind replied sweetly, saying, "You've been imagining things. I am no greater than the Mountain which stops me and doesn't let me blow with force, as I do in other places. It's to your advantage to make a match with the Mountain.

With joy the mouse went to the Mountain to ask him for his daughter, and said to him what it had said to the others. The Mountain replied, saying, "In fact, I should be finer than the others if the Marmot didn't burrow into me, making my whole body a mass of patches. It would be best for you to get the daughter of the Marmot for your clever son, especially because the Marmot has a great many relations. You and he suit each other in body, intelligence, cleverness, and agility."

The mouse went to the Marmot and asked him for his daughter. After he had promised to give him his daughter, the Marmot said, "In fact I should have been a fine person, if there weren't foxes, hawks and owls to keep me in hiding all day long just as your Lordship stays hidden from the cat. When you hear a movement by another animal, you keep very quiet because you think it is the wretched cat. You were right in not wanting to take a wife for your son from the land animals and in wanting to marry into a clean, care-free stock that doesn't stay hidden the whole day as we do in fear of our enemies. It was a splendid idea of yours to go to the heavenly bodies as well as to the Mountain. It was also a splendid idea of the Mountain to send you to me, who resemble you in family, body, and mind!"

The vain mouse felt ashamed as the Marmot spoke. The Marmot had made it understand that it had been foolish to exalt itself above the other animals.

A man should thus appraise himself correctly.

The Beardless Man Who Had Five Brothers-in-law

In a certain village there was once a beardless man, who was very rich and also very devilish. He was bachelor and asked for the hand of a girl in a neighbouring village, who was the sister of five brothers. Since these knew that he was very rich, they gave her to him. He gave a very big wedding party, because he could afford it.

We said that the beardless man was rich. One day he went to the fields to see if the grain was ripe. In one field he found two small hares, which he caught and took home to his wife.

When it was time for the wheat to be reaped, he called in the help of his five brothers-in-law, and they came. In the morning, before he and they went to start reaping, he said to his wife, "For lunch you must make a pastry and a wheat loaf. You must also have sour milk and a pot of whey for us."

As he went out to work with his brothers-in-law, they passed the hutch containing one of the hares and he ordered it to prepare this lunch for them. When his brothers-in-law heard him, they were much surprised and said to him, "How could a hare do such work?" He replied, "He is a clever son. You will see him at midday." He then let loose the hare, which ran off free into the field. His brothers-in-law explained that the hare had deserted, but he replied, "It is used to running about. It always comes home again." Such was the lie that he told to his brothers-in-law.

When midday came, the beardless man and his five brothers-in-law went home to lunch. The five men remembered his order to the hare and waited impatiently to see if they would be given all the things he had mentioned. When they saw them actually arrive, they were greatly surprised.

261

When they had finished eating, the beardless man said to his wife, "Wife, let me have the boy a little to caress." His wife gave him the second hare. When his brothers-in-law saw it, they were still more surprised and asked him to give it to them, but at first he pretended he did not want to. After they begged him hard to do so, he did, but not till they had paid very dear for it. When the harvesting was over, they went home very happy because they had acquired a clever son.

When the grain in the fields belonging to the brothers-in-law of the beardless man was ready to be reaped, they collected all the village to help them, for they, too, were rich and had many fields. They took along with them the hare which they had brought from the beardless man. They wanted to have it at hand to send home at lunch time to prepare their food.

In the morning, as they left for the field, the wife of the eldest brother had asked them what they wanted for lunch. They had said, "When lunch time comes, we shall send you word about that with the hare." She had replied, "Mind you don't disgrace us in the eyes of the village!" Then they left for their reaping.

When lunch time came, the eldest brother took the hare and began to caress it as the beardless man had done the other. They said to it, "Father's pet, run home and tell your mother to get ready for our lunch two pies, a big wheat loaf, some yoghourt and some whey. We are coming soon." He then let go the hare. It went and hid in a bush. Poor thing, it was very glad to escape.

When they had worked for some time, the brothers-in-law of the beardless man and the peasants went home for lunch. When they had sat down, the eldest brother ordered the food to be brought in. His wife replied, saying, "When I asked you in the morning what you wanted us to prepare for you, you said you would send us word by the hare. We waited for the hare. Where is it? You've disgraced us in front of the whole village." "What?" her husband exclaimed. "Didn't the hare come here to tell you what we had ordered?" "Of course, it didn't. What sort of wretched hare would come here?" she replied. The brothers-in-law then understood that the beardless man had made fools of them. In anger they sprang up and went to give him a sound thrashing.

262

Seeing them coming in the distance, the beardless man understood that they were angry and meant to thrash him. He at once killed a kid and caught its blood in a vessel. He filled the vessel with the small intestines and, hiding it in his wife's bosom, tied one end of the intestines round her neck in such a way that it could not be seen.

When the brothers-in-law arrived, they said to him, "You are a liar and you've disgraced us in front of the whole village. The hare could not do the things you said it could." The beardless man replied, "Brothers, you saw the hare yourselves, and it was you who begged me to give it to you. Is it my fault, then? It seems to me that your wives were afraid you might fall in love with the hare and give up your own children. It seems to me that they may have chased the hare away. Didn't you yourselves hear what I said to it? Didn't you see for yourselves how I gave it orders and how it carried them out? And let me tell you something else. Your womenfolk are wicked. My wife would never have learned to behave herself if I didn't kill her once a week. Just see here!"

The beardless man called his wife. "Wife," he said to her, "why didn't you cook the dinner better? I don't like it at all." Pretending to be angry, he got to his feet and snatched up a knife. Then he flung his wife on the ground and pretended to cut off her head, but only cut through the kid's intestines which she had tied round her neck. Blood gushed from it, his wife twitched her legs as though her head had really been cut off, and she pretended to be dead.

Her brothers, seeing this, were extremely sorry and began to cry and lament over their sister, whom they thought dead. "Don't despair," said the beardless man. He fetched a flute and began to play on it, saying that he was going to revive her. After he had played for some time, she began to stir a little as though she was gradually coming to life. When she had quite revived, her brothers forgot about the hare and began to ask the beardless man for his flute. He would not give it to them at any price. When they had begged him hard and offered him a large sum of money, they secured it. Their idea was to play on it and so to bring back their wives after they had killed them in a fit of anger.

263

The beardless man saw his brothers-in-law off in peace, having sold them nothing for something.

They went home very angry with their wives, because the beardless man had said that these had driven off the hare in order to make them love their own children. As soon as they arrived, they killed their wives. After a little they picked up the flute and played on it to bring their wives back to life. In vain! They played all day long, but achieved nothing. At last it dawned on them that the beardless man had fooled them again. This time they set off in earnest to kill him.

When the beardless man saw them coming heavily armed, he felt there was no escaping them this time and he ran for his life. As he ran, he met a shepherd with his sheep. The shepherd said, "What's all this hurry?" In reply, the beardless man said that the King had died and that the people who were chasing him, wanted to make him King, but he did not want this. The shepherd said that if they wanted to, they might make him King. The beardless man replied that if this was really his wish, they could exchange clothes. The shepherd liked the beardless man's idea and at once gave him his clothes and took his in return. When the beardless man had put on the shepherd's clothes and taken up his crook, he said to the shepherd, "Now run along towards the seashore until those fellows who have been chasing me catch you up."

Without having an idea of the beardless man's devilry, the shepherd ran off in the direction indicated by the beardless man. When the five brothers caught him up, they did not stop to see who he really was, but seized him and flung him into the sea, where he was drowned, poor man.

Three or four days later, the beardless man was walking along with a flock of six or seven hundred sheep, when he met his five brothers-in-law. They were surprised and said, "Didn't we throw this man into the sea? And wasn't he drowned? Where did he find these sheep?" They went up to the beardless man and said, "We thought we'd drowned you in the sea. Where on earth did you find these sheep?" "Ah," he replied, "you flung me into shallow water, near the shore, so I got nothing except these sheep. If you had only thrown me in a little farther out, you would have seen what a lot of mares, horses, oxen, cows and he-goats I should have collected."

"Do tell us about all this so that we can jump in and get things," his brothers-in-law pleaded. "All right," said the beardless man, "only you must plunge into deeper water and fetch out bigger animals. You are five but I was all by myself. What could I do alone?"

The beardless man fooled his brothers-in-law again. He took them to the seashore, where the shepherd had been thrown in, and he said to them that if they dived into the sea on the right, it was deeper and they would find all sorts of animals that they wanted, and many of them. One dived in, felt he was going to be drowned, and began to wave his arms and to shout. The beardless man then said, "Quick, jump in! Your brother is calling you. He can't do much alone." The four left

The Poor Woman Who Had Three Daughters

Once there was an old woman who had three daughters, and went every day to fetch firewood. Every night the girls asked their mother, "Mother, what is there to eat to-night?" "Nothing, nothing – bread and milk, broth, haricot beans, etc." the mother would reply.

Once the King issued orders that there should be no light in any house in the evening. These three girls lit a lamp in a corner and sat down, all three, to do embroidery. The eldest said, "If I married the King's servant, I should not want anything else." The second said, "If I married the King's cook, who knows how I should be?" The third said, "If I married the King's son, God would give me a son with a star on his forehead and a daughter with the moon on her forehead."

As the girls spoke, the King's servant heard them and went and told the King all that they had said. The King summoned the girls and asked if it was true that the third girl had said this. When it was confirmed that she had done so, he gave her in marriage to his son.

After some time she gave birth to a son and a daughter, too, exactly as she had said beforehand. The two sisters-in-law of the Prince took the children from her, put them in a box, and flung them into the sea so that they should drown.

A monster and a monstress who were husband and wife lived in the sea. They took the two children and reared them till they were nine years old. When the children grew up, they saw sense. They understood very well that they were not the children of this monster and monstress and said to each other, "We're not these people's children. They are black and look how we are!" And they said, "What shall we do? Come on, let's quarrel and when they see us, they will be annoyed and will put us out of their house." So they began to quarrel and in fact the monster and monstress put them out of the house.

As they walked along, the two children arrived at the King's palace, where they found a wonderful horse and a whole courtyard full of people who had not been able to mount the horse and had been petrified. The horse used to see its own shadow and the people could not understand what frightened it, and had been petrified.

When their two aunts saw the children, they pretended to pet the boy and said to him, "Get on the horse and go wherever you like." The boy turned the horse's head towards the sun and mounted. All those who were looking on and had not yet been petrified were astonished at seeing such a little boy able to mount the horse.

The two aunts said to the boy, "Off you go now and gather all the pumpkins people have." The boy mounted the horse along with his sister and off they went as far as the signpost. There they found a rose-tree and the horse said to the boy, "Get down now, gather all the pumpkins and cut off all the thorns of the rose-tree with scissors, and don't make a noise. Don't wake the *kulshedra* from her sleep." The boy dismounted, cut off the thorns and made his escape.

When he mounted the horse, it said to him, "When the *kulshedra* wakes, she will see that her pumpkins are missing, and she will follow us. When she catches us up, you must pull two hairs out of my tail, and then she will burst." After the *kulshedra* got up, she made after them. The boy pulled two hairs out of the horse's tail, and the *kulshedra* burst. The boy then returned to the King's palace.

When his aunts saw him, they were angrier than ever and said to him, "Go and fetch the Earthly Beauty." When the boy got on the horse, it said to him, "Go right into their house. You will find there two fountains, one flowing with honey and the other with grape juice. They will say, 'Take some and wash your face.' Wash yourself with the honey and wipe it with your handkerchief. Afterwards they will serve you with coffee, but don't drink it. They will look into your eyes, but avoid looking at them, seize the second girl, and run away." The boy did as the horse bade him. After he seized her, the Earthly Beauty said to him, "When they set food before us in the King's palace, don't eat it without first looking at me."

Well, then, he seized the Earthly Beauty and carried her home to the King's palace. There, food was set before them, and he looked at her between the eyes. She said to him with signs, "Throw the food to the dog." He did, and the dog began to throw itself this way and that, for the food was poisoned. They brought another dish, and he looked her in the eyes, and she said, "Eat it."

After they had finished the meal, the Earthly Beauty began to tell the story of the two children. When she had told it, the King understood from what she said that the stray boy and girl were his son's children. He said to them, "You are the Prince's children." "Yes, we are. Our aunts threw us into the sea," they replied. The King seized the two aunts and roasted them alive in the oven. He took the children into the palace, and when they boy grew up, he gave him the Earthly Beauty as his wife. The King also took back the mother of the children, and they lived a long and happy life and had heirs.

[told by Fani A. Cipi of Elbasan]

The Watermill

Once upon a time a man had an only son. Unfortunately, although the father was quite rich and honourable, his son was wicked and pleasure-seeking.

To pull up his son, the father gave him a considerable sum of money and urged him to go into business. Without much loss of time, the son dissipated all the money in evil and wicked ways. The unfortunate father had again to give him money to take up something else so that he should earn a little. To no purpose. In a short time the son made ducks and drakes of all this money as well.

The poor father did this three or four times, but seeing no good come of it, he was forced to leave his son idle. He saw that otherwise he would lose all his money with him.

One day the son unexpectedly saw a beautiful young girl. He tried with the help of an old woman to see her secretly and without her knowledge. In fact the old woman with her tricks brought him to her presence and he saw her. But what was the good? A fierce and fiery passion seized him so that he gave the old woman a goodish sum of money to give to the girl if only she would let him see her little finger but nothing more, through the crack of the door. The old woman promised to persuade the girl to do this and did so.

To get the promised money ready, the young man addressed himself to his father, saying that he planned to build a watermill on the bank of the river. In the hope that his son had grown tired of behaving badly, the father was forced to give him the sum he asked. Losing no time, the young man went to the old woman, money in hand, and gave her what he had promised. And so he got his wish to see the girl's finger.

After this, the young man tackled the old woman, asking her to persuade the girl to let him see her from a distance at her window, and

269

again promising her a goodish sum of money. Again the old woman promised to do what he asked and did it, saying to the girl, "What harm can come to you if he sees you at the window? We'll only get his money." The poor girl believed the old woman and promised to let the young man see her after they had got the money.

The young man went in haste to his father and asked him for the necessary sum, saying he had finished building the foundations and that the money was needed now for the roof. His father without delay gave him the money, and so the thing was done as he desired.

The third time he asked leave to sit for a little with the girl and to talk to her, accepting the hard condition that he must not touch her and must give her a much larger sum of money than the other times. The old woman promised to grant his wish.

The young man asked his father for money to complete the equipment of the mill, as he had quite finished the building. This time the father gave him the money without a word.

At last the young man asked leave from the old woman to stay with the girl when she was undressed and to lie down beside her if he wanted to, with the reservation, however, that he would go no farther. The old woman promised to arrange this, but wanted him to give her as much money as all the other times put together and to swear not to hurt the girl. He accepted her conditions with pleasure.

He again went to his father for the money. This time, the father was suspicious and would not listen to him. But he was persuaded to give him the money when he said he had finished the mill-wheel and was now going to let in the water. He gave him the money but followed him secretly to see the new mill.

The young man went straight to the old woman and together they entered the girl's room. She waited for him and stripped on the best possible bed made up in the middle of the room. They began their game, embracing and rolling each other over and over. The despairing father watched his son's behaviour through a hole.

When the young man began to caress the poor girl up and down, she could not stand it any longer and gave him leave to go the whole way. But the young man resisted her, saying they had arranged with the

270

old woman not to go all the way. But what was the use? The girl could not stand it. She offered him the money he had given her the first time. The young man would not have it. The second time, the third time, and the whole lot. The young man would not listen. At last the girl offered a sum from her own money as large as all of this gifts put together.

Then the father who was secretly watching could contain himself no longer and called out: "Let the water to the mill, you stupid fellow!" And with that the tale ends.

[told by Mehmet Nezimi, a teacher in Shijak in the district of Durrës]

271

The Three Pieces of Advice

Once upon a time there was an old man who had an only son. When the time came for him to die, the old man gave the young lad three pieces of advice. "Son," he said, "if you go into a shop, don't buy on credit. Don't make friends with officials. When you marry, see that your bride is from a family seven generations old." With these words the old man died.

After some time, the son, immature in years and mind as he was, forgot his father's advice.

One day he went to the bazaar and entered a shop. After buying 200 piastres' worth of goods, he said to the shopkeeper, "Expect me back in two weeks' time!" At the end of the two weeks he went to the same shop in the bazaar and bought an oke of paraffin for which he paid.

The shopkeeper said to him, "Why haven't you brought me the first 200 piastres?" The boy said, "Have patience for two days more," and went away. He went to his own village.

There he found a sergeant in government service and made such friends with him that they became foster-brothers. Three days later he went to the shop where he had bought goods for which he had not paid. There he found the sergeant whose foster-brother he had become. He said to the shopkeeper, "Give me some things." The shopkeeper did so, and he paid for them. The shopkeeper then said to the sergeant, "Sergeant, this boy owes me 200 piastres and doesn't want to pay them." In a great rage the sergeant said, "Why don't you give him the money, you rascal? Give the shopkeeper his money, quick!"

The boy replied – gently as the sergeant was his foster-brother – "Dear brother, I'll pay him in two days' time." The sergeant said, "Now, now, or I'll kill you." And he called to the gendarmes, "Take the

272

rascal and put him in prison – in the murderers' cell." As the sergeant bade them, the gendarmes arrested him and put him in the murderers' cell.

When the prisoners were let out for exercise in the prison yard, this young man was let out, too. The prisoners who had been sentenced, some to 25 years' and some to 100 years' imprisonment, began to sing and dance and amuse themselves.

The young man stayed apart, plunged in thought. The prison yard was opposite the Governor's office. The Governor came to the window to watch the prisoners as they played and sang, and he saw the young man deep in thought. He called his servant and sent him to the lieutenant of the prison guard to say, "Why is that young man deep in thought and why is he in prison?" So the servant went over, and later said to the Governor, "He owes a shopkeeper 200 piastres, that's why he's in prison."

The Governor sent back word to the lieutenant to send him the young man. The lieutenant sent the young man along with the servant. The Governor asked the young man, "Why have they put you in prison? Did you wound or kill anybody? And why are you so worried? All the other prisoners play and sing, but you worry." "I've neither killed nor wounded anybody," said the young man, "but I owe a shopkeeper 200 piastres, and they've put me in prison for that." The Governor said, "Do not worry so much about 200 piastres. See, I'll give them to you, and you can give them to the shopkeeper."

"No, sir Governor. I have the 200 piastres at home so don't bother about them. I am worried about some advice which my father gave me when he died. I had forgotten it but now it has come back to me, and that's what I'm thinking about." "What sort of advice did he give you?" asked the Governor. The young man repeated what his father had said, when he gave him the three pieces of advice we have mentioned above.

The Governor said, "Young man, go and ask in the village about my daughter and the family she's from. I'll give her to you to wife." The young man replied, "Please don't. I am poor and you are the Governor, and I can't marry Your Honour's daughter."

273

The Governor gave him the 200 piastres, saying, "Go and give them to the shopkeeper and then do as I said." The young man took the 200 piastres and gave them to the shopkeeper. Then he went home and asked here and asked there about the Governor's daughter and the family she was from. The girl turned out to have a pedigree 15 generations long. So the young man went and told this to the Governor. The Governor wrote a letter for his daughter, which the young man carried to her. She read it and said, "I accept the proposal," and she married the young man.

The young man had only a house and three fields. So he saw he could not make ends meet. He said to the Governor, "I must go abroad, because I can't make ends meet at home. Only I haven't money enough to go." The Governor replied, "Son, sell your house and fields and go abroad." The young man sold his house and fields for 300 Napoleons. He took 100 and went to Constantinople, and 200 he left with the Governor for his wife's support. The Governor lent this money out at interest in order to make it more.

The young man went to Constantinople and stayed there for eight years. At the end of the eight years he sent the Governor a letter, saying, "I'm coming home." The Governor replied, "Come along!" The young man arrived at the Governor's house and stayed one night. Next day the Governor said, "What did God do for you abroad?" The young man replied, "In eight years I've earned 600 Napoleons." "Good for you!" said the Governor. "With the money you left in my hands I've bought you land enough to need 250 kilos of seed-corn. I've also bought you a house, it's the one you see in front of you, and the fields are beside the house. And here are 200 Napoleons over and above." The young man took the money, and the Governor said, "Now go with your wife to your own house and live together in it." So he took his wife and went home and they lived happily and had heirs.

Motto: The advice of the old and the great should always be heeded.

[told by H. S. Kadulli, a teacher from Hudenisht in the district of Pogradec]

The Young Man Who Married the King's Daughter

Once upon a time there were a husband and a wife, who had a son. The husband died and left his wife and son alone. One day, the son said to his mother, "Did father leave us nothing?" "Only a rifle," she replied. "Let me see it," he said.

He took the rifle and went out shooting. He entered the forest and saw an eagle on a tree. As he took aim with his rifle, the eagle rose from the tree and lighted on the ground at his feet. "Please don't kill me. I have new-born eaglets in my eyrie and they will die without me," she said. "All right, I won't touch you," he replied.

Then the eagle said, "Pull out one of my feathers and keep it by you. When you are in trouble, come here and light a fire. Burn my feather and I will come at once to your help." The young man pulled out a feather as the eagle said and went away.

He next found a fox. As he aimed his rifle at it, the fox fell down and said, "Please, young man, don't kill me. I have new-born cubs in my den and they will die without me." She added, "Pluck a hair from my coat and when you need me, make a fire and burn the hair. I shall be by your side immediately." The young man went away.

He walked along the seashore and found a big fish with its head out of the water. When he aimed his rifle at it, the fish came to the edge of the water and said, "Please, young man, don't kill me. I have only just spawned and my babies will die without me." "Go away, I won't kill you," said the young man. The fish said, "Take a fin from my back and when you need me, build a fire here and burn my fin. I'll come to you at once." The young man went away, home to his mother.

"Haven't you shot anything?" asked his mother. "I didn't see anything," he replied. "Go to market, son, and find a job somewhere as

276

a servant. The rifle's not for you," his mother said. The young man went to market to look for employment.

When in the market, he heard the town-crier announcing, "Whoever wishes to marry the King's daughter, must send for her. The King's daughter has given orders, saying, 'Whoever wishes to marry me, must hide so well for one day that I can't see him. If I can't see him, I'll marry him'." The young man left the market place and went home to his mother.

Said he to his mother, "I heard the town-crier announcing to-day in the market place, 'Whoever wishes to marry the King's daughter, must send for her. But he must hide for one day and remain invisible. He must also go to the King's daughter and say to her that he will hide for one day. If she sees him, he cannot marry her. If she doesn't, he can marry her'."

His mother went to the Princess and said, "I have a son, and he has sent me to Your Highness to say that he will hide for a day." "Go and tell him to hide," the Princess replied. The mother went home and said to her son, "Go and hide, son."

The young man went to the forest where he had found the eagle which he had wanted to kill. On arriving he lit a fire and burned the eagle's feather. Thereupon the eagle came to him and said, "Why did you call me, young man?" He replied, "It was against this day, when I need you, that I did not kill you. I want you to hide me in a place where no one can see me." The eagle spread her wings and said to him, "Get on my back!" He jumped on her back and she flew away with him through the air. She kept him up in the air all day like an aeroplane.

The King's daughter was alone in her rooms. She went out into the garden and laid her mirror on the ground. She looked at land, mountains, fields and everything else but could not spy the young man. She turned the mirror towards the sky – and saw the young man.

The eagle lowered the young man to earth when evening came, and he went and said to his mother, "Please go and see the King's daughter to-morrow and find out if she saw me or not." And the mother went to the King's daughter next day and said to her, "My boy sent me.

277

Did you see him anywhere?" "I saw him on the eagle's back, high up on the air," the King's daughter replied. The mother returned to her son.

"She saw you, son," she said to him, "on the eagle's back, high up in the air." "Tell her I shall hide again," he replied. His mother went a second time to the King's daughter. "My son sent me again," she said. "He wants to hide a second time." "All right, let him hide again," said the King's daughter. The mother went to her son and said, "Hide, son!"

Next day, the young man went for a walk along the seashore and lit a fire. He burned the fish's fin and the fish came immediately to the shore.

"What do you want, young man? Why did you call me?" it said. "It was to have your help to-day that I did not kill you that day," he replied. "I want you to hide me in a place where no one will be able to see me." The fish opened its mouth and said, "Get into my stomach!" It took him into the sea and kept him at the very bottom of the sea.

The King's daughter went into the garden with her mirror. She looked at the land, mountains and fields, and saw nothing. She turned the mirror towards the sky and still saw nothing. She turned in towards the sea and spied him in the fish's stomach.

In the evening the fish brought him ashore again. "Young man," it said, "no one could have seen you. I had you in my stomach at the bottom of the sea." The young man went home to his mother.

He said to her, "Go and ask the King's daughter if she saw me anywhere." His mother went to see the King's daughter.

"My son sent me," she said to the Princess. "He wants to know if you saw him anywhere or not." "I did," the Princess replied. "He was in the stomach of the fish at the bottom of the sea." "She must be a devil, mother," he remarked when his mother told him the Princess had seen him. "Go again and tell her that I'm going to hide once more." His mother went to the King's daughter and said, "My son has sent me again. He wants to hide once more." "Go and tell him to hide once more," said the Princess. His mother went home and said to him, "Go and hide once more!"

He rose the next morning and went straight to the forest. There he made a fire and burned the fox's hair. The fox came and said,

278

"What's the matter? What do you need?" He replied, "I want to hide in a place where no one can see me. I have been raised high in the sky and been seen. I have been carried to the bottom of the sea and been seen. Where can you hide me?" "Tell me what your trouble is," the fox asked. "I want to marry the King's daughter, but she has a mirror which shows her the whole world," the young man replied. "Follow me," said the fox.

The fox led him into the garden where the King's daughter used to go. The mirror lay on the ground. Near it there were two apples, each of which weighed 40 okes. What did the fox do? She cut one apple in two and, putting it in her paw, she scraped away the inside till the apple was quite hollow. She then turned the young man into rubber and put him into the apple. "What have you done to me?" he asked. She replied, "You soared up into the sky and were seen. You sank to the bottom of the sea and were seen. I cannot find you a better hiding place than in the very hands of the King's daughter."

Next morning, the Princess went into the garden and found her mirror. She turned it towards the fields and mountains, but could see nothing. She turned it towards the sky, but could see nothing. She turned it towards the sea, but could see nothing. "What has become of this devil?" she asked herself. "Where has he hidden? He's not on the land, or in the sky, or in the sea. Let him come out now. I'll marry him as I've not been able to spy him."

The young man heard what she said and came out of the apple. When she saw him, she was frightened. "What's this coming out of my apple?" she asked. He said, "I hid in the sky and you saw me. I hid in the sea and you saw me. But here you could not see me."

She then gave a wedding party and married him. The son of the old woman who was poor and had no food to eat, became son-in-law to the King.

The Young Man Who Married a Log

Once upon a time there was a King who had three sons and three daughters. When he died, he left all his sons and all his daughters unmarried. The boys then said, "Let's get our sisters married and then we can marry ourselves."

The King of Fairies asked for the hand of one of the girls and was given it by her brothers. Another King, the King of Birds this time, asked for the hand of a second girl and was given it. Lastly, the King of Spirits asked for the hand of the remaining girl and was given it. So the brothers got all their sisters married.

Then the oldest brother married, and the second one. The pair next said to the youngest brother, "Let's find a wife for you, too." "Don't," he said. "I'm going to marry a log. I've dreamt that I'm going to marry a log."

He sent for the log and brought it home. Now it had a tortoise inside it, and inside the tortoise there was the Earthly Beauty. When the young man went out, closing the door behind him, the tortoise came out of the log and the Earthly Beauty came out of the log and swept and tidied the house. When the King's son came home in the evening, he found the house clean and tidy. He shouted to the servants, "Who has been in my room? Who opened my door?" "No one has been in your room," the poor fellows replied.

Next day he shut up his room and climbed on the rafters. He wanted to spy out who opened his door and came into his room. He saw the tortoise coming out of the log and the Earthly Beauty coming out of the tortoise. He jumped down from the rafters in haste and, snatching up the tortoise's shell, broke it. "What have you done to me?" the Earthly Beauty exclaimed. "What do you want with that tortoise shell? It's no use to you," he replied. "They will not let me stay here, they will

280

come and carry me off," she answered. "Who has the power to come here and carry you off?" he asked. "A man a hand high," she replied. "His beard is two hands long, and his horse has only three legs. He's coming this very minute to carry me off!" As she spoke, the man came and carried her off.

The King's son was dumbfounded. "What's come on me!" he wailed. Then he went to his brothers and said, "You must excuse me. I'm going away."

He hurried away from home, travelling fast and far till he reached the place where his brother-in-law, the King of Fairies, lived. He went to spend a night with his brother-in-law and told him of his trouble. "We three brothers married," he said, "but they carried off my wife. A man a hand high, with a beard two hands long and a three-legged horse, carried her off." The King of Fairies said to him, "It will be quite easy to find her," and sent out his fairies to search for her. They searched high and low but could not find her. The King's son then left the King of Fairies.

Some time later, he went to spend a night with his sister who had married the King of Birds. He told his trouble to this brother-in-law also. "They've carried off my wife," he said. "Who carried her off?" the King asked. "A man a hand high, with a beard two hands long and a three-legged horse," he replied. "We'll search and find her," the King of Birds replied. The King then sent out his birds, saying, "Go and look for this man and when you find him, come and tell me." The birds searched but could not find the man. The King's son continued his journey.

He went at last to spend a night with his youngest sister, who was wife to the King of Spirits. He told his trouble once again. "They've carried off my wife," he said. "Who has?" the King of Spirits asked. "A man a hand high, with a beard two hands long and a three-legged horse," he replied. "It will be quite easy to find her," the King of Spirits said.

The King sent out his spirits who found the little man at the end of the world, at the spot after which there is no more world. The King said to him, "Young man, you have no leave to go there. But I shall give you one of my mules, which will carry you there quickly." The young man mounted the mule and soon found the man at the end of the world.

A hut stood there, with the woman inside. The young man said to her, "Come, let's go." "I can't come," she replied. "Don't you see my husband working over there? He'll kill both of us." "Come on," he repeated. "Let him kill me!" He took her away and mounted her on his mule. But the man a hand high saw him. Riding on his three-legged horse, he dashed after him, caught him, and cut him into four pieces.

The woman said to the little man, "What you did was well done. Now load him on his mule so that everybody who sees him, will wonder and no one will ever dare to come here again." The little man did what she said, and the mule carried the four pieces of the young man back to his sister, the wife of the King of Spirits.

When his sister saw him, she was astonished and began to cry. The King of Spirits heard her weeping and came and asked her why she was crying. "For my brother who came here. They have cut him into four pieces," she replied. "Don't worry. I'll make him again as he was," he answered. He put the four pieces together and made him a man again.

"Go away, brother. You cannot get your wife back," his sister then said to him. But he replied, "I'm going after her again. I will not give her up." The King of Spirits again gave him his mule, saying, "Go if you must."

The King's son rode away on the mule and again found his wife in the hut. When she saw him, she exclaimed, "You are a fool. You were cut into four pieces once. Didn't you see for yourself the state you were in?" "Yes," he replied, "but just wait till I discover where the strength of this man lies." Then he hid.

When the little man returned from work, the woman said to him, "I want to know more about you. What gives you such strength?" "I've no strength myself," he replied. "My strength comes from my horse, which is the *gybylane*'s horse. It has a brother, which once kicked it and broke its leg and flung it down here. I caught it and trained it. Somebody should go and fetch its brother. But all the horses there are very wild. There is a fountain of running water there and every morning the horses come to the fountain to drink. When one of the brothers of

282

my horse drinks, it says, 'My God, isn't there a man who wants to ride me? I wish a man would come here and say, "This is a horse without a master. Shall I saddle it?"' If a man happens to pass the fountain and saddle this brother of my horse and ride it, then this man will plummet back into this world with this horse."

His wife remarked, "This business of the horse is very odd." The little man replied, "The man must go to that mountain and climb to the fountain. When the horse comes to drink and says, 'Oh God, is there nowhere a man to saddle me?' the man must reply, 'I can easily saddle you, only I'm afraid you will kill me.' The horse will promise not to touch him and will let itself be saddled by the man."

Next day, the King's son, who had heard all that the little man had said to his wife, went to the mountain and found the fountain. When the horse came to drink and said, "Oh God, is there nowhere a man to saddle me?" the King's son replied, "I can easily saddle you, only I'm afraid you will kill me." The horses said, "By God who has begotten me, who has given me life, I shall not touch you." The King's son saddled the horse and, mounting it, went straight to the woman, his wife, and found her in the hut. "Come, let's go now. I've found that horse," he said to her. He took his wife and mounted her on the horse.

The man a hand high saw him and, mounting his own horse, dashed after him. But his horse dared not approach the other one, being afraid of it ever since it had kicked it and broken its leg. The little man beat his horse, but the other one said, "What's he beating you for?" The little man's horse replied, "Because he wants to catch the man you have on your back and kill him." "Come close," said the wild horse. As it was its brother, the little man's horse obeyed. The wild horse caught the little man by the beard, shook him two or three times, and shattered him to bits.

The King's son carried his wife home and gave a wedding party.

The Fisherman's Son Who Married the King's Daughter

Once upon a time there was a fisherman, who had a son and a wife. One day his wife said to him, "Husband, take out your son and teach him how to fish." The son was young and did not know how to fish. The fisherman took him out as his wife had said.

They put out to sea. The fisherman cast his net into the water and caught a big fish. He pulled at the net, but could not get the fish in. Then he tied the net to a stick and said to his son, "Stop here and hold the net. I'm going to get some help. The fish is so big that it's difficult to haul in." "All right, go," said his son. When his father went away, he pulled in the net and a huge fish was drawn aboard.

The fish said to him, "Pick me up and throw me back into the sea, and I'll teach you a special trick." "All right," said the young man, "I can set you free, but what shall I do with the net?" "Throw it over here and I'll take care of it," said the fish. The young man took the fish out of the net and threw it back into the sea.

The fish then raised its head above the water and said to the young man, "You must say, 'The first word to God, the second to the fish, and the third to me,' then what you say shall be done. Now throw the net into the water and I'll take care of it."

The young man threw the net back into the sea. The fish tied it round a stone under the water, just before the fisherman and his helpers arrived. They began to tug at the net in order to catch the fish. They tugged and tugged. What happened to the net? It stuck in the sea.

The father beat his son. "You've brought me ill luck!" he said, and his son ran off along the seashore. Night caught him there. He stopped and cried. He then remembered the words which the fish had taught him and said, "The first word to God, the second to the fish, and

284

the third to me. God send me to Istanbul!" No sooner said then he found himself in Istanbul.

As he walked round the town, he stopped to look at the Royal Palace. As he stood gazing at it, the passers-by said to him, "Don't look there. That's the King's Palace, and he has shut up his daughter in it." "How should I know?" he said. "I'm a stranger here and I'm admiring the beauty of the palace."

The young man moved away. After walking some distance from the palace, he said, "The first word to God, the second to the fish, and the third to me. God send that the princess becomes pregnant!" and all in a moment, she became with child.

Two or three days later he said again, "The first word to God, the second to the fish, and the third to me. God send a son to the princess!" and sure enough a son was born to her. The King and the Queen were much surprised. "What man got into our palace?" they asked each other.

At the end of the week the young man again said, "The first word to God, the second to the fish, and the third to me. When I pass by the King's palace, may the baby call 'Dad' to me!" He then passed by the palace and as he had wished, the baby appeared at the window and called out "Dad, dad!"

They caught the young man and took him into the palace. They said to the King, "A young man passed by the palace and your daughter's son called 'Father!' to him. We've arrested the young man and have him in the palace now." "Bring him in," said the King. They brought him before the King. "Who let you into my rooms?" asked the King. "No one, sir. I've just come in. I am a stranger. I don't even know the way," the young man replied.

One of the members of the Royal Council said to the King, "You must order a big chest to be made. Then take the baby and your daughter and put them both, with the young man, into the chest, and throw them into the sea." The King made a fine, water-tight chest in which he enclosed his daughter, her baby, and the young man. He loaded it on a porter's back and had it thrown into the sea. It floated on the water and was carried out to the sea by the waves.

285

The young man opened the chest in the middle of the sea and put out his head. He could see no land at all, but only the sky and water. He then said, "The first word to God, the second to the fish, and the third to me. Let this chest come ashore in front of the Royal Palace!" The chest then came ashore as he said.

He then went to gather firewood because they were feeling cold. He lit a fine fire and they all three gathered round it. The princess and the baby fell asleep. Then the young man said, "The first word to God, the second to the fish, and the third to me. May a palace better than the King's be built here!" The palace sprang up at once. When the princess awoke, the palace was already complete.

When day broke, the King saw this palace and was amazed. "Such a big palace on the seashore!" he exclaimed. He was afraid that another King had come there to conquer him, and sent someone to see the palace and find out who was there.

The young man then said, "The first word to God, the second to the fish, and the third to me. May nails talk to nails, rafters to rafters, and tiles to tiles!" The King's messenger was afraid to approach the palace. He heard the noise of talking and ran home to the King and said, "Everybody there had gone inside. Who knows how many persons there are?"

Another man said, "I'll go and see what there is there." He set off to go to the palace, but this time the young man stopped the noise. The messenger went straight to the palace and found the young man. "Welcome. Come in!" said the young man. They took coffee together and talked for some time, and then the messenger went away. He went back to the King and said, "There's no one at all there except a woman with a baby upstairs and a young man in a room downstairs."

The man who had said to the King, "Make a chest," now said, "Invite these people here one night." The King sent them an invitation. The messenger went to the palace and said, "The King sends you his greetings and cordially invites you to come to-night with as many persons as you like, to take coffee with him." The young man laughed. "Why do you laugh?" asked the messenger. "Can the King supply enough food for me?" the young man asked. "Oh yes, come with as many people as you wish," replied the messenger.

The young man told the princess to get ready and said, "The first word to God, the second to the fish, and the third to me. May ten negresses come here!" He gave them to the princess, saying, "Go straight to the palace where you used to live." He then got himself ready and set off. Again he recited his prayer, "The first word to God, the second to the fish, and the third to me. May ten *araps* come here, and may one of them never find enough to eat!" He set off in earnest and went to the palace.

He left the *araps* in one room and went himself to find the King. There was coffee, there was talk, and dinner time came. They served food first to the *arap* who never found enough to eat. They set a huge tableful of meat in front of him. The *arap* snatched up the meat and swallowed it in one gulp. They served a huge tray of rice and raisins. He ate all that in one mouthful He alone finished all the food there was. There was nothing left for the others. As a result, they began to quarrel, but the young man who was with the King, came out and said, "Don't give the *araps* any food. They are never satisfied, and one of them eats human beings." The King was amazed. He stood there spellbound, and they all remained supperless that night. As soon as it was light, the guests got up and went home, leaving the King disgraced.

The young man then sent word to the King that he wished him to return his visit. He sent an *arap* to him, who said, "The young man kisses your hand and invites you to come to his palace with as many people as you wish." The King got together about a thousand people and went to the young man's palace.

The young man said, "The first word to God, the second to the fish, and the third to me. Let the table set itself. Let coffee serve itself. Let every imaginable good food come on the table itself." Dinner time came, and an *arap* entered. He shouted, "Prepare for ten courses. They are going to eat!" They prepared as he said. Tables were set and dish after dish followed. The company ate their fill and more, and still there was food left. They dined with the King.

287

When it dawned, the King made ready to go. The young man again said his prayer, "The first word to God, the second to the fish, and the third to me. When the King leaves my palace, let a spoon stick in his boot! When I call it, let the spoon reply!" The King put on his boots, mounted his horse and made ready to go.

The young man laughed at him. "Why do you laugh?" asked the King. "I laugh," said the young man, "because somebody has stolen from me. Somebody has stolen one of my spoons." "Let me search everybody," said the King. "No, I'll call the spoon," said the young man. "Call away!" said the King. "Short-handled spoon!" called the young man. "I'm in the King's boot," replied the spoon. "Oh, I have it here!" exclaimed the King. He pulled the spoon out of his boot and gave it to the young man. Then his party took their leave.

The King again called on the young man and recognised his daughter. He was much surprised. "This is God's doing!" he declared. He sent out invitations and gave a wedding party for them. He took his daughter home and they all lived together. Who was then as happy as the King?

The King's Son Who Married a Tortoise

Once upon a time there was a King who had three sons. When they grew old enough to marry, he gave them each an apple to throw wherever they liked. The eldest son's fell at the vizier's door and the second son's at a pasha's door, but the youngest son's apple landed in a bush. He found a tortoise in the bush and took it home. The Earthly Beauty was inside it.

When the boy went out, he left the tortoise in his room. The Earthly Beauty came out and did all the housework. This set the boy wondering, "I have nobody to attend to me. Who is doing the housework? I'll stay in one day and spy," he said to himself.

While he was spying, the Earthly Beauty appeared. The boy seized the tortoise shell and said, "I will burn it!" The Earthly Beauty said, "Don't, or the spoon will burn your lips." The boy did not heed her and burned the shell.

When the King heard she was the Earthly Beauty, he invited his three daughters-in-law to dinner. The wives of the two eldest sons said to her, "Think, tortoise, what sort of baklava will you make?" "I will make it with the droppings of hens and ducks," replied the Earthly Beauty. "What kind of make-up will you make?" the others next asked. "I will use the droppings of hens and ducks," she replied. She hid three doves in her bosom, they all took the baklava they had made, and went to the King's palace.

They set on the table the two baklavas which had been made by the two elder brides. They were uneatable because they had been made from the droppings of hens and ducks. The baklava made by the youngest son's bride was good.

As they ate, the Earthly Beauty fed the doves in her bosom. The other two noticed this and began to fill the bosom of their dresses with

289

bread and meat chops. The King saw them doing it and after dinner said, "Let the three brides dance until their waist belts burst!" As the two eldest danced, bread and meat fell from the bosom of their dresses. As the youngest bride danced, three doves flew out of her bosom. One dove went to the King, and the two others perched on the shoulders of her sisters-in-law.

The King was very pleased with his youngest daughter-in-law and wanted to marry her himself, his own wife having died. To compel his son to give him his wife, he demanded that he should bring him a carpet on which the whole of his army could stand while leaving half of it empty.

The young man went in tears to the Earthly Beauty. When he told her what the King had said, she answered, "Why did you burn my shell? The spoon will burn your lips. Go to the place where you found me and say, 'Give me the carpet which I left on the table.'" The young man went to the place, found the carpet, and brought it back to his father, who almost died in his anger.

His father then asked him to bring a bunch of grapes, such that the whole army could eat some and half of them be left over. The young man told his wife of this demand. She again said, "Why did you burn my shell? The spoon will burn your lips. Go to the place where you found me and say, 'Let me have the bunch of grapes which is at the door.'" The King was surprised to find that his whole army could eat some grapes from this bunch and that some were left over.

Finally, the King demanded that his son should find a child that should be born one evening and be able to speak by the morning. Following his wife's advice, the young man went to the spot she indicated and said, "Let me have the little child my wife gave birth to last night." He picked up the child and carried it to the King in a small box. "Just open this box," he said to the King.

The King did not believe he had succeeded, and opened the box. A child jumped out, sword in hand, and cut off the King's head. His youngest son succeeded to the throne, and he and the Earthly Beauty lived a long time and had heirs.

The Sulkumnixhi

Once upon a time there was a merchant who had a shop and three daughters. Once, when he was going to Istanbul to buy merchandise, he asked his eldest daughter, "What do you want me to bring you from Istanbul?" "A cloak stiff enough for its body part to dance while its sleeves play the drum," she replied. He then asked his second daughter what she wanted, and she asked for the same thing. Last of all, he asked his youngest daughter, and she said, "I want a *sulkumnixhi* and if you bring it, may your path be silver, but if you don't, may your path turn into a marsh and drown you!" "I will bring you the *sulkumnixhi*," he replied, and left for Istanbul.

There he bought merchandise for his shop and found cloaks for his two elder daughters that were stiff enough for the body part to dance while the sleeves played the drum. But he could not find what his youngest daughter had asked for. What could he do when such a thing was not to be found? "Let's go home," he said to his friends.

But on the way, his horse sank out of sight in mud. Said he to his friends, "Carry on, and a good journey to you! I'm going back to Istanbul." He returned there and asked again where a *sulkumnixhi* could be found. For he could not go home without one.

He went to a mountain to spend a night with the King of Spirits. "Will you take me in as your guest to-night?" he asked. "Yes, come in, and welcome to you!" they replied. They took him into the house itself, so honouring him. They then informed the King that a guest had arrived, and the King ordered him to be brought before him.

The merchant rose and went to the King, who said to him, "Why have you come here? No one ever comes here." The merchant replied, "I am in a difficulty about one of my daughters. She wants a *sulkumnixhi* and it cannot be found." "I have one," replied the King of

291

Spirits. "Stay a week with me and let's eat and drink, and then I'll give it to you." He kept him for a week, then gave him the *sulkumnixhi*, and said, "Here it is. And now a good journey to you!"

The king had a valet who looked after him. This man was a spirit and an *arap*. The King said to him, "Follow that merchant, and when the girl puts on the *sulkumnixhi*, catch her and bring her here." The *arap* followed the merchant. Being a shadow, he was invisible.

He followed the merchant and the *sulkumnixhi* all the way home. The merchant gave his elder daughters the cloaks they had asked for, cloaks stiff enough for the body part to dance while the sleeves played the drum. He gave his youngest daughter the *sulkumnixhi* and she put it on. But at that moment, the shadow seized her and no one saw him do it. He took her to the King.

The King married her. After she had lived five or six years with him, she got up from sleep one night and noticed that he had a lock on his stomach. She found the key and began to unlock it, saying to herself, "What does he have in his stomach?" But the valet who always stayed near the King, would not allow her to open the lock. "Don't, or I'll kill you," he said.

Next night she tried again, for she felt curious and wanted to see what there was behind the lock. But the valet held her back, saying, "Don't, or I'll kill you."

She tried again the third night and the *arap* said, "Don't, or he'll kill you." "Let him kill me," she replied and turned the key in the lock. She put in her hand and saw a market-place surrounded by shops. One man was making a child's cradle, a second was making swaddling bands, and some others were sewing clothes for the child she was about to bear.

She was amazed and locked it all up again. The King woke and said, "What have you done to me? Neither my father nor my mother ever opened my lock" He then gave orders to his valet, saying, "Take this woman, carry her up to the sky, and drop her so that she will be dashed to bits." The *arap* seized her and lifted her nearly up to the sun, where it was so hot that her hair almost caught fire. "What can I do?" the *arap* asked her. "I warned you, but you would not listen. Now I won't kill you, but I'll drop you from such a height that you'll be blinded in one eye." He dropped her gently and she lost the sight of one eye.

The *arap* went away, leaving her alone on the road. She did not know where to go. When a Kutzo-Vlach came by, she said to him, "Shall we exchange clothes?" "Yes, let's," replied the Kutzo-Vlach, "only your clothes are good and mine are no better than rags." "That doesn't matter," she replied. "Let's make the exchange." After she got the Kutzo-Vlach's clothes, she went away.

By dint of asking, she found her husband's house. She went to it and knocked on the door. A servant appeared. "Who's there?" he asked. "Night has overtaken me on my way. Please take me in for to-night," she replied. The servant opened the door, admitted her, and at once recognised her. He put her into a room apart.

He then went to the Queen Mother and said, "A Kutzo-Vlach woman has come. Let me wait up to-night." "All right, do," said the Queen Mother by way of consent.

At midnight God delivered the woman of a son who, like his father, had a lock on his stomach. The mother fondled her child, saying, "Your father would be furious if he knew that you were in this miserable room."

The servant went to the Queen Mother and reported this. "Come and look," he said. "The Kutzo-Vlach woman has given birth to a child." The Queen Mother rose and went to peep in at the door and heard what the young mother was saying to her baby. She opened the door and went in.

"Are you my daughter-in-law? Let me just look at the baby!" she said. One look was enough. She saw that he had a lock on his stomach. She rose to her feet immediately, carried the baby upstairs to a room all decorated with mirrors, and left him and his mother there, waiting for the King, her son, to come, from the special room in which he lived.

The King came towards his mother, who said to him, "What is worrying you, my son?" "My wife," he replied. "Why should she? You can easily find another wife. Come and see the one I've found for you,"

293

she replied. She took her son by the hand, her son who was the King, and led him upstairs to the room where his wife was.

She then said to the King, "Here is your wife and here is the son that God has given you. He has a lock on his stomach just as you do."

The King then gave a great party and they all rejoiced mightily that his servant had not killed the Queen.

The Girl Who Waked the Dead Man

Once upon a time there was a widow with an only daughter. The two lived together in a very poor hut.

The girl used to go to the front of the hut and sit there, working in the shade of a plum-tree.

One day when the girl was at work, a bird lighted on the plum-tree and sang, "Kirifiri, girl, kirifiri. You are destined to watch over a dead young man for three years." When the girl heard this, she ran into the house crying. "Dearest mother, did you not hear what the bird sang outside?" the girl said. "What bird, my daughter? What did he sing, my daughter?" replied the mother. In a trembling voice the girl told her what the bird had said. "It is nothing, my dove, it is nothing. You fancied it all. How could you hear the bird in your imagination?"

Her mother's words dispersed the doubts and fears in the girl's mind and she began to attend to the housework and to feel happy again, so that one wanted to keep looking at her and hearing her speak.

The following day the girl went outside again, this time to do her embroidery in the sweet spring sunshine. Before very long, our bird flew down as fast as lightning from heaven and began to sing again over her head, "Kirifiri, girl, kirifiri. You are destined to watch over a dead young man for three years." The bird sang this over and over again, and the girl cried and cried, then called, "Quick, mother, come and hear with your own ears and see with your own eyes! This bird is not like other birds and what he says must be heeded." The mother ran out but by the time she could look for it, the bird had become invisible. She heard what he sang, however, and, poor mother, she felt very sad.

She wanted to give her daughter courage and said, "Quick, daughter, don't be unhappy. And don't be afraid of what a bird says. Your friends will talk about you and make fun of you." But the girl was very worried and said in a faint voice like one suffering from apoplexy, "What can I say, mother? The Fairies have seized me. This bird did not come for nothing. Its words have a meaning, mother. God sent him to me." "My poor daughter!" exclaimed the mother with a sigh, "If the bird comes again to-morrow, there is nothing we can do except to bow to God's will."

Evening came and the night passed. Neither mother nor daughter ate anything in the evening or closed an eye during the night. They waited to see if on this, the third day, the bird with the gay plumage would sing the same sad song. At the very same minute as on the previous days the bird with its bright plumage arrived and began to sing the sad and sorrowful words, "Kirifiri, girl, kirifiri. You are destined to watch over a dead young man for three years."

The bird would not go away, but sang its sweet, sad melody and acted as though it wanted them to follow it. "Mother," called the girl, "look at the bird and listen to it! This is a sign from God. I feel in my heart that I should go with this bird. I cannot stay here any longer." "May God's will be done, my daughter!" returned the mother. "Praised be His name, and may He not let us perish. Let us get ready to go."

The bird did not go away but acted as if it was waiting for them, and sang the girl's song. Mother and daughter dressed before you could count three, put on iron sandals and, after praying to God, set out in the wake of the bird.

Here and there went the mother and daughter, following the bird closely, never looking back at their home. They reached a mountain which they had to climb. Both wailed aloud. Mighty mountains, dark forests – could man or woman cross them? They traversed them all. They crossed deserts – it seemed to them they were treading on cotton. Up and down, up and down they went, until they reached a forest of very tall trees.

There, mother and daughter felt terrified. Their hearts contracted with fear till they were as small as fleas. In the middle of the forest there was a small field – like the one at Pogradec, but covered with all sorts of flowers. In the middle of the field there was a vast palace, bigger than any ever built up to now and bigger than any that will ever be built to all eternity. The girl gazed at it and saw that the walls were silver outside but golden inside. Mother and daughter, beholding these wonders which are found only in tales, were dazzled and fell flat on their faces on the ground.

They did not stop to rest either a day or a night. How could they travel, you will ask, when it was dark? The bird became a star and, shining ahead of them, it showed them the way. As soon as sleep seized them, they awoke, but when they did so, the bird was no longer there. When they reached the door of a vast palace, they did not know what to do. They dared not knock. They came of distinguished ancestors, of glorious lineage, but such a door they had neither seen nor heard of.

Guided by a heavenly spirit, the girl finally knocked on the door with the golden hammer. Her heart was in her mouth. This hammer had been hung on the door expressly for knocking. As the girl knocked, the door opened. The girl entered and in a moment the door closed with great force as though pushed by invisible hands. The mother was left outside, while the daughter was shut up in the courtyard. She cried, and her mother cried, too. For this was an only daughter and her mother had lost her - how could she not be inconsolable? She felt so desolate, poor woman, that for a whole day she called out, "My daughter, my daughter!" She knocked, too, with all her might on the door, but it would not open. She called to her daughter to open it, but the girl could not hear her. The walls were so high that they could not hear each other.

At last the mother fell asleep from weariness. When she woke, she found herself at home. As she recalled all the wonders she had seen, she fell to her knees in prayer to God, invoking His name, imploring Him. "Take care of my daughter. As you took her away, so bring her safely home again. Life without my daughter is one long mourning for me."

Let us now see what happened to the girl. As soon as she entered the courtyard of the vast palace, the trees, the flowers, and the birds that were all around called to her with sweet melody, "Welcome to our mistress! Welcome to our mistress!" The girl was weeping but at length her face changed and, crying and smiling together, she replied,

"I am glad to be with you, dear ones. I am glad to be with you, beautiful ones."

She amused herself a little in the courtyard and was much amazed by the beauties she beheld. There were marble fountains – a host of them – there was a garden with many kinds of trees and sweet-smelling blue flowers. She was so happy that she forgot she was on earth. It seemed to her as though she was in the other world. Her heart led her to go into the house. She approached the door, whereupon its two halves opened, saying to her, "Welcome to our mistress!" The girl plucked up heart enormously. She began to realise that she was the mistress of the vast palace. By and by, the veil was quite lifted from her eyes. Her gaze grew wide, her carriage magnificent and proud like a Queen's. She entered a room, a second, a third, a fourth, a fifth, a sixth, and yet others. What did she see in the twelfth room? What she saw cannot be told. Anyone else would have gone out of her mind. The ceilings were of rare wood and blue, the nails with their golden heads were like stars, some larger, some smaller. The handle of the door was studded with diamonds. The three-legged chairs, the marble candlesticks, the pots, the trays – all were covered with silver and gold. So were the chairs and chests, the pegs and hat-racks, the tables and the plates, the beds with several kinds of mattresses, and the shining carpets.

The girl saw many thing that are not in our world. All greeted her as their mistress when they saw her, and bade her welcome. She entered the last room of all. And what did she see there?

A young man fallen from heaven was lying on a golden bed. And candles burned round him. The poor girl stood stock still in her amazement. But instantly fear left her heart like a cloud that is flown away. She remembered that the bird had prophesied that she should watch over this dead young man for three years. She went up to him and, after making the sign of the cross, kissed his breast, his forehead, and his right hand. She took a chair and sat down to keep watch over him. You will say, "Why should she guard him when the candles burned and were not consumed? When everything was all right?" But the dead must be watch because they become dust.

The girl with her beauty like a moon then said, "Where can I find incense, and where is the censer?" Instantly the incense and the censer were beside her. "Here we are, mistress," they said. When she set light to the incense, she undid her silken hair and let it fall to her shoulders. She tied a blue kerchief into the shape of a crown on her head. And she began to keen the dead with words so mournful that she made the household furniture wail and cry with longing for him. What did she not sing in her mournful dirge?

When she had wept until her eyes were swollen, she still did not understand the ways of the house. Exhausted and feeling ill, she said mournfully, "Where can the table be? And the bread and the cheese? The salt and the spoons? And the knife and the wooden water-bottle?" At once everything for which she had expressed a wish came to her of themselves.

When she had eaten, she wanted to clean the table. But what did she see? Everything began to go to its own place. Only the crumbs remained – unswept. "Where can the broom be?" asked the girl. The broom hopped across the room to the girl. When she tried to take it in her hand, the broom said, "Don't bother, mistress. I can sweep by myself." In three minutes the crumbs were swept up and thrown into the yard, where the birds ate them.

The girl no longer worried about her midday or evening meal. She uttered a single word and immediately what she wanted came. She had only one difficulty. With what? With sleep. For her watch was not for one, two, or even three days; it was for three years. The girl and the angels stood guard day and night by the dead youth's couch. Her eyes never closed for a minute and her face grew paler every day. How could she help growing pale? Poor thing! As one cannot live without food, so one cannot live without sleep.

The outside door of the courtyard called to the inside door to ask their mistress if someone who was knocking at the door should be admitted. From door to door the message was passed to the girl. She asked the big door if it was a good or a bad visitor. "A bad one," the reply came back. "What sort of visitor is it? Man or woman?" asked the girl. "A woman," was the reply. The girl stopped to think for a little,

299

and then said, "As it's a woman, what harm can she do me? For three years I haven't seen a human being or exchanged a word with a living soul. Welcome to this woman, who will help me to pass the time!"

She gave orders that the stranger was to be admitted. From door to door the visitor was passed, until she stood before her – a gypsy with clothes so threadbare and torn that there was no room for a dog to set his teeth in them. "Good morning, sister," she said. "Welcome, lady! I am glad God brought you here," the girl said. "I should say He did!" the gypsy returned. "As I went from town to town, I lost my way and took to the mountains. If I had not found this house, I should have died of hunger, and wild beasts would have eaten me."

"God does not leave anyone to perish," said the girl. "Thank you for letting me in and for not leaving me to get lost," said the gypsy, "but please do give me something to eat." "Wait a moment," the girl replied. The gypsy sat waiting. Before she could count three, the table was set before her by order of its mistress. The gypsy was astonished by the wonders she saw done. Though she was so hungry that she stuffed the food into her mouth with both hands, she hardly noticed what she ate, she was so surprised by the wonders she saw. She ate till she was full.

"I've had enough, sister," she said at length. "May you have my share of blessings. I have eaten so much that I shan't feel hungry if I have to go three months without eating. But, lady, may I stop with you here? You are so kind to me," said the gypsy. "I shall never forget your kindness. Shall I ever be able to repay you? But now tell me, who is this young man? Is he your husband or your brother? How did he come to die?" "He is neither my husband nor brother, sister," the girl replied. "What is he to you?" the gypsy asked. "Since you ask me, I will tell you, sister," the girl answered. "I will tell you all I have suffered and seen happen. Come closer and listen."

Angelically the girl began to tell her story from the beginning. With tears in her eyes she told how the bird from heaven had stuck to her and what she had suffered to that minute. She told the gypsy, the evil-minded creature, all she had been through. The wicked, black-hearted gypsy frowned as she listened to the story of the miracles and her eyes sparkled with joy when she heard that in three days' time the young man would come to life again.

"I am so dead tired, sister, that my eyes cannot keep open," the girl concluded. "Of course, you are dead tired. If you like, lie down and sleep a little," the gypsy said. "If you would stand guard over him while I take a nap, you would do me a great favour," said the girl. "Don't say another word about that, sister. You know what the trouble is?" said the gypsy. "No, what?" the girl returned. "Isn't it a sin and a shame that when I stand guard over this young man, this great gentleman, I should wear rags?" the gypsy explained. "What can we do? There are no other clothes in the house," said the girl. "If you are willing, lady, there is a way." "Why shouldn't I be willing, sister?" "I'll put on your clothes, and you'll put on mine, that's all," said the gypsy. "All? I have dedicated my life to this young man. Can't I give my clothes, too, for him?" the girl returned.

The pretty girl took off her own pretty clothes and put on the gypsy's rags. The ugly woman was delighted to put on the pretty girl's clothes. When she had put them on, she looked at herself and could not believe that it was herself. "Ah!" she said, "I won't part again with these clothes. From now on I'm not a beggar. I'm a great lady." The furniture heard what she said and was in despair. But the pretty girl heard nothing. She lay down to take a light nap only, but she fell into a heavy slumber because it was three years since she had slept at all. Not one or even two days did the poor thing sleep now. She slept three days in succession, showing no sign of life.

The afternoon of the third day, while she was still asleep, the young man stirred his limbs a little. The gypsy embraced him lovingly, then shook him, and said, "Get up, young man. You've slept long enough." The young man raised his hand, gave a little sigh, and said, "What a heavy sleep I have had! As though I'd slept in deep shade. I haven't shown a sign of life for twenty-four hours." "Ha, ha, ha! Only twenty-four hours?" laughed the gypsy. "What, longer?" said the young man. "I should say three years," said the gypsy. "Three years?" said the young man. "Have I been dead for three years? Is that the reason for the candles?" the young man asked. "Yes," the gypsy returned. "True, true,

301

fate's command was done," the young man said. "How was that? Do tell me, handsome young man," the gypsy begged. "I will," he replied. "My parents had any amount of worldly goods, as you can see, yet they were despairing and broken-hearted, for they had no children. They prayed to God to give them a son to keep the line from being broken. After many prayers and much fasting on their part, God heard their wish. Mother became pregnant and I was born. The third day after my birth, the Fates came to decree my doom. The eldest said, 'The baby shall grow to manhood, and when he is about to be engaged to be married, he shall die.' My mother overheard this, groaned heavily, but did not dare to utter a word. For things were always worse for those who overheard the Fates. The Fates knew this and pondered over it and swept such people off the face of the earth. It seems that the second Fate felt sorry about my doom and said, 'No, sister! Let him live and have a family, because his parents come of good stock and he is their only child. Perhaps they will never have another.' The eldest Fate was depressed and angry at this proposal. So the youngest Fate reflected for a moment, then said, 'Sisters, let there be no ill-will. I also think it reasonable to give the baby a better fate. He must die and remain dead for three years when he comes of an age to marry. After three years of death he shall come back to live. But his parents shall not kiss his marriage crown.' And so it was done. When I was old enough to marry, my parents were told by trustworthy friends of a widow living I don't know how many days' journey from here. She was of good family and had a daughter as fair as a star and as good as hot bread, milk, and honey. When my parents were about to send an engagement present, they died within a month of each other. I remember, too, that after a little I fainted and fell down here. I've been here for three years."

The young man then said to the gypsy, "You've heard of what stock I come. What about you?" The gypsy replied with the usual lies of a gypsy, "I am the daughter of a rich man. Destiny brought me here. For three years, I have been standing guard over you." The young man said to her, "Why do you have such a black face?" "Because I've suffered so much during the three years that I've been keeping watch over you," the gypsy replied. "All right then," said the young man, "this means that you are to be my wife." "It does," returned the gypsy.

The pretty girl was still asleep and had no idea what the black-faced gypsy was doing in order to marry the young man. The wedding took place and the guests left for their own homes. The young man then noticed the pretty girl. "Who is the woman that has stopped on here?" he asked his gypsy wife. "Oh, bless you, it's only a gypsy," his wife replied. "Let's send her to herd the fowl."

When the pretty girl awoke, she saw that the gypsy had appropriated her husband, but she dared not say anything for fear that the gypsy would kill her. They bought some geese and ducks and sent her out to herd them. The girl felt like committing suicide, but what could she do?

Easter was coming. The young man said to his gypsy wife, "Wife, what would the goose-girl like us to buy her for Easter?" "Oh husband, let the wolf eat her! What can she want? Bring her anything you can, and she will be pleased," his wife replied. "No, no," the young man said, "go and ask her what she wants."

The gypsy did not want to go so he got up and went to ask the girl himself. He found her crying, and looked closely at her. As soon as he saw her, he liked her, for she was the wife that God had ordained for him. "Never mind your crying now," the young man said. "What would you like to have for Easter, goose-girl?" "What should I like? Nothing," she replied. "No, no, say what you would like," he insisted. "I'd like," she replied, "and you must not forget to get them – I'd like a knife with three cutting edges, a whetstone with which to sharpen the knife, and a cotton rag with which to wipe the knife." "All right, you shall have them," he replied, "but what do you want such things for?" "I need them. Bring them," was all the answer she would make.

The young man went to market, bought all sorts of household necessities, but forgot the things she wanted. As soon as he left town, a heavy hailstorm came on, with each hailstone big enough to crack any head it fell on. The young man turned back and on reaching the hotel remembered the presents for the goose-girl which he had forgotten. He went at once and bought them. As soon as he had done so, the weather turned fine and he went home. He gave the goose-girl the three things for which she had asked.

When two or three weeks more had passed, the goose-girl went with the geese to the vicinity of the forest. There was a small lake there and the geese and ducks got into it and stayed there. The girl took the whetstone and knife and began to whet the knife. The weeping girl cried, "Be quiet, my heart, don't weep! Poor me, what shall I do? Shall I kill myself or not?" And she mourned as Christ's mother lamented for her son. From beginning to end she wailed her story aloud, because up to that day this had not happened to her.

After the young man had seen her for the first time, he wondered about her and said to himself, "Why, I wonder, did the goose-girl ask for these things?" One day he followed her when she drove out the geese. She went to the usual place and began to cry as before. The young man hid in a bush and listened to her crying. And she began to repeat her story aloud from the beginning. How the bird had come to her, how she had left her mother, how she had stayed three years watching over the young man, how the gypsy came and they exchanged clothes and she fell asleep – she repeated it all, point by point. The young man was much moved but said nothing to her and went home to think things over. His wife saw he was worried and said, "Husband, why are you looking so worried to-day?" "There's nothing the matter with me," he replied. Another day, however, he said to her, "Wife, I want to make the acquaintance of your people. Come along, take me to them, you know the way." "All right, I will," she said.

They walked along the road together. But she did not know how she had come because she had lost her way when she first arrived. So she led him into a forest, where they wandered backwards and forwards aimlessly. At last they returned to the road. There he said to her bluntly, "You are a gypsy and my wife's the girl who goes with the geese. What do you want? Two horses or a knife in your heart?" "Two horses," she replied. He tied her to the two horses and lashed them with a whip and they tore her in two. Then he married and had children by the goose-girl, the one who went through such suffering.

The King's Son Who Did Good to a Dead Man

Once upon a time there was a King, who had an only son. When the boy grew up, he said to his parents: "I say, dad! I say, mother! I want you very much to give me leave to go and seek my fortune!" "I won't let you go, son," said the King.

His son argued with them, saying, "I will go. I ask you only to give me a horse and ten pounds in money." They replied, "Our blessing then on you, son. Be careful and don't let any ill come to you." "I am not a child anymore," he answered.

When he was ready to leave, they remembered and said to him, "Ten pounds won't be enough for you. Take at least a bagful of gold." He refused their offer and, with only ten pounds in his pocket, set out to seek his fortune.

After leaving home, the young man travelled until he was overtaken by night near a cemetery. He tethered his horse and went to sleep among the graves. About midnight, he heard voices as he slept. He got up and went to see what was there. He found two men digging open the grave of a man who had been buried that day. The dead man had owed them money. The young man asked the men, "Why are you digging open this grave all night?" "He was in our debt," they replied. "Why don't you speak to his relatives instead of disturbing his grave? Can a dead man rise from the grave?" he asked. "He had no relatives," said they. "If that is so," he replied, "take these ten pounds of mine and go and leave him in peace. Though I've seen you digging him up, no one else has done so."

The young man returned home because he had no money left and had also torn his pocket. When his father and mother saw him, they said, "Oh son, you've been quick about seeking your fortune." "Please give me your blessing again, and also ten pounds more," he answered.

305

"My pocket got torn and I lost the first ten you gave me." "Son, it would be best for you to take a bagful of gold," his father said. But he would not listen, took only ten pounds, and once more left home.

Night again overtook him at the cemetery. He spent the night there and in the morning got up. As he prepared his horse to leave, the dead man rose from his grave. At first the young man was frightened, but he conquered his fear to some degree when the dead man said to him, "Don't be frightened! I shall never forget the good turn you did to me. Listen, from now on we are foster-brothers. We shall go wherever you please." "I will hold you very dear," the young man replied. Then they said together, "Let's go now." "Where shall we go?" the dead man asked. "I'm travelling for pleasure," the young man replied. "Whose son are you?" asked the dead man. "I am a royal prince," the young man replied.

Together they set out from the cemetery and journeyed on and on till they were benighted on a mountain. "Where shall we sleep?" asked the young man. "Don't be afraid, just wander about. I'll see to it that that house up there takes you in," the dead man replied. He pointed out a house on a mountain top which belonged to thieves. Indeed, forty thieves lived in it but he did not tell that to the young man.

So they went to the house and entered. The dead man ushered the young one into a room and said, "Stay here and sing. I'm going to shut the doors." "All right," said the young man. As soon as he was left alone, he began to sing. The dead man went out and took up his post on top of the outside door. The thieves saw a light in the house from a distance and said, "Whoever has gone into our house?" They hurried home to see. As they passed through the door, the dead man reached down from above and cut off their heads one by one. And so they died.

The dead man then returned to the young one, who said, "Where have you been, brother?" "Let's eat now. We are hungry," was all the dead man said in reply. When they had eaten, they lay down to sleep. But the dead man did not go to sleep. Instead, he lay awake to see that no one came. No one did. When day broke, he went the round of the rooms in the house. In some he found gold, and in others beautiful things such as one would expect to be found with thieves.

306

Just before they left the house, the dead man locked up all the rooms and took the keys with him when they started out. As they went outside, the young man saw all the men who had been killed and asked the dead man who they were. "Who knows?" the dead man replied. "Since you have me with you, don't be frightened. What a lot of good you will find me do you."

The two men travelled on until they reached Constantinople. "What shall we do here?" asked the dead man. "You came here for pleasure, didn't you?" "Yes, for pleasure," the young man replied. "Then let us go to the hotel," said the dead man. As they had taken a great deal of money from the house of the thieves, they enjoyed themselves very much. They then went to the coffee-house and tipped the waiters freely.

Once they were sitting in a coffee-house when they were seen by a King who had a daughter to marry. He said to his companions, "Who are these fine young men? It would be good to have one of them as a son-in-law." He called the coffee-house keeper and said, "Who are these men?" "Royal princes," the man replied. "Which is the older?" asked the King. "He is," said the coffee-house keeper, pointing to the dead man.

The King then sent the coffee-house keeper to ask them to come to see him in his palace because he wanted to talk to them. The coffee-house keeper carried the invitation to them. "We'll come next Friday. We haven't time now," they replied.

When Friday came, the dead man went to see the King. He was well received and afterwards the King said to him, "I like you and, God willing, I shall have one of you for a son-in-law." "God willing, you shall. Take my brother," the dead man replied. "I should like to," said the King, "only I am afraid. I have got her married twice and both times the bridegrooms were found dead next day." "Don't be afraid of anything," said the dead man. "God willing, this marriage will take place."

He got to his feet and returned to the hotel, where he said to the young man, "Brother, the King wants to marry his daughter to one of us. I cannot marry, but you are of an age to marry and must marry this

307

girl." "I won't displease you," the young man replied. "I will do what you wish. Betroth me."

The dead man went back to the King and said, "Good luck then. I have persuaded my brother. As for what you told me about your daughter, don't worry. I shall make her all right."

"I want," the dead man continued, "a golden knife and a pair of golden scissors, also your leave to be present in the room when the girl goes to sleep." All this was given him. When the girl went to sleep, a snake came out of her mouth and darted towards the bridegroom. But the dead man cut off its head with his golden knife. He did the same with two more snakes, and so the bridegroom escaped.

After the marriage, they spent about a week with the King. Then they said to him, "We must go now." The King then said to the dead man, "What do you want from me for saving my daughter?" "Nothing except twenty sacks and twenty horses and your leave to go," the dead man replied. The King gave him all this and saw the party off. Twenty horses carried the girl's trousseau and twenty horses belonged to the dead man. There were forty horses altogether.

They bade the King good-bye and left for home. On their way, they stopped at the thieves' house, where the dead man filled his sacks with gold. They continued on their way. The dead man's knees began to grow weak as they approached the grave. When they reached the cemetery, he said to the young man, "You really did do me a good turn, but I did you one, too. But for me, the thieves would have robbed you and the snakes would have bitten you. Now we must divide things. Either you take the girl and I the gold, or you take the gold and leave the girl to me." "As you please, we shan't quarrel over them," the young man replied. "Then it's best we should divide both the gold and the girl," the dead man said. As he spoke, he lifted his yataghan to cut the girl in two. Terrified, she let three snakes escape from her mouth for, though he had killed one set, she still had the head inside her. Then the dead man said to the young one, "All right, take both the gold and the girl. Long life and many children to you! And never hesitate to call me whenever you are in need."

308

The dead man vanished into his grave as he spoke. The young man took the girl, her trousseau and the gold, and went home to his parents. They were surprised to see the girl, but received both her and their son very well.

The Rich Pilgrim and the Poor One

Once a rich man made his mule ready, put a good deal of money in his purse, and set off on a pilgrimage to Mecca. As he came out of his house, a poor man met him and said, "I want to come with you, sir." The rich man said jestingly, "Splendid! But have you a beast to ride on? And have you brought a lot of money?" The poor man said, "I haven't either a beast or money. I mean to travel on foot." The rich man went on jesting till they reached a certain spot, and there he beat his mule and galloped away.

In the evening, the poor man slept in a village. When dawn broke, he miraculously found himself farther on than the rich man was. When the latter on his mule overtook him, he said, "Where did you sleep? Why did I not see you?" The poor man replied, "I slept in a village close by, and I started again this morning." The rich man said jestingly, "Where have you hidden your money? How much have you brought?" The poor man said, "It seems to me that you're joking. Don't you see me? I am poor, I haven't any luggage, I'm ill-shod, I couldn't be worse off! Where could I find money?" The rich man, having finished his jesting, struck his mule and galloped away.

After ten to fifteen days had elapsed, the poor man miraculously found himself near Mecca and met up with the rich man. Again the latter jested with him. They reached Mecca and, after doing their business, i.e. after completing the pilgrimage, they took to the road to return home.

After they had travelled three or four hours, the rich man saw ahead of his mule the poor man travelling barefoot. "A good journey!" said the rich man, and again began to jest with him, saying, "Did you do the pilgrimage? What did you think of it? Good or bad? And did you get a certificate that you had done it?" The poor man said regretfully,

"No, I did not get a certificate." Then he began to cry and wailed, "How did it happen that I tired myself out walking on foot all these days to get to Mecca and then wasn't given a certificate?" Still weeping, he turned back again to Mecca.

When he entered the sacred precinct, he prayed to God, saying, "Oh Almighty! Why did the rich man get a pilgrim's certificate while I, who am poor, did not? I pray Thee, grant me like the others a certificate." As he was praying, the good angel Gabriel came down from Paradise holding in his hand a certificate that was written in letters of gold. He gave this to the poor man and vanished.

The poor man took the certificate and kissed it. He closed his hand on it and, with a blessing on the rich man, hurried on his way.

That night, he reached a village where he slept in the mosque. Next day he found himself by a miracle ahead of the rich man. Looking back, he saw the rich man coming and stopped. "God forgive your sins," he said, "and God grant you a long life for what you said! I almost missed getting a pilgrim's certificate. There it is! Put it in your trunk. Put it along with yours." The rich man said, "Where is it? Let me see it." The poor man took it out of his shirt front and unrolled it. What should the rich man see? The sparkle of the gold lettering hurt his eyes and, struck by apoplexy, he fell from his mule and lay unconscious on the ground.

After two or three hours he came to himself and went to the poor man. He fell at his feet, begging him to forgive him. The poor man said, "What for? You did me a good turn." The rich man said, "I've often been in fault with you. Up to now I've only made fun of you. I didn't get a pilgrim's certificate. You have been beloved of God or you would not have had the luck to be given this certificate from Him." He begged the poor man to ride on the mule while he walked on foot. But the poor man said, "I'm not in the least tired. Ride on the mule yourself." In this way, they arrived home together. The poor man left the certificate in the rich man's trunk, because he had no place to keep it in.

Sometime later, when the rich man happened to be abroad, the poor man died. When the rich man came home, he looked for the pilgrim's certificate in the trunk, but he could not find it. Then he opened the poor man's grave, and found the certificate by his head.

[told by Shaban Hyseni, a teacher from the village of Plasa in the district of Korça]

Sultan Murat's Son

Once there were two young pickpockets. They went to the tailor, where one ordered a suit of clothes like those of Sultan Murat's son, and the other a suit like that worn by the Prince's adjutant. When the clothes came home, they embarked on a ship for Italy.

When they landed there, the captain of the steamer asked for their fare. The adjutant turned and said, "Who are you asking for money? Sultan Murat's son?" The captain said no more about his money, because people knew that Sultan Murat's son was very hot-tempered. As he was a well-known person, they were afraid of him. These men hadn't a single crown in their pockets, but lived by knavery.

When they landed in Italy, they went to the best hotel. The hotel-keeper made coffee for them, and sent it to their room. After they had drunk it, the Sultan's son broke the cups. The adjutant turned and said to the hotel-keeper, "Who did you make coffee for with those cups? For Sultan Murat's son?" Then he shouted at him violently, "Downstairs with you, pig!"

After a little, the adjutant went downstairs and said to the hotel-keeper, "Why did you make coffee with those cups? Don't you know that he is very hot-tempered?" "Poor me," said the hotel-keeper, "I did not recognise him." Then the adjutant said to him, "I'll make your peace with him, only you must give me 500 Napoleons." "All right," said the hotel-keeper. The adjutant took him to the room where his mate was, and made peace between them.

The King of Italy heard that Sultan Murat's son had arrived, and sent a couple of gendarmes to invite him to come and see him. The gendarmes went, but Sultan Murat's son would not hear of going to see the King.

313

"Good!" said the King of Italy. "Shall I go myself and see him?" The King himself set out to visit Sultan Murat's son in the hotel where he was. The King said to him, "I want to give you my daughter." "Grand," said the one who had made himself like Sultan Murat's son, "but I must see her first. Then if I like her, why not have her?" The King sent for his daughter, and she came. As she entered the room, she stumbled. The Sultan's son turned and said to the King, "Did you want to give me a lame girl?" "No," said the King, "she's not lame. She just stumbled in her shyness of you." "If that's so," said the Sultan's son, "good."

When the two pickpockets departed, they took the daughter of the King of Italy with them. The King gave them four steamers for their journey. The three embarked, and the steamers started straight for the palace of Sultan Murat.

The two young men talked together, saying, "What are we to do now?" "I know," said the adjutant. "You bid them stop the steamers for a little because your father knows nothing and you must let him know where you are. I'll go to Sultan Murat, and perhaps I can fix up something with him." "All right," said the other, the son of Sultan Murat. He shouted to the men, "Stop the steamer for a little! I want to let my father know where I am." Then the adjutant landed.

He set off to go to Sultan Murat, and said to him, "Look out of the window a moment!" The Sultan did so. "What are those steamer there?" he asked. "Please, we've done so-and-so. Either you save us or hang us." Sultan Murat laughed and summoned his wife and told her what the two pickpockets had done. Sultan Murat's wife said, "We have three sons. Let's make them four!" "All right," said Sultan Murat. And he sent three steamers to fetch them.

When they arrived, Sultan Murat greeted them with the rattle of musketry and the firing of cannons, and he adopted as his son the one who had called himself so. As for the other pickpocket, the so-called adjutant, he had some 800 Napoleons which he had made in Italy. With these he bought some eight shops and lived like a gentleman.

[told by Abdyrrahim Behluli, a teacher from Peqin]

The Three Liars

Once upon a time there were three liars in a town, who earned their living by telling people lies.

When some years had passed and the local people got to know their lies, they could not live there any longer because no one would believe anything they said. So one night they talked things over together. They decided to separate, each going to a different place.

Next day, as soon as it dawned, one of them left without telling the others where he was going. When he had travelled for some hours, he reached a large village. There he met some village elders who asked him where he came from.

"Where have you come from, dear brother?" said they. "From town," the liar replied. "What's the news there?" they asked. "Nothing," he said. "Only that a strong wind which blew this morning carried off all the donkeys in the town, and did not leave a single one in the place." At first the villagers were surprised by this news. But then they reflected that they would make a profit by selling their donkeys dearer. They then felt pleased that the liar had brought them this news and showed him into a room to spend the night.

About midday the second man arrived in the village, not knowing that one of his friends had arrived before him.

When the village elders saw this liar, they asked him, too, "Where have you come from, sir?" "From town," the liar replied. "What's the news there?" they asked. "Nothing," said this liar. "But we've been told that this morning a strong wind blew there and carried off all the donkeys," the elders said. The liar understood that one of his friends had been there and told them this lie. He decided to confirm the news and said to the elders, "That is so, but I did not happen to be there when the donkeys flew away. I saw their saddles falling down from the air, however. Now please show me a place to spend the night in."

When the villagers were convinced that the flight of the donkeys was true, they took the second liar to join their guest who had arrived that morning.

When the two liars saw each other, they pretended in front of the villagers to be strangers. After the villagers had gone, they questioned each other. "Where did you spring from?" said one. "Where did you spring from?" said the other. "I," said the first liar, "got here this morning and they asked me what was the news in town and I told them that a strong wind had blown and carried off all the donkeys in the town. Then the villagers brought me here and gave me food and drink. What did you say when they questioned you?" "I," said the second liar, "said when they asked me for news, that I had no news. When they told me what you had told them about the donkeys flying away, I replied that I had not seen them flying but that I was present when the saddles fell down from the sky." "Now, now," said the first liar, "you've confirmed my lie." "Yes," replied the second liar. "If I hadn't, we could not survive these days."

By dusk all the villagers had gathered in the church-yard and were commenting on the news from town, talking about how the donkeys had flown away and the saddles had fallen from the sky. At this moment, another man arrived and said, "Good evening, Gentlemen!" "Good evening and welcome, sir," the villagers replied. "How are you all?" "Quite well. And you, sir, how are you? Where do you come from?" "From town," the man said. "Ah! You do? What's the news there?" the villagers asked. "Nothing," he replied. "But we heard that the donkeys had all flown away and that their saddles had fallen from the sky. Isn't this true?" said the villagers.

As the third liar was even cleverer than the other two, he understood that his friends must have been in the village and invented this lie. He said to the villagers, "Oh, that's true. I was there when the donkeys flew away and when their saddles fell from the sky. But please find me a place where I can sleep to-night." The villagers were glad that the flight of the donkeys was true and they took the man to spend the night with the two others.

When the other two saw their friend, they inquired whether the villagers had asked him about the flight of the donkeys and his own reply. He said, "When the villagers asked me what was the news, I replied that what you had said was all true and that I had seen it with my own eyes. Be quiet now. I confirmed all that you said."

"Very good," said the two first arrivals. "From now on let's do this. One of us will go to a village and tell a lie. The second one will follow him and confirm what he said. About dusk the third one will go and confirm still further the lie told by the first two. In this way we think we shall get on very well."

That night, the villagers, happy in the thought that next day they would sell their donkeys in town for a bigger price, took very good food to the liars. The villager who was gladdest of all, took them a *gjysleme*. The liars had a great feast when they had supper. Never before had they eaten such good food. But they did not touch the *gjysleme* because they could not hold any more.

The first liar said to his friends, "I say, we can hold no more. Let's leave the *gjysleme* till to-morrow. Then whichever of us gets up to-morrow and tells the biggest lie, shall have the *gjysleme*." "So be it," said the others. All three then went to bed.

After three or four hours the third liar got up, found the *gjysleme* and ate it all. Then he went to sleep again.

Next day, after they all got up, the first liar asked his companions what they had dreamt. They replied that since he had been the first to arrive in that village, it was up to him to speak first. So he began his story. "Friends," he said, "I had a horrid dream. I dreamt that I was going up to God. Up and up and up I went. You can't imagine how high I went."

"What about you?" they said to the second liar. "What did you dream about?" "I dreamt," he said, "that I was going down, down, down, and I was very concerned about how I was to get up again. I was afraid that if I went on going down, down, I might arrive in hell."

The third liar then spoke. "You've both had really very bad dreams," he said. "But mine was even worse than yours." "Speak up, speak up!" entreated his friends. "Well, as I lay asleep, I dreamt that we were all three somewhere together, but you went away and left me alone. You," he said turning to the first liar, "went up ever so high into the sky. You," he said, turning to the second liar, "went down and down. I was left alone and wept because you had gone away without taking me with you. Suddenly I remembered the *gjysleme* and I said to myself, 'Since you've gone so far away, who knows when you'll come back? Dear, dear, the *gjysleme* will go bad. Hadn't I better eat it?' So I set to and ate it all. It gave me a tummy ache, but what could I do? Should I have left it to go bad? If you don't believe me, look at the tray at the end of the room."

When they saw the tray empty, the other two liars were very sorry at not having scrounged even a crumb from the *gjysleme* which was so good. With one voice they said, "Brother, you have ruined yourself. We don't want you as our friend anymore because you've stung us just like other people."

So the liars parted company that very morning. Each one went about his business. Each understood that it was impossible for them to live by lying.

This is not a story, but I have lied to you as much as I wanted.

318

The Muslim and the Christian – Albanians Both

Allah in his greatness, having created the world, made men also. Afterwards men multiplied and became divided into many races. God in his greatness recognised only four of these races – the Turks (or Muslims), the Infidels (or Christians), the Jews (or Israelites), and the Pharaonics (or Gypsies).

God in his greatness wished to give each of these four branches of the human race something that they desired. He graciously summoned the Turk first and said to him, "What do you want me to give you?" "An easy life," replied the Turk, and Allah granted him this.

God summoned the Christian after the Muslim and said to him, "And what do you wish me to give you?" "An easy life," said the Infidel. "Oh!" said God, "the Turk has got that." "Oh, what a business for us!" exclaimed the Christian. "All right, a life of business be yours!" said God. From that day to this, the Infidels are busy working, for the Turk's got the easy life.

The Infidel gone, God called the Jew and said, "And what do you want me to give you?" "An easy life," said the Jew. "The Turk has got that," God replied. "What a business for us!" said the Jew. "The Infidel has got business," God said. "Oh dear, what's all this give and take?" exclaimed the Jew. "All right, the give and take of money-changing be yours for all your life!" said God. And that trade the Jews have up to this day.

Last of all, God summoned the Pharaoh and said to him, "And what do you want me to give you?" "An easy life" said the Pharaoh. "The Turk has got that," God replied. "Oh dear, what a business for us!" the Gypsy explained. "The Infidel has got business," God said. "What's all this giving and taking?" asked the Gypsy. "The Jew has got the give-and-take of exchange," God said. "What's this knavery?" said the

319

Pharaoh. "All right, yours be the knavery!" said God. And knaves the Gypsies are to this day.

[told by Xhevdet Shehri, a teacher from Bitincka in the district of Devoll]

The Baldhead and the Crow

A Baldhead still had his father alive, and was given many lessons by him. He was very much a ne'er-do-well.

One day he passed by the church, and found a dead man being buried. "Good speed to your work, men!" he called to the mourners. "No speed to you, Baldhead!" they retorted. "Poor me, what ought I to say?" he asked. "You ought to say 'God give you strength to bear it!'" they replied.

Poor man, he set out once more on his way. He met a wedding party with a bride, and said, "God give you strength to bear it, men!" They beat him up.

Poor man, he went on his way crying and found a crow ill from the cold. He picked it up, put it in his bosom, and went to a house to sleep. When near the house, he called out, "Oh master of the house, will you let me come in for to-night?"

The woman would not let him come in, because her lover was inside. The Baldhead began to cry, and after a time they let him come in.

Two hours after dark, the husband came home. "How dreadful! He will find me!" exclaimed the lover, and the woman hid him in the horse's manger.

The master of the house asked the Baldhead what he had in his bosom. The Baldhead replied, "Don't ask me! It's a fortune-teller. Just speak to it and it will tell you what is happening." He squeezed the crow and it squawked.

The husband asked it, "What news is there? Tell us!" The crow replied, "There's a man in the horse's manger." When the husband went to the horse's manger, the woman opened the door and the lover ran away.

The husband asked her who it was. "A bad man who wants to steal your horse," she replied.

The husband bought the crow from the Baldhead. The latter warned him, "Don't let anyone throw water in its eyes, or it won't talk."

Later on, the lover went back to the woman. She exclaimed, "Don't come near me! My husband has bought a crow, and it talks. If you can throw water in its eyes, I'll let you come in.

The lover went and threw water in the crow's eyes. The crow caught his hand and cried *gaw, gaw, gaw*.

The master of the house heard it and said, "Stick to him! Don't let him go!" But he ran away, crow and all.

The husband called to the Baldhead, "Stay here and take your money. I want to give you more still." The Baldhead replied, "They have thrown water in the crow's eyes, and now it won't speak." The husband retorted, "Stay here anyway! I'll give you something extra as well." But the Baldhead departed, saying, "Wish me luck with what you've given me."

[told by Preng Bardhoku of the village of Gurëz-Bushkash in the district of Mat]

322

The Ogre at the Spring

Once upon a time, an ogre rose out of the King's spring and obliged the King to send a person to him every day to eat.

When the time came, the King sent his daughter. The young Saint George, passing by the spring, found the girl in tears and stopped beside her. She said, "What do you want here? Now the ogre will eat us both. Do go away." He then said, "Since your father has sent you here for the ogre to eat, I'll stay with you. The ogre can eat the three of us, counting my horse."

The boy sat down and, after bidding the girl look at his head, fell asleep. Afterwards, when the girl saw the water ruffled by the ogre as it came to the surface, she wept and did not want to wake the boy, because she pitied him. As she cried, her tears fell on his head, and he awoke. The ogre came out of the water and said, "God be thanked! Every day I've had one person to eat, and to-day I have three!" The boy called out, "Open your mouth wide so that we can all three get in at once." It opened its mouth, and the boy struck it with a club and killed it. All three were saved.

Then the boy cut off the seven tips of the ogre's tongues. That done, he told the girl to go home now. She did so, and told her father what had happened. He replied, "Why did you come away? Now the ogre will destroy us." The girl replied that a boy had killed the ogre and taken the seven tips of its tongues.

Then the King called all the people together so that the girl might recognise the boy. But he was not there. Another boy had secretly gone to cut off the other seven tips of the ogre's tongues, for the King had issued a proclamation that he would give his daughter and as much money as the bridegroom wanted to the man who had killed the ogre.

When this other boy produced the seven tips of the tongues, the girl said it wasn't he.

Next day, Saint George came at the gallop of his horse. From the palace window, the girl recognised him while he was still far off, and said to her father, "There's the boy who killed the ogre!" The King went out to meet him and said, "Now I want to give you my daughter and as much money as you want." Saint George produced the seven tips of the tongues and gave them to the King, but replied, "Thank you, I won't have your daughter and I have no use for money. Give your daughter in marriage to anyone you wish." With that he went away.

[told by Nikollë Gjetë Coku of Bregu i Matës in the district of Lezha]

The Vineyard

Once upon a time there was a man who had three sons and a vineyard. He divided the vineyard into three parts so that his sons could each have one when he died. And he said to his sons, "My boys, I am dying. I have nothing but a vineyard and I have divided it into three portions. If you don't get on together as well as brothers should, you can each take a portion and separate." With that, the old man died.

The brothers soon began to quarrel. At last one said, "Let's separate." "Let's," the others agreed. "It's easy. We have nothing but a vineyard and father divided that." So they separated, each taking his share.

Vintage time came and the vineyard was full of grapes. The eldest brother went to the vineyard and filled a basket with grapes from the youngest brother's portion. Passers-by asked him for grapes and he fetched some from the youngest brother's portion and gave them away. Then he took his basket and went home.

Next day the second brother went to the vineyard and he, too, gathered all the grapes he wanted from the youngest brother's portion and went home.

The youngest brother's wife said to him, "Go to the vineyard and bring me some grapes." "All right, I will," he said. And next day he went to his own portion of the vineyard.

A wayfarer came by and said to him, "Give me a bunch of grapes." "I will," he replied. He went to cut a bunch for him but the wayfarer said, "I don't want that bunch. I want that one," pointing to one in his brother's portion. "I can't give you that one," he replied. "It belongs to somebody else. If you want a bunch from this side, I can give it to you." "What about it?" said the wayfarer. "It wouldn't be a crime to take a bunch of grapes." "That's somebody else's property and I'm

325

not touching somebody else's property," the youngest brother said. "Then give me any bunch you like," the wayfarer said. The youngest brother picked a bunch and gave it to him. "You're very welcome to the grapes," he said as he placed the fruit before the man.

The bunch was so small (like a hand) but as the wayfarer began to eat the grapes, it grew so big (like a span). When he had finished the bunch, he rose to go. "God grant you increase of grapes!" he said. "Wait a little. I want to come with you," the youngest brother replied. "All right, come along," the wayfarer said.

They travelled together up to a certain point. There the wayfarer stopped and said, "Enough, young man! Where are you going? You ought to go home." "I won't. I'm coming with you," the young man replied. "You can't keep up with me," the wayfarer said. "I can," the young man insisted. "Then come along," he said. And they continued their journey.

On and on they went till they reached a road which was a blind alley. "Take that road and see how it is," said the wayfarer. The young man walked along the road up to a certain place, where he met another young man riding and dressed like a royal prince. When the newcomer saw him, he got off his horse at once and embraced him. "How are you?" he asked. After they had exchanged greetings, our young man said, "Who are you, sir? I don't know you." "But I know you. Don't you recognise me? If you can answer my twelve riddles, I will dig up a pot of hidden treasure for you." The young man replied, "Go and fetch the treasure. I'll tell you later about the riddles." But the newcomer said, "Oh no, I can't fetch it."

And what did the Devil do then, for the Devil it was. He dug a big, deep hole and put the young man into it. He then covered the hole with a rock to keep him from getting out.

His friend waited for him on the road. "Why is he so late?" he asked himself and entered the blind alley. After walking some distance he found the young man in the hole. "What are you doing here?" he asked. "A man dressed like a prince knew I was, say, Hysejn," the young man replied. "He said to me, 'If you can answer my twelve riddles, I'll bring you a gold treasure.' And I replied, 'I can answer the riddles. Go and fetch the treasure.'" His friend then said, "Do you know what reply to make to him?" "No, I don't," he said. His friend removed the rock that covered the hole, pulled out the young man, and said, "Come out and hide behind that tree and I'll get into the hole." He was as good as his word and got into the hole.

The Devil came, bringing a sack full of gold. "I've brought the gold. Now answer my riddles!" he said to the man in the hole.

"What riddles do you want me to answer?" he asked.

"The first," the Devil replied, "is, 'Who is he?'"

"Your master is behind you," the other replied.

"What is the answer to the second question?"

"The goat has two horns, and your master is behind you," was his reply.

"What about the third one?"

"The balance has three legs, the goat has two horns, and your master is behind you," was the reply.

"What about the fourth?"

"The cow has four teats, the balance has three legs, the goat has two horns, and your master is behind you," was the reply.

"What about the fifth?"

"The hand has five fingers, the cow has four teats, the balance has three legs, the goat has two horns, and your master is behind you," was the reply.

"What about the sixth?"

"There are six bright stars, the hand has five fingers, the cow has four teats, the balance has three legs, the goat has two horns, and your master is behind you," was the reply.

"What about the seventh?"

"There are seven planets, there are six bright stars, the hand has five fingers, the cow has four teats, the balance has three legs, the goat has two horns, and your master is behind you," was the reply.

"What about the eighth?"

"A bitch has eight teats, there are seven planets, there are six bright stars, the hand has five fingers, the cow has four teats, the balance has three legs, the goat has two horns, and your master is behind you," was the reply.

"What about the ninth?"

"A woman carries her child nine months, a bitch has eight teats, there are seven planets, there are six bright stars, the hand has five fingers, the cow has four teats, the balance has three legs, the goat has two horns, and your master is behind you," was the reply.

"What about the tenth?"

"A mare carries her foal ten months, a woman carries her child nine months, a bitch has eight teats, there are seven planets, there are six bright stars, the hand has five fingers, the cow has four teats, the balance has three legs, the goat has two horns, and your master is behind you," was the reply.

"What about the eleventh?"

"A buffalo cow carries her calf eleven months, a mare carries her foal ten months, a woman carries her child nine months, a bitch has eight teats, there are seven planets, there are six bright stars, the hand has five fingers, the cow has four teats, the balance has three legs, the goat has two horns, and your master is behind you," was the reply.

"What about the twelfth?"

"The year has twelve months, a buffalo cow carries her calf eleven months, a mare carries her foal ten months, a woman carries her child nine months, a bitch has eight teats, there are seven planets, there are six bright stars, the hand has five fingers, the cow has four teats, the balance has three legs, the goat has two horns, and your master is behind you," was the reply.

"And now may you burst and lie dead on your back!" the man in the hole shouted, and the Devil burst and died.

The man in the hole then came out and called the young man. "Come here and take the money. Did you hear how I replied to him?" he asked. "I heard you muttering something but I did not understand anything," the young man replied. "Take the money and go home," the wayfarer said. "There will be no end to your vineyard, either in winter or in summer." For our young man had a kind heart.

Lefkanili

Once there was a husband and a wife, who had a daughter whom they loved very much. After a long time, the girl's mother died and her father married again.

She was a good girl, and very pretty, too. In fact, she was so good and pretty that her step-mother took a great dislike to her. One day the step-mother said to the servants, "Take that girl away to the woods and let wild beasts eat her." The servants felt very sorry for her, but they could not disobey their mistress. They took the girl away to a mountain, left her there, and themselves came back.

The wretched girl was left alone. In her fear she cried with great sobs. Then she saw three pigeons and followed them. Before she had walked very far, she saw them enter a house. She went in after them, but they did not see her, and she hid.

They were no pigeons, they were three young men who became pigeons when they went out so as not to be recognised by people. In the same way, they never told their names.

When they had gone out, the girl swept the house, cooked food, baked bread and fetched water, etc. After she had done all this, she laid the table, putting on it food, bread, water, and many other things. When the young men came home, they were surprised to see the table laid, the house swept, etc., and they said, "Somebody has come into our house. If it is a boy, we'll adopt him as a brother. If it is a girl, we'll adopt her as a sister."

When next they went out, they left the oldest brother behind to watch and see who it was. But the girl saw the young man and did not appear. The young man waited for an hour, indeed for two hours, but the girl did not appear. Then he went to join his brothers. As soon as the girl saw he had gone, she came out, did all the work, and again hid.

329

After a little while the young men arrived, and were again surprised to see the house clean. As they saw the eldest brother could not catch the girl, they left the second brother behind. But the same thing happened to him as to the eldest brother, that is to say, he saw she would not appear, and he went away.

At last, the youngest son, whose name was Lefkanili, stayed at home, hiding behind the door. The girl did not notice him and came out to do her work. The moment he saw her, he caught her, saying, "You are my sister." And from that time on, she lived with the three brothers as their sister. Lefkanili and she grew very fond of each other and after a little while, they decided to get married, and did so.

When the girl's step-mother learned that she was living very happily, she became jealous. She dressed like an old woman to keep the girl from recognising her, left home and, going to the girl's house, said to her, "I'm an old woman, girl. Do ask your husband to-night what his name is." The girl was taken in and asked him. He said, "I'll tell you, but I'm afraid you'll tell somebody. If you do, I shall have to go away – a three years' journey away – and you will have to search for me with iron clothes and iron shoes, and you will have great difficulty in finding me."

The girl did not believe this and told the old woman his name. When she went back to the sitting-room, she found that Lefkanili had gone. She therefore put on a suit of iron clothes and a pair of iron shoes and started to look for him. For a whole year she had been travelling when she came to the house of a *kulshedra*. She went in and asked the *kulshedra* where Lefkanili's house was. The *kulshedra* replied, "I don't know, but my sister does. Here's a gold apple for you, and now go."

The girl took the apple and went away. After she had travelled for another year, she went to the second *kulshedra* and asked her where Lefkanili's house was. Like the first *kulshedra* this one replied, "I don't know, but my sister does. Here's a gold distaff for you, and now go."

The girl took the distaff and went away. It was the third year she had been travelling. When it was ending, she reached the house of the third *kulshedra* and said the same to her as she had said to her sisters.

This *kulshedra* told here where the house was and said, "Here's a gold broody hen and chickens for you, and now go."

After taking the hen and chickens, the girl went away. She stopped at a fountain, near which was Lefkanili's door. He had married another girl. After staying a little at the fountain, the girl got up and went to Lefanili's wife. "Is it possible for me," she asked, "to stay with you to herd the geese?" "Yes," replied Lefkanili's wife, "stay."

When Lefkanili's wife saw the gold apple, she asked for it. The girl replied, "I'll give it to you if you let me sleep a night in Lefkanili's room." His wife took the apple and gave her leave to sleep in his room. The girl put opium into the food he was to eat in the evening, to make him sleep. As soon as Lefkanili had had his supper, he went to his room to sleep, and fell asleep as soon as he lay down.

The girl went to his room and, crying all the time, said in a sorrowful voice, "Lefkanili dear! Where are you, dear? For three years I've looked for you, dear. With iron clothes and iron shoes, dear!" Having said this three times, she went away.

The servants were very much touched when they heard the girl say all these moving words to Lefkanili, and they waited for their master to awake to tell him about them. After a little he got up, and they told him. He suspected it must have been his first wife, but he said to the servants, "You've fancied this."

The next night his wife asked the girl for the gold distaff, and the girl replied as before. His wife took the distaff and let her go to Lefkanili's room. She went there, said the same words as before, and again went away.

The third night Lefkanili's wife took the gold hen and chickens, and the girl went to Lefkanili. That night the servants said to him, "Don't eat to-night if you want to hear what she says. She puts opium into your food to make you sleep." Lefkanili did as they said.

During the night the girl came and began to weep, saying, "Lefkanili dear! Where are you, dear? For three years I've looked for you, dear. With iron clothes and iron shoes, dear!" When she had said this three times, he got up and caught her, saying, "Do you see that I

331

really did go away? Why did you break your promise and tell my name?"

In spite of this, Lefkanili left his second wife and again married this girl. So they really suffered very much, but from now on they led a very happy and prosperous life together, and the step-mother did not get her wish for this girl.

[told by Aleksandër Xhufka of Elbasan]

The Priest and the Baldhead

There was once an old man, who had one daughter and three sons, one of whom was a Baldhead. Before he died, he left orders with his sons to give his daughter to any man who asked for her.

After a time a priest came and asked the young men for their sister. They gave him the girl in accordance with the orders left them by their father. The priest was a rich person, with farms and flocks.

Two or three months after the marriage, the brothers began to long to see their sister. So one day, the eldest got up and said to his mother, "I'd like to go to my sister's to-night." When his mother gave him leave to go, he set off and went straight to the priest's house.

The priest received him well. He killed a sheep for him and made some other dishes also as was the custom at that time. But when supper was brought in, they had not eaten more than two or three mouthfuls before the priest said to his wife, "Wife, we've had enough, and our guest has had enough. So take away the table, wife." Without delay, his wife caught the table and removed it, leaving her brother without food.

The priest himself did not stay without food. As soon as he saw that they had all gone to bed, he got up and went in the darkness of the night to the cupboard to eat like a madman.

The wife's brother, who had remained fasting, got up in the morning and without meeting either the priest or his sister, went home. When he came within earshot of the house, he called out to his mother in a loud voice, "I say, mother, make a dish of buttered maize. I'm dying for food." As soon as his mother heard him, she made the food and when he went into the house, he found it ready. After he had eaten it, he swore to his mother, "So long as the priest is alive, I shan't go to see my sister again."

333

After two or three months more, the second brother got up and went to see his sister at the priest's. He, too, had the same experience as his brother. As soon as supper was laid on the table and they had eaten two or three mouthfuls, the priest bade his wife remove the food. And he, like his brother, got up early the following morning and left for home. On getting near the house he called out to his mother in an even louder voice than his brother's that he wanted food.

When the girl had been married for a year, the youngest brother, who was called the Baldhead, got up to go and see her. He was a shepherd and a hunter. So before setting off for the priest's, he took three retrievers, his shepherd's sack and his gun with him, and set off straight for the priest's house.

For him, too, the priest killed a sheep and made some other dishes, as he had done for his brothers. When supper was laid, the priest, as before, bade his wife remove the food. But the Baldhead said, "You may get up if you like, but I'm going on eating." He sat on alone at the table and finished all the food, eating some himself, filling his sack and feeding the dogs. He did not leave a single mouthful for the priest to eat during the night.

When they had all lain down to sleep, the priest got up and went to the cupboard to eat, but he did not find a single mouthful and roused his wife to make a sort of porridge for him to eat.

The Baldhead stayed awake and heard what they said. When his sister put the pot on the fire to make the porridge, he sat up in bed and said, "What are you doing, sister?" "Putting on the pot to wash clothes," she replied. He then got up from bed and said, "That's fine. I've my drawers to wash." Taking them off, he threw them into the pot and mixed them up with the porridge.

Then he went back to bed and pretended to fall asleep. The priest thought that he had really fallen asleep and, his bowels rumbling with hunger, he bade his wife make a loaf and bake it in the hot ashes of the fire.

When she had made it and put it on the fire, the Baldhead got up and asked his sister what she was doing. She replied that she was lighting the fire because day was breaking. He took the tongs and said to her, "Oh, sister, to-night I dreamed that I was separating from my brothers. One said, 'We'll divide the land like this,'" – he cut the loaf in two with the tongs. "The second said, 'No, like this,'" – he cut the loaf in four. "And I said, 'Like this,'" – and he stirred the bits of the loaf in among the ashes.

When the loaf was lost among the ashes, the priest's bowels rumbled louder than ever. So he said to this mother to ask his wife what time the Baldhead got up in the morning. His wife replied that he got up when the cuckoo sang. The priest then made his mother climb a mulberry tree that they had in the courtyard, and begin to sing like a cuckoo.

The Baldhead, hearing her, got up, took his gun, went to the loop-hole in the wall opposite the mulberry tree, and fired on the priest's mother. When the priest's wife came in and said, "You've killed the priest's mother!" he replied that she shouldn't have climbed the mulberry tree.

When the priest saw that nothing came of this device either, he got up and went to the garden to eat leeks. But as soon as the Baldhead saw him go out to the leeks, he took his gun and, firing at him as if he were a wild boar, killed him outright. When his sister said to him, "You've killed the priest!" he replied, "He was a boar and not a priest."

The Baldhead then collected all the sheep and goats the priests had had, and returned home with his sister. He danced about and played the flute all the way home.

[told by Hajdar Biçoku of Elbasan]

The Vixen and the Wolf

Once a thorn stuck in Mrs Vixen's foot. When she got it out, she gave it to the baker and bade him take care of it. If he lost it, she said, she would have a loaf for a thorn. And the baker took the thorn.

Two days later, Mrs Vixen went to the baker and asked him for it. But the baker said, "I've lost it." The vixen then took a loaf, saying to the baker, "Didn't I tell you that if you lost the thorn, I'd take a loaf?"

After this, Mrs Vixen went to an innkeeper, gave him the loaf, and charged him to keep it in the bread-box. If he ate it, she said, she would have a filly for a loaf.

One fine day, the innkeeper noticed that the loaf was getting dry and, thinking that the vixen had forgotten it, waited no longer but took it out of the bread-box and ate it.

Next day Mrs Vixen came to the innkeeper and asked him for it. But the innkeeper said, "A mouse ate it." "Well done, mouse!" said Mrs Vixen. "All the same, bring me the filly, as we arranged." And the innkeeper brought her the filly.

After the vixen got the filly, she went home and left the filly there, saying, "You stop here. I'm going to fetch you fresh grass." And she charged her, saying, "Don't open the door unless they say, 'Filly, filly-o, open the door to Mother.'" With these instructions she shut the door and went away.

In the bazaar the vixen bought all sorts of things – salt, fresh grass – and came home and knocked at the door, saying, "Filly, filly-o, open the door to Mother." And the filly opened it. The vixen went inside and gave the filly food. Then she went away to steal something or other, saying the same words as before to the filly.

By bad luck, it happened that the wolf was near and heard what she had said. As soon as she went away, he came and knocked at the door, saying, "Filly, filly-o, open the door to Mother." And the filly was deceived and opened the door. The wolf flung himself on her and ate her up. He then filled the skin with stones, hung it up on the roof-beams, and went away.

After a little while, the vixen returned with grass and water for the filly. When she went inside, she saw the skin hung up and at once knew that the wolf had played her this dirty trick. She swore to take revenge.

One fine day, she sent the wolf an invitation to lunch. "Are you having a party, Mrs Vixen?" he asked. "No, Mr Godpapa. I'm not having a party, but I want to invite you. I suddenly thought of it," she replied. And Mr Godpapa did not disappoint her, but went to her house.

Before the wolf arrived, the vixen put several pots of water on the fire, and made a hole under the place of honour beside the hearth and flung a rug over the hole to keep it from showing.

As soon as Godpapa Wolf stepped inside the door of the house, he said to the vixen, "What have you made for us, Mrs Vixen?" "I've made you a little dove's flesh, a little bird's flesh, and a little wood-pigeon's flesh," she replied. And she added, "Godpapa Wolf, sit down in the chimney corner, as men guests do."

As he sat down where she bade him, the wolf fell into the hole. To make sure of killing him, the vixen flung over him the pots of hot water that she had ready beside the fire. The poor wolf screamed inside the hole and said, "What have you done this to me for, Mrs Vixen?" She said, "Bad luck to you! Do you not remember that filly of mine that you ate?"

Mrs Vixen then said to the wolf, "Do you know what to do, Godpapa Wolf? Go and roll on a heap of salt or in a lime pit and you'll be better at once." The wolf sprang out of the hole and went to do as she had said.

One day soon afterwards, Mrs Vixen saw a priest riding, with a bag full of sacramental loaves behind him. She jumped up on the crupper and gently untied the bag. Then she took out the loaves one by one, and flung them on the ground until she had emptied the bag. She then jumped off the horse and picked up the loaves she had scattered.

337

As she gathered them into a heap, she saw the wolf coming, all white with lime and looking like a ghost.

As soon as he saw the heap of sacramental loaves, he asked the vixen for a few of them. But she said, "They're not enough for me." Then the wolf said to her, "Where did you find them, Mrs Vixen?" And she said, "As I went along the road, some priests in a church I passed were calling out, 'Lord have mercy upon us! Lord have mercy upon us!' And I went in and called 'Lord have mercy upon us! Lord have mercy upon us!' and they gave me these sacramental loaves."

The wolf went to the church and began to call out with all the strength he possessed, as was his way. At once the dogs attacked him and bit him and made him all blood.

The poor wolf went limping to the vixen and said, "This time, too, you've played me a nasty trick, Mrs Vixen." "How so, Godpapa Wolf?" "Don't you know? I went to the church as you bade me, and began to call out like the priests. But that very moment, the dogs attacked me, and they bit me and made me all blood."

"Oh, Godpapa Wolf, how stupid you are! I did not tell you to stay outside the church. I told you to go in beside the priests. Then they would have given you the sacramental loaves."

[told by Pjetër Dashi of Elbasan]

338

The Three Girls and an Old Woman

Once an old woman and her daughters lived in a town. The girls were very pretty and dowered with every good quality.

The old woman was called Ilmiha, the eldest girl Hava, the middle one Ziliha, and the youngest one Zerhane.

One day, like the poor people they were, they went out into the courtyard and talked with each other about their needs. They hadn't even a brother to help and protect them if anyone spoke ill of them. So they never left their house.

One day, hearing a great noise, the three went to the door. At that moment the son of the King of that country passed. He was called Ismail and was very handsome and attractive. There was nothing wrong with them either, the three being as beautiful as mountain partridges.

The King's son liked them and looked closely at them, like a crazy person, one might say.

Then Hava said, "If I was married to that bey, I should clothe all the soldiers in the kingdom with three metres of cloth."

Ziliha said, "If I was married to that bey, I should feed the whole army with three okes of bread."

Zerhane said, "What are you saying, sisters? If I was married to that bey, I should give him two sons and a daughter with a star on their forehead and a moon on the arm."

Hearing these remarks, the King's son, Ismail Pasha, went joyfully home to the palace and told his father all that he had heard said. Besides that, he added that the girls were very pretty. "So, father, I want them," he said. The King said, "All right, son. If they are as you say, you have my leave to marry them. But perhaps they won't care to marry into our family."

339

The prince was delighted at this and at once sent a man to tell the old woman that the King's son wanted her daughters. The old woman did not believe what he said, and said to the messenger, "Go away, my son, and tell the King not to jest with me. I am an old woman and God knows my troubles and how things are with me."

The messenger returned to the palace and told the King what the old woman had said. Then Ismail Pasha took some horsemen and went with them to the old woman's house. "I'm the King's son, mother," he said to her, "and I really want your daughters. I'm not joking as you think." At these words the old woman fainted with joy and fell to the ground as if dead. In a few minutes she came to and, embracing Ismail, said, "I give both you and my daughters my sincerest blessing. They are lucky to be going to spend a happy life with you, and from now on I shall have a lucky old age."

So they arranged with the old woman as to when he would fetch the brides. The Prince returned to the palace and at once announced that he would get married on Sunday. That day, the officials great and small assembled, and guns and cannons were fired. Oh, oh, a great noise and din such as a pig like me who was at the wedding, not to speak of a gentleman, could not understand. This noise and din continued till the day the prince was married, but naturally was bigger on the wedding day. Goodness me! You know yourselves.

In this way, the King's son was married, and he began to test his wives to see if they were able to do what they said or not.

He first tested Hava, who could not clothe the army as she had said. He tested Ziliha also, and like the eldest sister she could not satisfy the army with three okes of bread. Ismail was extremely angry that the words of two of his wives turned out to be baseless boasts.

It now remained for him to test Zerhane, but her task was different as it took some time. In other words, Zerhane became pregnant and her husband, open-mouthed like a dead man waiting for the resurrection, waited to see what sort of child she would bear.

At the end of nine months her time came and she gave birth in the same hour to two sons and a daughter with a star on the forehead and a moon on the arm. Her sisters, however, hated her because she was

340

prettier and better loved by her husband. So as soon as her labour was over, the midwife and they took her children and put them in three boxes, which they threw into the river. In place of the children, they put puppies.

Ismail learned that his wife had given birth to her children and came and asked what she had had. "Three puppies," the other women replied.

The Prince was very much disappointed and in his anger gave orders that a hole should be dug in front of the door. Zerhane was to be put right down at the bottom of it, and everyone who passed was to spit in her face.

See what a trick her sisters played on poor Zerhane!

We said that they threw her children into the river. The river cast the babies up on one of its banks, but unfortunately very far away from the town in which they were born. A fisherman who passed by found the boxes with the children inside and took them home. When he opened them, he saw that the children were very pretty. Both he and his wife were very glad to have the children because they had longed for children and God had not granted them any of their own.

Poor as they were, they reared the three children until they were able to look after themselves. Then they sent them to school till they finished the fourth class in the elementary school. When they went to school, their companions mocked them, saying, "Go away, foundlings." Naturally, the children did not like such remarks. When they went home, they told the fisherman what had been said, and always asked him where he had found them. He did not tell them, however. After they had asked him again and again, with many embraces, he told them their story. "I found you on the bank of the river when you were little, and I reared you till I made you as you are," he said.

They understood it all very well and decided to run away, because things were impossible otherwise. Next day, while it was still rather dark, they got up and began their travels, although they did not know the way.

After they had gone some distance, they met a dervish who was a sort of saint. He asked them what their story was, and one by one they told him. He said to them, "My blessing on you! This road is a very good one and it will lead you to a good town, so don't worry."

In the end, the dervish gave them a stick and some advice, saying, "When you reach the town, jab this stick into four places in the ground and you'll have a big palace built. Inside the palace you'll find everything you want."

The brothers and sister again set out and two hours after sundown reached the town. They followed the street and did all that the holy dervish had told them. The palace was really built, and furnished with every beautiful thing that one could wish for.

When the King's wives saw this palace in the morning, they wondered and sent an old woman to find out about it. She came to the palace and found the girl alone and going through the rooms.

The old woman asked her how this palace came to be built bigger than the King's. The girl did not explain about the palace, but she did tell her all that had previously happened to them.

The old woman went to the palace and told the King's wives what the girl had said. She also told them of her beauty and of the magnificence of the rooms in the palace.

The King's wives had their suspicions roused by her story. To make sure, they went next day to the girl's new palace to wish her luck. But their purpose is known to have been different.

They talked with her at length and from her beauty and some lengthy questions they asked, they understood perfectly that she was their niece and that the boys were their nephews. For that reason they began to worry in case the news got about and their lives were endangered.

So after walking about the rooms of the palace for a little, they said, "This palace is very big and these rooms are very beautiful, but they would become still more beautiful if one of your brothers was to marry the Earthly Beauty."

The girl, being young, did not understand their intention and replied, "What you say is all very well, but what am I to do?" They said, "It's easy. Pretend to be ill and your brothers, if they love you, will find her. Otherwise, if they don't bring her, do them some harm." The wives of the King returned to their palace, and the girl fell ill enough to die as the good women had told her to do.

Her brothers came from the market and found their dear sister ill. "What's the matter, sister?" they asked. She replied, "I'm ill, brothers, and I won't get well if one of you doesn't do as I wish and marry the Earthly Beauty." "What are you saying, sister? Where can we find her? She has stout guards who will kill us," they returned. "I don't know about that. Only if you love me, find her. Otherwise I shall die," she replied.

You must know that no one went to see the Earthly Beauty because they knew they would be killed if they did. That's why the King's wives wanted to make these young men go to find her.

As they loved their sister dearly, one of the brothers mounted a horse and set off on his long journey to find the Earthly Beauty.

When half-way, he met a dervish who told him where to go and advised him not to wander this way or that, but to keep to the road.

As the dervish had bidden him, the young man went to the place in the hot hours of the day and found all the sentries asleep and went in and found the Earthly Beauty. When she saw him, she wondered. Then she called him to her and talked at great length with him.

The young man was very handsome and so was she. So they liked each other, and next day made ready to set off for the young man's palace, which they reached some days later.

The King's wives learned that the brothers had brought back the Earthly Beauty with them and began to be afraid.

One night they invited them all to supper with the idea of poisoning them. But the Earthly Beauty, who was very clever, said to them, "We'll go, but don't you eat until I say so, and give roses to the woman outside."

They set off and did as she said. The King welcomed them kindly and they began to talk. But the Earthly Beauty said that they must also bring in the woman who was outside by the front door. The King brought her in since they wanted her, although everybody else spat on her.

343

The first course was brought in poisoned, and the second one the same. The third came free from poison and all of them ate it together.

After supper the Earthly Beauty collected them all round her and bade them shut the door because she wanted to tell them a story. All the women – the King's wives and the midwives – who had acted so wickedly were also there. Zerhane told them one by one all the things that had happened to the children, saying to the King, "These are your children, this is your wife, and you are my father."

The King understood what had happened and gave orders for the evil-hearted women to be killed, and this was done. After he had had them killed, he grew old, and Zerhane and his dear sons whom he had so longed to see, had children.

[told by Lame Xhama of Fterra (Kurvelesh) in the district of Saranda]

The Two Poor Children

There were once a husband and wife, who had no property, but the husband worked and they ate and lived well.

God granted them a son and a daughter. They named the boy Veli and the girl Fatime.

After a time, the husband was killed in the war and the wife, having nothing to eat, married another man, who was a woodcutter.

The second husband did not work enough. So he had nothing with which to feed the children and his wife. One night found them with food, and the next without food. And the more time went on, the worse things went with them. Veli and Fatime's mother was sorry for the children, but the husband did not care a bit. That's to say, he didn't mind about them, because they were not his own children.

At last he grew tired of the children. And they were dying for want of food. So, one day that he went to the forest to cut wood, he took them with him with the idea of leaving them there. Their mother cried, but there was nothing the poor creature could do, as she had no food to give them.

When the husband set off with the children for the forest, Veli filled one of his pockets with grains of maize. And as they went, he dropped a grain here and there, until they reached the forest.

After the man had cut wood, he slipped away from the children, saying, "Stay here a little. I'm going over there to collect an armful of dry sticks." The poor children stopped where they were. After they had waited half an hour for him, they began to cry, saying, "Where shall we sleep to-night? A wild beast will eat us."

By this time it was almost night, but the moon gave a little light. At last Veli thought of the grains of maize he had dropped and he said to his sister, "Don't cry. We'll find the road." So, following the grains

345

of maize, they arrived home joyfully. Their stepfather was surprised to see them come back.

Next day he again took them to the forest. But since Veli knew that he would again leave them there, he took a piece of bread with him and, as they went along, he dropped crumbs here and there, as he had done with the grains of maize.

After their stepfather had cut his wood, he again slipped away from them, leaving them in the forest. Little Fatime began to cry, but her brother Veli said, "Don't cry, Fatime. We'll find the road again." But this time they could not find it because the crumbs of bread had been carried away by rain which had fallen a little earlier.

So the children wandered about the forest and cried. At last they saw a hut in front of them. This had walls of sweets and a roof of pastry. Veli and his sister ate some of it with enjoyment and satisfied their hunger, for they had had no food at all.

After a time, a giant with staring eyes and long nails came out of the hut. She was a *kulshedra*, and had built the hut with sweets and pastry to make people who passed that way and were hungry, stop and eat.

When she saw the children, she said to them, "Oh, you're my children!" She took them and kept them there. She shut Veli up in a cage to fatten him for eating, and kept Fatime with her to do the housework.

When Veli was fat, the *kulshedra* lit a big oven in order to roast him. When she did so, she said to Fatime, "Look at the oven and see if it's hot or not." But Fatime was very clever and said to her, "I can't reach it, it's too high. Go and look at it yourself." The *kulshedra* went to look at it herself. As soon as she went close to it, Fatime pushed her in and burned her to death. Then Fatime went joyfully to open the door of the cage in which her brother was shut up. Along with him, she ate and drank well with joy and, after taking some money, they ran away together.

As they went along, they met a peasant who knew who they belonged to. He took them to their mother, who was much delighted when she saw them alive. They built a house with the *kulshedra*'s money and lived happily.

Their stepfather had died some days before they came back. So everybody was surprised at their house, saying, "They hadn't food enough for one meal before. Where did they find the money to build this big house?" But the children never told them.

[told by Ibrahim Doraci of Elbasan]

The Beautiful Women of the Black Lake

Once long ago there was a shepherd.

Every day he took his sheep to graze beside the Black Lake, which lies between the villages of Valikardha and Martanesh. When the day grew hot, he led them to spend the noontide hours in a shady place nearby.

One day, when the sheep were resting at midday, he lay down himself in the shade to steal forty winks. Soon afterwards he saw two beautiful young women coming out of the lake with their hair loose and hanging down over their shoulders.

They did not notice the shepherd and, after walking about for a little, sat down on top of a rock and began to comb their hair.

The astonished shepherd got to his feet and began to walk towards them. The two young women turned their heads and, seeing him, at once sprang back into the lake.

This continued for several days in succession, say, for a week. The two young women came out of the lake and, when they saw the shepherd, they sprang back into the lake.

This astonished and amazed the shepherd a great deal so that he did not know what to do about it.

One day he happened to meet an old woman and told her what had happened to him. She told him that if he wanted to catch one of them, he should make a shift [slip] without a neck and leave it on the shore of the lake. When one of them passed the shift over her head to put it on, he should immediately catch her.

The shepherd did what the old woman told him. He made a shift of the kind prescribed and next day, when he went to graze his sheep, he left it on the lake-shore, while he himself hid behind a rock. As usual, the two young women came out of the lake and one of them slipped the shift over her head to put it on. Then the shepherd hastened to catch her, while the other sprang into the lake.

The one he caught was very pretty, and he took her home and married her. Unfortunately, however, she could not speak.

The shepherd tried many ways of making her speak, but in vain. None of them was of any use.

At the end of a year, a son was born to her. Then the shepherd thought of something else to do to make her speak.

When the boy was five or six months old, he filled an intestine with blood and, unknown to the mother, put it under the boy's throat. Then he took out his knife and, pretending to kill the infant, slashed through the intestine.

The mother, seeing her husband's hands covered in blood, thought that the infant had really been killed and she spoke. "My blood and the baby's be on your head!" she cried out. As she uttered these words, she fell dead, and along with her the little boy also died.

[told by Abdullah Keta of Shëngjergj in the district of Tirana]

The True Story of Pomegranate

Once long ago there were a husband and wife, who had no child except a daughter called Pomegranate.

It was not long before Pomegranate's father died, leaving the mother and daughter unprotected. Pomegranate was not more than seven years old. One day, the mother and daughter set off together to the orchard to gather figs. After they had finished gathering them, they sat down to rest and the mother began to search Pomegranate's head. Soon the girl fell asleep on her mother's knee. Then her mother, being a wicked woman, laid Pomegranate's head on a stone and went away.

After an hour the girl awoke, looked this way and that to find her mother, but could not find her. She was so little that she could not remember the road and began to cry. The King's servant heard her. He went up to her and asked, "Who do you belong to?" "My mother." "Where is your mother?" "I don't know." "Come on, then, let's go to my house." The two set off together and the servant took her to the King's wet nurse, who had a daughter and a son of her own.

The girl began to grow up and became a very pretty girl. The King's son liked her very much and said to his mother, "I don't want to marry any girl except this one. If I can't have her, I won't marry at all." His mother said to the King, "We can't find such a girl as this anywhere. I'd like to marry her to our son." And the King said, "Nothing could be better," and they gave her to their son to wife.

It was not long before the King and his wife died. God gave the King's son two sons, who grew up a little and went every day to school, and were very good pupils.

On the other hand, it happened that Pomegranate's mother went out to look for her and learned that she was the wife of the King's son. She went to Pomegranate's house disguised as a poor woman and knocked at the door. The women and servants answered the knock and told Pomegranate that an old woman had come. "Ask her what she wants," said Pomegranate. "Nothing," the woman replied, "only to be taken in to-night. Put me in the fowl or goose house." When Pomegranate saw her, she recognised her and with all speed went out and embraced her, greeted her and took her upstairs to her own rooms.

The mother stayed two or three days with her daughter and then said, "I'm going home to sell my house. I want to come and live here with you."

Pomegranate was more delighted at what her mother said than can be described.

After the mother sold her house, she returned to the King's palace. She brought three knives as presents, one for the King's son and two for her grandsons. Pomegranate, her mother and the two children went to sleep in one room. During the night the old woman took one boy's knife and cut the throats of both children. Then she put the knife under her daughter's head and again lay down to sleep. When Pomegranate rose in the morning, she saw the children dead. In haste she went and woke her mother and said, "I don't know who has killed my children." The mother at once went to her son-in-law and said, "My daughter has lost her reason and killed the children." The King's son came and put out his wife's eyes with the knife that had killed the children. He loaded the dead boys on her back and put her out of the palace and drove her off with the two murdered boys on her back.

Pomegranate walked along catching at one tree after another till she was able almost to reach a spring. There an angel took her by the hand and said, "Go to that spring and wash your face. Then your eyes will be restored to you. Wash the boys, too, and they'll come back to life."

Pomegranate did as the angel bade her. She washed her face and her eyesight was restored. She washed the boys also, and they came back to life. She looked for the person who had spoken to her, but could not see him, and then she prayed to Almighty God.

The poor woman with difficulty managed to find a hut in which she and her children could live. The boys were used to going every day to school. With difficulty they found books, and began to go to school. Their mother instructed them, saying, "If anyone asks who you are, don't tell them. Say, 'We're our mother's and our father's boys.'"

Things went on like this for two or three days. On the fourth day the King's son, their own father, saw the boys. He at once recognised them and stopped them. He kissed them and asked, "Who do you belong to?" The boys answered as their mother bade them, and ran off.

Next day the father again appeared, questioned them and was answered in the same way. In the evening he said to his mother-in-law, Pomegranate's mother, "I've seen two boys, who seem to be my sons." The old woman thought they might be so, and she began to confuse his mind, saying, "Don't look at strange children. It is not possible for your boys to have come back to life. God took them once and for all. Don't go, son, don't go, God may send worse troubles on you."

Next day the King's son waited once more for the boys in the road. When they appeared, he said to them, "Turn back and show me your house." The boys turned back and knocked on the door. "Who's there?" Pomegranate said. "Open up, open up! It's us," they answered. The door opened. The King's son had difficulty in recognising her, she had grown so pale from the loss of her eyes and from her grief. He greeted her and said, "Come, let's go home." "I'll come," she said, "but if you drive my mother from the house, may you live to weep over my dead body."

The two set off and went home. The King's son wanted to kill the old woman, but Pomegranate would not let him, saying, "Don't kill her. Send her away only." The King's son would not listen to his wife, but instead seized the old woman, cut her to pieces and flung the pieces to the dogs.

Next day he proclaimed a celebration for the boys and his wife and, that day, 101 guns were fired.

[told by Hakki Nesja of the Kruja region]

The Boy Who Learned to Steal

Once there were a husband and wife. After some time, the husband died, leaving three sons as well as his brother. Three or four months afterwards, the uncle went to offer his condolences to the family. When he got up to go, his brother's wife said to him, "Please take my eldest son and teach him your trade." The uncle said, "I will."

The uncle was a thief by trade. One day he took the eldest boy into a wood. When the boy was in the wood, he saw a goad for oxen and said to his uncle, "Oh, what a fine goad to steal!" The uncle said, "I don't want you. Go home. You're no good to me." The boy went home and his mother asked, "Did you learn anything?" "No," said the boy.

Sometime later, the uncle went again to see them, and as before, when he got up to go, his sister-in-law said, "Please take my second son with you." "All right," he said, "I will. But he won't learn anything either. These boys must follow their father's trade. But never mind, I'll take him with me." He led him in his turn into the wood. When the boy was in it, he saw a plough and said to his uncle, "Oh, what a plough to steal!" The uncle said as before, "I don't want you either," and sent him away. The boy went home and his mother said, "Oh, and you didn't learn anything either?" "No" he replied.

Again the uncle went to see them, and again his sister-in-law said, "The two boys you took with you didn't learn anything." "No," said the uncle, "Well, take the third one," she said. The third one was a Baldhead, and the uncle took him with him into the wood. There the boy saw a man leading a ram, and he said to his uncle, "Oh, there's a man leading a ram!" As they went on, the uncle said, "Ah, you're the boy for me!" The boy said to his uncle, "I'm going to steal the ram from him." "All right, go and steal it," said his uncle. The boy hurried off and

353

got ahead of the man. After he had passed him, he dropped a shoe. He then walked on for a little, and dropped the other shoe on the road, and himself hid at the foot of a tree.

As the man came on, he found the first shoe and said, "Oh, this is the very thing for my daughter!" Then he said, "There's only one. What shall I do with it?" And he left the shoe where he found it. When he had gone some way farther, he found the other shoe and said, "I've got the pair. I'll tie the ram to this tree here, and go back and get the other shoe." When the man was some distance away, the boy, who was hiding behind the tree, loosed the ram and went off with it to his uncle.

The uncle said, "How did you get it?" The boy said, "I hurried and got in front of the man, and after I had gone some way ahead, I dropped a shoe. I went on a bit and dropped the other shoe. The man found the first one and left it, but when he came to the second one, he said, 'Oh, I've got the pair. And they're just right for my daughter's foot.' He tied the ram to a tree and went to fetch the first shoe. I was hiding behind a tree and when I saw he had gone some distance away, I loosed the ram and took it."

Later on, the uncle went stealing. He entered a village and went right up to a goat-fold. The dogs saw him and rushed at him barking. He climbed to the top of a tree. The master of the house, seeing that the dogs were barking with great fury, came out, rifle in hand. But the boy's uncle cried *miaou, miaou* like a cat. The master of the house said, "The dogs are barking at the cat," and went back into the house. The uncle stole three or four he-goats and went to the wood where the boy was. When the master of the house got up in the morning, he saw that some goats were missing and said it hadn't been a cat after all, but a thief.

The uncle then went to another village, and in that village the dogs began to bark. Again the uncle mewed like a cat. But this time, the master of the house killed him.

In that village they had the custom when they killed anybody, of smoking him in the chimney. The uncle had a cigarette holder with him. The master of the house treated him according to the custom of the village. He took his cigarette holder and laid it on the wall under the eaves, and hung his body above the smoke in the chimney.

The boy learned that they had killed his uncle. Sometime afterwards, he filled a goat-skin with ashes and loaded it on his donkey. The donkey walked lame. After going some distance he reached the house of the man who had killed his uncle. This man was rich and the boy said to him, "Please, sir, let me stop with you to-night. My wife and children have nothing to eat." The rich man said, "Stop in that stable." The boy unloaded the donkey and went into the stable.

After he had gone into it, the rich man went into the house. After it was dark, they brought out *raki* and after the master of the house had drunk a little, he called the Baldhead. The Baldhead went upstairs and sat down. When he looked up above his head, he saw his uncle being smoked. He also looked under the eaves and saw the cigarette holder. He watched how the door closed, and he ate supper and went downstairs to the stable to sleep.

When the rich man had gone to bed, the Baldhead came out of the stable and went upstairs and opened the door of the house and entered. He emptied the ashes out of one goat's skin and put his uncle into it in their place. He then found the cigarette holder, put his uncle on the donkey, and went away.

On his way he came to a field of wheat, where three young men were threshing grain. Before he reached them, he set his uncle on the donkey as though riding it and put a forked stick at his back to support him. He pushed his bonnet to one side, and lighted a cigarette and put it in the holder and put that in his mouth. Then he freed the donkey's head so that it could bend and eat straw.

The donkey went along eating straw, while the young man hid close to the hedge. The three young men said to the uncle, "Stop the donkey, stop the donkey! God blind you!" The third, who was the youngest, fired at him, and the blast of the shot knocked him off the donkey.

The young man rushed out of his hiding-place shouting, "Oh, they've killed my uncle!" The three young men said, "Don't cry. We'll give you anything you want." He asked for twelve cartloads of wheat and they made them ready and took them to his house. In this way, the Baldhead became rich.

The tale for Lezha and health to us!

[told by Husain Maja of the Kruja region]

Gament Benegëpi of Damascus

There was once a young man of Damascus, who was called Gament Genegëpi. In his home town he had a house, his mother and one sister.

Gament was engaged in trade, buying and selling manufactured silks, and he was very rich.

Gament said to his mother, "Mother, I'm going to go to Constantinople to open a big business, always with manufactured goods. And you go on at home with the work we have here."

He took a large sum of money with him and went to Constantinople. As soon as he arrived, he hired a big shop, and filled it with manufactured goods. In another quarter of the town he rented a house, where he slept.

At that time in Constantinople, it was the custom that when a merchant died, all the other merchants went to the funeral. One day a merchant died and was being carried to his grave. This time was half-past eleven in the morning, Turkish style, and Gament went, according to the local custom. The funeral passed his shop, that is to say, they carried the corpse past his shop, and Gament went and joined them, forgetting to close his shop and leaving it alone, with nobody in it.

He went to the funeral. But when he went, the dead man was already buried, and all the merchants had gone back to their homes. Gament had been delayed on the way, and remained in the cemetery.

The time was almost one o'clock, Turkish style, after the call to evening prayer, and Gament wanted to find the way to leave the cemetery by which his friends had left. But he could not find his shop, and he had left it open. And so he found a tall palm-tree in the cemetery, and climbed it, to stay there all night until the mountains grew white with light, i.e. till dawn, and so to go back to his shop.

357

Then he saw some *araps* coming. There were three of them, and they were carrying a box. They reached the foot of the tree, sat down, and talked to each other, "We'll see if anybody is here in the cemetery." One of them got up and looked, but he saw nobody. "We'll look once more up in the palm-tree, to see there's nobody here." One of them climbed the tree, but did not see Gament, because the palm was very tall. So he came down, and said to his friends, "There's nobody there." He sat down at the foot of the palm.

They dug a hole, put the box into it, and covered it up. Then the *araps* went away home.

Gament came down from the palm, opened the hole quickly, took out the box and opened it. He saw that inside there was a very beautiful girl, with a great deal of jewellery round her neck.

That minute the girl recovered consciousness. She asked Gament, "Who are you, sir?" Gament said, "I am Gament Benegëpi, madam," and asked her, "and what is your name, girl?" She said, "Gulhelm Glubi." She said to Gament, "But where am I?" "Here, girl, in the cemetery. Three *araps* brought you." The girl understood and said, "All right. Now as soon as it is light, go to the bazaar to find an animal. Then come to fetch me and the box, and let's go to your house."

The girl understood that the King's wife had done this to her, because the King was away at the war. The Queen had done it out of spite, because the King wanted himself to marry this girl. He had brought her up and wanted to marry her, because she was very beautiful.

Gulhelm lived with Gament. They ate and drank and slept together. They did this for six months. For the first three months they slept together, but not one wicked act did the girl do with the young man.

After three months more, Gament said to the girl, "Gulhelm, to-night we'll sleep together and enjoy ourselves." Gulhelm replied, "No, I'm not yours. I'm another's." "Whose?" asked Gament. "The King's, and see, here's a ribbon which says, 'I am yours and you are mine.' That's the promise we have given each other."

So Gament separated from Gulhelm. They ate and drank together, but they did not sleep together. They slept in different rooms for many days.

Gament was much attracted by Gulhelm and he was a very handsome young man. After some days, Gulhelm said to Gament, "Gament, to-night, let's sleep together." Gament said, "I can't." "Why not? Why did you sleep at first with me, when you can't do it now?" Gament was afraid that the King wanted her. He was afraid of the King, because the ribbon had the King's signature.

Some days later, the King returned from the war. He saw his palace draped in black and asked, "Why have you draped the palace with black?" The Queen answered, "Poor Gulhelm is dead." "Where did you bury her?" "Because of the great love you bore her, we've buried her in her own room."

He went to her grave and ordered it to be opened. They opened it. When they did, he saw in it a body clothed with a shroud. When the King moved to put his hand on the dead body in the grave, an old man said, "Your Royal Highness, stop! With what face will you appear before God if you touch a dead body?" On hearing these words, the King took away his hand from the body he wanted to touch, and gave orders to cover it up. And it was covered up.

The King left. He went to his own room, and called two maids to massage his feet. As the maids did so, they talked with each other. One said to the other, "What a pity poor Gulhelm is dead!" She thought that the King had fallen asleep. But the King was lying in his bed, and he was neither awake nor asleep. He heard that the two maids were talking about the affairs of Gulhelm, saying she was alive and staying in the house of a man called Gament Benegëpi. One maid said to the other that she had found this out for certain. And so the King heard clearly all they said.

So he at once got up and called Gaferr. "Gaferr!" Gaferr came. "At your orders," he said to the King. Gaferr was the foremost general in the palace. The King said, "You will take soldiers and go to the house of a man called Gament Benegëpi from Damascus, to take Gulhelm and Gament Benegëpi and bring them here without delay.

Gaferr had some very bad soldiers. As soon as they went to the place, they stole right and left, and left nothing in that house.

When Gaferr's soldiers were near Gament's house, Gulhelm saw them and said to Gament, "Now you're lost, Gament!" Gament said to her, "What's up, Gulhelm?" "Soldiers are coming for us." Gament said, "Oh dear, what am I to do?" Gulhelm said, "Quick, Gament, take a woman's cloak. Put it on and put a bread-basket on your head and go out. If they ask you, say, 'I was in Gulhelm's house. I took her bread, because I work for a baker.' Say that and go, saving our life. As to the diamonds you have, don't worry. I'll save them for you."

When he appeared at the door, they asked him, "Where were you?" He said, "I was at Gulhelm's with bread." And so the young man escaped and ran away over mountain after mountain. He escaped from the clutches of Gaferr and his army.

Gaferr entered the house along with his army. Gulhelm appeared and said to Gaferr, "Gaferr, I have a little box. Please take it and sent it to the palace and put it in my room." Gaferr replied, "Certainly, madam."

The soldiers began to plunder Gament's house. They left him nothing but the four walls. Gaferr asked, "Where is Gament?" Gulhelm said, "It's been six months since Gament went back to his own home."

They then took Gulhelm and sent her to the palace to the King.

When the news came that they had brought Gulhelm, the King gave orders, saying, "Put her in prison in her own room." And he left her there for forty days without ever asking her what had happened.

The King gave orders again to Gaferr, bidding him go to Gament's house in Damascus. The soldiers went to the house, and asked Gament's mother, saying, "Where is Gament?" His mother said to them, "It's been six months since Gament went to Constantinople and started a business there."

As she said this, the soldiers went into the house and plundered it. Gament's mother, along with her daughter, began to beg from door to door in their poverty.

As Gulhelm sat in her room, she said to herself, "Your Royal Highness, I'm not sorry for myself for being shut up in my room, but

I'm sorry for Gament Benegëpi who preserved the honour of your palace. What sort of answer will you give God? The young man has gone, and it's not known whether he's alive or not."

As the King was walking by the room that Gulhelm was shut up in, he heard what she was doing and saying. The King at once called Gaferr and said, "Now open the door of the prison," that is to say, the room that Gulhelm was in. "Take her out and bring her here to me." Gaferr took Gulhelm out and brought her to the King.

The King said to Gulhelm, "Have I done you wrong?" "You couldn't have done me more wrong. Let alone your shutting me up in a room without making inquiries! There's Gament Benegëpi who preserved the honour of your palace, and now it's not known whether he's alive or dead."

The King said to Gulhelm, "Since I've done you wrong, what do you want from me?" "I want you to give me leave to go and find Gament and to marry him." And the King gave her leave, saying, "Go and find him, and bring him here to me."

She left carrying a great deal of money on her, and she gave the money to every poor person she found in the streets. Whether man or woman, if she saw them in the streets, she gave them money, so as to find her beloved Gament – or for the repose of his soul in the event of his being dead.

Gament from his aimless wandering had got into a very sorry state. One day he came to a village and stopped. There was a mosque there and when the villagers came to say morning prayer, i.e. before it was light, they found this young man, Gament, lying on the ground before the mosque door. What did they see? A handsomer young man could not be found. They were very sorry for him because he was so handsome. They took him and put him inside the mosque, and talked among themselves. "This young man, who's in such a state, must be in debt or at loggerheads with his government." This was the opinion of the villagers.

One of them went home, took a hot loaf and a dish of honey, and brought them to him to eat. As Gament ate, his mother and sister arrived. They were begging for food in the streets. The three met in the

361

mosque. But his mother and sister did not recognise Gament, and Gament did not recognise his mother and sister. And so he ate as much food as he wanted. The rest he gave to them, but he did not know that they were his own people.

His sister, however, said to her mother, "This young man is very much like our Gament, mother!"

When the villagers had prayed and come out of the mosque, they fetched a mule, set the young man on it, and took him to the state hospital to get cured. But the hospital was not open because it was very early and so the villagers left him at the door and went away.

The two women who were at the mosque and met Gament there, also went into the town.

At that moment, the Chief Watchman, that is to say, the chief of the night watchmen of the bazaar, was called the Sheikh because he stayed all night in the bazaar. He was on his way home as it was growing light when he saw the young man at the hospital door. He said to himself, "Suppose I take that young man, send him to my house and cure him. I wanted to do the pilgrimage, that is to say, go to Mecca. If I cure this young man, I've done the pilgrimage. If I leave him here at the hospital, they will kill him because he is very ill."

And so the Sheikh made up his mind and took care of the young man. He said, "Let me do this good deed." He took the young man and sent him to his house.

He said to his wife, "Wife, I found this young man at the hospital door. As I didn't like to leave him there, I took him to cure him myself. As I had decided to do the pilgrimage, if I do this good deed, I've gone on the pilgrimage."

His wife replied, "It couldn't be better. You've done very well."

Then the Sheikh went to the bazaar to get the doctor and bade him come every day to see Gament.

One day the Sheikh, that is to say, the head bazaar watchman, met a strange lady, who gave every poor person money for the repose of Gament's soul, in case he was dead. When the Sheikh saw this Gulhelm, he said to her, "Madam, I also have a sick young man in the

362

house. I found him at the hospital door, and so I took him to my house to cure him with my own money. Since you've come out and given money to the poor, if you like, come and see him."

At once she got up and went with the Sheikh. When she got to his house, she saw this young man and said, "A doctor will come at my expense." And so, two doctors came every day, one sent by the Sheikh and the other by Gulhelm.

One fine day, the Sheikh said to Gulhelm, "There are also two women begging in the market-place. But they seem of good family." And Gulhelm said to the Sheikh, "Take them, too, and bring them to your house. Their food will be my affair." Who these women were, nobody knew. And so they took them and the Sheikh brought them to his own house.

Every day Gulhelm went to the Sheikh's house, yet she did not know it was Gament and did not recognise him at all. The moment she saw the two women there in the Sheikh's house, Gulhelm asked them questions. She said, "What was the trouble that brought you into this state?" The two women could not tell her straight because they were afraid that this lady was a Princess. So Gulhelm said, "Tell me the truth because I am a woman who does good and not one who does ill." And the women began to tell her the truth.

"Madam, now I'm telling you the truth. I had a son who came here to Constantinople to trade. What he has done here, I don't know. Only when the King's soldiers came, they asked me where Gament was. I said he was in business in Constantinople, and was called Gament."

At once Gulhelm embraced Gament's mother and said, "You're Gament's mother?"

While Gament lay ill in bed, he spoke out and said, "Who is mentioning my name?" At once Gulhelm went over to Gament's bed and embraced him, saying, "You are Gament?" Gament said, "I am. And you, who are you?" "I am Gulhelm Glubi."

The four were thus together, Gament, his mother, his sister and Gulhelm Glubi, and four doctors then came in to see them. Not many days passed before Gament grew quite well.

363

When Gament was well, Gulhelm went to the King and said, "Your Royal Highness, I've found Gament." The King asked Gulhelm, "Where is he?" "He is in the house of the Sheikh of the bazaar watchmen."

The King gave orders and said to Gaferr, "Now go to the house of the Sheikh of the bazaar watchmen and fetch Gament Benegëpi. Take your best officers with you, and horses, too."

When the King said this, Gulhelm went at once to the Sheikh's house and said to her beloved Gament, "Gaferr is coming to fetch you and he'll send you to the King. Say all those sweet words to him that you know."

Gaferr went and fetched him with great honour. When he went to the King, the King said, "Come, boy, come and sit down here." And he made him sit down close by him, on his left hand.

The King began to question Gament, and Gament told him the truth. And the King understood it was the truth. He clapped Gament on the shoulders.

Gulhelm said to the King, "Your Royal Highness, Gament's mother and sister are also here." Then the King built another palace for Gament opposite his own, and said to Gament, "Now go. I have given you Gulhelm."

When the King saw Gament's sister, how beautiful she was! He sent a man and asked for her hand. Gament said to the person who came and asked him for his sister, "Please give our best greetings to His Majesty. Mother, sister, and I are his slaves."

For this speech of Gament's, the King gave him 7,000 gold Napoleons. First he married Gulhelm to Gament. Then he got married himself to Gament's sister.

And at that time, as they say, whatever person the King put on his left hand, was the King's deputy.

The King's wedding day with Gament's sister came. There was a great feast such as cannot be described.

Now, the tale has come to an end.

[told by Qazim Bakalli]

364

Black Mafmut

There was what there was. Once upon a time, there was an old woman who had only one son, and he was called Black Mafmut. He was a brave man and he dominated whoever talked with him.

One fine day, the King of that country called his mother and said, "See if you can send away your son. We'll look after you." In the evening the mother said to her son, "They want to send you away. Better go of your own accord." "All right, I will," he replied. But I want a club weighing 1,000 okes and a sword sharp enough to slice through a marble column." The mother went and told the King this, and he said, "I'll get them made for him." They went and ordered them, made them, and gave them to him

The young man set off. On his way he came on a marble column, smote it with his sword, and broke the sword. At once he returned home and said to his mother, "Get another sword for me. That one broke." She hurried to the King and said, "My son's come back because his sword broke." The King ordered a far better one for him, she gave it to her son, and he went away once more.

On his way, he came a second time to the marble column, smote it with his sword, and cut it in two. After he had sliced through it, he set off again.

On and on and on he went. He stopped to eat by a fountain under a shady tree. Unfortunately, that fountain belonged to the *jinns*. When he sat down to eat, some outlaws, thirty-nine in number, saw him and began to fire at him. But their bullets were like fleas on him, and their cannon-balls like fists. They went on firing all together, but still their bullets were like fleas and their cannon-balls were like fists, and he said, "There are fleas here! And who's hitting me with his fist?"

365

The outlaws came up to him and said, "Who are you there?" Black Mafmut replied, saying, "A man like you." They came close to him, and said, "Peace be with you!" "On you be peace!" he replied. They then said to him, "Shall we become partners?" "Yes," he replied. And so they joined forces. But Black Mafmut said, "Let me be the chief!" "All right," they said. They became partners.

One day, Black Mafmut and his companions went out. They met a man coming from the opposite direction and asked him if there was any news from the bazaar. He said there was none, except that the King had proclaimed that he would give anything he wanted to the man who came and killed the fairy in his bathroom. Black Mafmut hurried to the town and went to the lavatory and said to the guardian, "Let me go in." He went in, struggled with the fairy, seized her necklace of gold coins, and killed her.

He came out and said to the guardian, "I killed her!" The guardian said, "Will you sell the necklace to me?" "Yes," replied Black Mafmut. He sold it for thirty-nine purses, the guardian giving him ten down and promising to give him the rest another day.

Black Mafmut hurried to his companions and gave them the money. After three days, he went to ask for the rest of his money and found the guardian in the mosque, for he had promised to pay on a Friday. Black Mafmut went into the mosque and asked for his money. The King heard him and said, "What does he want?" The guardian replied, "Never mind. He doesn't want anything." Black Mafmut said, "Give me the money for the fairy's gold necklace that I sold to you." The King understood and killed the guardian.

He gave his daughter to Black Mafmut and treated him like his brother.

[told by Rexhep Alliu]

The Snakeskin

In bygone days there were two brothers, who were like each other in face and had playing on the *bullgari* for their trade.

One day one said to the other, "Shall we go to seek our fortune?" They decided to do so. As they started out, each gave the other a handkerchief, saying that when the handkerchief of one should drip blood, the other would have been killed. They set off, one towards the north and the other towards the south.

One of them went to a town. Entering the bazaar, he went to an innkeeper and said, "To-night I want to sleep in your inn." The innkeeper said, however, "At night *jinns* hang about the bazaar and they'll kill you." The young man would not be convinced and slept that night in the inn. He went into his room, sat down, and picked up his *bullgari* and played on it.

As he played, the *jinns* arrived. Opening the door, one after the other said, "Pleased to see you!" The young man was astonished. He heard voices, but could see nothing. In his surprise he stopped playing. The *jinns* begged him to continue. But he would not listen till they said, "We'll give you a servant called Snakeskin." When they said this, he began to play again. They listened a certain time and then went away, saying, "Good night."

After they went away, he thought a little and said to himself, "Shall I call to see if they have left something for me?" He called Snakeskin, who replied, "Yes, sir?" He then ordered, "Get my horse ready!" "Very good," the servant replied.

When it was still night, they left the inn and went for a walk in the bazaar, where they saw a tailor sewing in his shop and crying. As the young man passed by, he went into the shop and asked, "Why are you crying?" The tailor replied, "I've fallen in love with a daughter of the King. If you can bring her and let me see her for a little, I'll work three months for you." The young man said to Snakeskin, "Snakeskin, is it possible to bring the King's daughter?" "Yes," he replied. "Go and bring her then!" he commanded.

Snakeskin went and fetched the princess, who was sleeping. When he brought her to the tailor, the latter in his love let three teardrops fall on her face. But she did not wake up. The King of those days weighed his daughters every day, for if a princess was seen by anyone, she lost an oke in weight. Next day back in the palace, the princess who had been seen came out an oke less. "Who has seen you?" asked her father. "I don't know," she replied.

The next evening, the young man went again to the tailor and found him crying again. "What makes you cry?" he asked him. The tailor replied, "I want to see the King's daughter again. If I can see her, I will work three months more for you." The young man again fetched her with the help of Snakeskin.

Like the first night, Snakeskin went and fetched her and brought her to the tailor. As on the first night, the tailor let three teardrops fall on her face when he saw her, but she did not awake. Next day, the King found her again weighing an oke less and asked her who had seen her. "I don't know," she replied. "To-night stay awake and find out who sees you!" he commanded. As her father commanded, the princess stayed awake.

The third night Snakeskin went to fetch her. He did so and brought her to the young man, so that she saw him. Then Snakeskin took her hastily home. Next day, her father weighed her and she came out an oke too few. "Who is seeing you?" asked the King. "The young man who stays with the tailor," she replied.

The King sent to call the young man to the palace and said to him, "Will you marry my daughter." "Yes," he replied. He married her that night and went into her room, leaving Snakeskin behind the door. The girl, however, had a *kulshedra* inside her and as the young man sat with his bride, the *kulshedra* came out and killed him.

His brother's handkerchief began to drip blood. At that moment, the brother understood that they had killed his brother, and he set off in the same direction as his brother had done. He went into the bazaar of the town like his brother, and he went to the same inn and said to the innkeeper, "I want to sleep here to-night." The innkeeper thought it was the same man as had slept there once before. "All right," he said, "sleep here since you have already done so and the *jinns* did not kill you." The young man reflected and said to himself, "My brother must have stayed here!"

He went into the room and began to play on his *bullgari*. The *jinns* at once collected, opened the door of the inn, came inside and said, "Pleased to see you!" He was astonished for he heard their voices but saw nothing. The *jinns* said, "We'll give you Snakeskin once more, but don't let him go."

He thought to himself, "They've given him to my brother. I'll go on playing." He began to play. The *jinns* listened for a certain time and then went away, saying, "Good night."

After they went away, he said to himself, "Let me call Snakeskin just to see if they have left me anything." He called "Snakeskin!" who replied, "Yes, sir?" He said "See to the horse!" "Very good," he replied.

They left the inn and went to the bazaar, where they saw the tailor crying as he sewed. They went into the shop, and the young man asked why he was crying. He replied, "Is it possible to fetch the King's daughter once more?" "Yes," replied Snakeskin. "Go and fetch the King's daughter!" the young man commanded. Snakeskin went and fetched her and took her to the tailor. He looked at her and sent her back.

Next day, the King weighed his daughters. This one came out an oke too little.

On the second night, as on the first, the young man went out for a walk. Again he found the tailor crying, and again asked him why. "I want to see the King's daughter once more," he replied. Again the young man sent to fetch her. The tailor looked at her and sent her back. Her father weighed her the second day, and again she came out an oke too few. Her father asked her who had looked at her. "I don't know," she replied.

On the third night, as on the second, the young man went out for a walk. Again he saw the tailor crying and asked him why he did so. "I want to see the King's daughter once more," he replied. On the third night, however, the girl had stayed awake to see who fetched her. When Snakeskin went and fetched her and carried her into their presence, the girl saw the young man who had sent to fetch her. Then they sent her back home.

Next day, the father weighed his daughter, and she came out an oke too few. He again asked her who was seeing her. "A young man who lives with the tailor," she replied. The same day, the King summoned the young man and asked him to marry his daughter. "I will," he replied.

He married her. Both entered their bedroom after he had stationed Snakeskin in the chimney corner. As they sat there, the *kulshedra* again came out of the girl to kill the young man. But this time, Snakeskin caught the monster and said, "Either bring up the other man you killed, or I'll kill you!" The monster brought up the first brother. Then the two brothers lived and worked together.

The story for Lezha, and health to us.

[told by Riza Dervishi of the Kruja region]

The Wild Horses

In days long gone by, there were once three brothers who had one arable field in which they had sown maize. Wild horses got a habit of going night after night to that field and eating the maize.

One night, the eldest brother said, "I'll go and guard the field." But he could not manage. The second night, the second brother went and he, too, could not guard it.

The third night, the third brother, who was a Baldhead, went out to the field. He climbed a tree to which a horse came to scratch itself. The Baldhead climbed down very gently, jumped on the horse's back and rode it the whole night. When dawn came, the horse begged him to let it go, but he would not hear of it. Again the horse begged him, saying, "I'll give you three hairs, one white, one red, and one black." It added, "Whichever hair you burn brings a horse and clothes of the same colour."

The King of that country had made a trench twenty metres long, twenty metres deep and twenty metres wide, saying, "Whoever is able to jump across this trench, shall marry one of my daughters." The Baldhead's brothers went with a lame horse to jump the trench after saying to the Baldhead, "You stay at home and cook food for us, Baldhead." And he had answered, "Yes, I will."

As soon as he had cooked the food, he burned a hair. The horse and clothes appeared, he mounted the horse, and went and jumped the trench three times, and got one daughter of the King. No one recognised him, and he took the princess to the cellar of his house.

In the evening, his brothers came home and said, "Baldhead, bring us supper!"

Next day, they went away again after saying to the Baldhead, "Stay and cook the supper!" The Baldhead made supper and then burned a hair. The horse and clothes appeared, he mounted the horse and went and jumped the trench. He got the second princess and put her beside the first one.

When his brothers got home in the evening, they were downcast. When the Baldhead asked them if they had gained anything, they beat him with firebrands, and the Baldhead did not speak again.

The third day, they again went to the trench. The Baldhead cooked supper quickly and burned the third hair. Horse and clothes appeared, he mounted the horse, and went again and jumped the trench. He got the third princess and put the three together.

When his brothers came home in the evening, they said to the Baldhead, "Go down to the cellar and bring us some rice. We want to make soup." He would not obey and said, "Go yourselves." Then the eldest brother went down to the cellar and, when he saw the princesses there, he was surprised and called his brother, saying, "Come here! There are girls here, too!" The second brother went down to look. Then they called the Baldhead, who said to them, "Choose!" They chose the prettiest ones, left the ugliest one to him, and began to kiss their own choices.

Next day, the Baldhead's brothers went to the bazaar, and the Baldhead himself went with them. His wife went out into the yard to sew her embroidery frame, but an *arap* with a three-legged horse came and carried her off.

When the Baldhead came home in the evening, he asked his sisters-in-law where his wife was. They replied, "A man came and carried her off." The Baldhead did not stop a moment, but burned a horse's hair. A horse came with clothes, he got on its back and set out. He crossed twelve mountains and came out on a great plain, in the middle of which there was a house of the King of the Birds.

The Baldhead went inside, greeted them, and told them his story. The King asked all the birds and serpents and snakes to go and look for the Baldhead's wife and they set off. They all came back except the bat and reported they had seen nothing. When the bat arrived, the King questioned it. "I saw somebody," it replied.

The Baldhead wrote a letter to his wife in which he said, "Where shall we meet to-morrow?" and put it in the bat's beak. It carried the letter to her, and she returned the reply, "Let's meet at such-and-such a fountain."

Next day, the Baldhead mounted his horse and went to her. He went upstairs and there found the *arap* asleep. The *arap*'s horse neighed, saying, "They've stolen your wife!" The *arap* sprang up in a hurry, caught them on their way, and cut the Baldhead into little bits.

The *arap*'s wife said to her husband, "Shall I take these bits of meat and put them in the saddle-bags on the horse?" "Go on, take them!" he said. She collected them and put them in the saddle-bags. The horse set off and went to the house of the King of the Birds. The King took off the saddle-bags and took out the pieces of meat. After putting them together, he made the Baldhead a man as before.

The Baldhead said, "Oh what a long sleep I've had!" The King said, "You silly! They made mincemeat of you!"

Again the Baldhead sent a message to his wife, saying, "Ask him where he got that horse." His wife said to the *arap*, "Oh, what a lovely horse it is! It doesn't kick or bite. Where did you get it?" The *arap* said, "I got it where the four mountains meet. If you leave three rams and three ovenfuls of bread there, a horse with three legs comes out."

The Baldhead prepared four rams and four ovenfuls of bread and went and put them on the mountain. A horse with four legs came out. The Baldhead went back to the King of the Birds and then set out. He went to his wife, took her away and mounted the horse. The *arap*'s horse neighed, however. The *arap* sprang up and rushed after him. When the Baldhead saw him, he was frightened and said to his own horse, "He's caught us up." The horse said, "Don't be afraid. I'll kill both him and his horse." When the *arap* came up, the horse killed him and his horse. Then the Baldhead went to the King of the Birds. He bade him good-bye and the King filled his saddle-bags with money. Then the Baldhead set out and went home. The father of his wife gave a fine dinner-party to celebrate the arrival of his daughter and his son-in-law.

[told by H. Sheta of the Kruja region]

373

The Night Robber and the Day Robber

There was what there was. Be it as it may!

Once there lived a woman who was married to two husbands. Both of these lived by robbery, the first stealing by day and the second stealing by night. Neither of them knew that his wife had two husbands, because the night robber went away when the day robber came. So it never happened that they met. As the wife was afraid of them, she did not tell either that she had two husbands.

One day she made a loaf and roasted a fowl. Then she divided both loaf and fowl in two and gave one half of each to the day robber when he came home in the evening and the other half to the night robber when he came home in the morning.

Unfortunately for her, it happened that the two robbers met in a certain place that day for the first time in their lives. And as they did not know each other, they stopped to talk and to get to know each other.

It was lunch time when they met. After they had had a long talk together, the day robber, who was always ravenous at this time of day, took out of his robber's wallet the halves of the loaf and fowl which his wife had given him to eat. Then the night robber, like the day one, opened his wallet. This was almost filled with valuable and costly articles which he had acquire by his robber's trade. He then took out the halves of the loaf and the roasted fowl, which his wife had given him in the house.

The day robber, seeing that his friend had the same sort of food as himself, was extremely surprised and said, "What a strange thing, mate! You and I have both the same sort of food to eat!" "Yes," said the night robber, "and I'm very surprised at it. So let's measure the loaf and the fowl."

When they measured them, they saw that the length and size of both were the same. Presently the day robber, beginning to have a faint idea that they had one and the same wife, questioned the night robber, "I say, mate, what sort of house do you live in?" he asked. "I live in a house on the outskirts of the town," was the night robber's answer, and he also gave him the name of the quarter in which it stood. The day robber's idea was confirmed and with surprise in his voice, he said, "I live in that house, too. Who's your wife?" "My wife is very beautiful, and she's called Violet," answered the night robber. "But that's my wife," replied the day robber. "How has it happened that our houses and our wives are the same?" "I can't tell. I'm quite bewildered," said the night robber. "But to find out better about it, let's go home and see. If the house is both yours and mine, then let's go stealing and whoever proves the better man at it shall take wife, house and all the property."

This suggestion was accepted by the day robber and in a little they started for home.

After they had walked an hour and a half, they reached what was their common home. The wife came out to meet them, and was astonished to find that her two husbands had met that day for the first time. The day robber said, "Here's my house and my wife!" "But they're mine, too," said the night robber.

Since the both had the same house and the same wife, they were forced to do as the night robber had said earlier on. As soon as it was light next day, the day robber went away to steal. After spending the day in stealing many valuables, he returned home in the evening and found the night robber waiting for him.

As soon as darkness fell, the night robber, accompanied by the day robber, went out to steal. They decided to go to the treasury of the King of that country, and reached it after a short journey. Unfortunately, the King had not yet fallen asleep, although he was in bed and had one maid-servant at his head telling him folk-stories and another at his feet massaging his legs.

It seemed to the night robber that, to steal, he must not be heard or recognised by anyone as a robber. So he made himself like a poor person who had come that night for hospitality. The two maids saw him and said, "Come upstairs!" He obeyed and went to the room where the King was. He told the maid who was telling folk-stories to leave the room or he would kill her. And when she went away, he went to the King's head and began to tell him very good stories. From time to time, he mingled with the words of his stories such phrases as "Roast the goose!" And then he again continued with the story. The King liked his stories very much and all of a sudden fell asleep.

As soon as the night robber saw that the king was asleep, he rushed out to find the day robber, and the two went straight to the King's treasury to rob it. With great skill the night robber opened the door and after loading himself with money, shut it again. Then the two went away home, where they compared the goods they had stolen. As the night robber had more, he took property, wife and house.

After some time, God gave him three sons.

When they grew big, the father wanted to put them to a test to see which would make the best robber. So one day he took them to a big, dense forest. The two eldest were so frightened that they began to scream. The youngest, who was not in the least frightened, laughed at them. Then the father understood that the two eldest would be no good at robbing and that the youngest was fit to inherit his father's trade and would show himself, when grown up, a master-hand at robbing.

One night, after the youngest son had come to the age required for robbing, the father took him aside and said, "Son, to-night we'll go to rob the King's treasury. So you must show great skill in robbing, else they may hear us and kill us both." The son turned to his father and said, "No, father! Don't be in the least afraid about me. I'll try to show all the art you've taught me." "Splendid!" said the father and, after it was quite dark, they started for the King's palace.

When they reached it, they stole a great deal of money and went home delighted, because they had not been detected by anyone in the palace.

When the King got up in the morning, he saw that over-night a great deal of money had been stolen. So, to catch the thief, he decided to send a servant to walk through the streets of the town with a horse laden with gold; whoever should dare to steal the gold, would be proved to be the thief. So one fine day, one of the King's servants appeared with a horse laden with gold, and walked about the streets of the town. The night robber and his son saw him, and planned as follows to steal the money.

The father was to quarrel with somebody in the street. Then the King's servant, seeing them fighting, would go to separate them. This would give the son a chance to steal the horse and gold. They did as they had planned and the son stole the horse and gold, and took them home.

The King was astonished at the cunning shown by the robber and, to catch him, planned to strew the road beside the palace with gold; whoever would stoop to pick it up, would be proved to be the thief. But for this, too, the robber had an idea, which was as follows.

The Snake and the Peasant

Once upon a time there was a peasant who went to the forest to cut wood. He found the trees were all withered. So he left one for shade and set fire to the others. In the middle of the forest there was a tree with a snake in it. As the peasant watched the forest burning, the snake cried, "Son of man, please rescue me!" "How can I rescue you?" asked the peasant. "Reach up a long pole and I'll slide down it," said the snake. The peasant reached up a pole and the snake came down and curled itself round the peasant's neck and wanted to bite him.

"Now, now, what's this you want to do to me? I rescued you," said the peasant. "All right, we'll have a test. We'll ask other people what they think," said the snake.

The donkey was the first to appear. "Let's ask the donkey whether I should bite you or not," said the snake. "Mr Donkey," it said, "what shall I do with this son of man? Shall I or shall I not bite him?" "What are you waiting for? Haven't you bitten him yet? These fellows are my enemies. They load me up with a hundred okes, they ride on me, they load me with wool and as much flour as they can. Bite him!" said the donkey.

The snake bit the peasant. "Oh!" the peasant groaned. "Let's ask somebody else," said the snake.

A flock of sheep was passing by. As the ram passed, the snake said, "Ram, I've caught this son of man. Shall I or shall I not bite him?" "The Bey, my master, comes and feeds me well with barley and then he kills me. These men are our enemies. Bite the man!" the ram said.

Some pigs passed and they, too, said, "Bite him!"

Finally the fox passed. "This is the last time," said the snake, "that I'm asking anybody. I'm going to ask the fox if I should bite you or not." The fox was far away. The man beckoned to her and said, "Ten hens are yours if you rescue me from the snake." "How shall I manage?" said the fox. "Well, let's think it over quietly. First of all, how did it happen?" The fox turned to the snake and said, "Where were you?" "Up the tree," the snake replied. "I asked this man to reach up a pole for me to come down and save me from the fire. In this way, I escaped being burned." The fox said, "I don't believe you were up the tree." "I was," the snake insisted. "Well, climb up the tree once more and let me see," said the fox. The snake uncurled itself from the man's neck, let him go, and climbed to the top of the tree. The man ran away, leaving the snake up the tree.

The fox went and found the man. "I want the ten hens," she said. "Where will you bring them to me?" "I'll bring them to the flour-mill for you. I'll put them in a sack and bring them," said the peasant.

But the peasant did not keep his word. He went and found five fox-terriers which he put in a sack and carried to the other side of the river. The fox was waiting for him and saw him come. "Come along," she said. "The hens may escape. They may fly away." "Oh no," said the peasant. "Just come here, come here." The fox alternatively advanced and retired, she was afraid. The peasant advanced with the sack. "Come here," he said, "come here." He opened the sack and let the terriers loose. They ran after the fox, which ran away into a dense forest. She escaped the dogs but bled all over, torn by the bushes and thorns.

She climbed to a cliff in the forest where the terriers could not reach her. With one paw she beat her head, saying, "I rescued that son of man from the snake!" She lifted another paw and kissed it, saying, "But my quick legs saved my life."

The Advice of a Father

Once upon a time there was a very rich merchant who had a wife and an only son. He was old and said one day to his son, "My son, I am going to die. You must not make friends with government officials and you must never tell your wife what you are doing."

Sometime later, the old man died. A year afterwards, this son bethought him of his advice. "He told me never to make friends with government people and never to tell my wife what I am doing," he said to himself. The young man then made friends with a government man, a captain, and they became foster-brothers and very close friends.

What did the young man do next? One day he went to a butcher and said, "Have you got a nice fat ram?" "I have," the butcher replied. "Hold on to it then," the young man said. "I'm going to buy a suit of clothes and come here to kill the ram." He bought a man's suit, brought it to the butcher and said, "Now bring the ram!" The butcher brought it and said, "This is a really nice ram."

The young man spread the clothes on the ground and said, "Kill the ram on the clothes and let them get covered with blood." The butcher killed the ram and the clothes were covered with blood. Then said the young man, "Skin it and clean it. Weigh it to see how many kilos it is. I shall pay you for it." The butcher weighed it and it cost one hundred piastres. "Send it to the baker to roast," the young man said. The ram was roasted and brought back to the young man.

The young man then took some clean white sheets and wrapped up the ram so that it should not get dirty. He then drew the blood-stained clothes over it and made the package like a man. He loaded this on a porter's back and bade the man carry it to his house. He paid him his hire and went away to his home.

He called to his wife, "Come and help me carry this. I can't do it by myself." The two of them picked up the package and carried it down to the cellar. Then he said to his wife, "Don't tell anyone that I've killed this man!" As he said this, he pulled the clothes and meat out of the sack. His wife saw them and said in astonishment, "What have you done?" "Keep quiet," he returned. "Don't say a word. No one knows anything. I'm off to market."

He left the house and went to the market. His wife met a man and said, "Go and tell such-and-such a captain that the wife of so-and-so would like to see him." The man took the message to the captain.

The captain hurried to her, "Why has she summoned me? What has happened?" he asked himself. When he reached her house, he said, "What's the matter? Why did you call me?" "You don't know what my husband has done! He has committed a crime! He has killed a man!" she exclaimed. "Where is the man he killed? When did he kill him?" the captain asked. "Come and see," she replied. "He is down in the cellar. He brought him here and put him in the cellar." The captain went and saw the dead man and said, "What has he done?"

The captain then went to the police and, after collecting ten gendarme, went and searched the market for the young man. When at last he found him, he ordered him to be beaten. "What's this? What has he done?" the prefect asked. "He has murdered a man and concealed him in his house," the captain replied. The young man denied the charge, saying, "I've killed nobody." The captain said to the prefect, "Let's go and look. He has the man at home."

The prefect and a number of government people got up and went to the young man's house. The captain went to the cellar door and opened it, saying to the prefect, "Look at this!" The prefect went and looked and said, "He really has murdered somebody!" The prefect turned to the young man and said, "Here is a dead man! Why did you say you had not killed anybody?" The young man replied, "If I've been a murderer, I must be punished. But I should like to know who the man I have killed is."

They took the package out of the cellar and the young man said to them, "Undress the murdered man and let's see what sort of fellow he was!" They undressed the man and the roasted ram appeared.

The young man then said to the prefect, "Please come and eat the ram with me. My father advised me not to make friends with government people and not to tell my wife what I am doing. I had this ram roasted and then I arranged it like a murdered man. I waited to see what my foster-brother, who is in government service, would do. I was very fond of him. As for my wife and her loyalty, to see how much she loved me, I said to her, 'You must never reveal that I've killed somebody!' But she sent word to my foster-brother, saying, 'Come! My husband has murdered a man!' And my foster-brother got up and found gendarmes and arrested and beat me without identifying the person I had murdered. I was beaten because of a roast ram! And I found out what the love of my foster-brother and wife was worth. They loved me so dearly that they had me beaten! But I am grateful to my father for his advice not to make friends with government people and never to tell my wife what I am doing. I shall heed it from now onwards."

They ate the ram as hors d'oeuvres. And then, they beat and drove off the captain and degraded him.

The Fox and the Wheat

Once upon a time a fox, a pig and a bear became brothers and sisters and began to till a field. The fox stayed at home like a woman to do the cooking, and the pig and the bear tilled the field in order to sow it with wheat.

When the wheat was ripe, they reaped it. The bear and the pig winnowed it together and then wanted to divide it. The fox went to them and said, "Where is my share?" They replied, "You did not work with us so as to earn a share." She insisted, "Give me my portion. Otherwise I'll go and tell my brother. He has a twelve-shot rifle and he'll come and kill you."

On the threshing floor where they were winnowing, the wheat there was heaped up like a tree. The pig said to the bear, "I'm afraid the fox's brother will come and kill us. Climb to the top of the heap and keep watch that he does not come." The bear climbed up to the top of the heap. The pig stayed below on the ground.

As the bear kept watch, he saw a cat coming to chase birds or mice. He cried out to the pig, "The fox's brother is coming and he's got his rifle with him and will kill us." The pig replied, "You are safe up there, but where shall I hide?" The bear said, "Crawl inside the heap of straw!" The pig did so, but left his nose outside.

The cat came hunting mice, saw the pig's snout and pounced on it, thinking it was a mouse. The pig rose with a great roar *vu-u-u* and ran away in fear.

The cat was terrified and in its freight sprang up the heap in which the bear was hiding. At once the bear jumped down to the ground, terrified that the cat would eat him. In this way, the bear, too, ran away.

Bear and pig met far up the mountain. The bear said to the pig, "Did you see the fox's brother? As soon as he turned his back on you, he made straight for me. He wanted to eat us both." The pig and the bear were frightened away, and the fox went to the threshing-floor and took all the wheat.

Tort Leshi

Once upon a time there was a thief who was called Tort Leshi. One day he was going out to steal when he met two robbers, one of whom was called Tosku and the other Mosku. They were brothers. Tort Leshi went up to them and said, "Greetings to you!" "Welcome!" they replied. "A good journey to you!" he said. "Where are you going?" they asked. "To see a friend of mine," he replied. "You don't look as though you were going to see a friend. You seem rather to have robbing in mind," they said. "That seems truer of you than of me," he replied. "We'll make you our friend," they said.

Nearby, there was a large tree with an eyrie in which an eagle had laid her eggs. "Can you climb the tree and get the eggs without being noticed by the eagle and frightening her?" they asked. "If you succeed in that," they said, "we have a sister that we'll give you in marriage." "All right, I'll get the eggs," he said. He climbed the tree and reached the eagle, which was sitting on her eggs, and he took them from under her breast.

He then came down the tree and showed the other two the eggs which he had taken. One of them said, "We shall make you our friend." And they gave him their sister in marriage. He married her and gave a wedding party –such a party! They were wined and dined and then they went to return parties.

When the wedding parties were over, Tort Leshi stole a ram in the forest and took it home, and tethered it to a wooden post. Then he went out to steal again.

One day, Tosku and Mosku went to his house, where they found their sister. "Greetings to you!" they said. "Welcome!" she replied. "What's become of Tort Leshi? Where is he?" they asked. "He's out, but I don't know where he went," she replied. She prepared

385

lunch for her brothers and, when they had eaten it, they rose and went away again. "When Tort Leshi comes, give him our kind regards," they said.

Tort Leshi came home in the evening, and his wife said to him, "My brothers have asked me to give you their kind regards." "Why? Where they here?" he asked. "Yes, they were," she said. "Did they see the ram?" he asked. "I'm afraid they did," she replied. "Then bring a knife and let's slaughter it," he said. "They may come and steal it to-night." He took the knife and killed the ram.

He divided it into four parts which he put in a chest. He covered the meat with rags so that Tosku and Mosku could not find it if they came to steal it. Then he ate his supper and went to bed.

Tosku and Mosku rose during the night and came to steal the ram. They looked high and low for it but could not find it. The elder brother said, "Come, let's go. Who knows where he has put the ram?" "No, I'll not go away without the ram," said the other, taking off his clothes. Then he went and lay down between Tort Leshi and his wife as they slept. There he whispered to his sister, "Wife, did you cover up the meat properly so that they can't come and steal it?" She thought it was her husband who spoke to her and she replied, "I covered it up myself in the chest." The two brothers went to the chest, found the meat and carried it away.

After a little, Tort Leshi awoke and said to his wife, "Don't sleep as sound as the dead!" His wife replied, "Go to sleep. No one will come here. You've kept me without sleep all night." He rose and went to the chest, where he found no meat. It had been stolen. "Get up! They've stolen our meat," he cried out to her.

He followed in their tracks. It was still night when he entered a forest and came on a bad road, where he found them. The one who was carrying the meat was behind. Tort Leshi stepped between them and said to the one carrying the meat, "Come on, what's happened to you? Why are you dragging behind? Tort Leshi may follow us." "I can't carry the meat all night long. You take it for a bit," replied the other. "Give it to me," said Tort Leshi. The other one thought it was his brother who spoke and gave him the meat. "Come on, get in front of

386

me!" said Tort Leshi. Then he left them and returned home with the meat.

The other brother stopped and said, "Come on, what's become of you? Where's the meat?" "I gave it to you," said the other. "He has stolen the meat," exclaimed the first one. "How could he steal the meat?" said the other. "I gave it to you." "I won't give it up," said the first one and turned back and went back to steal the meat again.

He hastened straight to Tort Leshi's house. Tort Leshi had not yet arrived with the meat but was still on his way. In the meantime, the brother went and stole his sister's veil and came out of the door to greet him when he arrived, wrapped up in the veil as his wife might have been.

Tort Leshi arrived and passed into the house through the door. The disguised thief said, "Husband, did you see those rascals anywhere?" Tort Leshi dropped the meat to the ground. "Here it is!" he said triumphantly. "How dare they steal my meat?" He entered the house. Then the robber took the meat and, still wearing the veil, ran away. When Tort Leshi went into the house, he found his wife there. "What did you do with the meat?" he asked. "You never gave me any meat!" she said. "If you had, they would not have stolen it at the door." "I'll go after them again and get it back," cried Tort Leshi.

He followed them and found them in the forest, where they had lit a fire and were roasting the meat. He saw them but could do nothing, so he undressed and blackened his face with soot so that he became like an *arap*. Then he appeared suddenly in front of them where they sat by the fire, and he snarled like a devil. The younger brother said to the other, "Brother, who ate our father?" "An *arap* with white teeth," the elder brother replied. "Here's the Devil! He's coming after us!" the younger brother exclaimed. They ran off, dropping the meat. Tort Leshi then flung the meat over his shoulder and went home.

When he arrived, his wife said to him, "Husband, did you see those fellows anywhere?" "If you want meat, come and eat it. I'll not trust it in your hands again," he replied. He was afraid that the other two would steal it again. He and his wife then ate meat until they finished it all up.

The King's Daughter Who Was a Vampire

Once upon a time, there was a King who had three daughters and a son. All his daughters were married.

His eldest daughter used to turn into a vampire at night and come to her father's palace and eat one of his horses. Somehow the stable guard managed to inform the King that someone was coming and killing his horses. "Oh, how can they kill my horses?" the King exclaimed. "I don't know," the man replied. "I only find horse after horse dead – killed."

The King's son said, "Father, I will go and guard the horses to-night." And he did go to stand guard over them all night. The Princess who became a vampire came to the stable and, putting out her hand, opened the door. The Prince smote her with his sword and cut off her hand. She then ran away.

Dawn came and the Prince left the stable. He did not tell the King, his father, that he had cut off somebody's hand.

One night the King invited his daughters to supper. His eldest daughter came with her hand bandaged. When supper was brought in, she picked up her bread with her left hand. The King said to her, "Why are you eating with your left hand, daughter? What is the matter with the right one?" "This swine who calls himself my brother wounded me," she replied. The King seized a stick and beat his son. "Why did you hurt her hand?" he cried. "She is the person who is killing our horses," the Prince replied. "Out you go for saying so! Be gone!" the King exclaimed. And he drove off his son. And his son left the palace.

The young man then found a peasant woman who had a partridge. He said to her, "Will you sell the partridge to me?" "I will," she replied. "For a piastre." He gave her the piastre and took the partridge and put it in the bosom of his shirt and bade the peasant woman good-bye.

He then went to another country and there found that the King had dug a ditch as wide as a room and had issued a proclamation, saying, "I will give my daughter in marriage to the man who jumps the ditch." Many people from all over the country had gathered there, eager to jump the ditch but unable to do so because it was so wide.

When the young man arrived in that country, he looked round him and said, "What have all these people gathered for?" "They want to jump the ditch so that the King may give them his daughter," was the reply. The partridge said to the young man, "Jump! I will help you to get across." The young man then jumped the ditch. There was great rejoicing because a son-in-law had now been found for the King.

They said to the Princess, "We have found a husband for you. He is a stranger." She replied, "I don't want him if he is a stranger. I want him only if he can make me speak."

Well, they informed the young man of this, saying, "Can you make her talk to you?" "I'll see," said the young man. The partridge then said to him, "Let me go and enter the royal apartments. When you come in, say, 'I'm glad to see you!' and I'll reply 'Welcome!' And then we shall talk to each other. I will ask you to tell me something and you will say, 'I found three persons. One of them had made a tree and carved it into the likeness of a man. The second one had put clothes on the tree. And the third one had given it a soul and life. Now I want you to tell me which of these men is the best. The one who carved the tree into the likeness of a man, the one who dressed it up, or the one who gave it a soul?' I shall reply to you, 'The man who carved it like a man.' You will say, 'No, the one who dressed it up.' And don't mention the man who gave it life."

The young man went to the royal apartments and said, "I'm glad to see you!" The partridge replied, "Welcome!" Then it asked the young man to tell it something and he told it about the three persons he had found. When he asked which was the best, the partridge replied, "The one who carved it like a man." The young man said, "No, the one who dressed it up." The Princess then interrupted and said, "You are

389

both foolish. The best of the three is the one who gave it life." The partridge replied, "We know that. I just wanted to make you speak."

The Princess then married the young man. Some days later, she said to him, "Come, young man, let us go to your home." "All right, let us," he said. And they made ready. They took with them a lion and a tiger and travelled until they drew near the town where his father lived.

The town was deserted, the people having fled because of the Princess who haunted it and had killed everyone she could find. The young man said to his wife, "You stay here. I'm going to see what is happening there." He tied up the lion and the tiger and issued orders, saying, "When the lion and the tiger begin to quarrel, you must set them free. I shall be in difficulties. If I am in trouble and the vampire is about to jump on me, you must set the lion and the tiger free so that they may come and kill her." "All right," his suite said to him.

The young man went on and entered the town. There was no one there at all. He went straight home, and there he found the vampire, his sister.

As soon as she saw him, she sprang at him, crying, "Let me kill him!" He climbed at once to the top of a tree. She began to gnaw its trunk with her teeth and felled it. It fell on another tree. The young man clung to the topmost branches of this tree and again the vampire gnawed its trunk. But the lion and the tiger came running up and delivered him. "Seize the vampire and tear her to pieces," he ordered them. They seized her and tore her to pieces and killed her.

The lion and the tiger then went and fetched the bride home to the young man's house. Heralds announced on every hand, "Whoever is a native of such and such a town may now return home because the vampire has been killed." They all returned to their homes and this man became King.

The Old Man and the Seven Baldheads

Once upon a time there was an old man who had a son. The son wanted to take an ox to market and sell it, but the old man said, "Don't take it to market. The seven Baldheads who are there will turn it into a he-goat." "Oh, no," said his son, "they can't do that with me."

The son took the ox and drove it to market to sell it. One of the Baldheads went up to him and said, "Young man, how much do you want for this he-goat?" "This is an ox and not a he-goat," the young man replied. "Say, say, how much do you want for it?" the Baldhead repeated. "Five hundred piastres," he replied. "Won't you sell it for twenty?" the Baldhead asked. "No," he replied and the Baldhead went away.

Another Baldhead came up to the young man, for there were seven of them. "How much do you want for this he-goat?" he asked. "This is not a he-goat, it is an ox," the young man said. "How much do you want for it?" the Baldhead asked. "Five hundred piastres," the young man replied. "Will you sell it to me for twenty?" asked the Baldhead. "No," the young man replied and this Baldhead, too, went away.

Another one came and asked, "How much do you want for this he-goat?" The young man said to himself, "It seems that it really is a he-goat!" And he sold it for twenty piastres.

The young man went home to the old man, who said, "Did you sell the ox, son?" "It was a he-goat and not an ox," the young man replied. "I told you they would turn it into a he-goat," his father said. "But never mind! I will put it right."

Next day, the old man got a donkey and took it to market to sell it. But first he put a gold coin under its tail. A Baldhead went up to him and said, "How much do you want for this donkey foal?" "It's not a donkey foal. It's a donkey and it drops gold. You will see!" said the old man, hitting the donkey in the belly with his stick. In its pain, the donkey dropped the gold coin, which the old man at once picked up and showed to the Baldhead, saying, "Do you see, man, what my donkey does?" The Baldhead went away.

He went to find all his brothers and, having found them, said, "Come and see! An old man brought to market a donkey that makes gold coins." The Baldheads went to the old man and said, "How much do you want for this donkey, old man?" "One hundred Napoleons," he replied. "One hundred Napoleons for a donkey?" they exclaimed. "It makes gold coins, my friends," said the old man. So they bought the donkey for one hundred Napoleons.

"What must we do to the donkey to make it drop gold coins?" they asked. "Give it a lot of maize to eat and a lot of water to drink. Then prick its belly with a pointed stick as I did. Then it will drop gold," he said.

The Baldheads did as he said, giving the donkey a lot of maize and water. But the donkey only flung its legs up and died.

"Let's go and kill that old man," the Baldheads said.

The old man had lately caught two hares, one of which he kept tied up at home and the other he took with him when he went to work in the field. The seven Baldheads went to him and said, "What was this trick you played on us, old man? The donkey is dead." "How do I know what you did to it?" he replied. "Stay with me to-night and let's talk." As they spoke, he loosed the hare and said to it, "Run home and tell my wife to make a good pie for to-night. Tell her to kill some hens, too, and to roast them."

As soon as it was free, the hare ran off into the forest. The old man said to the seven Baldheads, "Come on, let's go home!" They set off with him and, on arriving at his house, saw the hare tied up. "Oh!" they exclaimed, "We don't want food from you, old man. Only give us this hare." "Don't mention such a thing," he replied. "The hare is a sort of telegraph between me and my wife." "We want it very much," the Baldheads said. "Well, I'll let you have it," he replied, "but I want fifty Napoleons for it. Money can't really buy it. Its head is worth one thousand Napoleons, but I'll let it go for your sakes." So the old man sold them the hare for fifty Napoleons.

"Here, take it," he said, "and keep it tied up close to you for a week till it gets used to you." The Baldheads took the hare home and kept it tied up near them as the old man had said. A week or ten days passed. Then one day, when there were in the market, they loosed the hare, saying, "Run home and tell the women to prepare a good meal for to-night." After they loosed the hare, the dogs in the market ran after it barking and it ran off at top speed into the woods.

When the Baldheads returned home in the evening, they said to their wives, "Where is the hare?" "There is no hare here," the women replied. "Let's go and kill that old man," said the Baldheads, and they set off for his house.

The old man had taken a couple of sheep's intestines and after filling them with blood, had hung them round his wife's neck. He also said to his wife, "When the Baldheads come, I shall ask you to make some good food for us quickly. You will shriek and scold me, saying, 'You get the same food every night.' Then I'll take a knife and cut the intestines round your neck and you'll fall down dead. I'll take the clarinet and come and blow in your ear. You will get up and begin to prepare the food." "All right," said his wife.

The seven Baldheads went to the old man's house to kill him. "Come out! Where are you?" they called. He came out and opened the door. "Come in, come in," he said. "A friend does not have to ask leave to come in." The seven Baldheads stepped inside.

The old man called to his wife, "Where are you, wife? Quick, get some good food for us! This and that!" He named some dishes. The old woman shrieked at him, "What? You get the same food every night." He drew out his knife, went up to her and, catching her by the hair, cut the intestines round her neck. She fell plumb to the ground as if dead.

The seven Baldheads said to him, "What? You've killed the old woman!" "I do it quite often," he said. "What do you mean? How can you kill her quite often? She's dead!" they exclaimed. "I'll revive her," he replied. He picked up his clarinet and, approaching the old woman,

393

blew into her ear. She soon got up to her feet and began to get dinner ready.

"If you don't mind, old man," they said, "we don't want anything to eat. We want nothing except your clarinet." "I can't give you that. My old woman might die then," he replied. In the end they bought his clarinet for who knows how many Napoleons. At least fifty.

They took the clarinet home with them and picked a quarrel with their wives. They drew out their knives and killed the women, who all fell down dead. Then they began to blow into their ears with the clarinet. They blew and blew, but it was no good. The women were dead and could not come back to life.

"He's killed our wives, this old man," they said. "Let's go and kill him!"

The old man had already dug a hole in the ground and said to his wife, "When the seven Baldheads come, cry and say to them, 'My old man's dead!'"

The Baldheads came and found the old woman crying. "My old man's dead," she told them. "When did he die? Where is his grave?" they asked. She pointed out the hole he had dug in the ground and said, "There is his grave!" "Let's go and stamp on his head!" they exclaimed. And they did this and then went home.

The old man later came out of his grave. When he made it, he had left a hole in it through which he could breathe.

The Poor Man Who Married the Daughter of the King of Italy

Once there was a poor young man, who went to the King's palace and shouted, "I have brains, but I haven't any money." The King heard him and ordered him to be brought to him. They called him and he went to the King.

"Why did you shout in the street that you have brains but no money? What would you like to do?" the King said to him. "I know what I want to do," he replied. "How much money do you need?" asked the King. "One thousand Napoleons," he replied. The King drew out his purse and gave him this amount of money.

The young man then went to the market, where he hired five young servants, paying them a wage of three Napoleons a month. "Come now and follow me," he said.

He set forth and went to Italy, where he went to a hotel for the night. Next day he said to one of his servants, "Ask the hotel-keeper to fetch for me the barber who shaves the King." His servant went to the hotel-keeper and said, "My master wants you to get him the barber who shaves the King." The hotel-keeper went to fetch this barber and brought him to the hotel. The barber shaved the gentleman and, having done so, gave him a mirror in which to look at himself, saying, "Your good health!" The young man laid down the mirror, put his hand in his pocket, and pulled out twenty Napoleons, which he laid on the mirror, saying, "Take this money, good fellow, and go!" With many a bow the barber withdrew to join the servant outside.

The barber asked him, "Who is this gentleman?" "Go away, go away, we don't know who he is," was the reply. He went away, returning to his shop.

Customers came to the shop. He said to them, "A Prince has come to the town and is staying in such-and-such a hotel. I went and shaved him and he gave me twenty Napoleons. The King doesn't give me more than one."

Next day the young man said to his servants, "Call the hotel-keeper!" They called him and he came. "You will now come and show me the baths where the King goes," the young man said. "Very good, sir, let us go," said the hotel-keeper.

They got up and went to the baths. The young man entered and had a bath in the bath-house. He then came out and dressed. The bath attendant handed him a mirror, saying, "Your good health!" The young man laid down the mirror, drew out thirty Napoleons and, after laying the money on the mirror, went away.

The owner of the baths stopped one of his servants and asked him, "Who is he? What sort of man is he?" "Take your money, take your money and leave him alone. He must not be named," replied the servant. The owner of the baths told the story to everyone that came to his baths, saying, "A Prince has come to the town and is stopping at such-and-such a hotel."

All the town heard the news. The King, too, heard it and asked one of his notables, a pasha, to go to the young man and bring him to see him. The pasha set out and went to the young man's hotel.

The young man had ordered his servants as follows. "Don't let in anyone who wishes to see me. Tell them all that I am busy and ask them to come the next day." For this reason, the pasha had to go back to the King without seeing the young man.

The pasha went to the King and said, "I went to see the young man but he would not let me come in. He said he was busy." "You must go again to-morrow to see him," the King replied.

Next day the pasha went again, and again the young man refused to see him. He was a Prince! The servants said, "Come to-morrow. Our master isn't busy to-morrow." The pasha went back once more to the King.

"He refused to see me again to-day," reported the pasha, "but I am to go again to-morrow."

When he went the following day, he walked straight in and went upstairs. The servants were outside the young man's door. The pasha said to one of them, "Is your master busy?" "No, he's not. Please come in." The pasha opened the door and entered the room. He found the young man seated on a chair like a prince and holding a newspaper. Yet he had no idea of how to read. The pasha stepped into the room, bowing reverently. "Please come in! Please sit down!" said the young man. The servants came in presently and served coffee. And then the young man and the pasha began to talk.

"The King has sent me to see you," said the pasha. "Why did your lordship go and stay in this hotel? The King is cross because you did not go straight to his palace." "Oh! Has the King heard I'm here?" exclaimed the young man. "He heard the day you arrived," said the pasha. "I did not want to reveal my identity because I wanted to leave soon. But since the King has heard about me, I'll go and see him," said the young man.

The pasha took his leave and went to the King and said, "He is coming to see you!" The young man soon afterwards took his servants and went to call on the King. He bowed once to the King, who shook his hand and embraced him. Then they sat down close together.

"How dare you come here and not call on me?" asked the King. "I'm not stopping long," the young man replied. "My father has written to ask me to leave soon." "I won't let you go just yet. I'll keep you here some days," said the King. And he did keep him for some days.

One day the King said to his notables, "Tell that prince that I wish to give him my daughter in marriage." The notables repeated the message to the young man, saying, "The King wishes to give you his daughter in marriage." "I cannot marry her without my father's permission," said the young man. "I will write to him about it. If God wills, I shall marry her." "Very well," they replied.

The young man stayed for some days with the King and then pretended to write a letter to his father. Yet he could not write at all. After he had stayed about a week there, the notables said to him, "Have you informed your royal father?" "I have," he replied, "and he has sent me word that he leaves it to the King here." In this way he married the princess.

397

He stayed quite a long time with the King. Then the princess said to him, "Let's go to your home, to the royal palace of your father." He had no house whatsoever, but she did not know that. "Let's go! Let's go!" she said. So they set out.

He sent word to the King of his own country, who had given him the one thousand Napoleons. "You are the King who gave one thousand Napoleons to a young man," he said. "He has married the daughter of the King of Italy and is coming to see you. Don't disgrace him! Don't let him down!" In reply, the King announced to all the town, "A son of mine is coming home. You are to go to meet him with a band and the army."

The young man went straight to the King's palace and the bride was taken in among the royal ladies in the harem. The King said to him, "You devil, how did you manage to marry this princess?" "I managed it by my cleverness," he replied. "I tipped the barber twenty Napoleons when he shaved me and I tipped the bath people thirty when I took a bath. Word went round that a prince had arrived and the King sent for me and offered me his daughter."

After this, the King adopted him as his son.

The Intelligent Brothers and the Stupid One

Once there was an old woman, who had three sons. Two of them were intelligent and one was stupid. The old woman always sent the stupid one out to work and kept one of the intelligent ones at home. The one who stayed at home was in the habit of washing and cleaning and changing his mother's clothes every day.

One day the stupid son said he wanted to stay at home. His brothers said to him, "You cannot do for mother as she likes." "I can take better care of her than you can," he replied. "Then stay at home to-day and take care of her," said his brothers. So he stayed at home. He filled a big boiler with water, brought it to the boil, and fetched the old woman to wash her. He then threw the boiling water over her and she died.

After she was dead, he dressed her up in new clothes. He found a distaff and stuck it in her belt. He hung a grindstone round the spinning wheel and set the old woman in the place of honour by the hearth.

When his brothers returned in the evening, they asked him, "How is the old lady?" "All right. She is laughing," he replied. "Laughing? How's that?" they asked. "Yes, yes, she is laughing. She is eating cream cheese and laughing," he said, for he had rubbed cream cheese on her lips.

The brothers went into the house and found their mother dead. "Oh, he has ruined us! He has killed mother!" they exclaimed. "The village will hear about this and tell the authorities and they will accuse us of murdering our mother. Quick, let us bury the old lady!" So they buried her somewhere and went home again. "Come, let us go," they said to their youngest brother. And they all left the house.

399

When they were outside, they said to the stupid one, "Pull the door to behind you." But he took the door off its hinges and carried it with him. He flung it over his shoulders and also the big spinning wheel, and followed his brothers.

When his brothers turned their heads to look at him, they saw that he was carrying the door and the spinning wheel. "Why did you bring these things?" they asked. "You told me to pull the door, too, behind me," he replied.

They went on and on and came to a place where there was a fountain, with big shady trees beside it. Night overtook them as they reached it. They climbed the trees because they were afraid to sleep on the ground.

That night some muleteers came there, bringing many loads of goods. They stupid brother said to the others, "Brothers, the door is slipping out of my hands." "Damn you, let it fall!" his brother replied. The door fell to the ground and the muleteers were so frightened that they abandoned their loads and ran away. The three brothers remained up the tree.

Monkeys came and seized the goods of the muleteers. "Mother's spinning wheel is slipping from my hands," said the stupid brother. "Let it drop!" said his brother. And so he did with a clatter. The monkeys were so frightened that they ran away.

Then the brothers came down the tree and got all the goods there. They became rich, the quantity was so large. And so, they benefited from their stupid brother.

The tale to Jatesh.

Health to us!

The Woman Who Cheated the Devil

Once upon a time, hodjas prayed for three years, trying to get the Devil into a bottle. It was not till after many efforts that they succeeded.

A woman went and asked them what they had in the bottle. "The Devil," they replied. "Oh nonsense! You say you have the Devil in it?" she exclaimed. "We had a hard time with him," said the hodjas. "We prayed for three years and could hardly get him in." "I can put him in it in no time," she said. She opened the bottle and let the Devil out.

After he came out, she said to him, "Where were you? Here in the bottle?" "Eh, of course I was," said the Devil. "I don't believe you were," she replied. "Yes, I was," he insisted. "The neck of the bottle is very narrow and you are a big man. How could you get in?" she argued. "Oh," he said, "I've been in already." "If you were in once," she said, "you could get in again, just to let me see how you did get in."

The Devil was tricked and climbed into the bottle. The woman immediately corked it and said to the hodjas, "You prayed for three years and had difficulty in cheating him. I managed to cheat him in one minute."

The Stupid Pasha

Once upon a time there was a King. There was also a Pasha, who was rather stupid. The King gave him a Napoleon and said, "Go out and buy a ram. Then bring me the ram, the Napoleon and a piece of meat from the ram." "How can I buy a ram like that?" said the Pasha. "Just do so, or I'll chop your head off," ordered the King. So the Pasha went out to buy the ram.

However, he went to hide in another town. On the way, he met another old man and said, "Where are you going, old man?" "To the town here," replied the man. "Let me come with you," said the Pasha. On the way, the Pasha noticed a field of wheat and asked the old man what it was. "Wheat," he replied. "Has the owner eaten it or is he going to eat it?" asked the Pasha. "He has not yet reaped it," the old man replied. "Come, let's go on," said the Pasha.

When they reached the town, the Pasha went to stay in a hotel and the old man went home. He had a son and a daughter to whom he said, "I travelled with a man who was stupid. We saw wheat on the way and he asked if the owner had eaten it or was going to eat it. And the wheat hadn't even been reaped!"

His daughter replied, "He was not making fun of you. The owner might already have eaten that wheat by selling it in advance or he might have borrowed money on it. Where is the man staying? In which hotel?" The old man gave her the name of the hotel.

The girl fried ten eggs and also baked a loaf of bread. She then gave the eggs and bread to her brother, saying, "Take these things to the man in the hotel. Tell him they are from father." Her brother took them from her and carried them to the Pasha.

402

On the way, the young man extracted an egg and ate it. He also broke off a piece from the loaf and ate that. The rest he took to the Pasha.

"These are from the old man with whom the Pasha travelled," was the message he gave. The Pasha replied, "My greetings to the old man and tell him the stars are few to-night and the moon is not fifteen days old." The young man returned home.

Said his sister, "Did you take the food to him, brother?" "I did," he replied. "Did he say anything to you?" she asked. "He said that the stars are few to-night and the moon is not at the full," her brother replied. The girl seized her brother and beat him. "You ate the eggs on the way!" she cried. "You also ate a piece of the loaf!"

The girl then said to her father, "To-morrow go and get the Pasha to come here. I'll see to getting supper ready." And next evening the old man went and fetched the Pasha.

When the Pasha arrived, he said, "You have a fine house, old man. Only your chimney is crooked." The old man's daughter was present in the next room and overheard him. "Reply to him, father," she cried, "that the chimney is crooked but the smoke goes out straight." The Pasha said to the old man, "Whose daughter is that?" "Mine," said the old man. "Call her in," said the Pasha. And her father did so.

The girl came into the room and the Pasha said, "How are you, daughter!" "All right," she replied. "I am looking for intelligent people," said the Pasha. "Why?" she asked. "What do you want them for?" "The King gave me a Napoleon," he said, "and told me to buy a ram. He wants the ram, the Napoleon and a piece of meat from the ram." "The King has been right to give you such a command," she replied. "Go out and buy a good ram and bring it here."

The Pasha went and bought a good ram and brought it to the girl. She took the animal and sheared it, then made a small rug from its wool. "Now take this and sell it," she said to the Pasha. He sold it for a Napoleon and, coming back to the girl, said, "I sold the rug and got a Napoleon." "Well, you have bought a ram and you've now got a Napoleon to take to the King, "she replied.

403

"He wants a piece of meat as well," the Pasha said. "Go and get a farrier to cut the ram," she returned. The farrier cut the ram and took out a piece of meat for the King. "Now take them all to the King," said the girl. The Pasha took them all with him and left the town.

He took the ram, the Napoleon and the piece of meat cut from the ram to the King. "Where did you learn to do all this?" asked the King. "A girl taught me, sire," said the Pasha.

"All you're fit for," said the King, "is herding cows."

Xhymert Ahmeti

Once upon a time Hizir went to a King. "Have you no children at all, oh King?" he said to him. "I haven't," said the King. "God hasn't given me any." "Do you want to have any?" said Hizir. "I do, even it if means my being blind and having no eyes," said the King. So Hizir gave him an apple, saying, "Eat half of it yourself and give half to the Queen. God will give you a daughter. When she begins to grow up, shut her up." "Why?" asked the King. "She will fall very deeply in love," said Hizir. God then gave the King a daughter.

The girl grew and became ten or twelve years of age. Then the King shut her up, giving her a servant to attend to her wants. One day she came out and broke a pane in the window. She put her head through the hole and looked at the snow that had fallen outside. Then she said to the servant, "What's that white thing that has fallen there?" "Snow," the woman replied. "Is there anybody as white as that snow?" the girl asked. "There is," said the maid. "There's a certain Xhymert Ahmet who is as white as that." The girl said nothing more and went back into her room.

Next day she came out again. Somebody had killed a fowl outside and there was blood on the snow. The girl called her maid, saying, "What's that red thing there on the snow?" "Blood," said the maid. "We've killed a chicken." "Is there anybody to be found as white as that snow and as red as that blood?" asked the girl. "Xhymert Ahmeti is as white and as red as they are," said the maid. The girl then re-entered the house.

Next day she came out again. Some raven's feathers had fallen on the ground. Again she called her servant. This time she said, "Is there anybody as white as that snow, as red as that blood, and with hair as

405

black as those raven's feathers?" "There's only Xhymert Ahmeti," said the maid.

"Go," said the girl, "and kill a goose. Clean it, pluck it, put it on a spit to roast, and bring it to me here." The maid went and killed the goose, cleaned it, and brought it ready spitted to the girl. "Now light a fire," said the girl. The maid lit the fire and made it ready to roast the goose. "Now go," said the girl. She did not want the maid to stay there because she wanted to say things.

The maid had spitted the goose and now the girl turned it over the fire, saying, "Roast, oh goose, as my heart is afire for Xhymert Ahmeti. Burn, oh goose, as my heart burns for Xhymert Ahmeti." But the maid heard her and went and called her mother, the Queen, saying, "Come and listen to what your daughter is saying." And the Queen went and listened behind the door and heard what the girl was saying. She set off to find the King and said to him, "The girl's all spoiled." "How so?" the King replied. "She's crazed about Xhymert Ahmeti," said the Queen. "Where has she seen Xhymert Ahmeti?" asked the King.

The King had a box made and put the girl inside it. "Take the box and throw it into the sea," he ordered. So they flung the girl into the sea.

Xhymert Ahmeti was travelling by sea and saw the box. He had a pretty numerous suite with him and said to them, "Catch that box!" and they caught it.

He was on his way to his sister's. He continued on his way, box and all. When he arrived, his sister came out to welcome him. "What's this box you have, brother?" she asked. "I found it in the sea," he said. "Open it and see what there is inside. If there's anything nice, keep it." She opened the box as he bade her, and found the girl. "What do you want here?" she said. "I want Xhymert Ahmeti," the girl replied. "Pooh, you idiot!" said the sister and shut the box again.

She then said to her brother, "Take away that box and throw it back into the sea." So when he left for home, he took the box with him and flung it into the sea.

A week later he came back again, this time to see his second sister – he had three altogether. Again the box turned up in his path, and

406

again he took it with him. When he went to his second sister, she said, "What's this box you've brought?" "I found it in the sea," he replied. "Open it and look inside. If it's got anything worthwhile, take it." And she opened it and found the girl inside. "Oh, what do you want here?" she asked. "I want Xhymert Ahmeti," the girl replied. His sister said, "Pooh, you idiot!" and shut the box again. She said to her brother, "Take the box away and throw it back into the sea where you found it." And he took it and flung it back into the sea.

The next week he came again, and again the box turned up in front of him. Again he took it with him and continued on his way to his youngest sister. When he arrived, she said, "What's this box you've got?" "I found it in the sea," he said. "Open it and look inside. If it's got anything worthwhile, keep it." His sister opened the box and found the girl inside. "What do you want here?" she said. "I want Xhymert Ahmeti," the girl answered.

"Come out of the box. I'll let you have him," the sister replied. And she took the girl to the kitchen. "You are to bring us coffee," she instructed her. "As you enter the room, slip and break the cups. I will get up and beat you. If my brother wants you, he won't let me hit you."

The girl carried the cups of coffee on a tray to the room. As she came near Xhymert Ahmeti, she slipped and spilled the coffee. His sister got up to beat her, but he caught her hand, "Don't touch the girl, but forgive her," he cried.

After a time, Xhymert Ahmeti wanted to go to bed and said to his sister, "Send me a girl to blow away the flies from me." She said to the girl, "Go and blow away the flies from Xhymert Ahmeti." He had lain down in a corner and the girl stood at the door to blow away the flies. He said, "Why, girl, do you blow away the flies at the door? Come closer and blow them away here." She replied, "If I burn like a torch and am scattered like ashes, I won't come near you."

He got up and said to his sister, "Where did you find this girl?" "It's for your sake she came here," his sister replied. So he married the girl made her his wife.

The tale for Godolesh.

Health to us.

407

The Talking Flea

Once upon a time there was what there was. There were an old man and an old woman, who had no children. They poured water into a pot and a flea came out of it. This flea could talk like a human being.

The old woman made a pie to take to her husband in the field. As she carried it to him, the flea was sitting on it and called out to the old man, "Oh father, how shall we go? Through the middle or by the edge?" His father shouted, "Through the middle." And the flea set to and ate the middle of the pie and finished it.

"Now, father, how shall we go?" he said. "Along the edge," said the father. And he ran along the edge of the pie and ate that, too.

The old woman reached the old man. "Where's my food, old woman?" he asked. "The flea ate it," she replied. "Why did you eat it, flea?" he asked. "You told me yourself to eat it," the flea replied. "You said, 'Go along the edge' and I ate the edge." "Get out of this! May I never see you again!" said the old man.

The flea went away. It went to the edge of a road by the bank of a stream and hid. At night three thieves came by and reached the edge of the stream where the flea was hiding. One said to the others, "I'll wet here." The flea said to him, "Don't wet me." "Who are you?" asked the thief. "A human being like you. What do you want here?" the flea replied. "I'm out to steal," said the robber. "And so are we," said the others. "Then I'll come with you," said the flea. And he went with them.

He went some way and entered a stable to steal the cattle in it. The robbers had said to him, "You steal them and we'll keep guard." The flea entered the stable and called, "Ho, ho!" to drive them off. But the master of the house heard him and went down to the stable. "Who's crying like this?" he said. He and the other men looked all round but could see nothing, so they went upstairs again.

Again the flea called, "Ho, ho!" to the cattle, but this time the people in the house said, "It's nothing. It's only our imagination. There's nobody in the stable." The flea then took the cattle and drove them away.

He joined his friends and they all went away together. After a time he said, "Now we'll separate. Give me my portion." So the robbers took an ox and killed it and gave him the tripe.

The flea got into the tripe and waited. After a little, dogs came to eat the tripe. He shouted, "Shaht, Shaht!" The dogs were frightened and ran away.

Then a wolf came and again the flea cried, "Shaht, Shaht!" But the wolf ate the tripe.

The flea climbed onto the wolf's back and hid in his coat. When the wolf went to eat the animals in sheepfolds, the flea cried, "The wolf is eating the sheep!" The shepherds came out rifles in hand, fired at the wolf, and made him run away.

The wolf then said to the flea, "Pity me! I'm dying of hunger. Go away and leave me alone." The flea replied, "Why did you eat my tripe?" "I'll bring you two rams for the tripe," said the wolf. "I don't want rams, oh no!" said the flea. "But take me to my own home. That will do." The wolf carried him to his own home at the old man's.

He called out to his father, "Father! Father! Come quick. I've caught a wolf." "Bring him here, bring him here," said the old man. "He won't come," said the flea. "Then let him go," said the old man. "He won't let me go," said the flea. So the old man came out and killed the wolf.

The Dervish and the Thieves

Once upon a time it was summer, and the fruit season. A man went to a certain dervish and asked him to write an amulet for him because he had a pain in his stomach. He had eaten a great many figs and could not digest them so he had a bad pain.

The dervish looked at him and understood his trouble. He said to the man, "Don't eat anything for twenty-four hours and do not stay in one place but walk about all day." He also gave him an amulet to hang round his neck.

The man did as the dervish told him and he recovered. He told everybody he knew that the dervish had cured him. As a result, the dervish had to write amulets every day for people and he won great fame.

One day, the King's money-box was stolen. The King summoned many wise men and asked them to find out who had stolen it. But they could not find the thieves. At length the King summoned a dervish and put pressure on him to make him find them. He even said to him, "If you don't find them, I shall kill you."

In great alarm, the dervish begged the King to give him leave to shut himself up for thirty days in his palace and meditate. He should also be sent good things to eat.

As soon as the dervish entered his room, he began to say to himself, "Thirty, thirty, thirty." He meant to say that he had only thirty days more to live. The next day, he said, "Twenty-nine, twenty-nine, twenty-nine." And the third day he said, "Twenty-eight, twenty-eight, twenty-eight." And so on he went, every day counting a day less.

The thieves who had stolen the money-box were thirty in number and were all in the palace the first day that the dervish came and they heard what he said. Thinking themselves discovered, they melted away in fear, one every day. Just as the dervish decreased daily the number of days he had to live, so did the thieves in their fear decrease their number daily.

At last, only one was left. He went during the night to the dervish and said, "Here is the money-box, but for heaven's sake don't tell the King." In his joy at escaping death the dervish promised that he would not tell the King.

The thirtieth day came. Proudly the dervish went to the King and announced that he had found the money-box. The King was very glad and ever afterwards kept the dervish in his palace and showered favours on him.

The Shoemaker Who Married a Princess

Once upon a time there was a King who had an only daughter. When she came of an age to marry, many important men asked for her hand but the King would not promise her to any of them.

One day, as he was passing through his capital, the King noticed a group of young men, who were shoemakers. When they saw the King, they rose respectfully to their feet. The King saluted them, and they returned the salute.

As he looked at them, he was pleased by the appearance of one of them. He called the servant who was in attendance and said, "Go and find out whose son such-and-such a young man is, in which quarter of the town his house is, and what its number is." The servant asked the young man for the information required and then he and the King bade the young man good-bye.

Early next morning the King told his police to go to such-and-such a number in such-and-such a quarter and to find so-and-so, the son of so-and-so, and bring him to the King. The police at once went to fetch the young man, saying to him, "Come along with us! The King wishes to see you."

As they walked towards the palace, the young man wept and said to himself, "Poor me! What have I done to make the King angry with me?" He thought that they meant to kill him.

As soon as he reached the palace, the King ordered his aides-de-camp to dress him in silver clothes, and this they did. The young man was much amazed. "What's all this?" he asked.

Then the King summoned him to his apartments upstairs and said, "Young man, don't be frightened. I have a daughter and want to marry her to you." The young man became calm and smiled. Next the King ordered that guns should be fired in all the towns of his kingdom.

412

It was done as he ordered and the people all asked, "What does this gunfire mean?"

The rumour soon spread everywhere among the people that the King had married his daughter to a low-class fellow, to someone quite unworthy. "He's given his daughter to a low-class rascal, his daughter that was wooed by such-and-such a prince of such-and-such a kingdom and by such-and-such a King!" they whispered.

They only whispered this in each other's ear and dared not say anything aloud. They knew that if they spoke out about it, the King's spies would hear and have them arrested and killed.

But no matter how secretly the rumours spread, the King got to know of them and learned that he was being criticised.

One day he issued a command to his prime minister, the head of the Mohammedans, and all the high dignitaries of the realm, saying, "Assemble in such-and-such a place on such-and-such a day. I have a message for you." So he assembled them.

All the important people in question gathered before the King arrived and, while waiting for him, said to each other, "What can this meeting be for? Do you know?" "No," the others replied. "We don't." And no one knew the purpose of the gathering. All anyone could say was, "Let's see what the King will say when he comes."

At last the King arrived. After greeting them he said, "Do you know why I have summoned you?" "No, sire, we know nothing," they replied. "I summoned you," he stated, "because you have criticised me for giving my daughter to such-and-such a young man, who was a shoemaker and a ne'er-do-well." "Far be it from us!" they exclaimed. "We are unworthy to mention your name, sire, much less to criticise you."

"I know you have criticised me," the King replied. "Think it over for a quarter of an hour. If you then tell me frankly that you have criticised me, you are free to go to your homes. If you do not, I shall have you all put to death by the executioner." With these words the King left the assembly.

In a quarter of an hour, the King returned and said to the gathering, "Well, have you decided anything?" "Yes, sire, we have," they replied. "Did you criticise me or not?" he asked. "Far be it from us!" they replied. "We did not criticise you. We only made one remark." "What did you say?" the King asked. "We said," they replied, "that such-and-such a King and such-and-such a prince had asked you for your daughter's hand and you had refused to give it. What do you see in this young man to make you give your daughter to him?"

"Now that you've told me the truth," said the King, "light your cigarettes and smoke. Be at ease and don't be afraid anymore. As for the young man to whom I gave my daughter, he has been a shoemaker, but in one or two years I'll make him a high dignitary, as are the others who asked for her hand. If he makes a slip someday, he'll lose the allowance which he receives from the Turkish Government. But that won't matter. He can take a shop and sew shoes in it all day. In the evening, he can buy an oke of bread and take it home to eat with my daughter. If I had given her to any of those who asked for her before and they had had their allowances stopped by the Turkish Government, they would have had no other profession to fall back on. No one would have hired them as labourers. They would not even have known how to hoe. For that reason, I gave my daughter to this young man, who was a shoemaker."

The notables exclaimed with one voice, "Long live the King! Long live the Kingdom of the King who has such wise thoughts!" They all clapped their hands in applause.

Gjini, the Foundling

Once upon a time three merchants were on their way to Durazzo to buy merchandise. They went as far as Kavaja where they stopped for the night at another merchant's. They were given food and drink that evening but otherwise were not well served by their host, to whom a son was born during the night.

When they got up in the morning, their host said, "Excuse me, gentlemen, for not attending properly to you. I have been busy with my wife."

The following night, angels came from Heaven to decree the length of the child's life and his fate. Two of the merchants were asleep, but the third one was awake. The angels talked to each other. One said, "This boy will live so many years but where will he get wealth?" "From this merchant who is awake," the other replied. The merchant overheard them and was frightened in case the boy would steal his property and pondered all night of what he should do to the boy.

At dawn, two of the merchants made ready to leave, but the third said, "I'm not coming. I've changed my mind." The two left. Then he said to his host, "Will you give me your boy? I haven't any children." He had really two sons and a daughter. "I'm willing to give him to you but it's for my wife to settle," said the father. He went to the new-made mother and told her of the merchant's request. "Let's give him the boy. God who gave us this child will give us others," she said. The father went back to the merchant and said, "I will give you the boy." The merchant mounted his horse, put the child on its board in front of him, and went away.

As he rode along a sombre mountain path, he flung away the child on its board. But angels caught the boy so that he was not hurt and

415

they put one stone on this side of him and another on the other, with the board resting on them both, to keep him from being hurt.

Close by there was a sheepfold. A ewe began to come and to let the child suck her. The head shepherd saw something was happening and said to his underlings, "Who's milking the ewe?" They replied, "We don't know." The ewe went every day and gave the child milk.

One day, the head shepherd followed the ewe, keeping her constantly in sight. She broke away from the flock, went straight to the child, straddled her legs and let him suck. The old man, still following her, saw the boy as the ewe fed him. He picked him up and took him back to the sheepfold.

In three months, the child grew as big as if he was three years old and was sent by the head shepherd to his own house, where he had five sons of his own, making six boys with this one. Because he had found him, he called him Gjini (Foundling).

The boy grew till he was fifteen or sixteen years old. Then the merchant who had flung him away on the dangerous road came to spend a night with the head shepherd. They ate and drank together that night and then lay down to sleep.

In the morning, the head shepherd got up. "How did you sleep, sir?" he asked the merchant. "Very well," was the reply. "Did the boys look after you well or not?" the head shepherd next asked. "Many thanks, they looked after me extremely well. But God spare you Gjini, because he looks so well after one. He is a clever boy," said the merchant. "Gjini is not my son," the chief shepherd replied. "I found him, an infant on a board on a mountain path."

The merchant realised that the boy he had flung away was alive and well. "He'll steal my property!" he said to himself. He reflected a little, then said to the chief shepherd, "For two months I haven't heard from home." That was a lie. "I'll write a letter and give it to Gjini to carry to my home," he went on. The chief shepherd said, "Send any of the other boys that you like, but not Gjini." "But it's Gjini that I trust," he said. "Let him take the letter."

Gjini took the letter and set off. On his way he met a dervish who said, "Young man, let me look at that letter you have," and Gjini

416

gave it to him. The dervish opened it and read it. The merchant had written to his sons, "As soon as possible, kill this person that I'm sending to my house. If you don't kill him, don't expect to see me there again." After reading the letter, the dervish tore it up and wrote another to the merchant's sons, saying, "As soon as possible, marry this man to my daughter." The dervish gave this letter to Gjini.

The young man carried the letter straight to the sons of the merchant. As soon as they read it, they married Gjini to their sister. "If father comes and finds them still unmarried," they said, "he will kill us."

When their father came, he said, "Did you do that job I wrote to you about?" "Yes, we married him to the girl," they replied. "What? Is that what I said?" he exclaimed. "Look at the letter you wrote, father," they retorted. He looked at the letter and recognised his own handwriting. "Well, never mind," he said.

He then gave orders to the shepherds, saying, "Any man I send to-morrow morning to the sheep you are to kill. Even if it's my own sons, kill them." "All right," replied the shepherds, and the merchant returned home.

There he said to his wife, "Get up early to-morrow morning and call Gjini. He is to go to the sheepfold and get a ram so that we can celebrate our daughter's marriage."

The merchant's wife got up early next morning and opened Gjini's door. She saw him and her daughter lying together in a close embrace and, like any mother, felt sorry to waken him from his sleep by her daughter's side. She said, "Why should I waken him? Why should I disturb him? I'll send my own sons." She went and called her own sons, saying, "Go to the sheepfold and get a ram. That's what father said." Her two sons got up and went to the sheepfold. When the shepherds saw them coming, they let fly at them with their rifles and killed them both.

When their father got up, he called to his wife, "Did you send Gjini for the ram?" "No," she replied, "I was sorry for him, sleeping side by side with our daughter. I sent our boys instead." "Oh, oh, you've murdered our boys!" he exclaimed. He leapt on his horse and rode off to the sheepfold. When the shepherds saw him coming, they exclaimed, "We've killed the aga's son, and he is now going to kill us! Let us kill him first." Without waiting any further, they fired at the aga and killed him.

So, his property came to Gjini together with his daughter.

The Violin

Once upon a time there was a very poor boy who had a mother and an only sister. For house he had a cottage thatched with straw. But he played the violin very well.

Close by there was an important man, a 'lord,' who had a grown-up daughter. She fell in love with the young man because of the splendid way he played the violin. He talked with her from a distance with his violin, he played so well.

The girl said to her father, "Father, I want to marry this young man." "Why, daughter? Are there no other lords?" said her father. "I want him," she said, "and if I don't get him, I won't marry at all." So the two were betrothed.

Some time passed with the young man still very poor. He said to himself, "The wedding day is coming and I've no money. I've also no house. I'll go abroad, perhaps to Istanbul, and earn some money."

He set off from home and before many days passed, came to a *teqe* [dervish lodge], where he stopped for the night. That very evening, the King of that country had died and it was the custom of that country that when the King died, the nobles should go to the *teqe* and elect as their King any man they found in it.

They found the poor young man in the guest-room. Once glance at him and they said, "You are our King!" He replied, "Kingship is not for me. I am poor and a stranger from abroad." "It doesn't matter," they said, "we accept you as is the custom of our country." And so they made the young man King.

After some time, the lord's daughter who was betrothed to the young man became very worried because so much time had passed without news of him. People said to her that he must be dead. And so, believing what they said, she engaged herself to another man. But not

419

with her heart. She did not want this engagement. It was her father who betrothed her.

Although she was engaged to another man, she hired a young man, giving him saddle-bags of gold and a good mule besides a gold pot on which her name was engraved. "Go and find the poor young man," she said. "Spend the money on your board and lodging till you find him."

The man set off and inquired here and inquired there in every country till he spent all his money and had to sell the mule. He was in the depths of poverty when he reached the very country of which the poor young man had become King. Because he had nothing to eat, he became a seller of *boza*. He often went to the bazaar to sell the drink, using the girl's gold pot.

One day, his road led him past the King's palace and the King saw him from his window and recognised the costume of his native country, which was considered outlandish in his new one. He also noticed the gold pot. At once he called to the orderlies he had, "Summon the *boza*-seller," and the orderlies did so.

The *boza*-seller trembled with fear, like the foreigner he was, in front of the King. "Tell me where you're from," said the King. But he saw that the man was very frightened and called, "Bring a doctor quickly to give him medicine and stop him from being frightened." When the man had drunk the medicine, the King said, "Tell me the truth! Where are you from?" "Albania," the man replied. "Tell me all about what has happened to you," said the King. "Pity me! Don't harm me!" said the man. "Don't be in the least afraid," said the King.

"The daughter of such-and-such a lord sent me," said the man. "She has lost her betrothed," he continued and mentioned the name. "She gave me saddle-bags filled with gold and a mule to pay for my expenses. She also gave me a pot to make so-and-so. I've spent the money and sold the mule and spent the money I got for it, too. As I hadn't any more food, I became a *boza*-seller. But I haven't found so-and-so."

"I am her betrothed," declared the King. He took off his robes and signs of rank and made the *boza*-seller put them on, and set him on

420

the throne in his stead. Then, dressed like a *boza*-seller, he jumped on his horse and set off for home. King as he was, he had plenty of gold.

He went straight to his own cottage. "I hope I find you well, old woman," he said to his mother. "Welcome, young man," she replied and he sat down in the chimney-corner. She did not recognise him as her son. "What are those drums beating for?" he asked. "Oh, young man, the daughter of such-and-such a lord is getting married. She was betrothed to my son," his mother replied and began to cry. "What happened to your son, old woman?" he asked. "He went abroad," she replied. "God knows if he's dead or alive. But I hope he's alive." "What else do you have, old woman?" he asked. "Have you any other children?" "I have a daughter, young man," she replied, "a young girl." "That violin hanging there, old woman, who does it belong to?" he asked. "Oh, young man, it was my son's," she replied. "Let me have it for a little to play on," he said. The old woman gave it to him. He played a little on it and hung it up again.

His sister, who was listening behind the door, thought as they were talking and realised that the man was her brother. "Mother," she cried, "this is so-and-so," mentioning her brother's name. With great joy she flung her arms round his neck.

"Is so-and-so alive?" he asked his sister. For he had always got on very well with that neighbour. "He's alive," she said. "Call him over and make him come and see me now that I'm here," he said. His sister gladly summoned their neighbour, saying, "Do come to our house. My dear brother has come back." The neighbour came joyfully and they embraced and kissed each other. The neighbour was poor and the wedding was now going on at the 'lord's.'

"Brother," he said, "here's some money. Go and buy a very good horse, a very good saddle, and a suit of the best clothes." His neighbour went to the bazaar and bought them all. Both of them became the same type and looked like Kings.

The poor lad took down his violin and cleaned it. "Come on, let's go to the wedding," he said. Off on their horses they went to the bridegroom's house, where they were well received. They entered the guest-room and sat down on the best chairs, but no one recognised the

421

lad. All took him for a stranger. The guests who were at the wedding said to him, "Sir, play us a tune on your violin and let's enjoy ourselves." He played a little, but badly, then said, "By your leave, we must go." "Do stay a little and enjoy the wedding," they pleaded. But the two men would not stay.

They mounted their horses, the violin in front of the poor boy. Straight to the bride's house they went. They entered the guest-chamber and were received well, but he was not recognised. For a time the guests made merry with the help of the wedding clarinets. Then they said, "Sir, play the violin a little for us." He played for a little, but not well.

The bride was in the next room separated only by a partition wall. She heard the violin and was struck by his playing, bad though it was. He sat still for a little, then played again, but extremely well this time, and called her by name. "Do you want me or not?" he called.

The girl called her father and said, "To-night my betrothed has come back, the poor boy. He is in the guest-room across the way, along with the other guests, and he's calling me with his violin." "Do you know him without seeing him?" said her father. "I do," she said. "We have our own signals. I won't marry that other man. I won't have him. I want my own betrothed."

Her father went to the guests. "Welcome, my friends." "We're glad to see you, master of the household," they replied. "You're so-and-so," he said. "I am," he replied, "But I'm now the King of such-and-such a country. So God willed it." "But my daughter? Will you marry her?" asked the old man. "I will. She's mine, by right of love," he replied. "Very good," said her father.

The poor but wise young man sent a message to the other man who was to have married the girl. "Don't send away the guests and don't stop the wedding party. I'm going to give you my sister. She is poor but I am a King to-day." "Very good," said the bridegroom.

The girl was pretty. The young King, having plenty of money, went to the bazaar and bought a whole trousseau for her and married her to the other bridegroom. The lord's daughter became his own wife. He took his mother with him, too, and went to the country where he was

422

King and gave a pension to the *boza*-seller he had left as King in his place.

The end.

The Robber

Once a robber went and robbed the King's treasury. He entered it by an unusual method. He climbed on the roof along with his father and made a hole in it. He was let down inside with a rope and fell on the ground in the place where the money was. He filled himself up with money and his father drew up the rope so that he got out, and they went away home with the money.

Next day the King learned that his money was gone. It happened that he had three robbers in prison, all A1 at robbing. He went and said to them, "To-day I've had the money in my treasury stolen. Let me profit by your skill. If I catch the two robbers who stole my money, I'll release you from prison."

The robbers questioned the King about what the robber had done when he stole the money. "He bored a hole in the roof of the building," said the King. "Go and hang a cask of tar below the hole," they said. "When he comes again to steal, he will drop down from the hole and will stick in the tar and next morning you will catch him alive," The King did as they said.

Again the robber and his father set forth and went straight to the hole. The father said, "Son, I'm going in this time. If you take a lot of money, I haven't the strength to pull you up. If I go in, you have the strength to pull me up."

So the father dropped down and fell up to the armpits into the tar. He struggled to get out but could not. "Son," he cried, "bend down to me. I'm stuck here and can't get out."

The son went to take hold of his father, but he could not pull him out. Then the father said, "Son, we've got money enough. Don't steal any more. Now take a knife to your father and cut off his head and bury it in the ground. When the authorities come, they will find me

424

headless and won't recognise me. If they catch me alive, they will cut me to pieces little by little and you, too, and all the family. If you do as I say, I'll die quickly and you others will escape." The son at once cut off his father's head and took it away and buried it in the ground. Then he went to the authorities and listened to what they were saying.

At dawn the following day, the authorities went and saw the robber headless and dead. They went to the robbers who were in prison and informed them that they had found the robber headless. The robbers said, "Take the man out of the cask and wash him thoroughly with water. Then tie a rope round his middle and drag him along the ground through the streets of the bazaar. Whoever he belongs to will see him dead and will cry over him. Catch whoever cries. His family will be the robber's."

The robber heard what was said and went and said to his womenfolk, "When father is dragged round the streets, don't cry or they will kill you." The women said, "When we see father in the street, we shan't be able to keep from crying." The young man said to them, "Each of you take two glass bottles in your hands and go to the fountain. When father comes along the street, quarrel with each other, break the bottle and cry enough to split your heads. 'Oh, my bottle!' let one exclaim, and Oh, my bottle!" let the other exclaim.

The women went out each carrying two bottles as he said. As the government officials came by, dragging the corpse, the women quarrelled with each other, broke the bottles and wept. "Oh, my bottle!" exclaimed one, and "Oh, my bottle!" exclaimed the other.

The government people came up and said, "What's making you cry? Are you sad about this man of yours being put on show by us?" "No, no, we're only sorry about the bottles." So the government people went away and the women went home weeping.

The government people went to the imprisoned robbers and said, "No one cried except two women who broke their bottles." The robbers said, "These were they. Why didn't you arrest them?" "Well, what are we to do now?" "Now take a camel and load it with money which can be seen and let gendarmes look secretly backwards. The robbers will come to steal some money." All this the robber heard as he knew what went on among the authorities.

He went home and said to his womenfolk, "When the camel comes to the door here, catch it and lead it into the yard, then shut the door."

The robber left the house and, accompanied by a friend, went some way up the street. When the gendarmes appeared with the camel that was loaded with money, he began to quarrel with his friend and they fired at each other. The gendarmes threw themselves between them because they seemed likely to kill each other. "Don't kill each other!" they exclaimed. The women caught the camel and pulled it into the yard, then shut the door.

When the gendarmes turned around to the camel, they found it gone, money and all. They went and reported to the authorities that the camel had been lost, money and all, in such-and-such a quarter.

The authorities went and asked the imprisoned robbers what they should do now that the camel, money and all, was lost. The robbers replied, "Send out an old woman, ninety-five years of age, to cry in that quarter, 'Who has camel meat for a medicine?'" The old woman soon found the robber's door and got some camel meat for her medicine. She then smeared the door with blood to mark it.

When the robber came home, he saw the stain on the door and asked the women about the meat. They said, "We gave some to an old woman for a medicine."

The robber immediately killed a fowl over a tray. Because the old woman had smeared one door with camel's blood, he smeared fifteen other doors in the neighbourhood with the fowl's blood.

The authorities came together with the old woman. She pointed out the blood on the door and said, "This is the door." They went in and searched the house but found nothing. They saw another door with a bloodstain and a third and yet another. They saw as many as ten doors all stained. They beat the old woman with a stick and went straight to the robbers in prison.

426

The robbers said, "Empty a basket of money on the ground in the four corners of the bazaar and let gendarmes stay in the neighbouring shops. The robber will come to take some of the money."

The robber learned of this and went home, where he put on a pair of big jackboots. After rubbing tar on the soles, he walked from corner to corner in the bazaar and trod on the money. He also bent down and picked up some coins. Then he went to his shop and pulled the coins from the soles of his boots and put them in his pocket.

Once, twice, thrice as he lifted his feet, they were yellow with gold. The gendarmes noticed him and soon arrested him. They shackled his feet and left him in a shop while they rushed to gather up all the coins on the ground. But since the robber's jackboots were big, he pulled them off, shackles and all, leapt up on the window-sill, jumped down and ran away.

When the gendarmes came back to the shop, they found nothing and went and told the King. He said, "Are you concerned about my money? Don't touch it. Let anyone take it. But hang on to the robber because he has stolen the lot."

So they went and told the story to the prisoners. They said to the King, "There's nothing else that we can do. What can we do? Put your daughter into a hotel and send out the town-crier to call, 'Whoever wants to, let him go to the King's daughter. She's turned out a bad lot.'"

The King did as they said. He sent out his daughter to a hotel and bade the crier call what the prisoners had advised. "The robber is a wastrel," they had said, "and goes with women like that. The Princess should ask every man who approaches her what trade he is. If she finds the robber, let her keep him. But let her send away any other."

The King's daughter went to the hotel and many wastrels went to see her. She asked each, "What is your trade?" They told her each their trade. When two or three days had passed, the robber, too, went to see her and was asked, "What is your trade?" "I robbed the King's treasury," he replied. "The authorities noticed and put a cask full of tar in the place and father stuck in it." The Princess wrote down all he said. "I cut off father's head and went to find out what the authorities were saying. I heard they were going to drag his body through the streets because his family would cry and I said to our womenfolk, 'Don't cry,' but they said, 'We must cry.' Then I gave them bottles to hold and they cried as much as they wanted. The authorities next sent a camel laden with money round the town. I went out and quarrelled with a friend. The women led the camel into the house and I killed it. Then the authorities sent a woman of ninety-five years of age to get camel meat for a medicine, and my womenfolk gave it to her. The old woman smeared blood on the door, but I smeared fifteen doors with it. Next the authorities put gold in the four corners of the bazaar. I put on a pair of big boots, smeared the soles with tar and walked over the money. The gendarmes saw me and arrested and shackled me. I pulled off the boots, shackles and all, and ran away. I heard what was being said day by day. To-day I've come to you. You will either treat me well or have me killed. I put myself in your hands."

The girl treated him well and he seduced her. It was her father's order that she should keep the robber only. After they had enjoyed themselves for four or five hours, they wanted to go to sleep. The girl said to the robber, "Promise that you won't run away from me during the night." "I shall never run away from you," said the robber. "Only let me go out for a moment." He went to the lavatory, jumped through the window and landed in a garden. There was a new-made grave in the garden. In all haste he opened it with his thief's fingers and cut off the dead man's hand. He took it with him and, as there was no other way out, he went back to the Princess.

Again they enjoyed themselves for a time and then they lay down to sleep. She said to him, "You'll run away from me during the night while I'm asleep." "I'll never run away from you," said the robber. "I don't believe you. Give me your hand to hold," said the Princess. He gave her the dead man's hand. She clasped it in both her hands and put it in her bosom and went to sleep with it still there.

Morning after morning the gendarmes had come to the door and asked if there was news. She used to say there was none. But that morning when the gendarmes came and asked for news, she called out, "I have him here in bed with me." The gendarmes entered, the girl lifted

428

the eiderdown and found the dead man's hand. "Oh, oh, oh! You've left me a dead man's hand here!" she exclaimed.

The Princess went to her father with the notes she had made from the robber and said to him, "This is what he did to us."

The King sent the crier out to call, "Who is the robber? Let him come and see me. I have pardoned him."

All the world went, saying, "I am the robber." But when the King questioned them, there wasn't one who could tell the story as it was in his daughter's notes and as it had happened according to the directions of the prisoners.

After two or three days had passed, the robber went and told the whole story as it had happened. The King called his daughter and asked her, "Is this the man or not?" "It is, father," she replied.

The King pardoned him and gave him his daughter in marriage as no one else would ever have the girl. He also gave him a great deal of gold.

The end. And your good health!

The Boy and the Dervish

Once upon a time a gentleman mounted his horse and after riding along the road dismounted and let the horse loose to graze on some grass, while he himself thought sorrowfully about his childless condition. A dervish came up. "What are you thinking about?" he asked. "Nothing," the man replied. "Come, come, tell me," said the dervish. "Well, I've been married for a long time but God hasn't given me any children," the man replied. "I'll give you something that will make you have children," said the dervish. "But if the first child is a boy, it is to be mine, and if it is a girl, keep it for yourself." "Right," said the man. The dervish gave him an apple, saying, "Eat half of it yourself and give the other half to your wife." The man ate the apple and gave the other half to his wife, who became with child and had a son.

When the boy was ten years old, the dervish met him one day and said, "Whose son are you, boy?" "So-and-so's," he replied. "Come with me. That's what your father promised," the dervish said. "I won't come with you," protested the boy. "Well," the dervish replied, "tell your father in the evening that the dervish he pledge his word to wants him to keep his pledge." The boy gave the message to his father, who bade him say he had forgotten to give it.

Next day the dervish met the boy again and said, "Well, did you tell your father?" "No, I forgot," said the boy. "Tell him this evening. And here's an apple to keep you from forgetting," said the dervish. The boy told his father, who told him to say to the dervish, "Find him and take him." He reported this to the dervish, who said, "Come along then. It's you I want!" He took the boy, who was in tears, with him.

He took him to a deep pond, for he was the Devil himself, and in it, he shut him up in a building with seven doors. As he shut him up, he said, "Here, boy, is where you are to have food and drink! Get up whenever you want to eat. I'm going to sleep for three years." And he lay down by the door to sleep.

The boy stayed there for a year. Then he could stand it no longer and, having the keys, opened the first door. Inside he saw quantities of gold. He opened a second and a third door until he had opened them all. In the last room he found a winged horse, which said to him, "Hallo, son of man, what do you want here? It's I who was fated to suffer like this." "I was, too," said the boy. "Can't we run away?" the horse replied. "The door's locked and the Devil has gone to sleep beside it." "I have the keys," said the boy. "Then open the door," said the horse. As the boy turned the key in the lock, the Devil heard him. "What's the matter, my son?" he asked. "What makes you want to run away? You have plenty to eat and drink, so come back." Once more he shut him up behind seven doors. As he gave him the keys, he said, "Wait! I need two more years of sleep."

The boy waited six months more, and then opened the doors and went to the horse. "Shall we run away?" he asked. "Yes, my son," said the horse. "Go and open the door!" The boy opened the door. "Mount me" said the horse, and the boy did. "Sit tight!" said the horse. "I'm going to put my foot in the Devil's ear, and he will hear us and chase us. Sit tight, I say, or you'll fall off. I'm going to fly." The horse put his foot in the Devil's ear and flew away with the boy. The Devil heard him and dashed off to catch them. The horse flew along with the Devil after him. At last the Devil caught him. "Get off!" he said to the boy, and the boy dismounted. "Why did you run away?" asked the Devil. "You had plenty to eat and drink. This horse, I suppose, had neither hay nor corn! Come along with me!" "I won't," said the boy and sprang on the horse's back. The horse flew away and the Devil cried, "Go, then. I won't worry you again."

The boy went away with the horse. When the time came for them to separate, the horse said to the boy, "Don't take this road. There's a *kulshedra* there. Take this other one, where there isn't a *kulshedra*." But the boy took the first road.

431

As he walked along the road alone, he met a *kulshedra*, who said, "Turn back, son of man, or I'll cut off your head." "Come and try," said the boy. The *kulshedra* came up and they seized each other by the throat. The boy threw the *kulshedra*. "Please don't kill me!" implored the *kulshedra*, for the boy wanted to cut her throat. "I'll give you three gifts – the power to turn firstly into a dove, secondly into a fly, and thirdly into wind." "Very well," said the boy, rising to his feet and letting her go.

"Farther on," said the *kulshedra*," you'll find my daughter. You may defeat her, but don't kill her. Still farther on, you'll find my son and he will defeat you. The first time turn into a dove, the second time into a fly, and the third time into wind. Then my son will say, 'By my mother's dugs I won't touch you.' Then come down because he won't touch you.

So the boy went on his way and met the *kulshedra*'s daughter. He defeated her but did not kill her. Again he went on his way and met the *kulshedra*'s son. "Go back," said the young *kulshedra*, "or I'll cut off your head. You defeated my mother and you defeated my sister but you can't defeat me." "Come on!" said the boy. They gripped each other and the *kulshedra*'s son threw the boy and pulled out his knife to cut his throat. The boy turned into a dove and flew away. "Come down. I won't touch you," called the *kulshedra*'s son. The boy came back to earth and turned into a boy again. Again the *kulshedra*'s son threw him. This time he became a fly and flew away. "Come down, I won't touch you," called the *kulshedra*'s son. The boy came back to earth and became a boy once more. Again, the *kulshedra*'s son threw him. This time he became wind. "Come down," called the *kulshedra*'s son. "By my mother's dugs I won't touch you." The boy came back to earth and went away as a human being.

He came to a village where he went to a gentleman with whom he took service as a shepherd. His master said, "Don't take the sheep to such-and-such a wood. There's a *kulshedra* there, and she'll kill you and the sheep." But the boy drove the sheep straight to the *kulshedra*'s wood. She called out, "Turn the sheep back or I'll cut off your head." "I'll take you on," he replied. They began to wrestle, but neither could

432

throw the other. The *kulshedra*, tiring, said, "If only I had the Earthly Beauty here, I know what I'd do to you." The boy said, "If only I had a loaf of sieved wheat flour, a roast chicken and the sheep-farmer's daughter, I know what I'd do to you." With that, the two separated. The boy drove his sheep home. He had already fallen in love with his master's daughter.

Every day before he had milked more than half the sheep, the buckets were filled. Because he had driven them to the *kulshedra*'s wood, they had more milk. When he had milked them all, his master said, "Where did you have the sheep, my son?" "Where you told me," he replied. He did not let on.

When he got up next morning, he drove the sheep to the *kulshedra*'s wood. But his master followed to watch him without his knowing. The *kulshedra* called to the boy, "Go on! Take your sheep out of this wood or I'll cut off your head." "I'll take you on," called the boy. The *kulshedra* came forward and they gripped each other. The *kulshedra* grew tired and said, "If only I had the Earthly Beauty, I know what I'd do to you." The boy replied, "If only I had a loaf of sieved wheat flour, a roast chicken and the sheep-farmer's daughter, I know what I'd do to you." The sheep-farmer heard what he said, and went away. The boy and the *kulshedra* parted. The boy found his sheep and drove them home. More milk than ever! His master asked where he had grazed the sheep. "Where you told me, sir," he replied.

The sheep-farmer rose in the morning and said to his wife, "Make a loaf of wheat flour, roast a fowl, and give them both to our daughter to take to the shepherd in the wood. He will kill the *kulshedra* if you send him these things." His wife prepared them both and gave them to her daughter, who set off for the wood.

When the boy reached the wood, the *kulshedra* called out, "Take your sheep out of this wood, or I'll cut off your head." He retorted, "Come along!" The girl did not see this because she had not yet arrived. The boy wrestled with the *kulshedra* till she tired and cried, "If only I had the Earthly Beauty, I know what I'd do to you." The boy called out, "If only I had a loaf of sieved wheat flour, a roast chicken and the sheep-farmer's daughter, I know what I'd do to you." That very

433

moment the sheep-farmer's daughter reached the boy, and so he resolved to take her to wife. In an instant he threw the *kulshedra*. "Please don't kill me!" she begged. "I'll marry you as the sheep-farmer's daughter has done." He spared her life and took her to wife, making two of them. He then drove the sheep home, his two wives following him. He entered the house and said, "I'm giving you back your sheep, sir, because I'm going away. I've killed the *kulshedra* and you can go and graze in that wood as much as you like now. The *kulshedra* has married me and so has your daughter. Now I'm going." With this, the boy went away.

The Earthly Beauty searched for the boy. She wanted to kill him because she was angry with him for defeating the *kulshedra*. She said constantly, "I want to find the boy and to marry him as the *kulshedra* and the shepherd's daughter did." She found the boy and said to him, "Will you marry me as you did the other two?" "All right," said the boy, "I will." And he married her.

When he went to the bridal chamber, the Earthly Beauty took out a knife to cut his throat, but he turned into a dove. "Come down! I won't touch you," she called. When he came down, she again pulled out a knife to cut his throat. He turned into a fly and flew away. "Come down! I won't touch you," called the Earthly Beauty. The boy came back to earth but the Earthly Beauty again took out a knife to cut his throat. He became wind. "Come down! By my mother's dugs I won't touch you," she called. He came down to earth, turned into a human being.

The boy went on his way, inquiring as he went until he reached his father's. Close by, the *kulshedra* built a better house for him than his father had. She built it during the night. When the father saw the grand building in the morning, he went to look at it, wondering what gentleman it was who had this fine house. He went into it and was welcomed like a father by the boy. He did not recognise him until the boy said, "I am your son who was carried away by the Devil." His father embraced him and said, "Come, son, let's go to my house," and the boy went there with him.

434

After they had had coffee, the father said to the boy, "Let's have a game of cards! But not for money. Whichever wins is to put out the other's eyes." They began a game and the boy beat his father. "Put out my eyes, son," said the father. "No, you're my father," said the boy. "Well, let's play again," said the father. Again the boy beat his father. "Come along, son, put out my eyes," said the father. "No, you're my father," said the boy. "Let's play again!" said the father. The third time the boy let himself be beaten. His father flung himself on him and put out his eyes, because he wanted to get his son's wives, who were beautiful.

His took his son and flung him into a hedge. Then he went to the women but they would not open the door. He gathered a number of soldiers to force his way in. The Earthly Beauty seized her sword and did not let anyone come in. Staying near the door, she killed them all with her sword.

Two small birds slipped into the boy's hand. He caught one and, rubbing his eyes with it, made himself see with one eye. He caught the other bird, rubbed his other eye with it, and saw with that eye also. He went straight to the women but, because he was all torn, the Earthly Beauty did not recognise him. The other two cried, "Don't kill him! He's our husband." He entered the house where the women were. The soldiers sent the news to his father, saying, "Come now. The door is open." The father came at once to go into the women but his son said, "Kill my father!" and the Earthly Beauty killed him.

A long time passed, and the boy became like a King. War broke out. During the fighting he was wounded and went to a lake to wash off the blood. He entered the lake, where the Devil caught him and shut him up. The soldiers went to his wives and said, "The King has been drowned in the lake." Said the Earthly Beauty, "Come and show me the lake!" The soldiers went and showed it to her.

She had taken three apples with her. She now went to the water's edge and began to play with the little apple. The Devil emerged and said, "Give me that apple. I have a little boy and he's crying." "Bring him out of the lake enough for me to see his head," she said. The

435

Devil raised his head above the water. She recognised her husband and gave the apple to the Devil.

The Earthly Beauty began to play with another apple, a bigger one. The Devil emerged and said, "Give me that apple! My child's crying." "Raise him high enough for me to see him down to the waist," she said. And the Devil raised him as far as the waist. She saw him and gave the apple to the Devil.

The Earthly Beauty then played with the third apple, which was finer than the other two. The Devil said, "Give me that apple, because my child is crying." She said, "Raise him to a palm's breadth above the water so that I can see him," and the Devil did so. But the boy did not understand. The Earthly Beauty said, "Fly, you pig! What are you waiting for now?" The boy immediately turned into a dove and flew away. The Devil rushed after him. But the Earthly Beauty struck him with her sword and killed him.

The boy came back to earth as a human being and they went away home together to the other two wives, and they all lived happily afterwards together.

[told by Xhafë Kuqi of Kuqan in the district of Elbasan]

The Sheikh with Bells

The sheikh with bells lived in Istanbul. He carried on as if he was a holy prophet, putting bells on his feet to frighten off the flies so that he should not tread on them. But on the other hand, he robbed all night and had forty thieves under his command. Night after night, robberies and losses took place in Istanbul, but no one dreamt that the sheikh was the thief. The authorities arrested people and tried and imprisoned them.

At last, a hodja from Albania discovered them, catching out the sheikh because he had had an experience at home. He had had a wife who prayed the usual five times daily and pretended to her husband that she was chaste. With the servant's help, however, he discovered that she was unchaste and he killed her. After that, he left home and wandered about at random until he came to Istanbul, where he tried to earn his living.

There he saw that losses kept occurring, that there was danger and that innocent people were being arrested. He guessed that the sheikh with bells was the robber. "My wife," he said, "gave me to understand that she was chaste, but she turned out to be unchaste. This sheikh who looks so saintly will, no doubt, be the chief robber in Istanbul."

So the Albanian said to a friend, and the news spread till the Sultan heard it and summoned the hodja. "Why did you say this and that?" he asked. "I did say it," replied the Albanian, "and it's true. The people who behave as so very religious and trustworthy are the lowest of all." "Can you expose this thieving?" asked the Sultan. "I can, if you will give me a government force," said the Albanian.

The Sultan gave him a good number of men, who went at night to the sheikh's monastery and surrounded it. After the business of

437

evening prayers was over, the visitors to the monastery dispersed and the sheikh was left alone. But he had forty men shut up in the cellar below. He at once opened the cellar door and called, "Come along, you forty men!" Out they all came into the mosque where the sheikh set them their different tasks, saying, "Ten and ten as you are, go out to this quarter and to that and rob."

Then the hodja who had been given government troops, called from his station outside, "Stand up, you and all your mates. There's nothing else you can do." The sheikh shouted rudely back, "Get away from here! I am praying in order to find black water here." The hodja said, "Whether you want black water or white water, put your hands up. You won't gain anything any other way." So the sheikh surrendered because he couldn't help it.

When they looked in the cellar, they found the most valuable of all the goods that had been stolen in Istanbul. The Sultan said to the hodja, "What trick did you use to catch him?" The hodja replied, "The man who has fallen from a fig-tree knows how it is to fall. The man who hasn't fallen, doesn't know. Something of the sort happened to me at home. Those who are over-religious are always the biggest thieves."

The Boy Who Paid a Dead Man's Debt

A boy went abroad where he stayed six years. He earned six grosh and saw that he couldn't earn any more. So he started for home.

At a certain point he found a dead man who was denied burial by the hodja because there was no one to pay his debts. The boy said to the hodja, "I stayed six years abroad and earned six grosh. I give the money to you, only bury the man." The hodja buried the man and the boy continued on his way home.

When he arrived, he said to his father, "Father, I stayed away six years and I couldn't earn more than six grosh, and these I gave for a corpse." "You did well, my son," said the father. "Only next time you go away, tell me."

When next he was going away, the boy told his father, who gave him three apples and said, "If a friend joins you, give him an apple. If he eats it all himself, don't take him with you."

A friend met the boy on his way, was given an apple, and ate it all himself, not giving one little bit to the boy. The boy parted from him and did not take him with him.

Another appeared and said, "Will you take me with you?" The boy gave him an apple and, like the other, he ate it all himself and did not give any to the boy. The boy parted from him, too, and did not take him with him.

A third man appeared and said, "Will you take me with you?" The boy gave him an apple and he divided it in two and they ate it together. So the boy took him with him.

They went to foreign parts and there learned that the King's daughter had had several husbands, who had all died on their wedding night. The apple friend said to the boy, "Shall we marry her together?" "We'll die," said the boy. "No, we shan't," said the apple man. "There

439

are two of us, so we shan't die." So they married the princess – two men to one wife.

The boy went to bed while the apple man stayed awake. In the night, an adder came out of the bride's mouth and was killed by the apple man. Then another came out and was killed, too.

When morning came, the King sent a minister to see if those two men were alive or not. Both were. The King sent for them and said, "What do you want from me?" "Nothing except that you should let us take your daughter to the place we're going to." And he gave her to them.

They set out for home and, on reaching a certain spot, the apple man said, "Let's divide things!" "How can we divide the woman?" asked the boy. "In two," replied the apple man. "Seize her by one arm and I'll seize her by the other, then we can divide her." They seized her, one on each side, to tear her in two. In her fear, the head of the adder that was inside her came out of her mouth.

Said the apple man, "The woman is yours! I am the man you buried for six grosh."

The boy took the woman and went home to his father.

[told by Lef Panshi of Valësh in the district of Elbasan]

The Faithless Wife and the Faithful Dog

Once upon a time there was a shepherd with his sheep. At midnight he heard a cry like "*waoo, waoo!*" At the sound, his dogs dashed out and barked and he seized his rifle and fired.

After a short time, a man came to the sheepfold. He was the Devil who had cried out. A wolf had caught him, for wolves eat the Devil, and this one had been about to eat him up. But when the shepherd fired, the shot frightened the wolf and he let the Devil go.

So the Devil came in the shape of a man to the shepherd and said, "What do you want from me?" "Nothing," said the shepherd. "I've nothing to do with you." The Devil said, "It was I who was out there. And you saved me when you fired. A wolf had caught me. So what would you like from me?" "Nothing," the shepherd repeated. "But I want to reward you for what you've done. Shall we become brothers?" said the Devil. "I agree," said the shepherd, "since there's nothing else for it." And the two became brothers.

The Devil said to the shepherd, "You must come and spend a night in my house." "Where is your house?" said the shepherd. "In a torrent-bed," replied the Devil, "at the point where there is a pool of deep water. But when you come, you must bring a very trusted person with you." "The only trusted person I have is my wife," said the shepherd. "All right, it doesn't matter," said the Devil, "bring her."

The shepherd took his wife, and set off with his dog following them. They went to the place indicated by the Devil. As soon as the Devil's companions saw them, they rushed forward to kill the shepherd. But the Devil who had made him his brother caught them back, saying, "This man is my brother. Don't touch him," and he began to prepare a good meal for them

441

The shepherd was tired by the journey and felt sleepy. So he lay down to take a nap. The Devil who was his brother went on preparing food and also brought out a lot of fine clothes for women, with a lot of coins strung on chains. Then he said to the shepherd's wife, "Which is better? All the lovely things you see here or your husband? "My husband," said the woman. "Don't stick to him," said the Devil. "Look at all the good things you have here." "What shall I do?" she said. "We'll kill your husband," said the Devil, "and you'll stay here." He beguiled the woman

The Devil seized a stick with which to kill the husband and raised his arm to strike. But the shepherd's dog was close by and saw that the Devil was about to hit its master. It flung itself on the Devil and tried to bite him. Its barking woke the shepherd. He shouted at the dog, which drew back. But he also saw that the Devil had raised his arm to strike him. The Devil was almost too frightened to speak. At last he said, "You haven't a trusty wife, but you have a trusty dog."

The shepherd took his wife and dog and, a shamed man, went home.

[told by Kov Qose of Valësh in the district of Elbasan]

Glossary

Aga
A landowner or wealthy individual.

Arap
Figure of Albanian mythology. The term, Alb. *arap*, def. *arapi*, Gheg *harap* 'moor,' is derived from the word 'Arab.' The *arap* is a figure also to be encountered in Turkey and in the other Balkan countries, ~ Rom. *arap, harap*. He is black or dark-skinned and is usually evil, though he is also capable of doing good.

Bald Maria
Alb. *Karrekacidhjara*. Mod. Greek *Μαρία Κατσιδιάρια*.

Baldhead
Figure of Albanian folktales and mythology, also known as the Scurfhead, Alb. *qeros*, def. *qerosi,* from Alb. *qere* 'ringworm, tinea, sycosis,' itself a loan from Lat. *caries* 'decay,' *cariosus* 'rotten.' He is an intelligent and artful character, but often proves to be deceptive and wicked. His fate is 'marked' either by his scurfy appearance or by an animal hide he wears as a disguise. His functions in Albanian folktales are much the same as those of the Barefaced Man. In Albanian folklore he often appears as the youngest of three brothers, who triumphs in the end.

Bilbil Gjyzar
Name of an imaginary singing nightingale. Alb. *bilbil* 'nightingale.' In Kurdish folktales, we come across the forms *bilbil sharur, bilbil*

443

sharura "singing nightingale," from which the Albanian form may be derived.

Black Mafmut
Mafmut is an Albanian dialect form for the Muslim name Mahmut, or Mehmed.

Boza
A fermented beverage popular in the Balkans and Turkey. It is usually made of millet or maize and sugar, and is drunk cold.

Bullgari
A four-stringed, lute-like music instrument, referred to in the tale "The Snakeskin."

Cadi
Muslim judge. Also spelt *kadi*.

Dërdyl
Figure of Albanian mythology. This being, Alb. *dërdyl*, def. *dërdyli*, or *derdyl*, def. *derdyli*, is envisaged as a mighty stallion or a powerful man. The *dërdyl* is associated at any rate with strength.

Durazzo
Modern Durrës, the main port of Albania.

Earthly Beauty
Figure of Albanian mythology. The Earthly Beauty or Beauty of the Earth, Alb. *E bukura e dheut* or *E bukura e dynjas*, is one of the most popular characters of Albanian myths and fairy tales. She is the quintessence of beauty, embodying either good or evil, though more often the latter. She can do magic and is as crafty as the ancient Greek sorceress Circe. Her magic powers derive from her dress. If she wishes, she can transform human beings into pigs, but she can also play the part of a good fairy and be very helpful. She also appears in the form of an

evil *arap* in a black skin. In a constellation of three sisters she appears together with the Sea Beauty, Alb. *E bukura e detit,* and the Heavenly Beauty, Alb. *E bukura e qiellit.*

Elbasan
Town in central Albania.

Fig-Bali
Name of an imaginary horse.

Gheg
A northern Albanian.

Gjysleme
A sweet pastry like baklava.

Godolesh
Village in the district of Elbasan.

Grosh
Unit of currency formerly used in central Europe (cf. German Groschen) and known in the Balkans.

Half-Cock
Half-Cock, also known as Half Rooster or Half Chicken, is a popular motif of Albanian folktales. Alb. *gjysmagjél,* def. *gjysmagjéli,* from Alb. *gjysmë* 'half' and *gjel* 'chicken, rooster.' He is a one-legged bird who has many an adventure in the course of its travels, carrying its weary companions on its back or in its belly. The companions later come to its assistance. The figure is reminiscent of the motif of the Town Band of Bremen in German folklore. The Half Cock motif exists in other cultures, too: 'κουτσόπεττος' in Greece, '*moitié de coq*' recorded in France in 1759, '*mitat de gal*' in Languedoc, '*de halve haan*' in Flanders, '*il galluccio*' in Italy and '*el medio pollo*' in Chile.

445

Hizr

Figure of Albanian mythology known to the Mat region. The *hizr* or *hizri* is a good being who goes from village to village and from door to door begging. He conveys the impression that he has been sent by God to test the generosity of homeowners. One must therefore be generous and give him money or food, for otherwise he will be angered and put a spell on the house.

Hodja

Also *hoja*; Albanian *hoxha*. A Muslim schoolmaster. From Turkish *hoca*.

Jatesh

Village in the district of Elbasan.

Jinn

Figure of Albanian mythology. This supernatural spirit, Alb. *xhind*, def. *xhindi*, from Turk. *cin* and related to Mod. Gk. τὰ τσίνια, is also to be encountered in Arabic and oriental folklore. It can assume both human and animal forms. Jinns are originally ghosts of the dead who have found no peace in the grave because of previous sins or because they have been insulted. It is said that they come out at night and take possession of the person who has insulted them, hence the expression, "He was taken over by the jinns," Alb. *e zunë xhindet*, i.e. he went mad. Jinns cannot normally be seen, although holy men sometimes know where they are to be found. Their presence is often signalled by the creaking of a door or the flickering of a candle. Sometimes they take possession of a whole house and, from that moment on, no one can live in it anymore. Jinns can react very aggressively if their parties are disturbed, if their children are trodden upon or if someone throws a pot of boiling water out of the window on them. In Albanian folktales, jinns live either on earth or in an underworld kingdom of their own. They can marry and have children, and have their own royalty.

Kalagjystan
Female mythological figure.

Kavaja
A town in Albania between Durrës and Elbasan.

Kulshedra
Figure of Albanian mythology. This female dragon, Alb. *kulshedër,* def. *kulshedra,* also known as *kuçedër,* def. *kuçedra,* derives from Latin *chersydrus* and Gk. χερσύδρος 'amphibious snake.' The term is also used in Albanian to refer to a quarrelsome woman. This *kulshedra,* usually described as a huge serpent with seven to twelve heads, is one of the most popular figures of Albanian mythology, being well known throughout the Albanian-speaking Balkans and among the Italo-Albanians or Arbëresh in southern Italy. She is extremely ugly. Her face and body are covered in red woolly hair and her long, hanging breasts drag along the ground. She lives in a mountain cave, in an underground lake or in a swamp, and spits fire out of all her mouths. When she moves, her skin scrapes over the rocks and, accordingly, any rusty-coloured water flowing from springs is thought to contain *kulshedra* blood. Comparable to the ancient Greek Hydra of Lerna, a *kulshedra* is basically frightening and evil, though in some folktales she can exhibit humour and occasionally even be helpful.

Lek's Kanun
System of customary law. The *Kanun* of Lekë Dukagjini, Alb. *Kanuni i Lekë Dukagjinit,* is the most famous compilation of Albanian customary or consuetudinary law. This initially unwritten code of law governed social behaviour and almost every facet of life in the isolated and otherwise lawless terrain of the northern highlands, and was adhered to throughout much of northern Albania for centuries. Indeed, it is widely respected even today. The heartland of the *Kanun* was Dukagjin, the highlands of Lezha, Mirdita, Shala, Shoshi, Nikaj-Merturi, and the plain of Dukagjin in present-day western Kosovo. Lekë Dukagjini (1410-1481), after whom the code was named, is a little

447

known and somewhat mysterious figure, thought to have been a fifteenth-century prince and comrade in arms of Scanderbeg (q.v.). Whether he compiled the code or simply gave his name to it is not known.

Lezha
Town in northern Albania.

Medjid
Albanian *mexhid*, Turkish *mecit*. A silver coin issued at the time of Sultan Abdülmecid (Abdul Mejid).

Nap
Abbreviation for a Napoleon (q.v.).

Napoleon
Unit of currency used in Albania in the old days.

Oke
Also *oka* or *okka*. Ottoman measure of mass, equivalent to about 1.3 kilograms.

Peri
Also *peria* or *perria*. Figure of northern Albanian mythology. This fairy-like creature, Alb. *perrí*, def. *perría*, also *pehrí*, def. *pehría*, from Turk. *peri* 'fairy, good jinn,' is envisaged as a maiden of exceptional beauty, wearing fragrant white clothes. She is protective and bedazzles humans with her beauty, but she can also do harm. If children are careless with their bread and spread crumbs all over, she will make hunchbacks of them. In popular speech, someone who is mentally deranged or talks to himself is referred to as having a *perria*.

Pilaf
A rice dish.

Raki
An alcoholic beverage, similar to Italian grappa.

Shkumbin
River in central Albanian that flows through Elbasan.

Shpat
Mountainous region of central Albania, south of Elbasan.

Sulkimnixhi
A garment of obscure origin, referred to in the tale 'Sulkumnixhi.'

Teqe
Also Engl. *tekke*. A dervish lodge or monastery.

Tosk
A southern Albanian.

Vashtëmia
A village in the district of Korça.

List of the Informants (Storytellers)

Informants of tales included in this volume

Ismail Haxhi Musaj, of Elbasan – 001
Stavre Xhimitiku, of Berat – 005
Peter Xhufo, of Elbasan – 015
Selman Ali, a teacher from Vashtëmia in the district of Korça – 016
Mahmud Verrçani – 003
Mehmet Gjavori – 012
Xhafë Kuqi of Kuqan in the district of Elbasan – 020, 030, 112
Qazim Kosma Tullumi, of Bujaras in the district of Elbasan – 017
Gjergj Simota of Grapsh in southern Albania – 018
Simon Nue. of Ungrej in the district of Mirdita – 019
Hasan M. Malishova – 022
Fridherik Caku. of Elbasan – 023
Jon Apostol Dede of Nezhar in the Shpat region of the district of Elbasan – 029
Tahir Jorgji Baduri of Shelcan in the Shpat region of the district of Elbasan – 033
Josif (Isuf) Kostandin Todja. of Elbasan – 024
Thomas Prifti of Bubullima in the district of Lushnja – 025
Jan Bocova, from near Fier – 026
Ferid Ngurrza – 027
Spiro Poppa – 028
Hamit Skilje of Elbasan – 031
Mehmet Myslim Starova of Dunica in the district of Pogradec – 032
Josif Sqapi of Elbasan – 035
Shaqe Zadrima Gera, a teacher from Fier – 034
Shaip Efendi Hoxha of Mbreshtan in the district of Berat – 036

Banush Demiri, a teacher from Braçanj in the district of Devoll – 038
Abdurrahim Ostreni from Dibra – 039
Thanas Bocova of Fier – 040
Kodhel Dede of Nezhar in the Shpat region of the district of Elbasan – 043
Halit Miraku – 044
Hilmi Dakli of Elbasan – 045
Harun Sefa of Lushnja – 046
Marije Mazja a teacher from Shkodra – 047
Jorgji Aleksi, a teacher from Niça in the district of Pogradec – 048
Mustafa Delimeta, a teacher from Elbasan – 049
Demir Koçi – 050
Marka Zef Ndoj of Laç in the district of Kurbin – 051
Kristo Vide of Verria in the district of Fier – 052
Aziz Mulla, a teacher from Mezhgoran in the district of Tepelena – 055
Foto Rumbo – 057
Olga Zallari of Përmet – 058
Urania A. Thanassi, of Elbasan (wife of a peasant) – 059
Ibrahim Riza, a teacher from Bicaj – 060
Tevfik Gjyli, a teacher from Haslikej – 061
Sulejman Hasita, a teacher from Kacul – 063
Fani A. Cipi, of Elbasan – 065
Mehmet Nezimi, of Shijak in the district of Durrës – 066
H. S. Kadulla, a teacher from Hudenisht in the district of Pogradec – 067
Shaban Hyseni, a teacher from Plasa in the district of Korça – 075
Abdyrrahim Behluli, a teacher from Peqin - 076
Xhevdet Shehri, a teacher from Bitincka in the district of Devoll – 078
Preng Bardhoku, of Gurëz-Bushkash in the district of Mat – 079
Nikollë Gjetë Coku of Bregu i Matës in the district of Lezha - 080
Aleksander Xhufka of Elbasan – 082
Hajdar Biçoku of Elbasan – 083
Pjetër Dashi of Elbasan – 084
Lame Xhama, of Fterra (Kurvelesh) in the district of Saranda – 085

Ibrahim Doraci of Elbasan – 086
Abdullah Keta, of Shëngjergj in the district of Tirana – 087
Hakki Nesja of the Kruja region – 088
Husain Maja of the Kruja region – 089
Qazim Bakalli – 090
Rexhep Alliu of the Kruja region – 091
Riza Dervishi of the Kruja region – 092
H. Sheta of the Kruja region – 093
Alfred K. Andoni of Elbasan – 094
Lef Panshi of Valësh in the district of Elbasan – 114
Kov Qose of Valësh in the district of Elbasan – 115

Other Informants (not included in this volume)

Mehmet Domi of Shijak
Liqë Nikë Meta (of Gurëz?)
Sefedin Mehmet, of Shumbat in the district of Dibra
Mark Liqe Nika (of Gurëz?)
Mara Liqe Nika (of Gurëz?)
Zef Trokthi, of Milot in the district of Kurbin
Mihal Sulkuqi
Mehmet Domi of Shijak
Fila Vasil Çerekaj
Shefik Suparaku
Mahir Domi
Refik Hari
Cen Pashaj of Elbasan
Hamdi Gokaj, a teacher from Shkodra
Simon Prendi
Adem Arifi, pupil of the military gymnasium of Tirana
Stefan Konstantin Dede of Nezhar in the Shpat region
Arif Karaj of Selta
Marka Pjetri, of Gurëz Kthella
Pal Kecota, of Gurëz-Shaljane

Kleoniqi E. Papanastas, of Përmet
Vasil Prifti, a teacher from Pojan
Adem Shehu, a teacher from Krahas
Andrea Ndrecolli of Berat
Aleko Llambri, a teacher from Halilem
Ibrahim Hyseni, a teacher from Baban
Jovan Jorgji, a teacher from Pleshtisht
Sulejman Zallo
Vasilika Dh. Shuka of the Normal School of Elbasan, native of Korça
Suleiman Zalla, a teacher from Preza near Shijak
Gjin Lleshi of Bushkash in the district of Mat
Selman Ndreu of Dibra
Frang Marka Noi of Mirdita
Nikoll Selala
Pal Laska
Ibrahim Kushta of Kanina
Hadi Vrioni of Berat
Mehmet Kaca of Kruja
Jashar Dedes
M. Emin
Ibrahim Shehi of Tirana
Riza Ndreu

Bibliography

Albanian Oral Literature

BELLIZZI, Mario. *Vallja e zaravet. La danza delle fate. Fiabe e leggende delle comunità italo-albanesi del Parco Nazionale del Pollino, Calabria e Basilicata* [The Dance of the Fairies: Fables and Legends of the Italo-Albanian Community of Pollino, Calabria and Basilicata]. A cura di Mario Bellizzi. Castrovillari: Edizioni Prometeo, 2000. 315 pp.
[Bilingual (Italian-Albanian) edition of fables and legends of the Italo-Albanians of Calabria]

BERISHA, Anton. *E Bukura e Dheut bahet nuse: përralla shqiptare* [The Earthly Beauty Becomes a Bride: Albanian Folktales]. Zgjodhi dhe përgatiti Anton Berisha. Skopje: Flaka e vëllazërimit, 1992. 159 pp.

BERISHA, Anton & MUSTAFA, Myzafere (ed.). *Anthologji e përrallës shqipe* [Anthology of Albanian Folktales]. Prishtina: Rilindja, 1982. 419 pp.
[Anthology of sixty Albanian folktales.]

ÇABEJ, Eqrem. Albanische Volkskunde [Albanian Ethnography]. in: *Südost-Forschungen,* Munich, 25 (1966), p. 333-387.

CAMAJ, Martin. *Racconti popolari di Greci (Katundi) in provincia di Avellina e de Barile (Barili) in provincia di Potenza* [Folktales from Greci (Katundi) in the Province of Avellina and from Barile (Barili) in the Province of Potenza]. Studi Albanesi 3. Rome: Istituto di Lingua e Letteratura Albanese del'Università di Roma, 1972.
[Collection of Arberesh tales with an Italian translation]

454

CAMAJ, Martin & SCHIER-OBERDORFER, Uta (ed.). *Albanische Märchen* [Albanian Folktales]. Düsseldorf: Diederichs, 1974. 275 pp.
[Albanian folktales in German translation]

ÇETTA, Anton. *Tregime popullore, I. Drenicë* [Folktales, I, Drenica]. Prishtina: Rilindja, 1963. 330 pp.
[Volume devoted primarily to Albanian folktales from the Drenica valley in Kosovo]

- *Prozë popullore nga Drenica* [Oral Prose from Drenica]. 2 vol. Prishtina: Enti i teksteve, 1970, reprint 1990. 331 & 347 pp.
[A collection of seventy-two folktales from the Drenica valley in Kosovo]

- *Balada dhe legjenda* [Ballads and Legends]. Prishtina: Instituti Albanologjik, 1974. 349 pp.

- *Këngë kreshnike 1. Letërsia popullore. Vëllim II* [Songs of the Frontier Warriors 1. Folk Literature, Volume II]. Prishtina: Instituti Albanologjik, 1974. 395 pp.

- *Albanske narodne balade* [Albanian Folk Ballads]. Prev. Esad Mekuli. Predg. Vladimir Bovan. Biblioteka Jedinstvo, 85. Prishtina: Jedinstvo, 1976. 167 pp.

- *Përralla 1* [Folktales, 1]. Prishtina: Instituti Albanologjik, 1979.
[Ninety Albanian folktales]

- *Përralla 2* [Folktales, 2]. Prishtina: Instituti Albanologjik, 1982.
[One hundred forty-four Albanian folktales]

- *Nga folklori ynë. Bleni II. Kallëzime dhe përrallëza* [From our Folklore. Volume II. Little Tales]. Prishtina: Rilindja, 1989. 410 pp.

ÇETTA, Anton, SYLA, Fazli, MUSTAFA, Myzafere & BERISHA, Anton (ed.). *Këngë kreshnike III* [Songs of the Frontier Warriors, III]. Prishtina: Instituti Albanologjik, 1993. 441 pp.

CINQUEMANI MARTORAMA, Micaela. *Fiabe e leggende albanesi* [Albanian Fables and Legends]. Illustrazione di Giuseppe Ferrara. Rome: Pompei, 1971. 131 pp.

[Albanian fables and legends in Italian translation]

COOPER, Paul Fenimore. *Tricks of Women and Other Albanian Tales.* Intro. by Burton Rascoe. New York: Morrow, 1928. 220 pp. [English translation of Dozon (1881) and Pedersen (1895, 1898)]

DINE, Spiro Risto. *Valët e detit prej Spiro Risto Dine* [Waves of the Sea by Spiro Risto Dine]. Sofia: Mbrothësia, 1908. 856 pp. [Important collection of Albanian folklore from the Rilindja period, including folktales and songs}

DOZON, Auguste. *Manuel de la langue chkipe ou albanaise par Auguste Dozon, consul de France. Grammaire, vocabulaire, chrestomathie* [Manual of Shqip or the Albanian Language by Auguste Dozon, French Consul. Grammar, Vocabulary and Reader]. Paris: Ernest Leroux, 1879. 348 pp. [Including twenty-four folktales in Albanian]

- *Contes albanais, recueillis et traduits par Auguste Dozon, auteur du Manuel de la Langue Chkipe* [Albanian Tales, Collected and Translated by Auguste Dozon, author of Manual of the Albanian Language] Paris: Ernest Leroux, 1881, reprint New York 1980) 264 pp. [French translation of the tales in Dozon (1879)]

ELSIE, Robert. *Dictionary of Albanian Literature.* Westport & New York: Greenwood, 1986. 171 pp.

- *Einem Adler gleich. Anthologie albanischer Lyrik vom 16. Jahrhundert bis zur Gegenwart* [Like an Eagle: Anthology of Albanian Poetry from the 16th Century to the Present]. Hildesheim: Olms, 1988. 303 pp.

- Albanian Literature in English Translation: A Short Survey. in: *The Slavonic and East European Review*, London, 70. 2 (April 1992), p. 249-257.

- *Anthology of Modern Albanian Poetry. An Elusive Eagle Soars.* Edited and translated with an introduction by Robert Elsie. UNESCO Collection of Representative Works, London & Boston: Forest Books, 1993. 213 pp.

456

- *History of Albanian Literature.* East European Monographs 379. ISBN 0-88033-276-X. 2 volumes. Boulder Social Science Monographs, 1995. xv + 1,054 pp.
- *Histori e letërsisë shqiptare* [History of Albanian Literature]. Tirana & Peja: Dukagjini, 1997. 686 pp.
- *Dictionary of Albanian Religion, Mythology and Folk Culture.* London: C. Hurst & Co. / New York: New York University Press, 2001. 357 pp.
- *Albanian Folktales and Legends.* Selected and translated from the Albanian by Robert Elsie. Dukagjini Balkan Books. Peja: Dukagjini, 2001. 240 pp.
- *Handbuch zur albanischen Volkskultur. Mythologie, Religion, Volksglaube, Sitten, Gebräuche und kulturelle Besonderheiten* [Handbook of Albanian Folk Culture: Mythology, Religion, Popular Beliefs, Customs, Habits and Cultural Particularities]. Balkanologische Veröffentlichungen, Band 36. Fachbereich Philosophie und Geisteswissenschaften der Freien Universität Berlin. Wiesbaden: Harrassowitz, 2002. xi + 308 pp.
- *Songs of the Frontier Warriors: Këngë Kreshnikësh. Albanian Epic Verse in a Bilingual English-Albanian Edition.* Edited introduced and translated from the Albanian by Robert Elsie and Janice Mathie-Heck. Wauconda: Bolchazy-Carducci, 2004. xviii + 414 pp.
- Zihni Sako. in: *Enzyklopädie des Märchens: Handwörterbuch zur historischen und vergleichenden Erzählforschung.* Herausgegeben von Rolf Wilhelm Brednich, Band 11. Berlin & New York: Walter de Gruyter, 2004., p. 1053-1055.
- *Albanian Literature: A Short History.* London: I. B. Tauris in association with the Centre for Albanian Studies / New York: Palgrave Macmillan, 2005. vi + 291 pp.
- *Leksiku i kulturës popullore shqiptare: besime, mitologji, fe, doke, rite, festa dhe veçori kulturore* [Lexicon of Albanian Folk Culture: Beliefs, Mythology, Religion, Customs, Rites, Feast and Cultural Particularities]. Përktheu nga anglishtja Abdurrahim Myftiu. Tirana: Skanderbeg Books, 2005. 282 pp.

457

- *Letërsia shqipe: një histori e shkurtër* [Albanian Literature: A Short History]. Përktheu nga anglishtja Majlinda Nishku. Tirana: Skanderbeg Books, 2006. 297 pp.
- The Rediscovery of Folk Literature in Albania. in: *History of the Literary Cultures of East-Central Europe: Junctures and Disjunctures in the 19th and 20th Centuries*. Volume III. Edited by Marcel Cornis-Pope and John Neubauer. Amsterdam & Philadelphia: John Benjamins, 2007, p. 335-338.
- Albanian Tales. in: *The Greenwood Encyclopedia of Folktales and Fairy Tales*. Donald Haase (ed.). Vol. 1, Westport CT: Greenwood Press, 2008. p. 23-25.
- *Historical Dictionary of Albania*. Second Edition. Historical Dictionaries of Europe, No. 75. Lanham, Toronto & Plymouth: Scarecrow Press, 2010. lxxiii + 587 pp.
- *Historical Dictionary of Kosovo*. Second edition. Historical Dictionaries of Europe, No. 79. Lanham, Toronto & Plymouth: Scarecrow Press, 2011. lvi + 395 pp.
- *Fjalor historik i Kosovës* [Historical Dictionary of Kosovo]. Përktheu nga anglishtja MajlindaNishku. Tirana: Skanderbeg Books, 2011. 436 pp.
- *Fjalori historik i Shqipërisë* [Historical Dictionary of Albania]. Shqip: Eva Bani. Tirana: Uegen, 2011. 735 pp.
- *Biographical Dictionary of Albanian History*. London: I. B. Tauris, in association with The Centre for Albanian Studies, 2013. ix + 541 pp.
- *Albanian Folktales and Legends*. Selected and translated from the Albanian by Robert Elsie. Albanian Studies, vol. 2. Charleston 2015, 186 pp.
- *Handbuch zur albanischen Volkskultur: Mythologie, Religion, Volksglauben, Sitten, Gebräuche und kulturelle Besonderheiten* [Handbook of Albanian Folk Culture: Mythology, Religion, Popular Beliefs, Customs, Habits and Cultural Particularities]. Zweite, verbesserte Auflage. Albanian Studies, Vol. 12. London: Centre for Albanian Studies, 2015. 482 pp.

458

- *The Tribes of Albania: History, Society and Culture*. London: I. B. Tauris, 2015. 382 pp.

GIAMPIETRO, Giuseppina. *Mala vila, 'piccola fata'. Fiabe, racconti e leggende italo-albanesi e serbo-croate* [Little Fairy: Italo-Albanian and Serbo-Croatian Tales and Legends]. Milan: Federico Motta Editore, 1992.
[Includes Italo-Albanian fables and legends]

GURAKUQI, Karl & FISHTA, Filip. *Visaret e kombit. Vëllimi 1. Kângë trimnije dhe kreshnikësh. Pjesë të folklorës së botueme* [Treasures of the Nation, Volume 1. Heroic Songs. Elements of Published Folklore]. Botimet e Komisjonit të kremtimevet të 25 vjetorit të vet-qeverimit 1912-1937. Tirana: Nikaj, 1937, reprint Prishtina: Rilindja, 1996. 323 pp.
[A masterful collection of heroic and epic songs]

FRASHERI, Stavro. *Folklor shqipëtar* [Albanian Folklore]. Durrës 1936. 387 pp.
[Collection of eleven folktales]

HAHN, Johann Georg von. *Albanesische Studien* [Albanian Studies]. 3 volumes. Jena: Fr. Mauke, 1854, reprint Athens: Karavias, 1981. 347, 169, 244 pp.
[One of the first publications to include Albanian folktales]

- *Griechische und albanesische Märchen* [Greek and Albanian Folktales]. Gesammelt, übersetzt und erläutert von J. G. v. Hahn, k. k. Consul für das östliche Griechenland. 2 vol. Leipzig: Engelmann, 1864, reprint Munich & Berlin: Georg Müller, 1918. 319 & 339 pp.

- *The Discovery of Albania: Travel Writing and Anthropology in the Nineteenth-Century Balkans*. Translated and Introduced by Robert Elsie. London: I. B. Tauris 2015. 222 pp.

HASLUCK, Margaret Masson Hardie
Këndime Englisht-Shqip or Albanian-English reader. Sixteen Albanian folk-stories, collected and translated, with two grammars and vocabularies. Cambridge: Cambridge University Press, 1931. xl + 145 pp.

[Sixteen tales in Albanian and English collected by Hasluck in Elbasan and appendixed to her now outdated grammar]

HAXHIHASANI, Qemal (ed.). *Këngë popullore legjendare* [Legendary Folksongs]. Zgjedhur e pajisur me shënime nga Q. Haxhihasani. Tirana: Instituti i Shkencave, 1955. 331 pp.

- *Këngë popullore historike* [Historical Folksongs]. Zgjedhur e pajisur me shënime nga Qemal Haxhihasani nën kujdesin e Zihni Sakos. Tirana: Instituti i Shkencave, 1956. 408 pp.

- *Epika legjendare (Cikli i kreshnikëve)* [The Legendary Epic (Cycle of the Frontier Warriors)]. Vëllimi i parë. Folklor shqiptar II. Tirana: Instituti i Folklorit, 1966. 592 pp.

- *Balada popullore shqiptare* [Albanian Folk Ballads]. Tirana: Naim Frashëri, 1982. 184 pp.

- *Epika legjendare* [The Legendary Epic, 2]. Vëllimi i dytë. Folklor shqiptar. Seria II. Tirana: Akademia e Shkencave, 1983. 376 pp.

- *Epika historike* [The Historical Epic, 4]. Vëllimi i parë. Folklor shqiptar. Seria III. Tirana: Akademia e Shkencave, 1983. 496 pp.

HAXHIHASANI, Qemal & DULE, Miranda (ed.). *Epika historike* [The Historical Epic, Vol. 2]. Vëllimi i dytë. Folklor shqiptar. Seria III. Tirana: Akademia e Shkencave, 1981. 764 pp.

- *Epika historike* [The Historical Epic, Vol. 3]. Vëllimi III. Folklor shqiptar. Seria III. Tirana: Akademia e Shkencave, 1990. 774 pp.

HAXHIHASANI, Qemal, LUKA, Kolë, UÇI, Afred & TRESKA, Misto (ed.). *Chansonnier epique albanais* [Albanian Epic Songs]. Version française Kolë Luka. Avant-propos Ismail Kadare. Tirana: Akademia e Shkencave, 1983. 456 pp.

HAXHIHASANI, Qemal & SAKO, Zihni (ed.). *Tregime dhe këngë popullore për Skënderbeun* [Folktales and Folksongs about Scanderbeg]. Tirana: Instituti i Folklorit, 1967. 288 pp.

JARNIK, Jan Urban. *Zur albanischen Sprachenkunde von Dr. Johann Urban Jarnik* [Study on the Albanian Language by Dr Johann

460

Urban Jarnik]. Programm der Realschule in Wien. Leipzig: Brockhaus, 1881. 51 pp.

- *Příspěvky ku poznání nářečí albánských uveřejňuje Jan Urban Jarník* [Contributions to a Knowledge of the Albanian Language]. Pojednání král. české společnosti nauk. Řada VI, díl 12. Abhandlungen der Königlich-Böhmischen Gesellschaft der Wissenschaften zu Prag, 12. Prague: Tiskem Dra. Edvarda Grégra, 1883. 65 pp.
[Folktales and anecdotes, mostly from Shkodra]
- Albanesische Märchen und Schwänke [Albanian Folktales and Anecdotes]. in: *Veckenstedts Zeitschrift für Volkskunde* 1884.

JOCHALAS, Titos P. [= GIOCHALAS, Titos P.]. *Arbanitika paramythia kai doxasies. Neraides, daimones, xorkia, psychiasmata* [Albanian Folktales and Beliefs]. Athens: s.e. 1997. 256 pp.
[Collection of folktales and beliefs of the Albanians (Arvanites) of Greece]

KAJTAZI, Halil. *Proza popullore e Drenicës* [Folk Prose from Drenica]. 3 vol. Prishtina: Enti i teksteve, 1985. 319, 341, 81 pp.

KOMNINO, Gjergj. *Këngë popullore lirike* [Lyric Folksongs]. Tirana: Instituti i Shkencave, 1955.

KRETSCHMER, Paul. *Neugriechische Märchen* [Modern Albanian Folktales]. Jena: E. Diederichs, 1919. xii + 340 pp.
[Includes a number of tales common to Greece, Albania and Turkey]

KULLURIOTI, Anastas [= KULURIÔTÊS, Anastas]. *Albanikon alfabêtarion kata to en Helladi homilumenon albanikon idiôma ekkatharisthen kai epidiorthôthen boêthêma tôn goneôn kai egcheiridion tôn albanikôn teknôn. Avabatar arbëror pas përgluhës arbërore si flitetë nd' Ejadë e përqëruar' edh' e përndrequrë ndihmës printvet edhe dorëmbaitôrë dielmvet arbërorvet* [Albanian Spelling Book on How the Albanian Language is Spoken in Greece]. Athens: Hê fônê tês Albanias, 1882. 164 pp.

461

[Contains folktales, poetry and proverbs in Albanian and Greek]

KURTI, Donat. *Prralla kombtare mbledhë prej gojës së popullit* [National Folktales Collected from the Mouth of the People]. 2 vol. (Shkodra 1940, 2nd edition Shkodra 1942)

KUTELI, Mitrush (ed.). *Tregime të moçme shqiptare* [Early Albanian Tales]. Tirana: Naim Frashëri, 1965, 1987, 1998. 254 pp.
[A collection of thirty-five legends]

- *Fiabe e leggende albanesi* [Albanian Fables and Legends]. Tr. E. Scalambrino. Milan: Rusconi, 1993. 185 pp.

LAMBERTZ, Maximilian. *Volkspoesie der Albaner, eine einführende Studie* [Folk Verse of the Albanians: An Introductory Study]. Zur Kunde der Balkanhalbinsel. II. Quellen und Forschungen 6. Sarajevo: J. Studnička & Co., 1917.

- *Albanische Märchen und andere Texte zur albanischen Volkskunde* [Albanian Folktales and Other Texts on Albanian Ethnography]. Schriften der Balkankommission. Linguistische Abteilung 12. Vienna: Wiener Akademie der Sprach-wissenschaft, 1922. 256 pp.
[A collection of 61 tales and legends in Albanian and German]

- *Zwischen Drin und Vojusa. Märchen aus Albanien* [Between the Drin and the Vjosa: Folktales from Albania]. Märchen aus allen Ländern, Bd. 10. Leipzig: Verlag der Wiener Graphischen Werkstätte, 1922. 177 pp.
[Twenty-four Albanian folktales in German translation]

- *Die geflügelte Schwester und die Dunklen der Erde* [The Winged Sister and the Dark Ones of the Earth]. Albanische Volksmärchen. Übersetzt und herausgegeben von Professor Dr. Maximilian Lambertz. Eisenach: Erich Röth Verlag, 1952. 225 pp.
[Includes twenty-seven Albanian folktales in German translation]

- *Albanien erzählt. Ein Einblick in die albanische Literatur* [Albania Narrates: A Glimpse at Albanian Literature]. Berlin: Volk & Wissen, 1956. 191 pp.

LESKIEN, August. *Balkanmärchen aus Albanien, Bulgarien, Serbien und Kroatien* [Balkan Folktales from Albania, Bulgaria, Serbia and Croatia]. Jena: Eugen Diederichs, 1915, 1919. 332 pp.
[Includes Albanian folktales]

LUTFIU, Mojsi. *Prozë popullore dibrane* [Folk Prose from Dibra]. Skopje: Flaka e vëllazërimit, 1988. 179 pp.

MEYER, Gustav. Albanische Märchen [Albanian Folktales], übersetzt von Gustav Meyer, mit Anmerkungen von Reinhold Köhler. in: *Archiv für Litteraturgeschichte,* Leipzig, 12 (1884), p. 92-148. Reprint: Cleveland ca. 1965.
[Fourteen Albanian folktales in German translation]

- *Kurzgefaßte albanesische Grammatik, mit Lesestücken und Glossar* [Short Albanian Grammar with Texts and Glossary] von Gustav Meyer. Leipzig: Breitkopf & Härtel, 1888. 105 pp.
[Includes southern Albanian (Tosk) folktales]

- Albanesische Studien. 5: Beiträge zur Kenntnis der in Griechenland gesprochenen albanesischen Mundarten [Albanian Studies, 5: Contributions to a Knowledge of the Albanian Dialects Spoken in Greece]. in: *Sitzungsberichte der philosophischen-historischen Classe der kaiserlichen Akademie der Wissenschaften,* Vienna, 1895, 134, Teil 7.

- Albanesische Studien. 6: Beiträge zur Kenntnis verschiedener albanescher Mundarten [Albanian Studies, 6: Contributions to a Knowledge of Various Albanian Dialects]. in: *Sitzungsberichte der philosophischen-historischen Classe der kaiserlichen Akademie der Wissenschaften,* Vienna, 1896, 136, Teil 12.

MIRACCO, Elio. *Favole, fiabe, racconti di S. Nicola dell'Alto, Carfizzi, Pallagorio, Marcedusa, Andali, Caraffa, Vena di Maida, Zangarona* [Tales, Fables, Told in San Nicola dell'Alto, Carfizzi, Pallagorio, Marcedusa, Andali, Caraffa, Vena di Maida, Zangarona]. A cura dell'Istituto di Studi Albanesi dell'Università di Roma. Rome: Bulzoni, 1985. xvi + 368 pp.

463

[Fables and folktales of the Italo-Albanians of Calabria]
MITKO, Thimi [= MITKO, Euthymios]. *Albanikê melissa (Bêlietta sskiypêtare). Syggramma albano-hellênikon periechon meros historias 'Dôra Istrias - hê Albanikê fylê', Albano-Hellênikas Paroimias kai Ainigmata, Albanika kyria onomata, Asmata kai Paramythia Albanika, kai Albano-Hellênikon leksilogion meta parabolês Albanikôn lekseôn pros archaias hellênikas* [The Albanian Bee]. Syntachthen hypo E. Mêtku. Alexandria: Typ. Xenofôntos N. Saltê, 1878. 257 pp.
[Including twelve Albanian folktales and legends]

- *Bleta shqypëtare* [The Albanian Bee]. E përshkroj me shkrojla shqype e përktheu shqyp dhe e radhiti Dr. Gjergj Pekmezi, Konsulli i Shqypërisë. Vienna: Rabeck, 1924, reprint Harper Woods, MI, 1988. 304 pp.
- *Vepra* [Works]. Tirana: Akademia e Shkencave, 1981. 756 pp.
MUÇI, Virgjil. *Përralla shqiptare për 100 + 1 natë* [Albanian Folktales for 101 Nights]. 2 vol. Tirana: Çabej, 1996. 259 + 254 pp.
- *Përralla shqiptare* [Albanian Folktales, 3]. Bleu i tretë. Tirana: Korbi, 2003. 272 pp.
- *Përralla shqiptare* [Albanian Folktales, 4]. Bleu i katërt. Tirana: Korbi, 2005. 272 pp.
- *Fiabe albanesi* [Albanian Folktales]. Nardò: Besa, 2006. 166 pp.
- *Shtrigat: Rrëfenjë* [Witches, Tales]. Tirana: Korbi, 2006. 70 pp.
- *Fiabe albanesi. Miti e leggende della migliore tradizione balcanica* [Albanian Tales: Myths and Legends from the Best Traditions in the Balkans]. Nardò: Controluce, 2013. 168 pp.
OMARI, Donika (ed.). *Përralla shqiptare* [Albanian Folktales]. I zgjodhi dhe i përgatiti për botim Donika Omari. Tirana: Naim Frashëri, 1990. 320 pp.
PALAJ, Bernardin & KURTI, Donat. *Visaret e kombit. Vëllimi II. Kângë kreshnikësh dhe legenda* [Treasures of the Nation. Volume II. Songs of the Frontier Warriors and Legends]. Mbledhë e redaktuem nga At Bernardin Palaj dhe At Donat

Kurti. Tirana: Nikaj, 1937; reprint Rilindja, Prishtina 1996. 286 pp.

PEDERSEN, Holger. *Albanesische Texte mit Glossar* [Albanian Texts and Glossary]. Abhandlungen der philologisch-historischen Classe der Königl. Sächsischen Gesellschaft der Wissenschaften. Vol. 15. Leipzig: Hirzel, 1895. 207 pp.
[Thirty-five Albanian folktales collected in Corfu and Albania]

- *Zur albanesischen Volkskunde von Dr. Holger Pedersen* [On Albanian Ethnography, by Dr Holger Pedersen], Privatdozent der vergleichenden Sprachwissenschaft an der Universität Kopenhagen. Übersetzung der in den Abhandlungen der königlichen Sächsischen Gesellschaft der Wissenschaften, phil.-hist. Cl. XV vom Verf. veröffentlichten alb. Texte. Copenhagen: Einar Moller, 1898. 125 pp.

PERRONE, Luca. *Novellistica italo-albanese* [Italo-Albanian Prose Tales]. Testi orali raccolti dal Prof. Luca Perrone ordinati e tradotti in italiano a cura dell'Istituto di Studi Albanesi della Università di Roma. Studi Albanesi, vol. 1. Florence: Olschki, 1967. 602 pp.
[Collection of one hundred seventy-nine Arbëresh folktales, fables and anecdotes from Calabria, in Albanian and Italian]

PHURIKIS, Petros A. [= PHOURIKÊS, Petros A.]. Hê en Attikê hellênalbanikê dialektos [The Greek-Albanian Dialect in Attica]. in: *Athêna,* Athens, 44 (1932) p. 28-76; 45 (1933) p. 49-181
[Folktales of the Albanian minority in Attica].

PITRÈ, Giuseppe. *Fiabe, novelle e racconti popolari siciliani raccolti ed illustrati da Giuseppe Pitrè* [Sicilian Fables, Short Stories and Folktales Told and Illustrated by Giuseppe Pitrè]. 4 vol. Palermo: L. P. Lauriel, 1875
[First collection of Albanian folktales from the Arbëresh settlements of Piana dei Albanesi (Piana dei Greci) and Palazzo Adriano in Sicily]

REINHOLD, Karl Heinrich Theodor. *Noctes pelasgicae vel symbolae ad cognoscendas dialectos Graeciae Pelasgicas* [Pelasgian

Nights or Notes for an Understanding of the Dialects of Aegean Greece]. Collatae cura Dr. Caroli Henrici Theodori Reinhold, Hanovero-Goettingensis, classis Regiae medici primarii. Athens: Sophoclis Garbola, 1855. 163 pp.
[One of the earliest publications of Albanian folktales]

RUCHES, Pyrrhus J. *Albanian Historical Folksongs 1716-1943.* Chicago: Argonaut, 1967. 126 pp.

SAKO, Zihni et al. (ed.). *Pralla popullore shqiptare* [Albanian Folktales]. Tirana: Instituti i Shkencave, 1954. 223 pp.

- *Mbledhës të hershëm të folklorit shqiptar (1635-1912)* [Early Collections of Albanian Folklore (1635-1912)]. Tirana: Instituti i Folklorit, 1961. 563 pp.

- *Proza Popullore* [Folk Prose]. Folklor Shqiptar, I-IV. Tirana: Akademia e Shkencave, Instituti i Folklorit, 1963, 1966, 1966, 1966. 462, 579, 580, 616 pp.

- *Chansonnier des preux albanais* [Songs of the Albanian Frontier Warriors]. Introduction de Zihni Sako. Collection UNESCO d'Oeuvres Représentatives. Série Européenne. Paris: Maisonneuve & Larose, 1967. 143 pp.

SAKO, Zihni, HAXHIHASANI, Qemal, LUKA, Kolë (ed.). *Trésor du chansonnier populaire albanais* [Treasure Book of the Songs of the Albanian Frontier Warriors]. Tirana: Académie des Sciences, 1975. 332 pp.

SAMOJLOV, David (ed.). *Starinnye albanskie skazanija* [Old Albanian Folktales]. Perevod s albanskogo, Moscow: Izdat. Khudozhestvennaja Literatura, 1971. 223 pp.

SHALA, Demush. *Këngë popullore legjendare* [Legendary Folksongs]. Prishtina: Enti i teksteve, 1972. 448 pp.

- *Këngë popullore historike* [Historical Folksongs]. Prishtina: Enti i teksteve, 1973.

- *Letërsia popullore* [Folk Literature]. Prishtina: Enti i teksteve, 1986, 1988. 352 pp.

SKENDI, Stavro. *Albanian and South Slavic Oral Epic Poetry.* Philadelphia: American Folklore Society, 1954, reprint New York: Kraus, 1969. 221 pp.

466

SOTIRIOS, K. D. [= SOTERIOU, K. D.]. Albanika asmatia kai paramythia [Albanian Songs and Folktales]. in: *Laographia,* Athens, 1 (1909), p. 28-106; 2 (1910), p. 89-120
[Includes Albanian folktales from Greece]

STANI, Lazër (ed.). *Me dymbëdhjetë çelësa. Përralla popullore* [With Twelve Keys: Folktales]. Përgatitur nga Lazër Stani. Tirana: Lidhja e Shkrimtarëve, 1994. 47 pp.

TREIMER, Karl. *Von Meer zu Meer. Albanische Volksmärchen* [From Sea to Sea: Albanian Folktales]. Tirana: Akademia e Shkencave, s.a.[1976]. 195 pp.
[Thirty-five Albanian folktales in German translation]

TRUHELKA, Ciro. *Arnautske price. Albanische Märchen. Proben albanischer Volkspoesien* [Albanian Folktales: Samples from Albanian Folk Poetry]. Bd. 1-2. Sarajevo 1905.

TUKAJ, Mustafa: *Faith and Fairies. Tales Based on Albanian Legends and Ballads.* Edited by Joanne M. Ayers. Shkodra: Skodrinon, 2002. 154 pp.

UHLISCH, Gerda. *Die Schöne der Erde. Albanische Märchen und Sagen* [The Earthly Beauty: Albanian Folktales and Sagas]. Leipzig: Reklam, 1987, reprint Cologne: Röderberg, 1988. 308 pp.
[Forty-eight Albanian tales and legends in German translation]

VLORA, Ekrem bey. *Aus Berat und vom Tomor. Tagebuchblätter* [From Berat and Tomor: Pages of a Diary]. Zur Kunde der Balkanhalbinsel I. Reisen und Beobachtungen 13. Sarajevo: D. A. Kajon, 1911. 168 pp.

WEIGAND, Gustav Ludwig. *Albanesische Grammatik im südgegischen Dialekt (Durazzo, Elbassan, Tirana)* [Albanian Grammar in the Southern Gheg Dialect (Durrës, Elbasan, Tirana)]. Leipzig: Johann Ambrosius Barth, 1913) xiv + 189 pp.
[Includes folktales from Tirana and Elbasan]

WHEELER, Post. *Albanian Wonder Tales.* With illustrations by Maud and Miska Petersham. Garden City 1936 / London: Lovat Dickenson, 1936. 255 pp.

Publications of Margaret Hasluck

HASLUCK, Margaret

The Shrine of Mên Askaenos at Pisidian Antioch. in: *Journal of Hellenic Studies*, 32 (1912), p. 111-150.

- Dionysos at Smyrna. in: *Annual of the British School at Athens*, Athens, 19 (1912-1913), p. 89-94.

- The Evil Eye in Some Greek Villages of the Upper Haliakmon Valley in West Macedonia. in: *Journal of the Royal Anthropological Institute of Great Britain and Ireland*, 53 (1923), p. 160-172; reprint in: A. Dundes, *The Evil Eye, a Folklore Casebook*, New York 1981, p. 107-123.

- The Significance of Greek Personal Names. in: *Folk-Lore*, 33 (1923), p. 149-154, 249-251.

- The Nonconformist Moslems of Albania. in: *Contemporary Review*, London, 127 (1925), p. 599-606; reprinted in: *Moslem World* 15 (1925), p. 388-398.

- Ramadan as a Personal Name. in: *Folk-Lore*, 36 (1925), p. 280.

- A Lucky Spell from a Greek Island. in: *Folk-Lore*, 37 (1926), p. 195-196.

- The Basil-Cake of the Greek New Year. in: *Folk-Lore*, 38 (1927), p. 143-177.

- Minorities in Serbian Macedonia. in: *The Fortnightly Review*, 125 (1 June 1929), p. 788-799.

- An Unknown Turkish Shrine in Western Macedonia. in: *Journal of the Royal Asiatic Society*, April 1929, p. 289-296.

- Traditional Games of the Turks. in: *Jubilee Congress of the Folk-Lore Society, September 19 – September 25, 1928. Papers and Transactions*, 1930.

- Nomad Shepherds of the Pindus Mountains. in: *Illustrated London News*, London 179 (1931), No. 4913 (18.07.1931), p. 100-101.

- *Këndime Englisht-Shqip or Albanian-English Reader. Sixteen Albanian Folk-Stories, Collected and Translated, with Two Grammars and Vocabularies*. Cambridge: Cambridge University Press, 1932. xl + 145 pp.
- Physiological Paternity and Belated Birth in Albanian. in: *Man, Journal of the Royal Anthropological Society*, London 32 (1932), p. 53-54.
- Bride-Price in Albania: a Homeric Parallel. in: *Man, Journal of the Royal Anthropological Society*, London, 33 (1933), p. 191-195.
- An Albanian Ballad on the Assassination in 1389 of Sultan Murad I on Kosovo Plain. in: *Gaster Anniversary Volume, in Honour of Haham Dr. M. Gaster's 80th Birthday*, Edited by Bruno Schindler in Collaboration with A. Marmorstein. London: Taylor's Foreign Press, 1936, p. 210-233.
- A Historical Sketch of the Fluctuations of Lake Ostrovo in West Macedonia. in: *Journal of the Royal Geographical Society*, Vol. 87, 4 (June 1936), p. 338-347.
- The Archaeological History of Lake Ostrovo in West Macedonia. in: *Journal of the Royal Geographical Society*, Vol. 88, 5 (Nov. 1936), p. 448-457.
- Causes of the Fluctuation in Level of Lake Ostrovo. West Macedonia. in: *Journal of the Royal Geographical Society*, Vol. 90, 5 (Nov. 1937), p. 446-457
- The Gypsies of Albania. in: *Journal of the Gypsy Lore Society* (Third Series), vol. 17, no. 2 (Apr. 1938), p. 49-61; no. 3 (July 1938), p. 18-30; no. 4 (Oct. 1938), p. 110-122.
- Baba Tomorri. in: *The Guardian* newspaper, 13 September 1939
- Couvade in Albania. in: *Man, Journal of the Royal Anthropological Society*, London, (Feb. 1939), p. 18-20.
- Dervishes in Albania. in: *The Guardian* newspaper, 9 June 1939
- Një kult i malit në Shqipnin e jugës [A Mountain Cult in Southern Albania]. in: *Shkolla kombëtare*, 1939, no. 23, p. 39-43.

469

- The Sedentary Gypsies of Metzovo. in: *Journal of the Gypsy Lore Society*, 17, 3rd series (1939), p. 168-170.
- Kulti i Malit të Tomorrit [The Cult of Mount Tomorr]. in: *Bota shqiptare*, Botim i Ministris s'Arsimit, Tirana, 1943, p. 82-84.
- *Albanian Phrase Book*. s.e., s.l. s.a. [London 1944?]. 100 pp.
- The Bust of Berat. in: *Man, Journal of the Royal Anthropological Society*, London, 1946, 29, p. 36-38.
- The Youngest Son in North Albania. in: *Folk-Lore*, 57 (1946), p. 93-94; reprinted in: L. Edmunds and A. Dundes (ed.), *Oedipus: a Folklore Casebook*.
- Firman of A.H. 1013-14 (A.D. 1604-5) Regarding Gypsies in the Western Balkans. in: *Journal of the Gypsy Lore Society*, 27, 3rd series (1948), p. 12.
- Oedipus Rex in Albania. in: *Folk-Lore*, 60 (1949), p. 340-344.
- The First Cradle of an Albanian Child. in: *Man, Journal of the Royal Anthropological Society*, London, 50 (1950), p. 55-57.
- *The Unwritten Law in Albania. A Record of the Customary Law of the Albanian Tribes. Description of Family and Village Life... & Waging of Blood-Feuds*. Cambridge: Cambridge University Press, 1954, reprint Hyperion Conn. 1981. 285 pp.
- The Albanian Blood Feud. in: *Law and Warfare, Studies in the Anthropology of Conflict*. Paul Bohannan (ed.), American Museum Sourcebooks in Anthropology. Garden City: Natural History Press, 1967, p. 381-408.
- Vështrim i përgjithshëm për të drejtën dokësore shqiptare [General View of Albanian Customary Law]. in: *Kultura popullore*, Tirana, 1993, 1-2, p. 139-144.
- *Once Upon a Time / Na ishte njëherë*. Tirana: Korbi, 2006. 140 pp.
- *Albanian Texts and English Translation*. Printed by Walter Louis, A.M. Cambridge: Cambridge University Press, 2011. 80 pp.

HASLUCK, Margaret (ed.)
Frederick William Hasluck: *Athos and its Monasteries*. London: Kegan Paul, 1924. xii + 213 pp.

-       Frederick William Hasluck: *Letters on Religion and Folklore*, London: Lusac, 1926. xi + 256 pp.
-       Frederick William Hasluck: *Christianity and Islam under the Sultans*. Oxford: Clarendon Press 1929, reprint Istanbul: Isis 2000.
HASLUCK, Margaret & MORANT, G. M.
       Measurements of Macedonian Men. in: *Biometrika*, 21 (1929), p. 322-336.

Publications about Margaret Hasluck and Lef Nosi

AMERY, Julian. *Sons of the Eagle: A Study in Guerilla War*. London: Macmillan, 1948. p. 27.

CLARK, Marc. Margaret Masson Hasluck. in: John B. Allcock & Antonia Young (ed.): *Black Lambs and Grey Falcons: Women Travellers in the Balkans* Oxford & New York: Berghahn Books, 2000. p. 128-154.

DAVIES, Edmund Frank. *Illyrian Venture: The Story of the British Military Mission to Enemy-Occupied Albania 1943-1944.* London: Bodley Head, 1952. 247 pp.

DAWKINS, Richard M. Margaret Masson Hasluck, née Hardie. in: *Folk-Lore*, 60 (1949), p. 291-292.

DEDURHAM, Mary Edith. Review of Këndime englisht-shqip or Albanian-English Reader, by M. M. Hasluck. in: *Man, Journal of the Royal Anthropological Society*, London, 32, 212 (1932), p. 173.

DESTANI; Bejtullah (ed.). *Our Woman in Albania. The Life of Margaret Hasluck, Scholar and Spy*. London: I. B. Tauris, forthcoming.

GOWIE, C. R. Hippolyta of the Albanians: Tribute to Margaret M. Hasluck. in: *The Aberdeen University Review*, Aberdeen, 33 (1950), p. 158 sq.

HAMMOND; Nichol Geoffrey Lamprière. Travels in Epirus and South Albania before World War II. in: *The Ancient World*, Chicago, 8, 1-2 (Oct.-Nov. 1983) pp. 13-46.

HIBBERT, Reginald. *Albania's National Liberation Struggle: the Bitter Victory*. London: Pinter, & New York: St. Martin's Press, 1991. 269 pp.

KLOKOT, Waltraud. Von Dora d'Istria zu Margaret Hasluck: Reisende Frauen und frühe Ethnographinnen [From Dora d'Istria to Margaret Hasluck: Travelling Women and Female Ethnographers]. in: Waltraud Klokot (ed.): *Pionierinnen der Ethnologie*. Trier: Kleine Schritte, 2002. p. 5-13.

MANN, Stuart E. Margaret Masson Hasluck. in: *Journal of the Gypsy Lore Society*, 29 (1950), p. 80.

NEWMAN, Bernard. *Albania Back-Door*. London: Herbert Jenkins, 1936. 315 pp.

SHILS, Edward & BLACKER, Carmen. *Cambridge Women: Twelve Portraits*. New York: Cambridge University Press, 1996. xix + 292 pp.

SHYTI, Migena. Lef Nosi nëpërmjet letërkëmbimit të tij. Letra të ndryshme drejtuar Lef Nosit [Lef Nosi in his Correspondence. Various Letters Addressed to Lef Nosi]. in: *Hylli i dritës*, Shkodra, 2010, 3, p. 159-171.

SMILEY, David. *Albanian Assignment*. London: Chatto & Windus / Hogarth Press 1984, reprint London: Sphere Books 1985. 170 pp.

STOCKER, Sharon R. Margaret Masson Hardie Hasluck (1885-1948). http://www.brown.edu/Research/Breaking_Ground/bios/Hasluck_Margaret%20Masson%20Hardie.pdf

WIEDENER, Michaela. Zwischen Folklore und Ethnographie: Margaret Hasluck und der Balkan [Between Folklore and Ethnography: Margaret Hasluck and the Balkans]. in: Waltraud Klokot (ed.): *Pionierinnen der Ethnologie*. Trier: Kleine Schritte, 2002. p. 110-125.

472

Recent Books Published in the Series "Albanian Studies," Edited by Robert Elsie

Volume 1
Tajar Zavalani, *History of Albania*. Albanian Studies, Vol. 1. London: Centre for Albanian Studies, 2015. ISBN 978-1507595671. 356 pp.

Volume 2
Robert Elsie, *Albanian Folktales and Legends*. Albanian Studies, Vol. 2. London: Centre for Albanian Studies, 2015. ISBN 978-1507631300. 188 pp.

Volume 3
Robert Elsie, *The Albanian Treason Trial (1945)*. Albanian Studies, Vol. 3. London: Centre for Albanian Studies, 2015. ISBN 978-1507709511. 348 pp.

Volume 4
Robert Elsie, *Gathering Clouds: The Roots of Ethnic Cleansing in Kosovo and Macedonia – Early Twentieth-Century Documents*. Second expanded edition. Albanian Studies, Vol. 4. London: Centre for Albanian Studies, 2015. ISBN 978-1507882085. 244 pp.

Volume 5
Robert Elsie, *Tales from Old Shkodra: Early Albanian Short Stories*. Second edition. Albanian Studies, Vol. 5. London: Centre for Albanian Studies, 2015. ISBN 978-1508417224. 177 pp.

Volume 6
Robert Elsie, *Kosovo in a Nutshell: A Brief History and Chronology of Events*. Albanian Studies, Vol. 6. London: Centre for Albanian Studies, 2015. ISBN 978-1508496748. 119 pp.

Volume 7
Robert Elsie, *Albania in a Nutshell: A Brief History and Chronology of Events*. Albanian Studies, Vol. 7. London: Centre for Albanian Studies, 2015. ISBN 978-1508511946. 93 pp.

Volume 8
Migjeni, *Under the Banners of Melancholy. Collected Literary Works*. Translated from the Albanian by Robert Elsie. Albanian Studies, Vol. 8. London: Centre for Albanian Studies, 2015. ISBN 978-1508675990. 159 pp.

Volume 9
Robert Elsie and Bejtullah Destani (ed.). *The Macedonian Question in the Eyes of British Journalists (1899-1919)*. Albanian Studies, Vol. 9. London: Centre for Albanian Studies, 2015. ISBN 978-1508696827. 311 pp.

Volume 10
Berit Backer. *Behind Stone Walls: Changing Household Organisation among the Albanians of Kosovo*. Edited by Robert Elsie and Antonia Young, with an introduction and photographs by Ann Christine Eek. Albanian Studies, Vol. 10. London: Centre for Albanian Studies, 2015. ISBN 978-1508747949. 328 pp.

Volume 11
Franz Baron Nopcsa, *Reisen in den Balkan. Die Lebenserinnerungen des Franz Baron Nopcsa*. Eingeleitet, herausgegeben und mit Anhang versehen von Robert Elsie. Albanian Studies, Vol. 11. London: Centre for Albanian Studies, 2015. ISBN 978-1508953050. 638 S.

Volume 12
Robert Elsie, *Handbuch zur albanischen Volkskultur: Mythologie, Religion, Volksglauben, Sitten, Gebräuche und kulturelle Besonderheiten*. Albanian Studies, Vol. 12. London: Centre for Albanian Studies, 2015. ISBN 978-1508986300. 484 S.

Volume 13
Jean-Claude Faveyrial. *Histoire de l'Albanie*. Edition établie et présentée par Robert Elsie. Albanian Studies, Vol. 13. Londres: Centre for Albanian Studies, 2015. ISBN 978-1511411301. xxiv + 530 pp.

Volume 14

Margaret Hasluck. *The Hasluck Collection of Albanian Folktales*. Edited by Robert Elsie. Albanian Studies, Vol. 14. London: Centre for Albanian Studies, 2015. ISBN 978-1512002287. 475 pp.

Made in the USA
Las Vegas, NV
23 April 2024

89063096R00262